Indulgence

Satisfy your craving for lush romance with these sexy stories by four of today's hottest romance writers.

CONNIE BENNETT
"Masquerade"

"Connie Bennett's powerful, fast-paced plot thrills us with passionate intensity and rich characterization sure to please discerning fans."

—*Romantic Times* for *Married to a Stranger*

THEA DEVINE
"Admit Desire"

"Thea Devine continues to reign supreme as the divine queen of sensually spicy love stories...a juicy hot romance coupled with a creative storyline..."

—*Affaire de Coeur* for *Secret Pleasures*

EVELYN ROGERS
"The Gold Digger"

"Evelyn Rogers delivers great entertainment!"

—*Romantic Times*

OLIVIA RUPPRECHT
"A Quiver of Sighs"

"The scorching sensuality could melt polar ice caps...."

—*Romantic Times* for *Love Game*,
writing as Mallory Rush

Other *Leisure* and *Love Spell* Anthologies:
LOVESCAPE
MIDSUMMER NIGHT'S MAGIC
LOVE'S LEGACY
ENCHANTED CROSSINGS

Indulgence

♥ *Connie Bennett* ♥

♥ *Thea Devine* ♥

♥ *Evelyn Rogers* ♥

♥ *Olivia Rupprecht* ♥

LEISURE BOOKS NEW YORK CITY

A LEISURE BOOK®

August 1997

Published by

Dorchester Publishing Co., Inc.
276 Fifth Avenue
New York, NY 10001

Printed in the United States of America.

Masquerade

Connie Bennett

To Evan Marshall, with thanks.

Chapter One

He looked enough like Dallas Kincaid to be his twin.
So much so, in fact, that when the sexy-as-sin movie
star look-alike paused on the dining hall stairs to get
his bearings, a medley of oohs, aahs, and breathy
murmurs swept through the Constellation Room like
a collective sigh. Every woman in the place sat up a
little straighter, and those with empty seats next to
them made sure their hairdos were unruffled and
their lipstick unsmudged.

The man was simply stunning. Breathtaking, even.
He was dressed as the hero from *The Buccaneer*, Dallas Kincaid's pirate adventure hit, in a blousy white
shirt open halfway to his waist and a pair of white
pants that clung to his well-muscled thighs like a
provocative second skin. His thick, unruly hair—as
black as the sash at his waist and the boots that
hugged his calves—tickled his collar and teased his

9

forehead. It seemed made for a woman's hands to run through, and there wasn't a lady present who didn't ache for the simple pleasure of brushing a lock of it away from his face.

A wave of applause rolled through the room as the handsome pirate moved down the stairs. Playing his role to the hilt, he acknowledged the accolade with a courtly bow and moved on, presumably in search of his assigned seat.

As it so happened, there was a vacant one beside Charlotte Nolan at the captain's table, but it never crossed Charlye's mind that the Dallas Kincaid look-alike would be seated next to her. Winning this all-expenses-paid Hollywood Masquerade cruise aboard the *Caribbean Star* and getting to spend fourteen days as her favorite movie character had stretched the limits of Charlye's luck. The most she dared hope for over the next two weeks was a suntan, a few duty-free bargains, and maybe a bingo jackpot or two. A close encounter with a heavenly hunk wasn't even in the realm of possibilities. Miracles like that didn't happen to Charlye, and she knew from experience that life was a lot less painful once you learned to stop wishing for them.

"My, what a striking costume he has on." The feminine voice that came from the other side of Charlye's table was soft, refined, and cracked with age.

The woman's voice that replied was all gravel and brass. "To hell with the costume. Look at what's in it. Now, that's what I call a *man*. I don't know about his swash, but even from here you can tell he's got plenty of *buckle*!"

"Hilda!"

Charlye smothered a grin and turned back to her table, leaving the ogling to the other ladies in the room. Seated across from her were the most unlikely man-watchers she'd ever met—two sweet-faced, white-haired ladies for whom age sixty was but a distant memory. That seemed to be about all the two friends had in common, though. The querulous one with the foghorn voice was doing a better-than-

Masquerade

passable impersonation of Lauren Bacall; she looked nothing like the aging movie star, but her voice and manner were right on the money. The other lady was spending a fortnight as the Agatha Christie sleuth Miss Jane Marple. Together, the two were adorable. Crotchety, but adorable.

"I'm not Hilda, you ninny. I'm Lauren. *Lauren Bacall*," the foghorn protested to her companion. "This is a masquerade cruise, remember? For the next two weeks we address each other by our character names only."

"Of course I remember," Miss Marple replied primly. "I'm not senile. *Or* deaf," she added pointedly.

Charlye had a lot of experience soothing ruffled feathers. It was almost second nature for her to head off the argument before it gathered any more steam. "No one would ever think that, Miss Marple," she told the angel-faced sleuth, and earned a sweet, beaming smile in return.

"How kind you are, dear. You must call me Aunt Jane," she invited. "You know, you remind me very much of Louisa Barnstable, the vicar's niece back in St. Mary Mead." She leaned forward confidentially. "She killed her lover, you know. Quite a sad tale."

"Tell it some other time," Lauren said dryly.

"Good evening, everyone. I believe this is my seat." The voice beside Charlye was so uncannily familiar that her heart skipped a beat. Her startled gaze flew up and she discovered that the sexy pirate who'd captured everyone's attention at the door not only looked like Dallas Kincaid, he sounded like him, as well. And he was here. At the captain's table. Right next to her.

Oh, brother.

Up this close, he was much too handsome to look at, and Charlye averted her gaze quickly before she could make a fool of herself. This gorgeous hunk was going to be sitting next to her? It was a nightmare. Sweet little old ladies like Jane and Lauren were something she could handle. Devastatingly handsome men were another matter entirely. What on earth would she say to him if he wanted to make polite dinner table conversation?

Across the table, the man beside Lauren rose. Even without his Horatio Hornblower costume his air of authority branded him the *Caribbean Star's* captain. "I believe you may be right, sir," he greeted the new-comer. "I'm Captain Jonathan Prior, at your service. And you, obviously, are Dallas Kincaid. Or should we call you Captain, too?" he asked with a gesture at the look-alike's costume.

"Please call me Dallas. There should never be more than one captain aboard any ship, and I gladly yield that responsibility to you, sir."

The real captain chuckled. "A wise decision, sir. Let me introduce you to your companions this evening. This gracious lady to my left is Miss Lauren Bacall, and traveling with her is the world-renowned sleuth Miss Jane Marple." Captain Prior continued the introductions around the table, which was set for eight, including a Madonna wannabe who positively purred when she greeted the newcomer, and a new-lywed couple who were spending their honeymoon as Hercules and the warrior princess Xena.

Then it was Charlye's turn. She could feel a blush creeping up her cheeks as all eyes, including—no, especially—Dallas Kincaid's, focused on her. Damn! Why did being shy have such an obvious and em-barrassing side effect? Charlye knew from experi-ence that her face was turning the color of ripe raspberries.

"And this young lady is something of a mystery to us," the captain said.

"Really? I love a good mystery." The statement was loaded with sensual overtones that sent a warm shiver down Charlye's spine. The handsome pirate pulled out the chair next to her and sat without tak-ing his eyes off her. Charlye kept her own gaze fixed on the cardboard movie camera that served as a cen-terpiece. She had to remind herself to breathe.

"We were just trying to guess her identity as you

arrived," the captain informed him. "Would you care to take a stab at it?"

"Oh, absolutely."

Charlye's face flamed even redder and she nervously fingered one of the spoons in the place setting before her. "Really, it's not that big a deal. I tried to tell them, but they wouldn't let me," she said softly.

"That's because half the fun is in guessing," Lauren said.

"And we had just established that she's portraying a fictional character," Miss Marple added.

"From the 1940s, obviously," Kincaid said.

"Yes." Charlye could feel the force of his curious gaze and wondered what he was seeing as he studied her profile. The heavily padded shoulders of the white, sequined jacket were a dead giveaway to the era when her favorite movie had been produced, but even with makeup and her light brown hair artfully upswept, Charlye looked nothing at all like Bette Davis, who had played the lead character. Davis was a striking, vibrant beauty who had instantly captured the heart of Paul Heinreid in that movie. Charlotte Nolan was a mouse, and no amount of makeup was going to disguise that fact.

Why on earth had she ever thought that winning a masquerade cruise was the best thing that ever happened to her? This was only the first night out of port, and already she was wishing she'd never come.

"Are you a character from a Fred Astaire movie?" Xena asked.

Charlye shook her head and darted a glance at the scantily clad young lady who was effectively decked out in a leather mini-dress with brass scroll breast plates. "No. I don't sing or dance."

Hercules, Madonna, and the others made incorrect guesses as well, but Dallas said nothing. He just continued to look her over as though he thought he might find the answer written on her somewhere—which it was, actually, if only he knew where to look and how to interpret the writing.

His steady gaze was unnerving in the extreme.

Charlye had seen enough Dallas Kincaid movies to know that the actor never simply *looked* at anyone. His distinctive blue eyes bored into you, into your very soul.

But of course this wasn't really Dallas Kincaid, the megastar who matched the rugged charm of Harrison Ford with the flawless good looks of Daniel Day-Lewis. This was just an ordinary person on vacation who happened to look like the movie star. He wasn't famous, probably wasn't rich, and never once had Charlye indulged in an embarrassing romantic fantasy about him as she had with the real Dallas Kincaid.

That rationalization should have helped ease her attack of nerves, but it didn't. Dallas Kincaid or not, the man studying her so intently had an aura of sensuality that rolled off of him in waves, engulfing Charlye. She'd never felt anything like it before. It was primal, and Charlye found it as frightening as it was compelling.

"Are you a character played by Katie Hepburn?" Lauren asked. "From *The Philadelphia Story*, maybe?"

"No. I'm sorry." Charlye shot her an apologetic look. "If you'll just let me tell you . . . I'm—"

"Ah-ah-ah," Miss Marple protested.

"But this is so embarrassing."

"Don't be silly," Lauren chided. "It's fun."

"Just give us one more clue, dear," Miss Marple suggested.

Dallas broke his long, speculative silence. "Oh, I think we have all the clues we need, Miss M. If I'm right, it's no wonder our lovely companion's identity is a mystery—it was in the movie she stepped out of, too." Before Charlye could fully grasp what was happening, the handsome doppleganger was leaning toward her, his face next to hers, his lips close enough to kiss.

"Isn't that right, Charlotte?" he whispered.

Charlye's heartbeat went into triple time. Either he had ESP or he'd figured it out. She looked at him, and while some logical portion of her brain registered the fact that the look-alike's eyes were brown, not blue, the part of Charlye that was all woman melted into a puddle of longing. An ache of desire settled low in her abdomen, startling her with its intensity.

Somehow she managed to answer his question with a breathy, "Yes," even though she wasn't absolutely certain what she was agreeing with. It didn't really matter. At that moment, she would have said "yes" to anything he asked.

Kincaid's arms went around her, not in an embrace, exactly, but he was so close it didn't matter. Charlye felt faint. She also felt a slight pressure on her shoulder and she reminded herself that this wasn't personal—he was just playing the masquerade game.

A moment later, he straightened and pulled away, taking all of the warmth in the room with him. He had also taken the little scrap of paper that had been pinned to the shoulder of Charlye's jacket.

"What is that?" Xena asked him.

Jane Marple cackled appreciatively. "It's a note telling her what shoes and accessories to wear with her gown. Isn't that right, dear?"

Charlye nodded, grateful that the mystery had been solved. Everyone's attention would shift off of her soon. "Yes."

The platinum-haired Madonna snorted disdainfully. "Why would anyone need that?"

"If I remember correctly, it's because her evening clothes are borrowed," the captain said, chuckling. "Well done, Dallas. You may give Miss Marple a run for her money as our resident sleuth."

Hercules shook his head. "Sorry, but I still don't get it. Who is she?"

"Charlotte Vale, from the Bette Davis movie *Now, Voyager*," Dallas replied, grinning appreciatively at Charlye.

"Never seen it," Madonna announced.

Lauren shook her head. "Somebody give this child an education in the classics, quick."

"My pleasure," Dallas said. "*Now, Voyager* is a movie about a shy young woman who's been so dominated by her mother that she has a nervous breakdown. She spends several months recuperating at a sanitarium and loses so much weight that she has to borrow clothes when her doctor insists that she take a cruise to South America."

"Oh." Madonna couldn't have been any less impressed.

"Shame on you, Mr. Kincaid," Miss Marple chided. "You left out the best part. About falling in love with Paul Heinreid."

Dallas nodded. "Sorry." He looked at Madonna. "And she falls in love with Paul Heinreid." Then he looked at Charlye, leaned a little closer, and lowered his voice to a seductive purr that sent chills down Charlye's spine. "*Desperately* in love. They have a mad, illicit love affair, and by the time Charlotte returns from the cruise she's no longer a shy, repressed spinster. She's a vibrant, confident woman who has experienced love in all its glorious incarnations."

Charlye swallowed hard and prayed that her face wasn't flaming again. Kincaid was only playing, but he was hitting alarmingly close to home. It was no coincidence that *Now, Voyager* was her favorite movie—the real Charlotte Nolan had a great deal in common with the fictitious Charlotte Vale, including growing up with a domineering mother and a whole boatload of insecurities. And as for being a repressed spinster—Charlye could have taught her fictitious counterpart a thing or two. Thirty-two-year-old virgins were a species facing extinction, but they hadn't died out completely. Charlye was living proof of that.

"And they lived happily ever after?" Xena asked.

Somehow, Charlye managed to find her voice. "Actually, they didn't. Jerry—Paul Heinreid—was married. His wife was ill and he was too noble to divorce her."

"Gee, what a crummy ending."

16

"I'm sure a Hollywood screenwriter could do a better job of it today, honey," Hercules told his wife.

"Why, what a fine idea." Lauren was looking speculatively at Dallas and Charlotte as she leaned toward Miss Marple and said, "I think it's high time that movie was remade, don't you, Jane?"

"Oh, absolutely," the diminutive sleuth replied. "And I can't think of anyone better for the Paul Heinreid role than Dallas Kincaid. Don't you agree, Charlotte dear? Wouldn't Dallas make a wonderful Jerry?"

There was no way Charlye could duck the question and she found herself looking at Dallas—really looking at him—for the first time. His brown eyes should have been blue, and now that he wasn't so close and Charlye wasn't quite so rattled, she could see lines and wrinkles on his face that didn't exist on the face of the real Dallas Kincaid. She could also see that this man wasn't as carefree as the teasing charmer he was pretending to be. Something was haunting him. Like everyone else, he had secrets and sorrows. Life had chewed him up and spit him out a time or two, just like all the other mere mortals on the *Caribbean Star*.

Suddenly, Charlye wasn't quite as intimidated by him any more.

"Yes, Aunt Jane, I agree. I think he'd make a wonderful Jerry," she said, holding Dallas's gaze. Then she grinned. "But let's not ask for the moon when we already have the stars."

The captain, Jane, Lauren, and Dallas all laughed at Charlye's quote from the movie's famous last line.

The other three looked grateful that the stewards chose that moment to begin serving dinner.

Chapter Two

Charlye stood at the rail looking out over the blue-black ocean, scarcely able to believe it was real. The stars weren't quite close enough to touch, and the moon was only three-quarters full, but it was a beautiful sight all the same. Best of all, she'd survived that embarrassing scene in the Constellation Room and actually made it through supper without calling any more attention to herself. The Madonna impersonator, who'd been seated on Dallas's left, had monopolized him and the dinner conversation while they ate. Afterwards, Charlye had engineered a subtle retreat as the band tuned up for the Get Acquainted Dance. A wallflower with two left feet had absolutely no business hanging around begging to be ignored. A walk on the deck had seemed less injurious to the ego.

Besides, she'd never seen the ocean before today.

It would take a lot more than two weeks to get her fill of it. Charlye propped her hands on the rail and swayed languidly to the distant strains of music that wafted over the deck. The only thing that could have made the moment more perfect would have been having someone to share it with.

Her thoughts went to Dallas Kincaid despite her best effort to rein them in. She replayed their introduction in her head, letting it loop again and again like a Moviola. As it played through, however, she rewrote the script until instead of just sitting there like a lump of raspberries, Charlotte Nolan was responding to Dallas Kincaid's flirtatious banter with the wit and charm of a woman who knew what it was like to be flirted with. Like a woman who knew what it was like to *be* a woman. To be wanted.

She rewrote the scene until it was perfect, letting an attraction build between the two lead characters until it sizzled off the movie screen in Charlye's head, setting the stage for romance. When the orchestra began playing, Charlotte didn't duck out. She stayed and basked in the knowledge that Dallas was going to hold out his hand and ask her to dance. And he did, of course, in a voice that had the bite of whiskey and the seductive allure of silk.

Charlye's own heartbeat quickened as her characters walked to the dance floor. She closed her eyes as Dallas took Charlotte into his arms and they began to dance. She sighed as the couple in her fantasy fell in love.

Of course, it was much too soon for them to *really* be in love. If she'd been writing the story for real—something she'd secretly been doing for years—she'd have engineered a strong conflict that interfered with their attraction, or turned the story into an action thriller by having terrorists choose that moment to hijack the cruise ship.

But tonight, with the stars shining down on the ocean and music floating around her, Charlye wanted her characters to be in love.

They danced, oblivious to everyone else in the

room, until the dance scene ran its course. She did a cross fade that moved the couple onto the deck where they strolled hand in hand in the moonlight.

But then she ran into a block. What should she have them do next? It was too soon for a kiss, even in a romantic fantasy. Maybe she could do a montage. A sequence of romantic images that led up to a kiss. Or she could let them talk.

And say what? What would Charlye Nolan have to say that could possibly interest Dallas Kincaid? For some reason, she couldn't recapture the confident Charlotte who'd entranced him at the make-believe dinner table.

Rats. The whole romantic scenario went up in a puff of smoke and was carried away on the breeze, leaving Charlye with the same empty feeling she always got when her daydreams evaporated and she had to face reality. And the saddest reality of all was that nothing had changed. Charlye had thought that coming on this cruise and pretending to be someone else for a while would give her the freedom to actually *be* different, but she saw now that that wasn't going to happen. Charlye Nolan was Charlye Nolan whether she was at home in Indiana or on a cruise in the Caribbean. She might as well get used to it.

"There you are. I had a feeling you were the stand-at-the-rail-looking-out-to-sea type. I was right."

Charlye's breath caught in her throat and she turned to find Dallas Kincaid beside her. How could she not have heard him approach? How could she not have sensed his presence? It was magnetic, over-powering. It made the air sizzle with electricity and stirred delicious sensations inside of her. Why hadn't she felt him coming?

It took her a second to find her voice. "You were looking for me?"

He nodded. "And finding you was no easy task, considering the amount of rail on this ship."

"Why?" she blurted out, then flushed with embarrassment. "I mean, why were you looking for me, not why is there a lot of rail on the ship."

Dallas chuckled. "Can't a gentleman seek out a beautiful woman without having an ulterior motive?"

Charlye turned her flaming face to the ocean. That was the second time he'd indicated that he thought she was pretty. She knew it wasn't true, but it was hard not to want to believe it. "If a gentleman could *find* a beautiful woman, I could understand his pursuing her." She managed to look at him. "But that doesn't explain why you came looking for me."

He cocked his head and Charlye could actually feel the force of his gaze again. He was studying her as though he'd found some new breed of animal and was trying to classify it. His close scrutiny was unnerving and thrilling at the same time.

"Are you fishing for a compliment, Miss Vale," he finally asked with genuine curiosity, "or do you really not know how pretty you are?"

Charlye felt something delicious and warm twist inside her, and she tried to distance herself from it. He was just taking the cruise's masquerade theme a little too seriously, that's all. He was playing a game, and Charlye reminded herself that it would be foolish—even dangerous—to take anything he said at face value.

She chose not to answer his question. Instead, she turned to the rail again, facing the ocean, and asked, "Why were you looking for me, Mr. Kincaid?"

He turned to the rail as well. "All right, I confess. I did have an ulterior motive. I wanted to apologize."

"For what?"

"The way I embarrassed you at the captain's table when we were introduced. After I thought about it, I realized that some of my comments were a deliberate attempt to put you on the spot because you have such a pretty blush. That was rude of me."

"No it wasn't," Charlye said, touched by his concern and consideration. "You were just having fun. Playing the game. I understood that. It's just that . . ."

"What?"

Charlye shrugged. "I embarrass too easily, but

21

that's not your fault. I don't much like being the center of attention."

"Everyone deserves to be in the spotlight from time to time, Charlotte."

"Only if they're comfortable in the light. And I'm not."

He cocked his head to one side and a lock of dark hair fell onto his forehead. "Is that a polite way of telling me to get lost?"

"No!" she said too quickly. He smiled in response, but there was no mockery in it. Just an apparent pleasure that his company was welcome. "I—I'm just afraid you'll find me a very dull companion," she confessed.

"Why would you think that?"

"I'm not exactly a social butterfly."

"That doesn't mean you're not an interesting person," he commented mildly, then stepped back from the rail. "Come, take a stroll with me and I'll prove it."

A smile that was part humor, part excitement tugged at Charlye's lips—and her heart. "How is a stroll on the deck going to prove I'm not boring?"

Dallas grinned, too. "You're right. It won't. But if talking to you proves so tedious that I feel compelled to throw myself overboard, I'd rather not be this close to the ship's propellers." He crooked his elbow and held it out to her. "Now, shall we walk?"

Charlye's smile was fully formed now and her heart was pounding a mile a minute. How could she possibly refuse? "All right," she said, slipping her hand through the crook of his arm. The silk of his shirt was a cool contrast to the warmth of the flesh and muscle beneath her hand. "But when they find you in the water masquerading as shark bait, don't blame me."

"It's a deal," he said with a chuckle as they began their leisurely stroll. "Now tell me about yourself—and don't be any more boring than absolutely necessary. Is this your first cruise?"

"It's my first everything. First cruise, first airline

flight, first evening gown, first masquerade party . . ." *First walk in the moonlight with a man who takes my breath away.* "Until this morning, the farthest I'd ever been away from home was Indianapolis."

"Where's home?"

"A little town in Indiana."

"What do you do there—besides blush when someone pays you a compliment?" he asked with a grin.

Charlye didn't waste time telling him that her experience with compliments was limited. "I work for a chain of residential health care facilities and nursing homes."

"What do you do for them?"

"Coordinate resident activities to be sure that the seniors stay active in the community."

Dallas slid his hand absently over Charlye's, trapping it between the silk of his sleeve and the roughness of his palm. "Like how?" he asked.

It suddenly became a struggle for Charlye to remember what she did for a living. "Oh . . . we have a Grandparents' Program that matches seniors with kids who need attention, guidance. And I make sure there's a steady stream of volunteer work that needs doing to keep them busy—and visible," she added. "We're one of the only societies on earth that shuts its elderly away as though it's a crime to get old. I've made it my personal mission in life to see that none of the seniors in my care are ever cast aside."

"That's quite a mission," he said, giving her an appreciative sidelong look. "One of the most worthwhile I've ever heard."

The respect in his voice warmed Charlye all over. She shrugged. "It keeps me busy."

"All the time? Don't you have any hobbies?"

Charlye thought of the laptop computer that was waiting for her in her cabin. "I write. A little," she confessed, and then wondered why on earth she'd told him. Her scribblings were part of a secret she'd kept separate from the rest of her life since she was twelve years old.

"Poetry?" he guessed.

23

Connie Bennett

Charlye laughed disparagingly. "Do I look like a poet to you?"

Dallas chuckled. "I don't know. What does a poet look like?"

"I have no idea," she said sheepishly. "Just not like me."

"Okay. Then what do you write?"

She shook her head vaguely. "Just . . . stuff." There was no way she was going to tell him the truth. "Nothing that will ever be published."

He respected her reticence and didn't pursue the topic any further. They came to a staircase and he guided them up to the Compass Deck where the only canopy over their heads was the moon and a sky full of stars. It was an appropriate setting, since all the areas of the *Caribbean Star* were named according to a celestial theme.

As they strolled the Sunwalk past the Eclipse Snack Bar and the Stargazer Lounge, they laughed about some of the other cleverly named places in the shipboard community, like the Aries Sports Arena, the Gemini Twin Cinema, and Cosmo's Hair Salon, which wasn't actually a celestial reference to the universe. The head stylist just so happened to be named Cosmo—as Charlye had discovered this afternoon when he'd enthusiastically created her ultra-forties, Bette Davis hairstyle.

"All right, I want the truth," Dallas said as they started their second revolution on the Sunwalk.

"About what?"

"Why you chose to spend the cruise impersonating Charlotte Vale," he replied. "You had almost a full century of screen personas to choose from. Why this one?"

The question took her by surprise. "*Now, Voyager* is my favorite movie, and since it's about a sea cruise it seemed somehow . . . appropriate."

"Why is it your favorite movie? What do you have in common with Charlotte Vale?"

Let me count the ways . . . "Our names, for one thing."

24

"You real name is Charlotte?"

She nodded. "But my friends call me Charlye."

He stopped at the rail and looked at her with a hopeful smile. "Then may I call you Charlye, too?"

Charlye felt the impact of that smile all the way to her toes. "Of course."

"Okay, Charlye. What else?"

It took her a second to catch up with the conversation. "What else do I have in common with Charlotte Vale?" The answer to that question covered territory Charlye didn't want to discuss—not on this wonderful, surreal, too-perfect-to-be-true night. "Nothing," she told him. "I just happen to like stories where the heroine undergoes a Cinderella-like transformation, and *Now, Voyager* is the best of that genre. What about you?" she asked, hoping he'd allow her to change the subject. "What are you doing on this cruise?"

He grinned devilishly. "I would have thought that was self-explanatory. With a face like this, I couldn't very well come aboard and impersonate Harrison Ford."

Charlye blushed. "That's not what I meant. It's obvious why you chose Dallas Kincaid. I meant, why do something as silly as a masquerade cruise?"

He shrugged. "It was mostly a matter of timing. I needed a vacation badly, and this sounded like a lot of fun."

"A vacation from what?"

A cloud passed over his face, as though her question had sent him to a place he'd rather not go. Charlye ached to call her question back even before he said, "From talking about what I do for a living, for one thing."

Charlye flushed with embarrassment. "I'm sorry," she said, turning to the rail. "I forgot the rules. For the next two weeks, you're Dallas Kincaid. End of story. I shouldn't have asked."

She pushed away from the rail, but Dallas caught her arm and kept her beside him. When she looked into his eyes she discovered genuine remorse. "No,

Connie Bennett

I'm the one who's sorry. I didn't mean to be sharp with you. And *I'm* the one who broke the rules with all those questions about where you're from and what you do for a living. You had every right to ask me the same." He slid his hand lightly down her arm until their palms touched and his fingers curled around hers. "Please don't be angry with me."

Charlye's mouth was as dry as cotton. "I'm not."

"Good."

His gaze held hers and the air between them seemed to be alive with something Charlye couldn't begin to name. It wrapped around her and curled inside her. It was wonderful. It was frightening. It was much too perfect to be real.

But please, God, let it be real . . .

"What are your plans for tomorrow?" Dallas asked, his voice soft and sexy.

Charlye could barely think. "Tomorrow?"

He nodded. "Tomorrow. You know, Friday. The twenty-four-hour period that usually comes right after Thursday."

Charlye grinned sheepishly. "Oh, *that* tomorrow."

"Yeah, that one." Dallas sandwiched her hand between both of his and raised it up. For an instant, she thought he was going to press a kiss to it, but he only held it next to his chest, with the silk of his shirt brushing lightly against her fingers. "How are you spending the day?" he asked her.

"Why?"

"Because I want to spend it with you."

Charlye was so mesmerized she could only ask the same question again as she searched his handsome face. "Why?"

Dallas smiled. "Because you don't know how to pretend."

She thought about the fantasy she'd been indulging in before he'd found her, and she couldn't help chuckling. "If you only knew," she muttered. "I've got enough imagination for everyone on this boat."

"But not an ounce of artifice."

Charlye could tell he meant it as a compliment, but

26

it didn't feel like one. She slipped her hand out of his and turned toward the ocean. "You mean, not an ounce of sophistication, don't you?"

Dallas stepped closer. "Sophistication is only the ability to pretend we're something more than we really are—smarter, sexier, more experienced, more powerful . . . You don't know how to be anything but yourself."

Charlye found the courage to turn her face up to his and look into his dark eyes, but her voice was little more than a whisper. "The way you say it, I could almost believe that's a good thing."

"It is, Charlye," he said softly, dipping his head toward hers. "It's a *very* good thing."

Charlye's breath caught in her throat and the world seemed to tilt a little to one side. He was going to kiss her. This funny, intelligent, insightful man with the face of an angel and a smile that could put the devil to shame was going to kiss Charlye Nolan. His lips closed in on hers, his hand slid around her waist. The other hand came up to touch her cheek, and Charlye could smell the musky scent of his aftershave, could feel the heat that radiated from his body.

His thumb brushed across her lower lip, sending a cascade of sensation rippling through her, and then his lips were there, sending more sensations chasing the first. His mouth was soft and warm, the kiss was undemanding. His lips simply lingered on hers, pressing lightly, teasing her mouth with the faintest pressure imaginable until every nerve ending in her body suddenly shifted to her lips. Then his tongue began a gentle exploration, and Charlye was lost.

She opened to him eagerly, and in the space of a heartbeat the kiss changed from sweet and uncomplicated to something hungry and impatient. Dallas gathered her to him and needs blossomed inside Charlye that she'd never felt before. What had for years been vague, restless longings became insistent demands that begged to be met, fires that needed immediate quenching. Passions Charlye hadn't known she was capable of feeling swept through her, scorching her with their intensity.

It was too much for her—too much sensation, too much hunger . . . Dallas's mouth was plundering hers in a sensual imitation of an even more intimate mating dance, and reality finally slapped Charlye in the face.

This couldn't be happening. Dynamic, handsome, sexy men like this one weren't attracted to boring, unimaginative, mousy little nobodies like Charlotte Nolan. Why, out of all the women on this cruise, had he chosen her? There had to be a reason why she was in his arms, why she could feel his heart beating wildly beneath her hand. There had to be a reason why, when his mouth finally left hers and he raised his head, the look in his dark eyes conveyed a hunger as strong as Charlye's. There had to be a reason . . .

"Are you part of the prize?" The breathless question popped out before Charlye had any idea that she was even thinking it.

Dallas looked a little dazed. "Prize?"

Charlye cleared her throat and stepped out of his arms. It was the only hope she had of thinking clearly enough to explain. "This masquerade cruise. I won the trip, the costumes, a beauty makeover, everything, in a contest." She took a deep breath to steady the quaver in her voice. "Are you part of it? Are you an employee of the cruise line?"

Dallas stared at her in disbelief. "You think someone is paying me to be with you?"

"Not just to be with me. To . . ." Heat flushed Charlye's face again. She looked out to sea. ". . . you know."

"No, I don't," he protested, taking her arm and forcing her to look at him. "To what?"

Charlye had never felt like such an idiot, but she'd started this line of questioning and he wasn't letting her off the hook. "To flirt with me. To romance me. To do . . . whatever it was that you were doing."

Dallas leaned against the rail. "Well, if you don't know, I must be losing my technique."

Charlye couldn't get a fix on what he was thinking or feeling. At first, he'd seemed disbelieving, then irritated, but now she wasn't sure. He seemed almost . . . amused. "Oh, there's nothing wrong with your technique," she assured him, without bothering to add that though she didn't have a lot to compare it with she couldn't imagine how anyone could have done it better.

"That's good to know," he replied and Charlye could see a definite twinkle returning to his eyes. "I'm glad it was recognizable as a kiss—because it certainly felt like one to me," he added.

Did it ever. "Then you do work for the Star Cruise Line, right?" she asked tentatively. "You're a celebrity impersonator and they pay you to mingle with the guests."

His amusement vanished. "You're not joking, are you?" he asked with a frown.

"No. Are you an employee here?"

Dallas looked at her so long and so intensely that Charlye had the feeling he was trying to see inside her, to crawl inside her head and find out what made her tick. Logically, she knew that he didn't have that power, but logic hadn't played much of a role in her life this evening.

She turned away from him, denying him access to the windows to her soul. People had been rejecting Charlye all her life—people like her father, who'd walked out of her life when she was seven years old. And her invalid mother, who'd spent the twenty years that followed blaming Charlye for Don Nolan's desertion. If she gave this Dallas Kincaid look-alike access to her soul, he might see, like everyone else, that there was nothing inside her worth sticking around for. It was easier to turn away than risk rejection.

But Dallas didn't let her escape. "Who did this to you?" he asked after a long moment.

The question startled her. "Did what?"

"Convinced you that you're so worthless as a woman that no man would want to kiss you unless he was getting paid for it."

Charlye flushed with shame. When he said it out loud like that it was so humiliating that she couldn't do anything but deny it. "Don't be ridiculous. That's not what I think."

"It's what you just said."

"Well, that's not what I meant," she said with more bravado than she felt. "I am not *worthless*."

"Of course you're not. But the irony here is that I'm a total stranger and I believe that more strongly than you do."

It was a simple declarative statement, but Charlye had never felt more threatened by anything in her life. "You don't know anything about me," she said defiantly as her flight instinct kicked in.

"But I want to."

"I don't think that's a good idea." She pushed away from the rail.

"I disagree."

"Sorry, you don't get a vote. Thank you for the walk and the conversation and the kiss. You can tell your boss you definitely earned your pay this evening. Good night."

"Wait a minute," Dallas commanded as she started for the stairs. When she didn't obey, he fell into step beside her. "Charlye—"

"*Charlotte.*"

"Oh, good grief. Charlotte, will you please slow down? Or even better, *stop*, for crying out loud."

"It's late, Mr. Kincaid—or whatever your real name is. It's late, I'm tired, and I've lost my appetite for this game we've been playing."

"Game—"

"That's right, game. I don't want to play any more," she told him flatly. "Now, please leave me alone."

She quickened her pace toward the stairway and heard Dallas's footsteps falling away until he came to a stop.

"Charlotte!" he called out impatiently.

But she didn't look back.

Chapter Three

Charlye felt like ten kinds of a fool. The way she'd literally run away from Dallas Kincaid last night was as humiliating as the things he'd concluded about her. Was she really that much of a coward? And was she that transparent to the rest of the world? Did she wear her insecurities on her sleeve for all the world to see, or was the handsome stranger who'd romanced her in the moonlight gifted with some special ability?

Or had she just imagined the whole thing? Had she been living in fantasies inside her head for so long that one of them had slipped out and become real?

No, Charlye decided. She was shy, insecure, and probably a little naive, but she wasn't crazy. The man who looked like Dallas Kincaid had flirted with her. He'd held her hand and assailed her with idle flattery. He'd been charming as all get-out, and then he'd given her that mind-numbing, earth-shattering kiss.

Which she had run away from just as surely as she'd run away from his insights into her personality. If that wasn't cowardice, the word didn't mean what Charlye thought it meant.

"There she is! See, ladies? I told you she was the sit-in-a-deck chair-and-read-a-book kind of gal."

"You were right, as usual, dear boy," Aunt Jane said.

"Charlotte, darling!"

Charlye dropped the novel she'd been pretending to read into her lap. Sauntering down the deck sandwiched between Lauren and Aunt Jane was the cruise line's replica of Dallas Kincaid.

Charlye swallowed hard. Today, he looked as though he'd walked straight out of the movie *Court Martial*, wearing the crisp dress whites of a Navy officer. No man in uniform had ever looked better.

Charlye forgot for a moment that she had been dreading seeing him because of the way she'd humiliated herself. In fact, she found herself drinking in the sight of him. What she found in his eyes surprised her. Where she might have expected mockery or disdain she saw only caution.

"Good morning, Charlotte," he said politely as the trio stopped near the end of her chaise.

Charlye struggled to meet his gaze calmly, as though nothing intimate or embarrassing had passed between them the night before. "Good morning, Mr. Kincaid, ladies," she replied.

Lauren disengaged her hand from the crook of Dallas's elbow and moved to her. "Charlotte, darling, we've been looking absolutely everywhere for you. What are you doing here? You're much too young to be lolling about like this."

"I'm getting a tan," Charlye replied equitably. "That's a perfectly acceptable pastime on a cruise ship, Lauren."

Jane looked up at the canvas awning that provided a canopy for this entire section of deck. "In the shade, dear?"

32

Charlye could feel Dallas's eyes on her, but she did her best to pretend otherwise. He had assumed the "at ease" position with his hat beneath his arm, and he was studying her in the same penetrating, unnerving manner he had studied her the previous night.

Her '40s-style bathing suit was modest in the extreme, but Charlye was glad she'd donned the white sleeveless cover-up that matched it. It made her feel less conspicuous. Her legs were showing, though, and Dallas seemed to be inspecting them thoroughly. She refused to squirm under the examination.

"I burn easily, so I have to work at tanning in stages," she told Lauren. "I moved out of the sun a few minutes ago."

"Then you're not tanning anymore, are you?" the elderly siren said wisely. "You can join us."

Charlye's heart tripped in alarm. If it had been just the two ladies, she would have agreed, but they weren't alone. "Thank you, Lauren, but I already have plans."

"Sitting in the shade reading a book does not constitute a plan, dear," Jane informed her primly.

"*Other* plans," she lied, but Dallas didn't let her get away with it.

"Don't believe a word of it, Aunt Jane," he said. "She's just avoiding me because she thinks I'm a gigolo in the employ of the cruise line."

Jane turned a pair of sharp blue eyes up to him. "Are you?"

"Jane! What kind of a question is that?" Lauren exclaimed with exasperation.

The frail looking old lady in the filmy summer frock and floppy-brimmed straw hat was completely unrepentant. "A very good one, I think. Though I've been grateful for Mr. Kincaid's company this morning, one must wonder why the most handsome, eligible young man on the cruise would choose the company of two dotty old ladies."

"Speak for yourself," Lauren demanded. "I may be old enough to be his grandmother, but I'm not *dotty*."

"I'll say." Dallas was chuckling as he came forward and draped his arm around Lauren's shoulder. The old lady positively beamed at the attention he paid her. "Escorting the three most beautiful women on this cruise doesn't make me a gigolo—it makes me lucky." He looked at Charlye. "If you'll join us, that is."

Idle flattery came too easily to him, and Charlye knew better than to trust it. Or him.

"Yes, Charlotte, you must join us," Jane chimed in. "We're going down to the Evening Star to take gambling lessons."

"And directly after lunch, we're all going to sign up for Murder on the High Seas," Lauren added.

Charlye had been attracted by both activities when she'd looked over the extensive list of shipboard festivities. In fact, signing up for the murder mystery role-playing game had been on her mind when she'd told them she already had plans.

"That sounds nice, but I'm not dressed for the casino," she said lamely.

"Oh, you're more than presentable for any daytime shipboard activity," Dallas assured her. "And most of the nighttime ones, too."

Was she imagining it, or had there been a hint of sexual innuendo in his voice? she wondered. When she glanced at him sharply, he looked as innocent as a newborn babe.

"Come join us, Charlotte, please," Jane pleaded.

Charlye looked at the sweet-faced octogenarian and found that she couldn't refuse. More than that, she didn't really *want* to. She liked both ladies very much, and despite her embarrassment and a lingering distrust of Dallas, she liked him very much, too. Probably way too much.

"All right. Count me in." She slipped the paperback into her oversize beach bag, and stood.

"Wonderful!" Lauren exclaimed.

"Indeed it is," Dallas said with a smile for Charlye that warmed her all the way down to her toes.

Charlye felt an accursed blush creeping up on her

again, but if Dallas saw it, he didn't comment. Lauren took him by the arm and started off briskly toward the elevators, leaving Charlye with the pseudo Jane Marple.

"It was sweet of you to think of including me in your plans, Aunt Jane," she said as they followed the other two. Charlye adjusted her speed to the elderly woman's snail's pace without even thinking.

"Oh, you mustn't thank Lauren or me, dear," Jane replied. "Inviting you to join us was Dallas's idea. A most welcome one, of course, but all his own. When your name came up at breakfast, he expressed a sincere concern that you might spend too much time alone on this cruise."

Charlye wasn't sure how to feel about that. It was just one more instance of the man's uncanny insight into her personality. "Not everyone's a joiner, Aunt Jane," she said by way of explanation.

"And there's nothing wrong with being a private person, to be sure, but there's a difference between being a loner and being alone." She tucked her hand into the crook of Charlye's arm and asked shrewdly, "Which are you, dear?"

Charlye found she couldn't look into those perceptive blue eyes and lie. "Maybe a little of both."

"Then don't even consider saying no the next time our handsome Mr. Kincaid requests the pleasure of your company," she advised. "He's genuinely smitten with you, dear. Why, last night when he realized that you'd left the Constellation Room, he was very disappointed. He danced one dance with Lauren, then extricated himself from the clutches of Miss Madonna and went looking for you. I hope he found you."

Charlye nodded. "Yes. He did."

Jane inspected her closely, frowning. "Dear, if I was forty years younger and had a handsome young man like that courting me, I'd look much happier about it than you do."

"But I don't know anything about him, and the

rules of the cruise prohibit asking any questions," Charlye found herself confessing.

"Oh, pishtosh," the old lady scoffed. "Knowledge is vastly overrated. You can look into a man's eyes and know everything you need to know about him."

"I'm not so sure that's true."

"Trust me. It is. And besides, he told us all about himself at breakfast, and there's no great mystery. He owns a greenhouse and nursery in California. And he also picks up a little extra income by acting as a celebrity impersonator from time to time."

Charlye felt simultaneous urges to shout "aha!" and to cry. "Then I was right. He is in the employ of the cruise line!"

Jane frowned again. "Oh, I don't think so, dear. He mentioned something about having been in dire need of a long vacation. He's just a tourist, like us."

Which left him without a motive for trying to seduce Charlye. Unless, of course, he really was attracted to her. "Did he happen to tell you his real name?" she asked hopefully. "It seems so odd calling him Dallas Kincaid when that's not who he really is."

"No, sorry," Jane answered, and then added helpfully, "but he's divorced and he has no children—though he'd very much like to start a family someday. I'd say that makes him a prize catch, wouldn't you?"

Charlye caught her lower lip between her teeth and shrugged. "I suppose so."

"You don't sound convinced."

"I just wish I could be sure of his motives," she confessed.

"For pursuing a sweet, attractive young woman? I should think his intent would be perfectly obvious to anyone."

Except me, Charlye thought.

Jane patted her hand. "Just relax and enjoy the cruise, dear. Let nature take its course."

Charlye winced. "I think nature may be vastly overrated," she mumbled.

But Jane's hearing was as sharp as her mind. "Oh,

my. If you believe that, you're much younger than I thought, dear."

"Not young, just naive," she replied glumly.

Jane chuckled. "Good for you! Some men find a touch of naivete very attractive. Now, cheer up! Stop trying to analyze our Mr. Kincaid and enjoy his attention. There's no law that says you have to fall in love with a man just because he gives you a wink and a tickle."

"Hey, you slow pokes! Move it!" Lauren commanded from well ahead of them.

"Oh, dear," Jane muttered, picking up the pace. "We'd better kick it into high gear, or we'll never hear the end of it. Hild—er—Lauren can be a real tyrant when you're on her bad side. Come on, Charlotte, shake a leg."

Charlye laughed as she quickened her steps to keep up. Jane was absolutely right. It was time to stop dissecting every situation and start living. "Yes, ma'am. I'm shaking as fast as I can."

Charlye had never received better advice in her life. With Jane and Lauren as a buffer, she was able to relax and enjoy herself. The result was one of the best days of her life. Under the tutelage of the casino staff, she and the ladies learned the basic rules of craps and roulette, but it was Dallas's able coaching that added finesse to their play. Lauren and Jane had delightful—and sometimes scathingly pithy—comments on every topic under the sun, and the four of them laughed through the remainder of the morning, through lunch, and a healthy portion of the afternoon.

A part of Charlye tried without much success to be suspicious of Dallas, but he was not only a perfect gentleman, he was also the ideal companion for three women. He was like a master juggler keeping three delicate vessels in the air all at once and having a great time doing it.

Lauren and Jane positively glowed at the attention he paid them, and Charlye found herself trusting

Connie Bennett

him more and more as the day wore on. If he had
ulterior motives for paying attention to her, they
didn't apply to Lauren and Jane; there was nothing
phony about his regard for them. Charlye had spent
enough time around the elderly to know when someone was genuinely comfortable, and Dallas wasn't
faking any of his enjoyment of their company, their
stories, and their delightful idiosyncracies. This Dallas Kincaid wasn't a real movie star, but he was definitely one of the good guys.

That's what finally helped her become really comfortable around him: She got past his uncanny resemblance to America's hottest sex symbol and saw
him as a real person—handsome, funny, and kind,
to be sure—but just an ordinary guy.

Charlye was having so much fun that she hated to
see it end, but Jane and Lauren had signed up for
the Senior Bridge Tournament that began that afternoon. Dallas seemed almost as reluctant as Charlye
to let them go when they escorted the ladies up to
the Saturn Room on the main deck.

"Now, don't forget, eight o'clock!" Lauren said,
though it was more of a command than a reminder
that the foursome had made a date to visit the casino
to put their lessons to good use.

"Eight it is," Dallas replied, then waggled a finger
at Lauren. "And don't *you* forget to wear your dancing shoes. I need a partner for the fox-trot."

"I'll be ready."

Jane shook her head at them as she gave Lauren a
little push toward the door. "Don't believe it. She's
never been ready on time for anything in her life."

Dallas bent and gave the diminutive lady a kiss on
the cheek. "Then you'll have to be my dance partner."

"Oh, pishtosh," she said, but she was beaming and
her cheeks were blushing pink as she disappeared
inside.

Charlye looked at Dallas and something con-
stricted in her heart. How could she not feel warmly
toward a man who had such a gift for making sweet
little old ladies feel special?

38

"They adore you," she told him as they began ambling down the corridor. "You're just wonderful with them."

Dallas seemed genuinely pleased by the compliment. "You're pretty high on their list, too. And I can understand why—has anyone ever told you that you have a wicked sense of humor?"

Charlye flushed. "No, not *wicked*."

"Well, I haven't had this much fun since—" He thought it over and shrugged. "—since I honestly can't remember when."

"Me, too."

He rubbed his hands together. "So . . . what do we do now?"

Charlye was undeniably pleased that he wanted to spend some more time with her. "We?"

His dark eyebrows shot up. "You're sick of me already? I thought we were doing pretty well. You haven't bored me into suicide and I haven't chased you away with any unwanted advances."

Charlye supposed it was inevitable that he bring up what had happened last night. She felt compelled to tell him, "I'm sorry about that, Dallas—the way I ran away from you."

He shook his head. "I was coming on too strong. I deserved to be abandoned. What do you say we take a swim and forget last night ever happened?"

Forgetting that kiss would be a lot easier said than done, but Charlye was happy to agree. "All right. Last one into the pool is a rotten egg."

Dallas laughed and looked down at his dress whites. "Very funny. I have a better idea. Why don't you walk with me up to my cabin while I change?"

That didn't sound like the best idea Charlye had ever heard. "I don't think—"

Dallas read her mind. "Don't worry. It's a suite," he said, taking her hand in his. "I promise you'll be perfectly safe. You can stay in the sitting room with the companionway door open while I change."

"Or I could wait for you at the pool," she suggested.

"True enough. But then I'd miss the pleasure of

your conversation and your sweet smile."

Charlye tried to restrain the smile he seemed to like so much. "Careful, Dallas. Don't lay it on too thick—the cruise line can't be paying you *that* well."

He sighed heavily. "Are we back to that? You still think someone is paying me to become totally besotted by you?"

Charlye's heartbeat quickened and a rush of heat flushed through her. "Besotted?"

He shrugged. "I've only known you for a day, and you're given to running away when pushed too hard. I can't very well say that I'm falling in love with you, now can I? You might throw yourself overboard."

His eyes were twinkling merrily, and Charlye wanted to tell him not to make jokes about things like falling in love, but doing so seemed ridiculous. Men made outrageous, flirtatious statements to women all the time—it didn't mean the woman had to believe they were true. As Jane had said, Charlye didn't have to fall in love just because a handsome man paid a little attention to her.

And anyway, what if she did fall just a little bit in love? So what? Where was the harm in that? This was a two-week cruise, and at the end of it she and Dallas would go their separate ways—if the relationship even lasted *that* long. He would probably get bored and move on in a few days, anyway.

In the meantime, a handsome, funny, kind, considerate, sexy guy wanted to treat shy little Charlotte Nolan to a little romance, so why shouldn't she enjoy it?

Charlye knew there was a flaw in her logic somewhere—it had something to do with guarding her heart and not falling *too* hard—but she didn't want to stop to examine the wisdom of her newly made decision. She wanted to have fun. She wanted to be wined and dined and treated as though she was someone special.

What was it Dallas had said last night? Everyone deserved to be in the spotlight from time to time. Well, this was Charlye's time in the spotlight, and she was going to bask in it for as long as it lasted.

"All right, Mr. Kincaid. Lead the way," she said.

She must have sounded uncharacteristically co-quettish, because Dallas's dark brows went up in surprise. "To my suite?"

She caught his gaze and held it steadily. "To wherever you want to lead."

Dallas cocked his head to one side and studied her. Charlye wondered if her eyes were betraying any of the excitement she felt. Could he sense what a daring step this was for her?

"That could take us to some ... interesting places," he said cautiously.

Charlye's chin came up as though rising to meet the challenge. With more daring than she'd ever dreamed she possessed, she told him, "I hope so, Dallas. I certainly hope so."

Chapter Four

Her satin evening gown shimmered in the light of her vanity mirrors as Charlye checked her hair one last time. It had looked better yesterday after Cosmo styled it, but it wasn't too bad tonight. The unswept spirals seemed a little more natural—probably because they weren't shellacked into place with a jumbo-size can of hair spray—but they would do.

Her makeup wasn't as dramatic as it had been last night, either, but in a way, Charlye liked it better. It was more natural, more like her, and she was beginning to think that despite everything her mother had ever said to her, being Charlye Nolan wasn't such a bad thing.

Last night at the captain's table, she'd wanted to be sophisticated Charlotte Vale; not only had she failed miserably, she'd had a miserable time. Today, with Jane, Lauren, and Dallas, she'd been plain, ordinary Charlye Nolan, and she'd had the time of her life.

There had to be a lesson in there somewhere, and Charlye was trying to learn it.

A knock on her door drew her away from the mirror and the philosophizing. She hurried into the main salon and looked around. Everything seemed to be in order. Room service had set out the hors d'oeuvres, and the luxury suite was equipped with a wet bar. Charlye had never in her life served cocktails before dinner, but she regularly hosted a variety of reception-type events for the residents at Green River's various retirement and nursing care facilities. She'd calmed her nervousness earlier by convincing herself that playing hostess to Dallas, Jane, and Lauren was just like a Green River tea party, only on a much smaller scale.

It was a deception that worked reasonably well. She was only moderately terrified when she opened the door to her guests. Her terror fled when she saw Dallas in his black tuxedo looking as if he'd stepped out of a James Bond movie. He really was too handsome to be from this world.

All Charlye could think to say was, "How is it possible that there could be *two* of you?"

A look of puzzlement crossed his face and he looked over his shoulder. "Two of me?" Then realization lit his eyes. "Oh, you mean my doppelganger—the real Dallas Kincaid. Frankly, I think his looks are overrated."

"That's because you're a man." Charlye stepped back so that he could enter.

"*You* on the other hand," he continued, as though she hadn't spoken, "look absolutely stunning."

"It's the dress. Another Bette Davis knock-off," she said modestly as he made a half-circle around her, appraising the gown and the woman in it—and giving every appearance of liking what he saw. Thanks to her '40s-style underclothes, the midnight blue gown fit her like a glove and gave her curves that

were considerably more generous than nature had
bestowed on her.

"There is nothing second rate about you, Charlye.
I swear."

She smiled at the compliment and the warm regard in his eyes. "Thank you." She started to close
the door, but realized that something was missing.
"Where are Lauren and Jane?"

"I'm afraid it's just us. Our friends are having dinner in their cabin tonight and then they're going to
turn in early."

"What? Why? I thought they were really looking
forward to an evening in the casino."

"They were, but Lauren says that Jane over-
extended herself playing shuffleboard, and Jane says
that Lauren had one too many gin and tonics at the
bridge tourney."

"Oh, no." Charlye's heart tripped in alarm and she
began searching for her beaded clutch purse. "I have
to check on them, Dallas. I was a little worried after
lunch that they were doing too much. Obviously I
was right."

Dallas caught up with her before she could expand
her search into the bedroom. "They're fine, Charlye,
I swear," he said, reassuring her. "I just came from
their cabin, and to tell you the truth, I think they're
doing a little not-so-subtle matchmaking—giving us
a chance to be alone."

Charlye had grown too fond of the ladies to shake
her concern easily, but it was not hard to believe Dallas's conjecture. "That certainly sounds like something they'd cook up, but it wasn't necessary."

"No, but it's very sweet." He gestured toward the
wet bar in the corner. "Shall we have a drink or
would you prefer to go on up to supper now?"

This changed the whole character of the evening,
but Charlye found she wasn't disappointed. "Drinks
would be nice, if you'll do the honors. I'm afraid I
haven't had much experience as a bartender."

"Glad to." He moved behind the bar. "What'll you
have?"

"Just a diet cola."

"Oh, come on," he cajoled, as he opened the refrigerator and looked inside. "Throw caution to the wind. Live dangerously!" He held up a can and grinned. "At least have a ginger ale."

Charlye laughed. "You cad! You're trying to ply me with carbonation so that you can take advantage of me."

"Curses. My plan has been discovered. You're entirely too shrewd for a scoundrel like me," he said, as he began fixing Charlye's cola and a scotch and water for himself. "Speaking of scoundrels, did you get your instructions for Murder on the High Seas?"

The role-playing game they'd signed up for earlier had been personalized for each player and instructions had been delivered to their cabins. One of the fourteen players had been assigned the role of murderer and the other thirteen had the job of ferreting him—or her—out.

"I'm supposed to be a mysterious, reclusive heiress with a dark and terrible secret," she told him. "How about you?"

"A daredevil, fortune-hunting playboy," he said, cutting her a courtly little bow. "Which gives me a perfect excuse to continue my relentless pursuit of you."

Charlye wanted to ask him if he really needed an excuse, but was afraid to be that brazen. Besides, she knew him well enough by now to realize that he was just making flirtatious small talk.

"When do you suppose the 'murder' will take place?" she asked instead, accepting the glass he held out to her.

"The Karaoke Singalong tomorrow night in the Orion Lounge," he replied.

Charlye was surprised by how definite he sounded. "Was that in your information packet? They gave me a list of shipboard activities that all of us are supposed to attend if we want access to all the clues, but they didn't get specific."

"No, it's just a guess," he replied, gesturing toward

Charlye's private patio as he came around the bar.

Charlye didn't take the hint. She looked at him through narrowed, suspicious eyes instead. "Are you sure you're not the murderer?"

"Positive."

She tilted her head to one side, trying to evaluate his answer. "I don't suppose you'd tell me even if you really were."

Dallas flashed her the devilish grin that set her pulse racing. "Not bloody likely. But it's not me, I swear." They moved outside to enjoy the gold-and-magenta sunset as he explained, "I got the same list you got and some interesting biographical data I'm supposed to be able to reveal if anyone questions me. I just think the karaoke night would be the perfect time. Everyone will be very relaxed and ready for anything."

They sat on the padded white wicker love seat. Charlye burrowed comfortably into one corner and crossed her legs, her body angled naturally toward Dallas. Being with him seemed so natural that she couldn't imagine what had prompted her to run away from him last night.

"I'm really looking forward to it," she told him. "I suppose it's silly, but I've always wanted to play one of these mystery role-playing games."

"They're great fun," he assured her. "You can buy kits, you know. They have all the roles and clues already established—you just give the information packets to your guests as they arrive."

Charlye nodded. "I know. I've seen them, but you have to have friends in order to play them."

Dallas looked at her in disbelief. "Oh, come on, Charlye. I can't believe you don't have any friends."

She realized how that sounded and flushed with embarrassment. "Of course I have friends. Good ones. But neither of them enjoy playing games," she told him, then realized that she hadn't really done anything to correct the image of a barren lifestyle. Two friends didn't exactly constitute a full dance card. "I mean, I'm just not a very social person."

"All it takes to be social is getting out and doing things, Charlye," he told her, but she shook her head.

"No, it's not as easy as that, Dallas. You have to know how to be frivolous, make small talk, be comfortable around groups of people. . . . I don't. That's a talent I never acquired or had a chance to practice."

Dallas cocked his head to one side. "Let me get this straight. You only have two friends, you don't know how to be frivolous, and you're uncomfortable in groups. What? Have you been locked away in a nunnery all your life?"

"Something like that," she admitted.

He looked even more shocked than when she'd insinuated she didn't have any friends. "A nunnery? Really?

"No, of course not! I'm sorry," she said, wondering how she'd gotten into this mess. "I just meant that I've lead a pretty . . . sheltered life."

"For any particular reason?"

"A very specific one, actually." She hesitated a moment before telling him, "When I was eleven my mother was crippled in a car wreck, paralyzed from the waist down. We couldn't afford much in the way of nursing care, so I had to do most of it."

Dallas's face was a mask of sympathy and concern. "Most of what?"

"Anything that needed to be done. Mother was a very—" Charlye struggled for the right word. "—needy person to begin with, and where other people might have tried rehabilitation, Mother chose to depend on me. And the older I got, the more responsibility I assumed. I went to school, then came straight home to take care of Mother. I didn't go to football games, I didn't go to dances, I didn't date. . . . By the time I got out of school mother's health had deteriorated to the point that she needed round-the-clock care, so I stayed home and took care of her because I couldn't earn enough with only a high school diploma to pay for nursing care."

Dallas shook his head as though he were trying to imagine what living like that would have been like,

Connie Bennett

but couldn't quite grasp it. "Charlye, that's not a life, that's slavery," he said.

She shrugged. "I did what I had to do."

"But you were just a child!"

She shrugged. "Children have to grow up eventually. It just comes sooner for some of us. But that's why I don't have a gaggle of girlfriends and I'm pitifully inept in most social situations."

"You're not inept, Charlye—you just feel that way," he assured her. "Where is your mother now?"

"She died three years ago."

"And you went to work for that health-care group?"

"Yes."

He reached out and took her hand in his. "That must have been a very confusing time for you. Losing a parent is devastating, but after being so closed in—"

Charlye knew where he was headed and she didn't want to go there. The price she paid for her freedom was a tremendous amount of guilt. "I adjusted," she said, cutting him off. "I adapted."

Dallas nodded and let it drop. "What about your father?"

Charlye took a sip of her cola and wished she'd been a little more daring in her choice of beverage. Even after all these years she couldn't think about him without feeling a sharp stab of pain. Adding it to the feelings she'd just stirred up about her mother made her wish she'd found a way to avoid this discussion.

She was still looking at the ice in her glass when she confessed, "My father left us when I was seven. He was a stock car racer who liked to travel the circuit year-round. When I had to start going to school, he couldn't handle settling into one place. He went off to a race in New Mexico one day and never came back."

"Oh, Charlye . . ." Dallas squeezed her hand. "I'm so sorry."

A nervous little laugh bubbled in her throat. "I

know. It's pathetic. If you threw in a blizzard and a buzz saw, my life story would read like something out of a bad melodrama." Dallas chuckled generously at her attempt at humor, and Charlye was encouraged to add, "All I need now is for you to start twirling your moustache like Snidely Whiplash."

He held up one hand. "Hey, I've only got white hats in my closet, I swear."

She smiled at him, but she knew that there was a touch of sadness in it. "I hope that's true, Dallas."

"Trust me."

"That might be easier if I knew your real name." The statement popped out before she could censor it, but after the way he'd reacted to her question about him last night, she knew she had to call it back. "I'm sorry. We agreed last night that that subject was off-limits. I didn't mean to say that." She stood up quickly. "Can I get you another drink? Or some hors d'oeuvres?"

She stepped to the door, but Dallas came to his feet and blocked her hasty retreat. "Charlye, it's okay. My real name is—"

She held up her hand. "No. Don't tell me."

He looked at her with obvious surprise. "Why not?"

Why not, indeed? She wanted to know his name, but in a way, she didn't want to know, either. She felt like a princess in a fairy tale, and part of her wanted to know who this Prince Charming really was so that she could believe that what was happening to her was real. But there was also a silly, niggling fear that knowing the truth would burst the magical bubble that encased her. Somehow, it suddenly seemed safer to maintain the element of fantasy.

"Because if you tell me your name," she explained, "that's how I'll think of you, and I'm bound to slip up and call you that when there other people around."

"So?"

"So, it's not fair. You came on this very expensive cruise and invested in some wonderful costumes so that you could spend two weeks as Dallas Kincaid, Famous Movie Star. I have no right to spoil that for you."

"You're not spoiling anything, Charlye. It's no big deal, really. Like the old saying goes, 'it doesn't matter what you call me—so long as you *call* me.' My real name is—" He paused and sighed, an amused grin tugging at his lips as though he could hardly bring himself to say the words.

Charlye found herself leaning toward him expectantly. "Yes?"

"Dwayne Lewis Hadjepetris."

Charlye straightened and stared at him. "You're kidding, right?"

He shook his head. "Nope."

"Hatchi . . . Ha—"

He laughed at her attempts to wrap her tongue around the outrageous name. He spelled it for her, then pronounced it again. "Hadjepetris. It's Greek."

"I'll say."

He laughed again. "See why I wanted to be Dallas Kincaid? I don't envy his fame or fortune, but I sure do like his name. My friends and family call me Del— I wish you would, too."

"Del." She tried it on for size. It didn't fit him quite as well as Dallas, but it was better than Dwayne. Charlye still had vivid memories of a bully by the same name who'd made her elementary school years sheer torture. "I suppose it's derived from your initials—D. L."

"Exactly. And it's close enough to a nickname for Dallas that no one will think twice if they hear you call me Del."

She knew his name now, and the magic hadn't disappeared. Did she dare try for more? "Would I be pushing my luck if I asked about your family?"

"I think I can accommodate that request, but you'd better bring out the hors d'oeuvres. I can't recite the Hadjepetris family history on an empty stomach."

Charlye did as he suggested and Del replenished their drinks as he began telling her about his great-grandparents, Greek immigrants who came to America just after the turn of the century. By the time he'd brought her up to the present generation who operated a family-owned greenhouse, the sun had long since set, the ocean was deep black, and Charlye felt as though she'd just made friends with Del's entire boisterous family.

"What about your brother? Does he look like Dallas Kincaid, too?" she asked.

"No," he said, with a shake of his head. "He got Mel Gibson."

Charlye laughed. "Did he get a better name, too?"

Del raised one black eyebrow, but let the gibe go unchallenged. "He doesn't think so. He says anyone who would name a kid Krispin should be drawn and quartered."

"Krispin?"

Del shrugged. "At least it's Greek. I don't know where they came up with Dwayne."

"Your family sounds wonderful. And big." He had a brother, three sisters, six nieces and nephews, seven assorted aunts and uncles, and more cousins than he could "shake an olive branch at," as he'd put it. For someone like Charlye who'd always dreamed of belonging to a big, loving family, it sounded like paradise.

"You'll have to meet them someday," Del said.

"I'd like that." Charlye knew he was only being polite, but it reminded her that once this fortnight cruise was over, she'd never see this wonderful man again. She could tell already that the parting was going to be incredibly painful.

"So, do you feel better now that you know who I am and where I came from?" he asked.

"I didn't feel bad before, Del. I just didn't feel like I knew who you were."

"Now, you do. Disappointed?"

"Why would I be?"

"My life isn't glamorous like Dallas Kincaid's."

Charlye shook her head. "Glamour is highly overrated," she told him. "And it's also very intimidating.

I wouldn't know how to deal with an honest-to-goodness movie star like Kincaid, but a farmer from Fig Garden, California . . . That's someone I can relate to."

Del's arm slid along the back of the love seat as he leaned closer. "Then you won't run away next time I kiss you?"

Charlye's breath caught in her throat when it appeared that he was going to match the deed to his words. "No. I won't run," she managed to whisper.

"Good," he said brightly as he leaned back and reached for a canapé.

The abrupt change in mood startled Charlye. "You mean you're n—" She caught herself this time before she could say anything embarrassing.

Del looked at her, his black eyebrows raised, his expression too innocent to be real. "Not going to what?"

Charlye blushed and stood. "Nothing. Never mind." She picked up the hors d'oeuvres tray. "We should probably go up for dinner."

Del stood as well, blocking her exit. "Not going to what?" he pressed, plucking the tray out of her hands and returning it to the table. He straightened and looked at her. "Not going to kiss you? Is that what you were going to say?"

He was teasing her, and enjoying it entirely too much. "You know very well what I was thinking."

Del slipped one arm around her waist, holding her only very lightly. "And am I to infer from your question that you would *like* to be kissed?"

Charlye tried to keep her voice and her breathing steady. She could only half-manage it by avoiding his dark eyes and the wicked grin that was teasing the corners of his full lips. "Only if you want to," she replied, knowing she didn't sound at all indifferent. "I mean, if it's not a *strain* or anything—"

Del pulled her tight against him, stealing Charlye's breath away. She looked into his face, and everything inside her melted.

"Kissing you would never be anything but intense

pleasure, Charlye," he whispered. "Very intense." And then his mouth was on hers, proving how true that was. Charlye's lips parted automatically, inviting him in, welcoming him to take what he wanted, and he did. Somehow rough and gentle at the same time, he plundered her mouth and her senses. Without even thinking about it, Charlye's own tongue mirrored the intimate liberties of his and she was thrilled by the low moan that rumbled in Del's throat.

Knowing she had done something to please him made her want to do more, and Charlye wrapped her arms around Del's shoulders, arching into him as she wove one hand into his thick hair. Del's arm around her waist tightened, and his other hand moved impatiently down her thigh and up again. His lips left hers so that he could press fevered kisses along her jaw and down her throat, and Charlye groaned with pleasure when his roving hand found her breast and cupped it, kneaded it, caressed it until a hard pinpoint of heat blossomed and spread outward.

Charlye was vaguely aware that she murmured something . . . it might have been Del's name or a plea that he continue. Whatever it was, it earned another rumbling moan from Del and a searing kiss that Charlye returned with equal fire.

"Oh, Charlye . . ." Del's mouth left hers but his arms sealed their bodies together. One hand moved lower to cup her buttocks and fit her hips even more tightly to his, letting her know exactly what he wanted. "Charlye, we have to stop now, or I won't be able to. God, how I want you."

Charlye couldn't bear the thought of stopping, either. She had never made love with a man before, but she knew that the anticipation his skillful lips and hands evoked had a natural conclusion. She didn't want to step out of Del's arms until she had experienced that climax fully—in every sense of the word.

Charlye couldn't imagine why a man like this would want her, but there could be no doubt that he

Connie Bennett

did. She could feel the long, hard ridge of his masculinity pressing against her abdomen and just the thought of feeling it inside her made the ache between her thighs unbearable.

She chased Del's lips and pressed a breathless kiss to his mouth. "Don't stop, Del. Please."

"Mmmm . . ." His teeth nipped at her lower lip. "Charlye, are you sure?"

Her body shifted, rubbing against him intimately out of pure instinct, giving him all the answer he needed. His lips branded hers one last time, then he pulled away abruptly, taking her hand to guide her indoors, through the sitting room and into the bedroom.

The lights were off, and the only illumination came from the vanity in the dressing room next door, casting a golden glow that was almost like candlelight. Del stopped by the bed and Charlye looked into his dark eyes. The raw hunger in them thrilled her and moved her at the same time. She'd spent a thousand restless, lonely nights dreaming of being wanted like this. Now it was happening. It wasn't a dream.

She couldn't help herself. She reached for him, searching for his lips, but Del evaded her. Instead, he turned her away from him and began a sensuous search for the pins that held her hair. She felt them skitter to the carpet one by one as strands of her shoulder-length hair came tumbling down. Del ran his hands through it, then gathered it into a mass that he pulled to one side, exposing Charlye's throat.

Her breath hissed between her teeth when he pressed a kiss behind her ear, then nipped at the lobe playfully until it was as sensitive as every other place Del had touched tonight. His lips worked magic down the column of her throat as his hands unfastened her gown. A brush of his hand slipped it off her shoulder and a second later it was a pool of midnight blue satin at her feet.

A shiver went through Charlye, but it had nothing to do with her sudden state of undress. Rather, it was the way Del slowly unfastened her bra and let it fall to the floor. The way he lightly, almost casually, brushed his fingertips across the hard, sensitive pinpoints of her nipples, then moved lower to divest her of the remainder of her restrictive underclothes.

And then she was finally naked, standing there trembling with need and the terrible fear that he wouldn't be pleased by what he had unveiled. But he didn't look. Instead, he let his hands discover her. His lips nuzzled her ear as his hands traced the angles of her shoulder blades. His tongue tested her pulse as it quickened when he filled his hands with her breasts, kneading them, savoring their weight, brushing his thumbs across the crests and making Charlye moan.

Her knees wouldn't hold her, and she leaned back against him. "Del, please . . ."

"Please, what, Charlye?" he muttered against her throat, but he knew exactly what she wanted because one of his hands moved lower, down her abdomen until his fingers were sliding through soft curls of hair, then deeper still, into the very center of the fiery ache burning inside her.

Charlye gasped Del's name as his hand began to move, building the fire to an inferno. She arched her back, instinctively grinding her buttocks against the hard ridge of his arousal. With his other arm, Del pinned her to him as his fingers danced inside her and urged her to higher plane of arousal. Charlye rocked against his hand, straining toward the pleasure that was building.

"Del, please . . . please . . . oh, God . . . Del . . . yes . . . *Del*." She cried out his name again and again as the heat of the climax coursed through her.

The pleasure blinded her, set her senses ablaze. She had no idea how it happened, but as the wave of pleasure passed, she found herself in Del's arms, facing him this time, his lips claiming hers as though he were trying to drink in the sound of his own name as she cried it. And then the wave died away and Charlye found herself being lowered gently onto the

Connie Bennett

bed. She was only vaguely aware that the bedclothes had been thrown back and she didn't stop to wonder when—in the midst of all this magic—he'd had the chance.

"Del . . ."

"Shhh . . ." He hovered over her, pressing a gentle kiss to her lips, then left her quickly and began tearing at his own clothes with far less finesse than he'd used with Charlye. There was grace and power in his movements, and Charlye understood why. His torso was lean and muscled, a sculpture of masculine perfection. Dark, curling hair dusted his chest and formed a perfect V that automatically drew her eye to the fly of his trousers.

He bent to slip off his shoes, and the idea of touching Del as intimately as he'd touched her set Charlye on fire again. Without thinking about it for fear she'd lose her nerve, she got to her knees on the bed. When Del straightened, Charlye was there, brushing away his hands, placing her own on the button of his trousers, slowly sliding the zipper down, sending the trousers to the floor. He grabbed Charlye's shoulders as her hands slid between his briefs and his skin, and then he was as naked as she.

A sudden burst of shyness washed through Charlye, but her curiosity and her need overwhelmed it almost instantly and she reached out to touch the shaft of his manhood. It was soft and hard at the same time; silk and steel. She ran her hand down the length of it and back again.

Del gasped and his fingers bit into Charlye's shoulders as he brought her mouth up to his. He laid her back against the bed, kissing her wildly, using his mouth and his hands to arouse her all over again, and then he left her one last time to sheathe himself in a condom.

When he returned, one knee slid between Charlye's and she opened to him. His hand skimmed her buttock and thigh, encouraging her to fold her legs around his. She closed her eyes and arched upward, but he only hovered above her, withholding the plea-

56

sure that she wanted more than she'd ever wanted anything in her life.

"Look at me, Charlye. Look at me," he commanded, his voice harsh and husky with desire. "I want to see your face, your eyes . . ."

She opened her eyes and looked into his. The heat and hunger in them thrilled her. "Please, Del . . ." Her hand ran down his body, seeking his manhood and finding it, wrapping her hand around it, guiding him to her, into her.

Charlye's breath came in a long, hoarse moan as he filled her slowly and fully. He held still there for what seemed like an instant and an eternity, drinking in the expression of ecstasy on her face, and then he began moving. Slowly at first, almost pulling all the way out of her and then filling her again, until his thrusts came harder and faster, and Charlye couldn't breathe, couldn't think. She could only feel, and the feelings were exquisite, overwhelming. . . .

A pleasure so intense that it was painful twisted through her, curled inside her, blinded her with its power. It built to a crescendo with every thrust of Del's manhood until the pleasure exploded. He swallowed her hoarse cry of ecstasy with a deep kiss as his own climax rocked him, sending him over the same precipice.

Del's lips left hers as the wave of pleasure passed and they gasped for air and sanity. He slipped out of her, away from her, rolling onto his back beside her, but he reached for her hand and wove his fingers through hers.

Charlye was suddenly keenly aware of being naked, but she didn't want to cover up. She didn't want anything coming between her and Del. She needed to savor this moment, the intimacy of it, the power of it. She squeezed his hand tightly and bit her tongue to prevent herself from telling him how much she loved him.

He wouldn't want to hear that. She knew it instinctively. And besides, it couldn't be true. They had met only twenty-four hours ago. They were virtually strangers, and people didn't fall in love in a day, did they? Of course not. And "a good girl," even in this day and age, didn't fall into bed with a man on the first date—not where Charlye came from, anyway . . . not unless she wanted to be branded the town tramp.

Charlye wasn't ashamed of what she'd done, but a chill snaked down her spine and she reached for the sheet to cover herself.

"Del . . ."

"Are you cold?" he mumbled sleepily, reaching for the sheet, too, and tucking it around both of them as he pulled Charlye into his arms.

She rested her head on his shoulder and her hand drifted of its own accord across this chest. "Del . . . I need you to know that I don't—" She was at a loss for words. "—that I've never gone to bed with a man on a first date. In fact, I've never . . ."

She stopped abruptly, suddenly afraid to make the ultimate confession.

Del brushed a lock of hair off her face and wrapped it absently around his fingers. "You've never what?"

No. She couldn't tell him. "Never mind."

Charlye sat up abruptly, shielding her breasts with the sheet, and Del's posture of languorous contentment evaporated. He stopped her with a hand on her arm before she could slip out of the bed.

When she saw the way he was looking at her, Charlye knew that he knew. "Charlye, was this your first time?" he asked with a mixture of wonder and incredulity.

She turned her face away from him, and apparently that was all the answer he needed. Del sat up. "My God, Charlye, why didn't you tell me?"

"Would it have made a difference?"

"I don't know. I might have waited. I might have . . . done something different, made it more romantic . . ." He shook his head.

Charlye found the courage to look at him. "Then

I'm glad you didn't know. I couldn't have asked for anything more, Del. It was perfect."

A ghost of a self-satisfied grin teased his lips. "As compared to what?"

Charlye grinned, too. "Compared to anything I could have dreamed or imagined or hoped for." She cocked her head to one side. "You're not sorry we did this, are you?"

"God, no." Del gathered her into his arms and lay back on the bed.

Charlye snuggled her head into his shoulder. "Are you . . . disappointed?"

His arms tightened and a deep chuckle rumbled in his throat. "Disapppointed? My God, Charlye, I didn't think I'd ever feel this way about a woman again. You're such an intoxicating combination of innocence and fire that you make me feel like I'm fifteen and just discovering what love is all about."

"Don't you mean sex?" she ventured to ask.

"No, I mean love, Charlye. I don't normally jump into bed on a first date, either. But last night when you looked at me as I unpinned that note from your dress, I felt as though someone had hit me in the chest with a sledgehammer. I haven't been able to stop thinking about you since. I don't know what it means or what's going to happen tomorrow or the day after, but for right now, I feel like a kid in love and I want to enjoy every blessed second of it." He rose on one elbow and looked into her eyes. "Now, tell me how you feel, and be honest."

She couldn't do otherwise when he was looking at her with such tenderness. "I feel like Cinderella at the ball in the arms of her handsome prince."

Del smiled. "And when the clock strikes midnight?"

She shrugged. "My coach will turn into a pumpkin, my gown into rags, and I'll run back home to sit by the hearth and polish my memories."

Del bent his head and pressed a kiss to her lips. "Well, don't forget to leave your slipper on the stairs so that I can find you," he whispered. "It may not be that easy to get away from me."

He kissed her then, and Charlye gave herself over to it, concentrating on his lips instead of the way her heart wrapped around the words he had spoken. It was more charming flattery, without a doubt, and she knew better than to believe that their relationship might last beyond the stroke of midnight. But until then . . .

Chapter Five

The next week wasn't a fairy tale; it was heaven. By day, Charlye and Del indulged in every luxury the *Caribbean Star* offered. By night, Del introduced her to love "in all its glorious incarnations," as he'd so eloquently phrased it the night they'd met. Only then, he'd been talking about the fictitious Charlotte Vale. It was the real Charlotte he made love to every night, and it was the real Charlye who fell hopelessly in love.

They laughed, they played. They squired Jane and Lauren to karaoke night and gambling at the Evening Star. They became Nick and Nora Charles, pooling their resources to hunt down the clues to the identity of the murderer on the High Seas. They sunned on the beach in St. Bart's and basked in the rich history of St. George's in Grenada.

Gradually, the harsh worry lines around Del's eyes

disappeared, as though he'd cast off the problems that had followed him on board. For a solid week, the real world ceased to exist and heaven took its place.

Because of his resemblance to Dallas Kincaid, Del had to take a few precautions whenever they went ashore. In an attempt to look like the kind of loud, obnoxious tourist that everyone avoids like the plague, he wore the gaudiest tropical print shirts imaginable, baggy bermuda shorts, a big straw hat, and sunglasses. It was inevitable that he be "recognized," of course, but the odd costumes of the other *Caribbean Star* masqueraders made it easy to convince would-be fans that Del wasn't the real Dallas Kincaid.

Until they made port in Curaçao. That was where they ran into the Robertsons. The vacationing couple—Bob and Junie—spotted Del early in the day, and no amount of persuasion would convince them that he was just an ordinary guy with a famous face. Bob followed them with a camcorder and Junie snapped roll after roll of film, until finally Del and Charlye were forced to cancel their walking tour of historic Willemstad. They took the first shuttle back to their ship, and even then the Robertsons tried to follow them. Unsuccessfully, thank goodness.

"My God, how does the real Dallas Kincaid stand it?" Charlye was still fuming as she unlocked the door to her cabin and preceded Del inside. "Can you imagine him being pursued and harassed like that every time he goes out in public?"

"Actually, I can," Del said dryly as he shut the door. "That's not the first time this has happened to me. I'm just sorry it's upset you so much."

Charlye tossed her colorful straw bag onto the sofa. "Yes, but you're not really *him*, and the people you're around most of the time know it. You don't get accosted like that everywhere you go, whereas Dallas Kincaid—" Charlye smothered the urge to hit something. "I just can't imagine how he copes with it."

Del moved to the bar and began fixing two heavily iced diet colas. "Well, according to the interviews I've seen him do, he says it's the price he pays for making fifteen million dollars a picture for doing something he loves so much he'd do it for free."

"But it must get to him," Charlye insisted, joining Del at the bar. "Honestly, those people were absolutely horrible! Don't they realize he has a right to privacy?"

Del stopped pouring and looked at her with purely artificial irritation. "Hey, why are you feeling sorry for him? *I'm* the one Bob sneaked up on at the urinal in the men's room. Toss a little of that moral indignation in my direction."

"You're right. I'm sorry. It's just so absurd. How do you—I mean, how does he . . . that is . . ." Del's laughter brought her to a confused halt. "Oh, pishtosh. You know what I mean."

Del swept her into his arms. "Yes, I do, and only my sweet, beautiful Charlye could feel so much outrage on behalf of a man that wealthy and influential."

Charlye wrapped her arms around Del's waist and snuggled against him. "I'm just glad you're not the real Dallas Kincaid. Very, *very* glad."

Del pressed a kiss against her forehead. "Me, too," he said, then released her abruptly. "Listen, if you were serious about wanting to take that dance class this afternoon, I'd better shower and change."

A little chill ran down Charlye's spine as Del moved away from her. "All right," she said tentatively, but he didn't seem to notice. "Listen, Del, if you don't want to take the class—"

"Don't be silly. It'll be fun." He checked his watch as he moved to the door. "Why don't I swing by in about an hour and a half, okay?"

"Sure. I'll be ready."

"See you then."

He opened the door and was gone.

Charlye couldn't suppress a feeling of panic. Something strange had just happened between her and Del, and she didn't have a clue why. It was the

Connie Bennett

first time he'd ever been in a hurry to leave her arms. Usually it was just the opposite. An embrace led to a kiss, and kisses led to the sensual magic that Charlye had become addicted to and only Del could supply.

If they were going to take Texas two-step lessons this afternoon instead of their planned tour of Willemstad, it was only reasonable that they go their separate ways and get ready, but Charlye couldn't escape the feeling that he was making an excuse to leave her.

Why? Had she done something to displease him? If so, she couldn't imagine what. They got along so well that it was almost uncanny—they had similar tastes in books and movies; they enjoyed puzzles and word games. Charlye had dreamed for so long of experiencing new things that she was game for anything Del proposed, be it scuba diving, wine tasting, or the delights of making love in the gigantic shell-shaped bathtub in her luxury cabin. Why, they'd even delved into the treacherous waters of politics and religion and hadn't found any serious breaches between their opinions and beliefs.

They were perfect companions—or so Charlye had thought. Had she just been fooling herself? Was Del growing tired of her? Had he finally become impatient with her lack of sophistication in and out of bed? Was he getting ready to dump her and go trolling for another conquest? There were only five days of the cruise left, after all. If he was looking for sexual trophies—

No. Charlye refused to let herself go there. Del wasn't a predator. He wasn't a phony, insincere lech making notches on his bedpost. He was a kind, considerate, loving, down-to-earth guy who didn't have an insincere bone in his body. What's more, he genuinely cared about her, and one abrupt hug didn't mean that he was dumping her.

Charlye thought it through logically and quieted her fears. It was inevitable that she would lose Del at the end of the cruise, but their affair wasn't over

64

yet. She was sure of it. She still had five more days
with Del.

Five more days in heaven before she was consigned to an eternity in hell without him.

The message light was flashing on Del's telephone.
He saw it as soon as he entered the cabin and was
tempted to ignore it. It wasn't likely to be a message
from Charlye—not so much because he'd just left
her, but because she was so careful not to crowd
him. Her confidence and self-assurance blossomed
daily, but she hadn't reached the point of believing
that she had a right to ask for things from him and
expect her needs to be met. She'd even been hesitant
to ask him for something as simple as taking a dance
class with her.

So the call probably wasn't from her, and if that
was the case, Del wasn't really interested in talking
to anyone else—particularly if it was a summons
from someone beyond the confines of this ship. He
loved the insular world he and Charlye had inhabited
this past week, and he hated the thought of anyone
intruding on it.

But Del had a big family, and there was always the
possibility of an emergency. . . .

He dialed the Passenger Communications Center
to pick up his messages, and sure enough, his
brother had called three hours ago. It took only
about five minutes to make the arrangements to return the call.

"Fig Garden Nursery. Kris Hadjepetris speaking."

Del breathed a little sigh of relief. His brother's
voice sounded completely normal, no signs of undue
stress. "Kris? It's Del. I had a message that you called.
Is everything all right?"

"Hey, Del! Everything's fine," Kris assured him.
"Mama's going nuts planning Leah's baby shower
and Trina called off her engagement to Bobby
Lupo—again—but other than the usual insanity, life
is good."

Del sat on the sofa and propped his feet on the

coffee table. "You called halfway around the world to tell me we have a crazy family?"

He could almost hear his brother nodding. "And to find out how your vacation is going. You were so stressed out when you left, I wanted to see if the masquerade cruise is everything you'd hoped it would be."

"That and more, Kris. I'm doing great. Really, really great."

"Ooh, that sounds like you're getting more than a good tan."

Del chuckled indulgently. "Crass as that comment is, little brother, you are correct. I've met someone really special. She's the kind of sweet, unaffected woman Mama tried to fix me up with before, during and after my disastrous marriage. You'd love her."

"That's great, Del. Does she know—"

"No. And I'm trying keep it that way," he said, cutting his brother off in midsentence. That was territory Del didn't want to wander into. "How's the business?"

"Growing—literally," Kris replied. "Joseph Andropolis has finally agreed to sell us those four acres Grandpapa's been coveting since the end of World War Two."

That was good news, indeed. "Hallelujah! I hope you're not going to celebrate this joyous occasion without me."

"How can we? This is a family partnership. We need your signature in order to close the deal."

Del chuckled. "And a little extra cash, too, I'll bet. Old Man Andropolis wouldn't let that land go cheap."

"Exactly. So when are you coming home?"

"Well, the cruise ends on Sunday. I'll probably head back to California a day or two after that," he replied, thinking of Charlye and the whole open-ended question of what was going to become of their relationship once the *Caribbean Star* docked. It was a subject they'd both avoided like the plague.

"And you're coming here after the cruise?"

Del frowned at the question. "Why wouldn't I? It's my home."

"One of them, anyway," Kris said dryly. "I've had at least a half dozen phone calls from Avery this week wanting to know where you are and when you're getting back to the big bad city. Somebody named Grayson is pressing him for an answer and Avery wants to know if you're going to sign off on the deal."

"I don't know, Kris. I haven't made up my mind."

Kris made a sound that Del knew was exasperation. "Why not? Isn't that why you went on that cruise? To decide whether this project would be a twenty million dollar mistake?"

"And I still haven't decided." Del felt a tension in his neck that hadn't been there since the first time he'd made love to Charlye. Damn Kris for bringing this up. And damn Avery Clark for getting his little brother involved. "You didn't tell Avery where I am, did you?"

"Of course not."

"Good. Keep it that way." Del rubbed his right eye gingerly because there seemed to be something in it. "The last thing I need is Avery chasing me down at our next port of call and demanding an answer I don't have."

"Del . . . this woman you mentioned. Does she have anything to do with the reason you've been avoiding making a decision?"

"Only peripherally. I'm having fun, I'm relaxing, I'm enjoying my life for the first time in ages, and it's all because of Charlye."

"This doesn't sound like a shipboard romance," Kris said with a touch of suspicion.

"I don't know what it is or how it's going to end," he confessed. "We live three quarters of a continent apart, but it just feels right, Kris. Really right."

"Del, how can it feel right if she doesn't know the truth about you?"

"She knows *me*, Kris. The real me, and this is the first time that's happened in longer than I can remember."

"Then maybe it's time to come clean."

Del thought of the conversation he'd just had with Charlye, and of a half dozen times she'd said something similar in the past week. "Not yet, Kris. I can't risk it. Where Charlye comes from, people like me aren't real—all we do is go to parties every night, get chauffered around in limousines all day, and drink nothing but champagne. Or so they think."

"But if she knows the real you—"

"I can't tell her yet, Kris. I'm too afraid she'd freeze up on me." Del's eye was driving him crazy. Rubbing it hadn't done more than stimulate the tear gland. Unable to bear it anymore, he cradled the receiver between his shoulder and his chin so that he could remove the continuous-wear contact lens that was causing the irritation. While he was at it, he popped the other one out, too.

The distinctive blue eyes that had been hidden beneath the tinted brown lens felt better immediately.

"Del? You still there?"

"Yeah. Sorry. I was just getting rid of my contacts."

"I guess they're doing their job, keeping you anonymous."

"Yes, they are. And that's the only reason I was able to get to know Charlye at all. She's falling in love with Del Hadjepetris," he told his brother. "If she knew the truth, I'd lose her for sure."

"But—"

"No 'buts,' Kris," Del said firmly. "I did too good a job pulling off this masquerade. I'm not taking the chance of losing Charlye now by telling her that I really *am* Dallas Kincaid."

Chapter Six

"I agree with Lieutenant Commander Data. Major Buffington was murdered by that ne'er-do-well Dallas Kincaid," Indiana Jones said, tipping the brim of his fedora in Del's general direction. The Aquarius Cafe had been gussied up to look like the smoking car from *Murder on the Orient Express*, and all of the High Seas players were gathered for the unmasking of the killer.

Del tipped an imaginary hat back at the portly, good-natured, five-foot-three-inch Indiana Jones impersonator. So far, "Indy" was the sixth player who'd tried to pin the murder on him. There had also been two votes for Lauren, two for *Star Trek*'s Commander Data, and one for the immortal Sherlock Holmes.

"And what reasons do you have for suspecting Mr. Kincaid?" Holmes asked.

"He was acting very strangely at the karaoke—re-

Connie Bennett

member? He sang 'I've Got a Crush on You' not five minutes before we found Major Buffington's body backstage, smashed beneath those counterweights. How did he know the manner of Buffington's death if he wasn't the murderer?"

A murmur of conjecture rippled through the gamers, but Indy didn't pause long enough for anyone to argue with his conclusion. He rattled off a litany of clues that had been dropped over the past week, but Del was having trouble concentrating on the accusations against him. He was a lot more troubled by some of the things his brother had said on the phone yesterday afternoon. They'd argued for a good ten minutes before Del had finally hung up in irritation and frustration.

Damn Kris's ethical hide. Del had been doing great before the call, happily ensconced in the bubble of utter contentment he'd found with Charlye. True, a moment of guilt had chased him out of Charlye's arms when she'd said she was glad he wasn't really Dallas Kincaid, but he'd handled many such moments in the past week. If Kris hadn't called, Del would have convinced himself once again that his little white lie wasn't hurting anyone.

But was that really true? Was the deception he'd perpetrated going to backfire once he told Charlye that he hadn't been completely honest with her? He didn't know, and he was afraid to find out.

One thing was certain, though. She wasn't ready to hear the truth right now, and he wasn't ready to tell it. He'd come on this cruise as a way of hiding in plain sight because he needed to escape the pressure of being Dallas Kincaid. Since everyone assumed he was just a passenger who looked like the movie star, people on the ship treated him like the ordinary guy he was. Most of the time, even onshore, no one pestered him for autographs. Before the Robertsons' assault yesterday, not one person had shoved a camera in his face without asking permission to take his picture, and no one had followed him into the men's room with a camcorder, either. Del couldn't say the

70

same about an ordinary day in his "real" life.

He had been free to be Dwayne Lewis Hadjepetris, a better-than-average-looking guy who'd chosen to go into acting rather than run the family's truck farm or the nursery or the greenhouse. He'd gotten lucky and become a star, and most of the time he accepted the price that had to be paid for his success. But there were also times when it got to be too much and he ached to be treated like a normal person.

And that was what he had with Charlye. She was falling for the man, not the movie star. If he told her the truth now, she'd be intimidated by him and by the blinding glare of the spotlight he lived in. She'd treat him differently, react to him unnaturally. Their relationship would change, and Del couldn't bear that. They had four days left, and he wanted Charlye to see him as "Del" for as long as possible, because he had no idea whether she could love him as Dallas Kincaid.

"That's a very interesting indictment against our Dallas, Mr. Indiana. Quite persuasive, I must say," Jane said as Indy completed his presentation. Del forced his attention back to the game, hoping he hadn't missed too much.

"Aunt Jane!" he exclaimed. "I thought you were on my side."

She reached out and patted the arm he had draped casually around Charlye's shoulder. "I am, dear, but evidence is evidence. If you prove to be the murderer, I'll make certain you get a good lawyer."

"Now, who's next?" Holmes, their self-appointed leader, asked. "We've yet to hear from Miss Vale and Mr. Kincaid. Who do the two of you think murdered the Major?"

"Miss Scarlet with the lead pipe in the conservatory," Charlye announced.

Everyone but Commander Data laughed, and Holmes said, "No, seriously, Miss Vale. Who do you think it is?"

Charlye glanced at Dallas for support and he nodded at her. Everyone knew that they had been working as a team, so he didn't expect anyone to be surprised that they'd reached the same conclusion. "Actually, after careful investigation Del and I have decided that the murderer is none other than our adorable Aunt Jane."

"Oh, pishtosh!"

Del shook his head at her. "Now, now, Auntie. Profanity won't prove your innocence—or get you a good lawyer." He proceeded to outline all the reasons why he and Charlye had come to suspect Jane. Everyone was suitably impressed, but no one seemed inclined to change his or her own conclusions.

But there was still one player left to make an accusation. The most recent suspect herself.

"Why, it's absolutely elementary, as our good friend Mr. Holmes would say," Jane told them with a Cheshire cat grin and a twinkle in her blue eyes. "There is absolutely no doubt that the murderer is our mysterious heiress, Charlotte Vale."

"What?" Del gasped.

Titters of laughter went round the room—nearly everyone had agreed earlier that Charlotte was the least likely suspect of all, but when Jane outlined the reasons for her accusation no one was laughing any more. The sly little "sleuth" had had the foresight—and insight—to ask questions of Charlye that no one else had thought to ask. Not even Del.

By the time she'd finished, Del was seriously wondering if he'd been hoodwinked by his so-called "partner." He watched her as Holmes declared that the week-long investigation had come to a conclusion and demanded that the real murderer confess. Everyone looked from face to face, waiting expectantly until the culprit finally stood up.

Del couldn't believe it. Jane was right! "Charlye! You sneak!"

She was blushing to the roots of her dark hair. "I'm sorry," she said to him, but clearly she was delighted that she'd managed to surprise everyone. Or almost everyone. "I was just playing the game."

"Yeah, brilliantly," he said grumpily, though he was genuinely delighted by the way she'd pulled off her deception.

Most of the other players came to their feet, gathering around Charlye to congratulate her on her masterful charade, and Del sat back, enjoying the glow of pleasure on her face. Jane found herself in the limelight, too, as debates began raging about which clues had been genuine and which had been red herrings. It was at least an hour before the group began to break up.

Del and Charlye escorted Lauren and Aunt Jane down to their cabin, then went up one deck to Charlye's.

"Well, this is a fine how-do-you-do, I must say. Some partner you turned out to be," Del groused as he closed the cabin door and locked it behind them. "When I think of all the times you accused me of being the murderer . . ."

Charlye was chuckling as she slipped out of her sandals. "I figured that was as good a way as any to throw you off the scent. And as for the rest of the players, I just kept a low profile and let them come after you."

"You used me as a decoy!" he accused.

"I most certainly did."

Del shook his head. "This is unbelievable. When we weren't together, I just assumed you were out shopping—and all the while, you were busy framing me for murder."

Charlye grinned. "I did some shopping, too." A hint of hesitation came into her eyes. "You're not really angry, are you?"

Del pursed his lips in a teasing grimace. "I don't know if I am or not," he replied with a touch of petulance. "Maybe, if you could think of a way to make it up to me tonight . . ."

He left the statement hanging in the air. "Make it up to you, like how?" she asked innocently as she sashayed over to him.

Connie Bennett

Del wiggled his eyebrows at her. "Like . . . you figure it out."

Charlye slipped her arms around his waist. "Oh, you mean if I do something like this—" she arched up and traced his full lower lip with the tip of her tongue, then settled back on her heels "—you'll forgive me?"

He affected a bored sigh, though he was anything but. "Oh, please. That doesn't begin to make up for your deception."

Charlye snuggled against him and let her hands at his waist drift lower, cupping his muscle-sculpted derriere and kneading lightly. "How about that?"

Del swallowed hard. "Ha! I scoff at your pitiful attempts at restitution!"

"Hmmm . . ." Charlye pursed her lips thoughtfully and it was everything Del could do to keep from kissing her. He restrained himself, though, because the game they were playing was utterly delightful, and he was more than moderately interested in which of them would win it.

"Well, how about this?" she inquired, sliding one hand between them to cup Del intimately.

"That's . . . that's . . ." She massaged him gently, and Del sucked in his breath as he hardened in her hand. It was almost impossible for him to think, let alone keep up his end of their teasing banter.

"Hmmm?" Charlye prompted. "What did you say?"

"I said . . ." Del grabbed her hand and stilled it. "I say that if you have any hope of sharing what's coming, you'd better stop that right now."

Charlye's eyes widened dramatically as she withdrew her hand. "Then by all means, I'll stop. I do so enjoy . . . sharing with you."

Del laughed as he swept Charlye off her feet. "And I enjoy coming with you, my darling," he assured her, as he carried her into the bedroom so that he could prove it to her.

They undressed quickly and came together in playful passion, teasing and cajoling, until the moment Del filled her and their playfulness vanished. His thrusts brought her closer to the brink and she called out his name breathlessly.

"Look at me, Charlye," he demanded, as he had every time they made love because he needed to see her face at the moment of her release. She was nearly there—he could tell it by her body's response to his—but this time he needed more than to see ecstasy in her eyes. He needed much more.

"Tell me you love me," he commanded, his voice harsh with the tension of holding back his own release as he thrust into her. "Tell me, Charlye."

"Del . . ." Her voice was no more than a whisper.

"Say it, Charlye." He thrust again, driving into her, and a breath shuddered through her.

"Del, I . . ."

"Say it!" She'd never uttered the words before, and Del had to hear them. "Say it!"

"I love you!"

His thrusts quickened. "Again."

"I love you."

"Again."

"I love you."

"Again . . ."

The litany repeated as their pleasure built to a crescendo and they both cried out in release. Del collapsed onto her, bearing his weight on his arms as Charlye's tightened around him. He kissed her cheek, her jaw, her lips, and then he raised his head to look into her eyes.

"I love you, Charlye. No matter what happens, don't ever doubt that," he said more harshly than he intended. Then he claimed her lips again.

When Charlye awoke the next morning her bones still felt like Silly Putty. Del was on his back beside her, sprawled pretty much in the same position he'd fallen into after the second time they'd made love, as though he'd been too sated to move after he'd withdrawn from her.

Charlye recalled that at one time he'd had a corner of the sheet draped over his lower torso and thighs,

Connie Bennett

but she'd apparently pulled it off him sometime in the night. He was gloriously naked, and Charlye drank in the sight of him, marveling at his sheer masculine beauty and greedily memorizing every line and plane of his body.

Their lovemaking last night had been . . . astonishing. Too powerful for words, really. What had started as playful had taken on an urgency that none of their other couplings had had. The way Del had begged her—no, forced her—to admit that she loved him had almost frightened Charlye with its intensity, but she wouldn't have taken back the words even if she could have.

She *did* love Del, with all her heart. And he loved her, too. Or so he'd said, and the urgency in his eyes and his voice had convinced her that he'd meant it. But the other part . . . "no matter what happens . . ."

Charlye didn't have a clue what he'd meant by that. Was it his way of telling her good-bye? That he wanted her to know, even after they'd gone their separate ways, that she'd been special to him?

What else could it mean? There were only three days left, and she could hardly bear to think about it. Her life had begun the moment Del had walked into the Constellation Room. It would end when they docked in Miami. The trials that had come before and the desolation that would come after were only preface and footnote.

But the last page wasn't written yet, and Charlye refused to dwell on what was to come. She was determined to savor the here and now for as long as it lasted.

Unable to help herself, she reached out and ran her hand lightly over Del's chest. He sighed at her touch and stirred, then went still again.

She wove her fingers into the dark curls in the V of his abdomen. A low moan rumbled in his throat.

Her hand moved lower still, and his body responded with the first stirrings of arousal.

"My god, Charlye . . ." Del mumbled, his hips moving restlessly as he pried open his eyes and looked at

76

her. She was propped on one elbow watching him, and her questing fingers paused as she searched his face for approval. "Oh, don't stop on my account," he encouraged her sleepily. "I can think of lots worse ways to be awakened."

The telephone beside the bed chirped. "And that's one," he said with a groan.

Charlye laughed and twisted around to answer it. That was when she caught her first glimpse of the clock. "Oh, my God, Del! It's seven-thirty. We promised Jane and Lauren we'd meet them for breakfast at seven."

"And go with them into Ocho Rios at eight," he added, scrambling to the edge of the bed to search for his clothes.

Charlye answered the phone, apologized to Lauren profusely and promised that she and Del would be ready to disembark in a half hour. It was a miracle, but they actually made it, arriving just as the last of the day-trippers were being helped aboard the Ocho Rios water bus.

The view of the Jamaican harbor was breathtaking, and even from a distance the city of Ocho Rios was an eye-catching blend of the old and the new. This was the first shore excursion Jane and Lauren had taken, and the ladies had a guidebook and a carefully thought-out sightseeing plan, which Lauren outlined for them in detail as the boat made its way to Pier Four.

"But of course you and Dallas mustn't feel obligated to stay with us all day," Jane said as Charlye helped her up the steps and onto the pier. "Gardens and plantation tours may be a bit too tame for you."

Charlye laughed at the very idea of abandoning their friends. "Don't be silly. Besides, you two may be the ones to ditch us if there are any tourists like the Robertsons in Ocho Rios."

"Oh, heavens, I hope not," Jane said. She and Lauren had heard all about the obnoxious couple who'd plagued them three days ago in Curaçao.

"Careful, Charlye, or you'll jinx us," Del said with

Connie Bennett

a chuckle. He was right behind her with Lauren on his arm.

Charlye glanced back at him. "Don't worry, no one could be as bad as the Robertsons. Although . . ." She caught her lower lip nervously when she realized that she and Del had been so rushed this morning that he hadn't had time to go back to his room to dress. After a sixty-second shower he'd slipped into one of the casual changes of clothes he kept in her room because he spent so many nights there.

He looked wonderful in the crisp white shirt and trousers, but he didn't have so much as a pair of sunglasses to provide a disguise. He had never looked more like Dallas Kincaid.

Charlye's little joke didn't seem so funny any more. "You may be right, Del," she said as they began moving down the pier. "If we don't do something to divert attention from that face, we won't have a moment's peace today."

He nodded in agreement. "I was just about to suggest that our first stop be at the tackiest vendor stall we can find."

"Oh, my," Jane muttered. "It may be too late for that."

"What do you mean, Jane?" Charlye asked, following the lady's glance to the knot of camera-toting tourists on the other side of the gate twenty yards ahead of them. There were thirty of them at least, and they were all looking their way, studying the crowd of day-trippers who were pouring off the water taxi.

"That woman in blue, dear. The one right by the gate," Jane replied. "That's Isabelle Michaels from that TV show *Hollywood Exposé*. And there's a man with a big camera with her."

Charlye loved movies, but she didn't watch Hollywood gossip shows. There was no denying, though, that the woman Jane pointed out had a cameraman attached to her side—and a microphone in her hand as well. What on earth was happening? Had someone decided that their masquerade cruise was wor-

78

thy of major press coverage? That didn't seem likely.

Charlye scanned the crowd and saw two more TV cameras. Not only that, nearly every person pressed against the fence had two or three cameras around his neck, and there were at least a half-dozen distinctively dressed Jamaican bobbies keeping the mob behind the barrier. These weren't tourists. It was the press!

And smack in the middle of the pack were Bob and Junie Robertson!

"Oh, Del! I don't believe this! Do you see them?" Charlye turned to Del, but she couldn't stop because they were all being carried along by the swell of *Caribbean Star* passengers who were anxious to get off the pier and begin their shore excursion.

"I see them," Del replied grimly. "Charlye—"

"This is just absurd!" she ranted. "Those two idiots must have somehow spread the word that the real Dallas Kincaid is on the *Caribbean Star*."

"Charlye—" Del's brow was furrowed and his eyes were dark with an emotion Charlye had trouble deciphering. Concern? Fear?

"What is it, Del?" she asked as the tide brought them to the gate.

"There he is! That's him!"

"Dallas! Over here!"

"Hey, Kincaid!"

"How 'bout an interview!"

"Is it true you're turning down a twenty-million-dollar deal with Universal?"

Two dozen voices all clamored at once, telescoping into an almost indecipherable symphony of chaos. Cameras began snapping and grinding, and the mob surged forward as Charlye, Del, and their elderly companions went through the gate. The police tried to keep them back, but it was hopeless.

Charlye found herself being shoved against Jane, nearly knocking her down, and she dug in her heels, shoving back because it was the only way to protect the frail little lady beside her.

"For God's sake, tell them, Del!" she begged, shouting to be heard over the cacophony of questions. "Get rid of them before someone gets hurt."

"Dallas! Hello! What are you doing in Jamaica?" Isabelle Michaels and her cameraman were at the head of the mob that closed in on the foursome like a pack of hungry wolves. She shoved a foam-covered *Exposé* microphone in his face.

The crowd seemed to suddenly quiet and Charlye looked at Del expectantly, waiting for him to explain the mistake. He glanced at her and that look of fear was still there, but as he turned to face the cameras it disappeared behind a thousand-watt smile.

"Hello, Isabelle," he said. "I think a better question would be—what are *you* doing in Jamaica?"

The beautiful blond reporter laughed. "Well, Dallas, there's a great rumor going around that you're taking a luxury masquerade cruise disguised as yourself. Is that true?"

Del laughed. "I'm vacationing, Isabelle. That's all."

"Then what's with the brown contacts?" the reporter asked, but before he could answer, she shoved the microphone in Charlye's face. "You were seen with Dallas in Curaçao, where you both denied that he was Dallas Kincaid—did you meet him on the ship? Are you two dating? Did anyone on the cruise really buy his story that he was just a celebrity look-alike?"

Charlye couldn't breathe. Reporters were snapping her picture as they waited for her to pick a question and answer it, but she couldn't think beyond the enormous wave of pain that was streaking toward her like an ocean swell, sucking the life out of her as it built into a monstrous tower that came crashing over her.

Everything was a lie. The long talks, the lovemaking, the laughter, the joy . . . It was all a lie. The last ten days hadn't been a fairy tale, or heaven, either. They were a never-never land of deception and betrayal.

Charlye wanted to die.

"You bastard," she whispered, fighting back a flood of tears.

"Charlye—" He put his hand on her arm, but she yanked away from him.

"So you didn't know!" the reporter demanded.

Charlye shoved the microphone out of her face. "Get away from me." The microphone came back and she shoved harder this time, elbowing her way through the crowd. Questions were shouted at her, and even when she finally shoved free a knot of reporters and paparazzi followed her.

"Leave me alone!" She broke into a run, and behind her she vaguely heard Del's voice raised to announce an impromptu press conference. The reporters paused, clearly torn as to what to do, but Dallas was the celebrity. Charlye was a nobody. The reporters broke off their pursuit and returned to the pack, leaving Charlye hurrying blindly past street vendors and tourists. She had no idea where she was going or what to do when she got there.

She could run from the reporters, but she couldn't run from the truth or the betrayal. Or the pain.

Chapter Seven

It appeared that Jamaica had swallowed Charlye whole. Del was sick inside and he wanted nothing more than to find her so that he could explain—so that he could erase that horrible look of pain and loathing in her eyes. Searching for her was impossible, though. Finding her would only have brought her back into the spotlight and he couldn't subject her to that again.

The most he could do was send Jane and Lauren off to hunt for her while he led the vultures away from the pier, keeping them distracted until the water bus made its next run to the *Caribbean Star* at noon. Del was certain that Jane and Lauren would have found Charlye by then and gone with her back to the ship, but when he finally made his own escape on the two o'clock water bus, Charlye hadn't returned.

Masquerade

Jane and Lauren had searched all morning, even contacting the police and the hospitals, but to no avail. They were frantic, and so was Del. Charlye was alone and distraught in a strange city in a foreign country; God only knew what had happened to her, and it was all Del's fault. He had to find her. He had to make her understand. He had to make her believe that he loved her.

Not knowing what to do or who to turn to, he went to the ship's purser to ask for help, and that was where he finally learned what had happened.

Charlye was gone.

Shortly after nine that morning she'd called the purser's office from shore claiming that she had to return home immediately because of an emergency. Though she hadn't detailed her plans to the purser, he speculated that she'd taken a bus to the airport in Kingston on the other side of the island. Housekeeping had orders to pack up her belongings and ship them to her.

And she'd left strict orders that the cruise line not release her real name and home address to the media—or anyone else.

Del felt as though he'd been kicked in the stomach, but he knew it was nothing compared to what he'd done to Charlye. He'd hurt her so desperately, humiliated her so thoroughly, that she hadn't been able to face him or anyone. Somehow he had to set things right.

"Did she leave a message for me?" he asked the purser.

The handsome young man looked sightly embarrassed. "Not exactly, sir. But there was something. . . ."

"What?" Del prompted eagerly.

"The lady had purchased an item at the Glass Menagerie, a curio shop on the Mall. It was paid for, but she hadn't picked it up because it was being encased in a special glass box."

Del was confused. "What does that have to do with me?"

"Apparently, it was meant to be a present for you at the end of the voyage. She wanted you to have it now, though." The purser turned and unlocked a cabinet behind the desk as he continued, "She had special instructions for what she wanted me to do with it before I gave it to you, but I just couldn't do it, sir."

He removed a small cardboard box from the cabinet and set it on the desk between them. Del opened the flap, brushed away the packing, and pulled out a delicate glass box about five inches square. Inside it, on a tiny cushion of red velvet, sat a perfect crystal slipper.

A lump rose in Del's throat and he stiffened his jaw against the memory that put it there.

"I feel like Cinderella at the ball in the arms of her handsome prince."

"And when the clock strikes midnight?"

"My coach will turn into a pumpkin, my gown into rags, and I'll run back home to sit by the hearth and polish my memories."

"Well, don't forget to leave your slipper on the stairs so that I can find you. . . ."

She was leaving him a slipper. . . . Did it mean she understood? That she was willing to forgive him? Twin shafts of hope and relief spiked through Del as he picked up the fragile glass box.

"You said she left instructions. What were they?"

The purser ducked his head, clearly embarrassed. "Well, sir . . ."

Del looked at him. "What? Spit it out."

"She wanted me to break it, sir."

The glass in his hand turned as cold as ice. "Break it?"

"Yes, sir. Her exact words were, 'smash it into a million pieces.'"

Just as Del had smashed her heart.

"Damn."

Charlye was late for her meeting at the Green River Retirement Community. She was scheduled to conduct a guided tour of the facility for two prospective residents, but her Hug-a-Pet session at the Valley Nursing Home had run longer than expected. She was going to be late, and there was nothing she could do about it; she considered it a miracle that she was functioning at all.

She'd been home two weeks now, and there was nothing good about being back in the little town of Blessing, Indiana. She'd darted home like a scared, wounded rabbit seeking the safety of its burrow, only to find that home wasn't safe any more because she was a celebrity now. Bob and Junie Robertson had sold their pictures of Charlye and Dallas in Curaçao to every supermarket tabloid and TV gossip show in the nation.

All the reporters thought it had been a stroke of genius for Dallas to take an anonymous vacation by impersonating himself, but according to the media, the country was rabid to discover the identity of the "mystery woman" he'd become involved with on the cruise.

Charlye was of the opinion that it was only the reporters who wanted to know—if there was any rabid curiosity about her in the country, it was being manufactured by the media. Fluff-reporters interviewed *Caribbean Star* passengers, who were only too happy to provide details about the "torrid love affair" they'd witnessed, and when they didn't have details, they made them up. Luckily, though, no one on the ship knew her real name or where she lived, so the press hadn't found her yet.

As for Dallas Kincaid, he seemed to have vanished, too, but Charlye didn't care. He certainly wasn't going to come looking for her—he'd had his fun, and at least he was gentleman enough to do his laughing in private. After the impromptu press conference Charlye had fled from in Jamaica, Dallas had refused to grant interviews to anyone, and Charlye was praying that the furor would die down as soon as the press realized she'd been nothing more to him than a good laugh and an easy lay.

Connie Bennett

After the first week, Charlye stopped watching the magazine shows and refused to look at the tabloids. She also refused to answer questions from the townspeople of Blessing when they accosted her on the street demanding to know if she was "the one."

Even her two best friends didn't know the truth—that she was dying inside. That she felt used, cheap, and dirty. She had allowed herself to be seduced by a handsome lecher who was so far removed from the realities of the world that he thought common people like Charlye were nothing more than playthings to be used for his amusement and then discarded like garbage.

Scenes from their relationship—words, touches, laughter, glances—played through her head endlessly, sending her emotions careening from shame to rage to a grief so deep she didn't know how she'd ever recover. All she could do was slip back into the drab, colorless life she'd been living before the cruise and pray that someday she would forget the joy, the passion, and the love that had been only illusions.

In the meantime, she moved like a sleepwalker between the main office of the health-care group she worked for and its two local facilities, the Valley Nursing Home and the Green River Retirement Community. Even the simplest functions were difficult for her, but she was surviving.

"Hello, Mrs. Kelly. I'm sorry I'm late," she said to Green River's head nurse as she hurried into the office.

The prune-faced tyrant lowered her head, glaring at Charlye over the rims of her Ben Franklin glasses. Francis Kelley was unfailingly gentle with the residents, but she was the type of person who had only a short supply of kindness. That was why the staff called her Godzilla behind her back and hated to see her coming. She'd been particularly surly to Charlye these past two weeks; she knew that Charlye was "the mystery woman" who'd engaged in an illicit love affair with a movie star, and her disapproval had been eating its way to the surface for days.

86

"Charlotte, there are two prospective residents waiting for you," the nurse informed her coldly.

"Jeanette Dorchester and Hilda Brimley. I know. I'm sorry. I couldn't get away from Valley." Charlye slipped out of her coat and hung it on the rack in the corner. "Where are they?"

"In the receiving room, of course," the nurse snapped. "Charlotte, this kind of behavior does not reflect well on our facility. If you think that your new celebrity status entitles you to take liberties, you are sadly mistaken."

Being chastised so harshly would normally have sent Charlye scurrying for cover, but she suddenly found herself standing up to the tyrant. "I'm not a celebrity, Francis, and I've already apologized for my tardiness. Twice. If you've got a problem with that, call Mr. Vickers—he was with me at Valley. He'll tell you why I was late. Now if you'll excuse me, I have an appointment."

Charlye spun on her heel and stalked out, leaving a speechless Francis Kelley behind her, puffing in air like a blowfish.

Charlye moved on down the carpeted corridor, taking a deep, calming breath. She'd never done anything like that before in her life, but she couldn't deny that standing up for herself felt good. Maybe she should try it more often. After all, her reputation in Blessing had turned to mud. What was the harm in spouting off to some of the town bullies?

She was thinking about just who she'd like to tell off next when she opened the door to the spacious sitting room where some of the residents preferred to receive guests.

"Mrs. Dorchester and Ms. Brimley, please forgive—" Charlye stopped and stared at the two very sweet, very familiar faces that turned toward the door.

"Hello, Charlotte dear."

"Lauren. Aunt Jane . . . What—How—?"

"Actually, honey, it's Hilda and Aunt Jeanette," Lauren said, as she and Jeanette rose to their feet.

Charlye gave them both hugs and found her eyes

stinging with unshed tears. Funny. She'd thought her tears had dried up after those first few terrible days, and now here they were again. She fought them back, though she knew very well that her two dear friends would understand if she lost the battle.

"What are you doing here?" she asked as she guided them back to their seats and took one herself.

"Well, it's not for a tour of the facility," Hilda replied with typical bluntness. Apparently her tough-as-nails Lauren Bacall routine hadn't been much of an act.

"No," Jeanette agreed, though more softly. "And we're terribly sorry for the deception, dear. We were afraid you might refuse to see us, so we arranged this subterfuge."

"I would never refuse to see you," Charlye assured them. "But how did you find me?"

Hilda and Jeanette exchanged pensive glances. "Dallas," Jeanette said.

Charlye felt sick inside. Just the sound of his name made her stomach clench with revulsion. "How did he know? I never told him where I live."

"Apparently you mentioned the state of Indiana and the fact that you worked for a senior citizen's health care facility. That was enough for us to track you down," Hilda replied.

Us. Meaning Hilda and Jeanette, not Dallas. He had the means of locating her, but he hadn't bothered.

What should have been relief cut through Charlye like a knife. A fresh wave of hatred for Dallas washed through her. "No offense, ladies, but why did you go to so much trouble? Once you found out I live in Blessing, you could have called."

Jeanette reached out and patted Charlye's arm. "We had to see for ourselves that you're all right, dear. We were all frantic when you disappeared in Jamaica, and with all the publicity since . . . We just couldn't bear the thought of you suffering though this alone."

"I'm fine," Charlye assured them.

"But finding out about Dallas's little deception in that fashion—"

Something exploded inside Charlye. "*Little deception?* That's what you call the way he made fools of us?"

"Charlotte, no one was made a fool of!" Hilda insisted.

"How can you say that? How can you not be angry with him? He deceived everyone on that ship!"

"On the contrary. He told us he was Dallas Kincaid, and he is. That hardly constitutes deceit," Jeanette said shrewdly.

Charlye came to her feet. "Well, that's not what he told me," she informed them coldly. "He made up a ridiculous name and wove an intricate fairy tale about his huge, loving, wonderful family—his brother Krispin, his sisters . . . their business, their celebrations, their squabbles—"

Charlye realized that tears were streaming down her cheeks. She'd fallen in love with his big, raucous family just as surely as she'd fallen in love with Del Hadjepetris.

"But it was a lie," she cried as a sob caught up with her.

"Oh, Charlotte . . ." Jeanette said as she and Hilda stood. "Dear, Dallas Kincaid is only a pseudonym. The name he gave you and the family history he shared were both entirely legitimate. In fact, nothing he ever said to you was a lie."

"How can you say that? You don't know!"

"Of course we do," Jeanette insisted. "Dallas told us everything."

Hilda chuckled. "Well, probably not *everything*, honey. But enough to know that he never wanted to hurt you."

"Well, he did, and I hate him for it," Charlye said viciously.

"No, you don't, dear. You love him."

She shook her head. "No. I loved a man who doesn't exist."

"My mother would be very upset to hear you say that."

Charlye whirled toward the door she'd left ajar. Dallas Kincaid was standing there in a designer suit with an overcoat draped casually over one arm. He looked like the movie idol he was, too handsome for words, with a magnetic presence that filled the room even before he entered it. Charlye's knees felt as weak as they had the first time he'd kissed her, and two weeks' worth of carefully constructed walls came tumbling down. The pain of his betrayal and her own humiliation washed over her in fresh waves, nearly knocking her off her feet.

"What . . . what are you doing here?" she managed to ask him.

Dallas stepped into the room. "Well, my cracker-jack scout team seemed to be coming under direct fire, so I thought I'd better step in and take the heat myself. After all, I'm the one who deserves it." He put a hand on Jeanette's arm. "Can you give us a minute, Aunt Jean?"

"Certainly."

"Thanks for trying."

Charlye turned her back as he kissed both women on the cheek and escorted them to the door. Seeing the three of them so chummy just made the hurt dig in even deeper—she was the outsider, just as she had been all her life.

There was only one door to the room. No way to duck and run as she had in Jamaica. She was going to have to face him, and she didn't want to. Not once had she let herself fantasize about another meeting with him. Once she had learned the truth, she hadn't ever wanted to see him again—not even to hear an explanation or an apology. There was no excuse for what he'd done, and a mouthful of platitudes wouldn't take away her pain or make her feel any less used.

Charlye heard the door close on the other side of the room. She was alone with him.

Suddenly, she couldn't bear the silence. "All right,

Dallas. Say it," she demanded, turning to face him. "Tell me you're sorry. Say you didn't mean to hurt me. You were just playing a game and it got out of hand." She spread her hands. "There. It's done. You've apologized. I forgive you. Now, *get the hell out of my life*."

Del cocked his head to one side and studied her. "Well, you're about three-quarters right."

"Three-quarters?"

"I am sorry. I certainly didn't mean to hurt you. And it damned sure got out of hand," he said, ticking them off on his fingers. "But it was never a game, Charlye."

He dropped his overcoat onto one of the chairs and Charlye saw that he'd been carrying something in his hand. He stepped to the middle of the room and put a little box on the oak library table.

It was the glass slipper.

Tears welled in her eyes and she steeled her heart against them. "That was supposed to be broken before you got it."

"It was too beautiful. The purser couldn't do it."

Charlye glared at him through a shimmer of tears. "I can."

"I don't doubt it," Dallas said with a nod. "Right over my head."

"Don't try to be funny," she advised him. "I've been vaccinated against your charm."

He raised one dark eyebrow. "You mean you lied?" he asked.

"*I* lied? About what?" she gasped.

Del took a step toward her. "When you said you loved me that last night we were together on the ship."

The image of that moment was branded on Charlye's heart and soul. More than any other moment, she'd tried to forget that one, but no matter how hard she worked at putting it out of her mind, it kept coming back to her, playing endlessly, haunting her, driving her crazy, because it was impossible to run from something that part of her heart was clinging to with all its might.

"You made me say that," she accused him. "You forced it out of me. Was that your crowning achievement? Getting silly little Charlotte Nolan to spread her legs and humiliate herself at the same time."

Every ounce of civility left Del's face. "Don't you say that!" he all but shouted, crossing the room in two strides and grabbing Charlye so forcefully that she caught her breath in alarm. His blue eyes were blazing with anger. "Don't you ever say anything like that again, do you understand me? *We made love.* It wasn't just sex. It wasn't a fuck, a screw, or a roll in the hay. You were the best thing that ever happened to me, and I won't let anyone cheapen it—not even you!"

He gave her one last hard shake, then released her.

Charlye sucked in a breath and tried to calm the flow of adrenaline in her veins. Some perverse part of her wanted to applaud his performance, but an even bigger part of her wanted to believe it wasn't an act, that she could really have been that special to him.

"I'm sorry," he said when he was calmer.

Charlye swallowed hard. "Why are you here, Dallas? What do you want from me?"

He looked at her. The flash of anger had burned out, leaving nothing in its wake but sadness. "I want you to forgive me."

"I can't."

"You have to."

She glared at him defiantly. "Why should I?"

"Because you love me."

Charlye stiffened. "I loved a guy named Del Hadjepetris."

Dallas spread his arms wide. "That's me."

"You're Dallas Kincaid."

He nodded and dropped his arms. "When I have to be. And when I'm in front of a camera, I become Captain Fleming or Roderick Benton, or Coop Hawthorne—whatever the script calls for, that's who I

92

become. But there's a handful of people in Fig Garden, California, who know me as Del Hadjepetris, and they treat me like a human being, not a millionaire movie star or a tool to be exploited by every Tom, Dick, and Harry who can possibly get a piece of me.

"I love my family, Charlye, because they let me be me, and they don't ask anything in return but my love and my loyalty."

Del stopped to clear his throat and Charlye felt tears coursing onto her cheeks as he continued, "You were like one of them, Charlye. Loving, trusting, so damned easy to be with, and at the same time you made me feel like a kid again."

He stepped to her, and Charlye was too mesmerized to move away from him. "A kid in love," he added softly. "I love you, Charlye, and I don't want to lose you. No matter what it takes."

Something inside Charlye melted, draining her anger and carrying it away. She wanted so desperately to believe him. She *needed* to believe. He'd deceived her, true, but maybe he hadn't lied to her about the important things—like the way he felt for her. Maybe she wasn't a total fool. Maybe she hadn't given her virginity away to a cold, callous bastard after all.

There was so much love and tenderness in his eyes that Charlye could almost allow herself to believe that the illusion of love she'd found in Del's arms hadn't been an illusion at all.

And she would have believed it if those loving eyes had been brown instead of blue.

"Shall I give you the Oscar now, or can I mail it to you?" she asked, steeling herself against the need to believe in fairy tales.

Del looked as though she'd slapped him. He took a step back, froze for a second, then caught a deep sigh. "I deserved that."

He moved across the room to pick up his coat. He carefully placed a business card on the chair where it had lain. "This is my private address and phone number, Charlye. At home in Fig Garden. You can always reach me through my family, no matter where I am."

Charlye glared at him defiantly. He was getting ready to walk out of her life, and that was exactly what she wanted, so why did she feel like throwing herself into his arms and begging him to take her with him?

"I don't have any use for your phone number, De—Dallas. Or your address."

"Fine." He folded his coat over his arm and faced her. Apparently, the cold stare he received in return made him think better of whatever he'd been going to say. He turned to the door. "If you'd like to say good-bye to Hilda and Jeanette, you'd better do it now. There's a private plane waiting for us at the airport over in Millhouse."

Charlye was too close to breaking down to be able to stand saying good-bye to them. "You . . . uh . . . say good-bye for me. Please."

"Whatever you want." He put his hand on the doorknob, then withdrew it and turned.

"You know, Charlye, you're not worthless, no matter what your mother might have said to the contrary."

The statement stunned her. "What does my mother have to do with this?" she asked, frowning in confusion.

"The night we met I asked you who was responsible for the fact that you had no idea how special you are. You never said so outright, but during our time together, I figured it out. It was your mother," he told her, regret and sorrow coloring his voice. "She chipped away your self-esteem so that you'd never even think about leaving her."

Charlye couldn't deny it, but she shook her head at him. "That has nothing to do with us, Dallas."

"It has *everything* to do with us, Charlye," he said with a touch of desperation. "You don't believe I could love you because you don't think you're worthy of love. You don't see how sweet or funny you are, or how a man could possibly need your warmth and your incredible passion. Your mother robbed you of the first half of your life, Charlye, and you're throwing the rest of it away. And you're destroying both of us in the process."

He opened the door. "Good-bye, Charlye," he said softly, and then he was gone.

Charlye's trembling knees wouldn't hold her up. She sank onto the floor, and the tears she'd been holding back came out in a great flood of anguish.

Del was gone. She'd sent him away. It was over.

Damn him!

Why had he come? Why hadn't he left things alone? What satisfaction did he get from perpetuating his deception? Why on earth had he told her he loved her?

Because he does, you idiot.

Charlye couldn't tell where the voice came from—whether it was her head or her heart—but she listened to it.

He loves you and he wants to be with you, so why are you sending him away? What have you got in Blessing, Indiana, that you couldn't have in Fig Garden, California? Other than a life, that is—because you've got no life here. No life at all, Charlye.

Something between a sob and a laugh of triumph bubbled in Charlye's throat as she sprang to her feet. Del loved her. She stumbled to the library table, then on to the door, down the hall, past the office, picking up speed as she made straight for the exit.

"Charlotte! Where are you going?" Mrs. Kelley demanded.

Charlye wiped tears off her face with the back of her hand.

"To California, Mrs. Kelley! With occasional side trips to heaven!" she shouted as she hit the doorway running. She burst out of the building and ran as hard as she could run to the parking lot where the man she loved was helping two sweet little old ladies into a big black car.

"Dallas, wait!" she screamed as fresh tears flooded down her face. "Don't you leave me!"

Connie Bennett

He looked up as she streaked toward him, and then she was in his arms, her feet were off the ground, the world was spinning dizzily, and Del—or was it Dallas?—was kissing her lips, her cheeks, her eyes . . .

Her tears turned to laughter, and Charlye suddenly found herself back on her own two feet looking up into eyes that were movie-star blue. They would take some getting used to, but she could do it. Just like she could get used to the rest of his life.

"Do you really love me?" she asked breathlessly.

Del looked like he was having trouble believing she was in his arms. "Yes."

"Well, what are you going to do about it?"

A huge smile made his face almost too beautiful to look at. "If I thought you'd say 'yes,' I'd ask you to marry me."

"Ask," she commanded.

"Marry me." He said it as a demand, not a request.

"I will," she said, holding up her hand. In it was the glass box containing her crystal slipper. "At the stroke of midnight, so we'll know that the fairy tale will never end."

"It's a deal," Dallas said, sealing the promise with a kiss as two beaming fairy godmothers looked on.

Admit Desire

Thea Devine

To John, Tom, and Michael—my heroes.

Chapter One

"Let me get this straight," Nick Shields said through gritted teeth into the phone. "You have asked Francesca Doran to marry you."

"That covers it perfectly," his younger brother said easily.

"The same Francesca Doran who jilted me."

"Oh, now Nick—she says you jilted *her*."

Nick clenched his fist. "The same Francesca who swore she would sooner be cloistered and take the veil than marry someone named Shields—"

"Hyperbole," his brother said calmly.

"The same Francesca who instigated a fight and then poured the engagement party punch all over me just before she walked out on all our guests."

"She was younger then, Nick."

"The same Francesca who is two years older than you—"

101

"I'm mature for my age, big brother."

"Have you lost your mind?"

"I'm a happy man, Nick. I was hoping you would wish me well."

"What I wish is you would get some therapy. You definitely are not *well*."

"I'm sorry you feel that way, old man. I was hoping you would stand up with me."

"What?!"

"I want you to be my best man, Nick."

"I'll be your worst nightmare," he muttered. "You've lost it, Bobby."

"You think so, huh? Let me tell you—I've found it." Bobby Shields smiled as he heard the low growl of Nick's disapproval. "We're getting married as soon as possible."

"Dear God—"

"So you have to come."

"I know I'm going to regret asking this—but how soon is soon?"

"Tomorrow wouldn't be too soon."

Nick growled again. *Foolish Bobby. His baby brother. Personable, self-made millionaire, and as volatile and impulsive as they came. He had spoken to him not a month ago. So when the hell had they gotten together?* "Forever would be too soon."

Bobby pretended not to hear him. "Next month, soonest we could arrange it. I really want you to be here. You'll just have to shift things around and take the time. It's going to be a big wedding. A monster wedding. Francesca will have nothing less."

"As far as I'm concerned, she can have less than nothing."

Bobby ignored that. "You really should curb that hostility, Nick. I'm the last person I thought I'd see walking down the aisle with all the bells and whistles, and to my amazement, I'm really looking forward to it."

"Oh yeah, you're a real amazingly forward kind of a guy."

"Nick, I detect a note of disapproval."

"You're imagining things, Bobby. I'm overjoyed that the woman I once was planning to marry is now to become my flaky sister-in-law. Nothing to disapprove of there. I'm thrilled to death we're going to be one big happy family."

Bobby waited a beat. "So when can you come?" He heard Nick's hand slam against the desk and then a long irritated pause as he riffled through his calendar.

"I can fly in next weekend."

"Oh—" Bobby began. "I was hoping—No. Forget that. You never were one for parties. Just to let you know, though, Dad's throwing a huge formal reception for Francesca Friday night. Everything from soup to nuts—"

"*You* are nuts," Nick said dampingly.

"But Nick—it's *Francesca*."

"Exactly my point."

"You know what she's like."

"She isn't *like* anything . . . or anyone."

"Precisely."

"And she isn't *likable* either."

"Hey—don't be a bastard just because you lost, Nick. She's mellowed a lot."

"She's a damned bulldozer, Bobby, and it looks like she's rolled all over you."

"Now you're being flat-out nasty. Forget it, if you're going to talk about Francesca like that. Just come when you can; we'll talk then."

"You bet we will."

"I didn't hear that, Nick. I'll see you soon."

"You're damned right you will." But he was speaking to the dial tone.

He hung up and impatiently paged through his calendar again. *Too damned many meetings. Too damned many brothers thinking that because they conquered Wall Street, they could tame the tigress.*

He grabbed the phone and punched in the extension of the company travel representative. "Hi, Ellie. It's Nick. Listen—I need a seat on the red-eye to New York tomorrow night. Sunday return." He leaned back in his chair resignedly, as if hearing the sound of the words finally made the thing real.

He was going to New York when he had sworn he would never go back there again, and his baby brother, of every eligible fool on the planet, was marrying Francesca, the hellcat who still haunted his dreams.

He shook himself in response to Ellie's next question. "No, not business. Nope—I'm going to a party."

This was the reward of his family's forty years of hard work: a townhouse in Gramercy Park that was lit up like a jewel on this autumn evening.

He stopped the cab at the corner, tipped the driver generously, hauled his suitcase over his shoulder, and started walking down the block.

The air was brisk, and he felt the vibrance of the city seep into his bones. Everything was motion, motion, motion. He wasn't used to it. He had forgotten it. He felt himself embracing it even as he resisted it.

And he loved the sight of the house with light pouring out of every window.

He had left it two years before because of Francesca. And he was coming back to it because of her.

The irony floored him.

And he suddenly could not understand why.

He mounted the steps slowly. He hadn't seen his father in over a year; in an annual ritual his father flew out to Chicago so that he would not have to come to New York.

And this is what I missed; so who was I punishing after all?

He could hear the music even before he opened the door, and underlying it, the sibilant sound of animated conversation.

He dropped his suitcase in the vestibule and marched past the closed parlor doors down the hallway to the dining room.

There were a hundred people, maybe more, dressed in the height of cocktail elegance, crowded around tables serviced by attentive waiters at ten buffet stations around the room.

And still more waiters precariously balancing trays of hors d'oeuvres passing through to the parlor.

Bobby was nowhere in sight.

He pushed through the crowd into the parlor.

This room, which was some fifty feet long by thirty feet wide, was also jammed with guests, most of whom were dancing or drinking.

And right in the center of this crowd, just where he would have expected to find her, he saw Francesca Doran.

She was magnetic, as she had always been, and still model-slender, with her milky skin and thick auburn hair tumbling around her shoulders. She was wearing a slip of a dress in matte gold silk and he was certain she was wearing nothing under that.

And she wore a gold circlet around her throat, and gold on her ears, around her wrists, and one ankle.

And a huge diamond ring on her left hand.

He felt his stomach curdle, and he moved toward her slowly, not at all certain he wouldn't just strangle her on the spot.

She didn't see him at first, but then she turned to take a glass of champagne and she fairly bumped into him.

And he said the first thing that came into his head.

"Gold digger."

She looked up at him calmly, took the flute and sipped delicately without missing a beat.

"But—we weren't talking about James Bond, Nick darling. Have you had some champagne? It's excellent. Do take some. There you go. Isn't this a lovely party?"

"No. It's too crowded and too noisy."

"Just what I like," she said, daring him to contradict her.

"I remember."

"I bet you do. Whereas you are perfectly content to be a party of one, preferably up a mountain that no one could possibly climb. We do hold true to type, don't we?"

"Some of us do," he growled.

"What are you doing here anyway?"

"Best man."

"Excuse me?"

"You heard me."

"That's the worst excuse I ever heard for butting in."

He needed that champagne badly, but the waiter was already across the room. "Bobby's idea; I would have thought he cleared it with you."

She thought about it a minute. "No," she said darkly. "No. He must have had a brainstorm. I think there was a full moon the other night. He really needs to be in restraints once a month. What the hell was he thinking?"

"Mending fences, darlin'," Bobby's voice interposed, and then Bobby's lips grazed Francesca's cheek, and he extended his hand to Nick. "Nick—so glad you made it."

"Wouldn't have missed it," Nick murmured insincerely. Bobby—when had he last seen Bobby? After the breakup? Before he had left for Chicago? Robert Shields, suddenly the good son, who had returned to the family corporate fold after the heir apparent had defected. Bobby looked seventeen years old, freshfaced and still growing, and he was managing the venture capital fund—and he'd made millions doing it on his own.

"Of course not," Bobby said as a camera flashed across the room. "I knew that. Come, Frankie, time to dance."

Frankie? Frankie!

"Yes!" She handed her champagne flute to Nick. "You know how I love to dance."

He knew. Too well, because he hadn't. Wouldn't. Didn't want to look like a fool. But not Bobby and Francesca.

They moved to the center of the room as the music

escalated to a thumping, pulsing beat. They moved right into it without missing a step.

Nick took a deep sip of Francesca's champagne. Bobby didn't look like a fool. Bobby was loose and sleek. Bobby knew just how to do it.

Damn him.

He handed the empty flute off to a passing waiter and edged out of the room and away from the grinding multitude.

"Son." His father, coming around a corner, looked as elegant as ever. He was superbly dressed by the designer of the moment, and he was a man who always looked as though he had somewhere to go.

"Dad." They embraced.

"You saw Bobby?"

"Right inside."

"And Francesca."

"Couldn't miss her."

"Excellent. So glad you came."

"Wouldn't have missed it," he said again, but he didn't miss the gleam of skepticism in his father's eyes.

"You look wonderful," his father said. "Here—" He stopped a waiter and took two flutes from the tray. "A toast. To your return and Bobby's wedding."

"And to the fact that the old man looks as young as his sons."

"Now, Nick—"

"You haven't aged a month, Dad."

"Bless you."

"Neither has Bobby," he added, turning to look at him and Francesca as they moved sinuously around the front parlor.

"Ah, yes. The rebel has come to rest on terra firma. It's rather a sight to see," his father murmured. "He financed her recording studio, you know."

"What?" Dear God, the studio—the music—everything that had come between them—and Bobby had been the one to hand it all to her on a silver platter.

Who was the fool?

"Well hell, son—she had a plan. Wrote it all up tidy

as a Christmas present. You knew she was going to do it. Moonbeam Studios. Over in Brooklyn . . ."

He was barely listening. Moonbeam Studios. A monument to his cavalier rejection of her dream. Fairy dust and moonbeams, he'd called it.

He remembered the whole scene distinctly, painfully. And he still didn't see where he was wrong.

She had come to work for Shields and Company. She was an astute investor, specializing in entertainment stock, and she had risen to Vice President and head of her own group in three years. She had won every major award and she was a much courted speaker and interviewee.

She was also a musician whose forte was stringed instruments. She played everything from guitar to cello and keyboard on the side, but her great loves were the electric violin and jazz.

They had been a clear case of opposites attracting. She was like helium—with her, he could cut loose and float free; with him, she could fly high and still stay tethered to the ground.

They were a team, they had a common goal, they were getting married. They were having catastrophic arguments and fights. He wanted to save for their future. She wanted to invest in the here and now.

She walked into his office very early one morning and said, "I just quit."

He had been absolutely flabbergasted. "You just—what?"

"Quit," she said flippantly. "You know—resigned, gave it all up, said good-bye, adios, farewell, and adieu."

He was speechless. Elegant Francesca, in her perfect corporate gold-trimmed black silk suit, with her wild auburn hair neatly knotted into a soft chignon at her neck, brilliant gorgeous corporate vice president Franscesca Doran was telling him she was leaving Shields and Company.

"And why is this?" he asked roughly when he got his bearings back.

"I woke this morning and I asked myself, as I always do—and as you know—do I want to make money this morning or do I want to make music? And you know what my answer always is. And this morning I decided there was no reason why I couldn't make music."

His mind raced over the previous, perfect evening to see if there was anything that could have set her off. They had gone to an off-off-Broadway show, a kind of folk gospel presentation with lots of guitars and things, and then dining and dancing.

She had loved the show; he'd been bored. But surely that wasn't nearly enough to make her turn everybody's life upside down like this. This was a whim, a pie-in-the-sky yearning. She could do it as a hobby. He thought they had already discussed it, and that she had come to terms with it. They were building something together. And for nothing she wanted to just throw it all away.

"Look, Francesca . . ."

"I don't want to hear this lecture again, Nick. I'm young. I have money. I can take risks. I have a business plan. I know what I'm doing."

"That's a bungee jump to nowhere," he said harshly.

"Fine. And if I continue here, I'll suffocate. I vote for the adrenaline rush, Nick. And you vote for the down quilt."

"That makes me sound puffy and enveloping."

"Maybe you are."

He stiffened. "Maybe we should talk this out over dinner."

"Oh God, no. No more discussions. I know you think this is good communication, but I'm telling you, Nick, you have not been listening."

He drew in a deep, hissing breath. "You want to make music."

"You're a regular parrot, you are. But *you* didn't hear that. You heard Francesca wants to make music and that's fine with me as long as it doesn't interfere with my life. And guess what, Nick. That's fine with me, as long as it doesn't interfere with *my* life. Hear this: We don't intersect, you and I."

He heard it, and he felt his veins turn to ice. She was angry, she meant it. This was important, and he had never wanted to believe it was important. He knew why too: She already had a *real* job, and he didn't understand why she needed anything else.

"Francesca . . ."

She had just walked out.

Still, that hadn't been the end of it. They had talked about it and talked about it, and he had thought that they had finally negotiated a truce.

It lasted just until the night of their misbegotten engagement party.

And then he finally and completely understood that she was never going to give up that dream, that she had made her choice and she was going to make him choose.

He could either accept her decision or walk away.

And he had arrogantly and stupidly decided to walk away.

. . . *Francesca* . . .

Moonbeam Studios . . .

His father was still talking, describing how she had spent the first year performing, researching, pinpointing her audience, finding studio space, equipment, and a distributor.

And then Bobby had stepped in. Clever, resourceful Bobby, with imagination, vision, and faith. Fairy dust—waving his wand and making it all happen.

But what had happened, after all? She was still performing and now had a cult following. The company's catalogue was a dozen releases a year, one of them hers, and all of them on a shoestring. Reviews were good. Sales were good to brisk. Her staff was dedicated. And she was thriving. She was happy. She hadn't needed an anchor. She had needed to fly free.

Moonbeam Studios . . .

She looked as though she could walk on moonbeams. His father adored her. And Bobby—he wished he were as young and fearless as Bobby. He was three years older and felt as if he were a hundred as he watched them.

"Francesca is going to play later," his father said.

He took a deep breath. "I can't wait to hear her."

His father skewed a look up at him. "Really, Nick?"

"Really, Dad."

"She's great on stage. Plays regularly at the one of the jazz clubs downtown. Just a knockout. Jazz fiddle."

"I know, Dad."

"Do you now? The wind brings glad tidings even in Chicago?"

"I keep in touch," he said darkly, but what he meant was that well-meaning friends kept him in touch, and had sent him her first CD, which he hadn't taken off the changer since it arrived.

"Well," his father said heartily, "then you have some idea. And you're in for a treat. Now, have you eaten?"

"On the flight."

"That's not eating, dear boy. That's ingesting. Come, let me at least feed you." He clapped him on the shoulder. "By God, it's good to have you home again."

He ate. There was a buffet that would have fed the whole population of the city. There were too many people, crowds of people jostling, excusing, murmuring introductions and identifications. . . .

Ah, yes, he had gone through this before. The night of the ill-fated engagement party. All those people. All those never-to-be-taken-back words. And him, sopping wet in punch, watching Francesca storm out the door.

And into her future. And his past.

He lost his appetite suddenly.

His past . . . he was her past . . .

He had never quite thought about it like that before.

"Nick!" More friends, business acquaintances—past lives. Why had he ever gone to Chicago?

Thea Devine

It was so easy to be swept into conversation and catching up. He didn't have to think about Bobby and Francesca and what might have been.

He had thought he was over that anyway.

"You can't let her marry Bobby."

He was in a quiet corner by himself, watching the ever-shifting crowd.

"Nick?"

"I hear you, Missy."

"So, what are you going to do about it?"

"I guess I'll just go tell her I can't *let* her marry Bobby."

"This is *not* a joke."

Oh, now she sounded just like Francesca, as only a younger sister could.

Except there was a note in her voice which made him look at her sharply. "Not a joke? Come on, Missy."

"Look at them, Nick. She adores him because he's been her knight in shining armor—and because he looks so much like you. Try to picture them two years down the line. Or with children . . ."

Oh God—children . . . he had desperately wanted children—with her, with her long lean lines and that thick coarse Francesca hair, and those eyes and mouth and skin . . .

"*He's* a child. He's playing at being a financier and a fiancé."

"If he is, all his cards are on the table. I'm the best man."

"Yes, you are," Missy said tartly. "And you just up and left her. We won't even talk about how stupid *that* was."

"We don't know each other well enough for you to talk to me like that," Nick said, keeping his tone light. But he meant it.

"Well, someone has to. Your dad wouldn't. You walked out. And she would never beg. And who won? We both know who didn't. And who's been miserable? She was. You've been—"

"Now wait a minute—"

112

"Oh, please . . . I don't want to hear about the good life in Chicago, Nick. I'm sure it's been wonderful. We all know you're a great success. You're probably engaged to someone, too. But just don't let her marry Bobby."

There it was again: that *let* business, as if he could control Francesca. As if he could ever have controlled her.

But I always wanted to . . .

The thought shocked him. *Did I?*

"How does one stop Francesca from doing anything she wants to?"

"Not the way you did it."

"Damn, Missy." And anyway, she wasn't serious. She couldn't be, not about something like this.

"They haven't set the date. She hasn't wanted to."

"Bobby said next month."

"That's news to me, and I'm the maid of honor."

"Everything is news to everyone," he muttered.

"Well—that shows you how well-planned *this* event is going to be. And that's because it's not Bobby she really wants."

"Hold it . . . hold it. Damn it, Missy. You have no right to do this."

"I've been waiting two years to do this, for Pete's sake. Don't throw this opportunity away."

A knife straight to his heart. "Meaning what?"

"You know what, Nick. That whole blow-up was so stupid. And you just let her go. Have you learned anything in two years? I hope so. I'm telling you: don't let her marry Bobby."

"Missy . . ."

But she ignored the warning tone in his voice; she turned before he could protest further and just melted into the crowd like some fairy godmother.

Maybe she was.

Maybe he was dreaming because when he looked for her again, she was gone.

Francesca stood on the dais with the band, waiting for the milling crowd to quiet.

"Shhh . . . shhh . . . shhh . . ."

Like a wave, slowly, front to back, the voices of the guests murmured down to nothingness until there was absolute silence.

Francesca lifted her violin, the band struck the note, and she began to play.

And then it was Francesca in motion, body, mind, spirit, her mobile face expressing everything she felt as she drew out the music—*her* music: complex, dissonant, rich, lush . . .

And romantic . . . which he thought was pure Francesca. Her music was romantic and passionate, and it resonated in his gut.

. . . *Don't throw it away* . . .

Ridiculous. Impossible. There was Bobby, leaning against the parlor doors, watching her with love-struck eyes. And his father, always so fond of her, so proud of his prospective daughter-in-law. Twice over.

And Missy. He caught sight of Missy toward the back of the room, a carbon copy of Francesca with her thick auburn hair that she wore angled and short, her pert features, and her long, lean Doran frame.

Missy hadn't been serious. Missy was trying to stir up trouble. Maybe Missy wanted Bobby. A dozen scenarios occurred to him as he studied Missy's serious face.

She was so much like Francesca. And so unlike. Why would she goad him like that after all this time? Two years ago she had been a bespectacled college freshman to whom he had paid scant attention at the requisite holiday functions at which they usually met.

And he wouldn't have listened to her anyway if she had spoken her mind back then. She had been all of seventeen or eighteen. Not a woman of the world. Certainly not one who knew anything of affairs of the heart. Or *his* heart, in any event.

To him, she had been an unformed version of Francesca who had yet to become fully defined. He wouldn't have taken one word of advice from Missy two years ago.

But now . . . now—

No . . . no—

That was fairy dust and moonbeams, to think that there was anything that could be rescued, that there was anything left.

He didn't believe in things like that. He didn't, but Missy's comments had rocked his boat to the point that he felt as if he were drowning . . . drowning in Francesca's music, drowning at the sight of her, her beauty, her swaying body, and her joy in her playing, in her life, and in herself.

He felt as if he had fallen overboard all over again, just as he had when he had first met her, but now it was far, far too late for anyone to save him.

Chapter Two

She played three of her compositions, and the applause didn't stop for a full fifteen minutes.

When she was done she handed her fiddle to one of the band members and then stepped down off the stage and into the crowd. Everyone reached for her, and she took everyone's hand and accepted their compliments as royally as any queen.

But then, she had always thought it was merely a matter of educating people.

Educating Nick . . .

No—she wasn't going to go there.

She slanted a look at him from across the room. Maybe she would go there; he was looking delightfully vulnerable, almost as if the music had moved him.

She was still filled with it. She felt it in every pore,

the pure exhilaration of both her playing and her guests' response to it.

Nick's response to it.

She moved toward him slowly and deliberately, although he wouldn't have known that. But she wanted to see it up close, she wanted to hear it—*his* response.

His capitulation . . .

No, she was over that. That was over, years ago. Contact broken, with only his father as intermediary to assure her that he was well and he was doing well. Unforgivable, that. And all over her decision to make music.

He'd just gone into a hole and never come out. And she was not going to beg.

She wanted to rub his nose in it, which she supposed she had. What better evidence than the slow steady success of Moonbeam and the affection and adoration of her audience, albeit one admittedly hand-picked for the occasion?

But still—the expression on his face. She had covertly watched him as she played. Yes, he had felt the music.

But what else he'd felt, she could not tell. Almost immediately after, he had put on his trader's face, the one that admitted nothing and gave away nothing.

He was the most memorable man in the room. No one stood as ramrod straight or wore a suit like Nick. No one had that map of a face that made you just want to stare at it, or that thick, gray-streaked hair that you just wanted to bury your fingers in.

And she was being dispassionate about it. Every woman in the room was staring at him—at *them*—as she went toward him, willing him to be the first to say something, anything.

It had been like this the first time she met him. Every woman wanted him; no one could claim him. Nick Shields, son and heir, patrician, impassive, implacable, unobtainable.

117

Except for the light flaring at the back of his eyes, the infinitesimal indication of fascination and interest. She saw it there now. Again. For her.

And as if to underscore the moment, the band began to play.

The music was slow, seductive, romantic.

"Dance with me, Nick."

Francesca's voice was whipped cream. Delectable. Tasty.

And the look in her eyes challenged him. *Do it. Don't make a scene. Don't be a fool. . . .*

Or was he reading all that into something that wasn't there?

He hated dancing.

But he wanted no scenes. He had come home to be civilized and forgiving.

He *hated* dancing.

He held out his arms and she walked into them as naturally as if she had been there an hour ago.

Her slender body was *that* close; they were hip to hip, thigh to thigh. Her dress was so thin, it was as if she were wearing nothing. He knew every inch of her, and he didn't know her at all.

She was so warm. She moved so easily, so subtly, and he found himself moving, too, easily, coherently, rhythmically.

Not a fool . . .

Her face was radiant. She wasn't classically beautiful, but there was something about her that made him just want to look at her all the time. And it had always been like that.

If she could have been as pliant and tractable in life as she was on the dance floor . . .

No. There was no point to thinking like that. She was what she was: beautiful, talented, determined, and a gambler.

And he wasn't.

She had made the right choice, and she and Bobby would live happily ever after.

But that thought did not mitigate the rhythmic feel of her body moving against him, or his own response

118

to it. And her scent. And her beauty. And everything there had ever been between them.

He felt the firm nudge of her leg against his, and immediately he had the disconcerting vision of her long bare leg wrapped around his hip when they were naked and tightly wound together in bed, sated with sex, and whispering to each other.

Those lips, those knowing eyes—she flashed him a curious look as he faltered.

God, he could almost feel the smooth slide of her bare foot on his leg. And had he not held her this way, sprawled naked on top of him, with nothing between them but their insatiable need for each other?

He pulled back on the thought, on the mounting desire, on the keen edge of need. All of that was buried, long dead, and not to be disinterred and displayed.

But to hold her close like this was torture. And to know she was aware of his body's every betrayal was sheer torment.

She was like quicksilver in his arms. There—and not, sliding away from him, just as she had before, when he most needed to contain her.

She was the embodiment of Eve, elusive, mysterious, so outrageously feminine, so utterly oblivious to the havoc she had wrought.

And everyone wanted her: As the music wound down, there was a chorus line of available partners waiting for him to relinquish her.

With a shimmering look over her shoulder, she went to join them, leaving him bereft on the sidelines, with a hard-on that would have tumbled a building.

He watched her from a suitably discreet position as she turned on the dance floor with another guest.

That sleek, slender body . . . he could see every contour beneath the tissue-thin material of the dress. He could see the flex of her buttocks as she moved, and the jut of her hips, and her taut nipples just outlined beneath the form-fitting bodice of her dress.

And if he could see, everyone could see . . .

Which was none of his business.

He had to get out of there. He was losing perspective. He wasn't there for Francesca, he was there because he was the best man, he was family, he was Bobby's big brother.

That was enough; that had to be enough.

He took another glass of champagne and meandered through the downstairs rooms. There must have been a hundred and fifty people there, and he knew at least half of them.

There was plenty to divert him. He settled himself in the library to talk with old friends, all of whom knew his and Francesca's history and were very careful to talk around it.

It was a pleasure not to hear about Francesca. He talked about his life in Chicago and the successes of the newest branch of Shields and Company. And yes, he was very happy for Bobby, and yes, it was both ironic and fortunate that Bobby had joined the company. And no, he wasn't thinking at all of coming back to New York.

All he was thinking about was Francesca, how she had felt in his arms, how she had moved, how she had looked, how she had once loved *him*.

No. He couldn't allow himself one minute of regret. None. Ever.

He lifted his gaze toward the door, and he could just see her in a crowd beyond the threshold. Her face was in profile, and she was listening attentively to whomever was speaking.

Francesca . . . she had looked at him like that dozens of times across his desk, a restaurant table, a crowded room . . . with that amused lift of her eyebrow, that glint in her eye, that unspoken invitation to kiss her—*damn, blast, and hell . . . this was a bad idea, a catastrophically bad idea.*

And then she was there, tall and slender and luscious, standing in the doorway. "Hey, everyone."

"Hey Francesca—wonderful music . . ."

"Beautiful . . ."

"New? I didn't think I had heard . . ."

". . . is the next concert?"

She held up her hands, laughing. "Friday night, guys, at the Cookery . . ."

Well, he wouldn't be there, and he felt a jolting and unexpected sense of regret.

She vanished before he could examine that unaccustomed sensation, and everyone started talking about her—her beauty, her talent, her success, her upcoming nuptials.

And there was no way he could gracefully withdraw. It would have looked as if talk about her upset him. As if he still cared. Well, yes—he cared. But he was over Francesca, and listening to them discussing her would not upset him at all.

At all.

"I swear, she's never been more productive than since she and Bobby got engaged," one woman commented. "She just glows with it. And the music . . . well, didn't we all think that was just a pipe dream . . . and now look . . ."

"I heard there's been some interest from the megalabels."

"No kidding. Jeez . . ."

"No, Francesca's hanging on. She's not thinking of selling out any time soon. Anyway, I heard she's going after . . ." And the woman whispered a name that was well-known in New York jazz circles.

He used that moment of astonishment and awe to make his escape, and he headed purposefully for the kitchen on the basement level.

The world of his childhood. The long steps down. The family dining room at the front of the house, and the huge white-tiled kitchen at the rear.

No longer; now it was a model of professional efficiency, a beehive swarming with caterers and waiters working at stainless steel tables and a six-burner restaurant range.

And he was in the way. He swiped a shrimp toast and popped it in his mouth, and wandered through the kitchen to the adjoining ell with its powder room and storage, and out into the garden.

The guests were congregated in the garden as well. There were knots of people at the picnic tables arranged around the planting beds, and more going up the steps to the deck, and still more in and out the door into the rear parlor.

There were people everywhere, and they were all talking about Bobby and Francesca, and he had made the biggest mistake of his life thinking he could handle coming home again and seeing her.

He was over her. He had made it his mission to get over her. And it had been easy—in Chicago, where he slowly and determinedly had carved out a life for himself.

But not here. Here, she was everywhere he looked, and he hadn't been home three hours yet.

Here, he felt the essence of her seeping into his pores. Here, he couldn't avoid his memories, his feelings, his responses.

Or was it just Missy and her insinuations? He shouldn't have let her say one word against Bobby. Or Francesca.

"Nick—" Francesca's voice, from the deck above, fluty and flirty.

He looked up and she was leaning over the rail like some screwball-comedy heroine.

"Hey you. Come on up."

That face, he knew that face, that expression; instantly he flashed on the first time he had ever kissed her, holding her head, digging his fingers into that thick auburn hair, tasting the heat and honey of her mouth.

His body reacted and he gritted his teeth as he mounted the steps slowly. *I have to stop thinking like this. She's Bobby's fiancée now. She made the decision—both decisions—and it's too late to go back now.*

"So talk to me," Francesca said, handing him another champagne.

"Oh, I'm sure you're up on all the details," he murmured.

"Now, Nick," she chided. But she was. "All right, let me see. Shields and Company is a huge success. You love Chicago. You're not involved, at least as far as Jonathan knows—or are you?"

He was watching her full red lips and hardly concentrating at all on her words, so her sharp question caught him off guard. "My father's a damned gossip. No. Nothing serious."

"Let me see—you work twelve-hour days, but still you find time to be a patron of the symphony and the Art Institute. You have a season pass to the Bears, and you just moved into a new apartment on Lake Shore Drive—did I miss anything?"

"I think Dad got it all."

"Sounds delightful."

"It is."

"Glad to be home?"

"I could say I have missed New York."

"How long will you stay?"

"Not sure yet."

"I see." She looked down into her champagne flute as if it were a crystal ball. "And you'll be back for the wedding."

He felt something congeal inside him. "That I will."

"That's good, then." She slanted a look up at him, and he had the strongest urge to both shake her and kiss her.

He had to ask. "Have you set the date? Bobby was talking about next month."

"Well, yes—yes . . ."

"Ummm—the music . . . I loved the music."

Again, that quick, flashing look. "Did you?"

"I really did."

"I'm glad." A long awkward moment of silence, and then, "Ah—a new guest. Excuse me, won't you?"

He watched her glide away. That dress was indecent, obscene. And that body . . . pure Francesca, and—he had to come to terms with it—no longer his.

* * *

The next he saw her, she was in the parlor, lounging on the thick rolled arm of a leather sofa, one arm balanced on the back, one long bare leg showing through the slit in her dress, a pose he had seen a hundred times as she lay languorously beside him in bed.

Francesca . . . dammit, dammit, dammit—

What did he see but her long legs wrapped around him, and him joyously thrusting and pumping into her gorgeously responsive body until the explosive moment of surrender. . . .

He had to stop this, he had to—

She was Bobby's now.

And anyway, he was forgetting the arguments, the disagreements, her irritating way of just riding all over him when he wanted to do something. Her quitting the company and her high-powered position to pursue her music.

There. Of everything, that betrayal had cut the deepest because she had gone ahead without telling him, without discussing it, without considering the consequences.

And of everything, he was a man who always considered the consequences. Except this time. But he wasn't going to think about why. He just wasn't.

And if the party seemed like it was going on for months, well, that was just because he hadn't expected that seeing her would raise all those old feelings.

But he was a grownup. He could cope.

He grabbed another champagne and got out of the parlor as fast as he could.

"So how do you think it's going?" Missy whispered in Francesca's ear as she was going downstairs to the powder room.

"It's a disaster."

"Shoot. I was hoping . . ."

"Come downstairs with me before he sees us talking. He's got on his martyr expression. I don't know, Missy. I don't think this is going to work."

124

"Well, it worked enough to get him here."

"I can't even talk to him. You should have heard that conversation. It was awful. Like two people on a blind date with nothing to say."

"Now, wait—look. I grant you that we've taken drastic measures. But before we abort the mission, I think you have to count your blessings. He's *here*."

"Oh sure, and look what it took."

"Exactly how you planned it, Franny, although it's an awfully convoluted way to get him back. You can't expect he's going to jump on his charger and carry you away just on my say-so. I gave him something to think about. And God knows, you've given him a *lot* to think about. He looks like he wants to lock you up and throw away the key. I think that's very encouraging."

"Do you?" Francesca murmured. "You know, Jonathan thought I was crazy. But maybe you're right. Maybe this is a baby steps thing. Maybe my expectations were too high."

"You read too many romances," Missy said darkly. "This is real life in which the manipulating ex-fiancée schemes to get back the man who ran away."

Francesca shot her a simmering look. "Okay. So we found the trick to getting him back here. I've sashayed around here like a high-priced hooker. You've warned him. And all he's doing is wandering around and *looking* . . . and not *doing*. So now . . . now I think I'm going to become the sweetest, most amenable fiancée there ever was in the world so he can get a taste of what he's missing. What do you think?"

"I think I feel very sorry for Bobby for having to put up with this."

"Bobby's fine about this. Bobby volunteered to do this. I'm going to be sugar sweet and defer to Bobby. It'll be easy to do that. What did Nick call me? An autocrat? Because I have opinions, ambitions, and a point of view? You know, some things never change. But that's okay. I'm perfectly willing to be retro for the rest of the night."

Missy didn't like the gleam in her sister's eye. "So he'll be jealous of Bobby?"

"Missy . . . we just want him to come after me. Maybe if I put on an apron?"

"Right."

"Okay. You might see how he's feeling now, Miss Missy."

"My pleasure."

"And don't get any ideas."

"Oh, God—not about him. You're about the only one I know who can handle him."

"Except I didn't, and look at what happened."

"A failure to communicate is all," Missy said airily. "And of course, he ran. But that's another component to be dissected another time."

"Right. Okay." Francesca wriggled her body and then looked at herself in the powder room mirror. "I am now in my deferential fiancée mode. I really owe Bobby for this. Come on, let's put on a show."

There was something about Nick: Nick belonged in elegant places, surrounded by beautiful things. He was so tall and austere and of this place where he had been raised that she could never picture him anywhere else.

In all the years he had been away, she had always envisioned him in some similar townhouse, living in a similar style, involved with similar people.

He was a man who would always attract attention, and as she surreptitiously watched him, she saw that he had not changed at all; even in a crowd, he still focused in as if the person he was speaking to were the most important person in the world.

And he had always been the best listener, the best friend.

She wondered yet again when and where it had all gone wrong. Seeing him here now was the most natural thing in the world. He was meant for her, made for her, and never in all the two past years had she thought differently.

But she *had* had a different agenda than he, one

he hadn't wanted to hear about. One he hadn't taken seriously.

Because he hadn't understood it. Because it interfered with his plans and ideas.

She hadn't lost sight of that in the past two years and she mustn't forget it now. It hadn't been a perfect relationship that had gone sour. It had been a relationship in which one member could not support the ambition and dreams of the other.

That problem shouldn't have been too hard to fix. But she had never found it easy to talk to Nick about the music. Never. It was too amorphous for him. It wasn't something he could grasp, touch, or quantify. And there wasn't a bottom line, and Nick always dealt in the concrete and the profitable.

Nevertheless, she still wanted him. And now she was two years older and two years more successful, and she was in a position to go after what she wanted.

She hated subterfuge, but not even Jonathan had been able to make his son give up the luxe city life in Chicago to come home for a visit.

It had called for major strategy, the statesmanship of a diplomat, and the unanimous cooperation of Nick's entire family, who all wanted to see him back in New York and married.

To her.

Jonathan especially, and they had even tossed around the idea of pretending she was engaged to *him*—

Dear Jonathan, willing to sacrifice his lovely house and his regimented life to the exigencies of her plots and schemes . . . and he would have done it, too, if Bobby hadn't gallantly volunteered for the job.

And there Bobby was—his bolt-blue eyes meeting hers across the room as she entered, after which he broke free and came to her, and she wrapped her arms around him, and clung to him.

"What do you think?" she whispered as they moved into the room together.

"I think you've lost your senses."

"No . . . no . . . I just thought Nick ought to see a different side of me."

"Ahhh . . . what side is that, Francesca? Just keep hanging on, darlin'."

He swung her into a slow dance to the music that was ongoing in the adjoining room.

"I love dancing," she murmured.

"I think we did this routine already. How do you think it's going?"

"Darned if I know. He keeps getting up and walking around, and the one conversation we had sounded like a bad script for what not to say on a first date."

"Sounds like things are percolating right along."

"So now—" she went on as if he hadn't spoken, "you and I are going to do dominant submissive stuff."

"Oh yeah? Which of us is which?"

"Guess."

He swung her around in a wide-arcing circle that just grazed Nick's feet as he stood in the threshold watching them.

God, she looked happy. Bobby made her happy. He could even make her laugh while he was dancing. Bobby loved to dance.

Nick turned away.

Francesca watched him, her lips thinning. Same old Nick. Why had she thought that two years would make a difference? Because she wanted it so badly?

She smiled brilliantly at Bobby. "I'll tell you what, Bobby. I'll let *you* choose."

Chapter Three

At midnight, the remaining guests adjourned to the family dining room for a sit-down dinner.

There were twenty altogether, digging into a huge pile of spaghetti and meatballs like a bunch of kids.

His father was at the far end of the table, with his back to the bay window, and Bobby sat at the head, with Francesca to his right and Nick directly across from her.

He wished they had seated him a mile away from her. As it was, she was directly in his sight. And it was painful to watch her playing hostess, and to be thinking about all the might-have-beens.

She was gorgeous by candlelight, impish and serious by turns, her conversation encompassing everyone at the table, including him.

She and Bobby were perfect together; he was as

outgoing as she, and with him she was soft and giving.

Soft . . .

Cancel that thought. She had never been *soft*.

But still, just by the way she touched him, and leaned over to whisper to him, and turned her face up to him, he would have bet his life they never argued over anything. Bobby was so easygoing, so loose. Nothing was critical with him. He took everything in stride.

And more than that, Bobby had given her a moonbeam.

He pushed aside his food. He knew what he was hungry for, and it wasn't pasta.

It wasn't on the menu.

And it wasn't possible.

So there he sat, with that disapproving look she knew so well, barely speaking, hardly eating, and such a dissonant presence, she felt like shaking him.

Missy was right; she had expected too much, even if she hadn't defined in her own mind exactly what she thought he would do.

But then, she had never been able to predict what his responses would be. Look at the disaster she had made of leaving the company.

Well, she hadn't thought it was a disaster then. Only after, after the recriminations and the outrage and his insistence that he hadn't believed she was serious, that what he understood was that she was going to undertake music as a *second* career.

Oh, lord—when she remembered that, she wondered why she had ever put this ridiculous plan into motion. And why she couldn't have fallen in love with Bobby.

She smiled up at him with all the intensity she could muster, and Bobby leaned toward her and patted her arm.

"What do you think?"

"I think he's ready to bolt."

Admit Desire

"You could be right. Why don't you rub my cheek? That should get him crazy."

"Gee, Bobby, you know him so well," she murmured, as she caressed his face, putting a little extra into the indulgent expression with which she was gazing at him. "He looks ready to pop."

"Well, did you ever rub his cheek?"

"Not in the last two years. Or is that a euphemism? Bobby—be serious!" She smacked his hand lightly as he started laughing.

"Dad'll keep him here. He's getting ready for a long round of toasts."

Jonathan clinked his glass and stood up.

"It is time to salute the prospective bride and groom. My children—and Francesca is as dear to me as if she were my child—my children, I can't tell you what great joy I feel at your impending marriage."

". . . your impending doom," Bobby whispered under the *hear hear*'s, and she laughed out loud.

Nick eyed them over his wineglass. They were whispering under the ongoing toasts and giggling like teenagers.

Happy. Bobby makes her happy. . . .

But when dinner was over and all the guests had left, he was stunned to find out that Bobby and Francesca were staying at the house.

He watched them climb the staircase together, Francesca leaning against Bobby's arm, her long dress trailing the steps behind her.

He turned as he felt his father's hand on his arm.

"I can't tell you how happy I am to have my family home again," Jonathan said quietly.

He said what had to be said. "I'm sorry it took so long."

"No. You did what you had to do, son. I'm glad you're here now."

And only then did he lie. "So am I, Dad. So am I."

A grown man didn't have wet dreams.

What was it about Francesca? He couldn't get her out of his mind. And he couldn't sleep because she

131

was in the house. Why the hell had his father invited her and Bobby to stay?

He came down to breakfast early, and still she was there before him, looking freshly scrubbed and businesslike in an ivory silk blouse and taupe tweed trousers. And Bobby was there, and his father, and they were all nestled companionably in the library reading the papers and watching the weekend *Today* show.

Like a family.

He felt like an intruder.

He took his coffee and settled down near the TV.

"So," his father said, "it was a wonderful party."

"Lovely," Francesca murmured, raising her coffee cup.

"Most appreciated," Bobby said. "But now the question is, how long is Nick going to stay and how are we going to entertain him?"

Nick waved the question off. "Probably until Sunday, and you don't have to do a thing. I have a whole city to catch up with. I'll just wander around today, maybe go to the Met and take a walk down Fifth Avenue."

He caught Francesca's glance.

"I wonder . . ." she said hesitatingly, "I wonder if you'd like to see the studio."

He didn't think twice; he didn't blink. He said the only possible thing: "I would like to." But he wasn't at all sure he would.

She smiled beatifically.

"But you and Bobby must have plans today."

"Nope." Bobby answered for her. "I'm back to the office this morning, and Frankie's on her own."

Frankie! . . . To his credit he didn't wince.

"We'll meet for lunch—or dinner," Francesca said.

"Dinner, I think. Call me later." Bobby took a last sip of his coffee and got to his feet. "God, I don't know how I got up this morning. Nick—" he touched his shoulder. "See you later." He leaned over Francesca to kiss her. "Don't overwhelm him."

"I don't think that's possible," she murmured. "I'll call you about five."

"That's fine. See you all." And Bobby was gone, and with him, it seemed, all the lightness and air.

His father was next. "Church meeting."

Church? But he didn't have time to question it; Jonathan was out the door before Nick's surprise could register.

And then it was just the two of them, the fragrance of the coffee, the breakfast fixings, the TV, the papers, and the sudden sense of intimacy and home.

He forcibly pushed it away. Not his home. Not his.

He picked up the paper. He watched the morning show. He ate a piece of sticky sweet pastry he did not want, all to avoid speaking to her.

She was engrossed in *Billboard* magazine and didn't even notice his heavy-handed machinations.

He was woefully out of practice, he thought resignedly. Tied up in knots by Francesca; but that had always been his state of mind when he was around her. Nothing had changed.

No, something had. Today they were going to be on her turf, and he was finally going to face the demon.

They had strategized all night. Had telephone consultations with Missy. Roused Jonathan from his sleep. And this was the best she could do: corral him at breakfast and force him to go with her to Moonbeam.

The truth was, she *hadn't* planned anything past the party. And she was usually so good with business plans.

But Nick Shields wasn't a business. He was a damned monolith.

And she really hadn't thought he would show up.

Or that she would be sharing coffee with him in his father's house in a setting that was almost as intimate as his bedroom.

She still couldn't believe it, because last night had

been something out of a fantasy. She could have dreamt it.

And now she had to deal with it. Bobby had suggested she get him to the studio. The empty studio.

She had thought that would be tricky, very tricky. That he would resist.

What she didn't know about Nick Shields . . .

Except she knew that wary look in his eyes. That she knew very well.

They had planned for every contingency. All she had to do was get him there.

There was time. They were alone in the house, except for the housekeeper. It was only seven o'clock. She was hungry. She couldn't quite gauge what he was feeling.

But he had agreed to come. And that was all she needed.

"More coffee, Nick?" It was the best she could do when they had no conversation whatsoever.

"Half." He watched her pour. Those long slender fingers that made such magic on strings. The fall of her hair over her profile. The bend of her body, and the utter concentration that she brought to every small task . . . "Thanks."

"We'll leave about eight?"

"That's fine." Damn, he couldn't think of a thing to say to her. "Where is it, by the way?"

"Oh. Brooklyn. Greenpoint."

"Greenpoint . . ." he said faintly. Wherever that was—another planet for all he knew.

"Don't worry, Nick. We'll drive."

"I wasn't worried. I've already put myself in your capable hands."

Damn . . . he shouldn't have said that.

There was a slight smile playing around her lips as she went back to the magazine.

He shook himself, picked up the paper, and immersed himself in the sweet silence that followed. The only sound was the low hum of the talk on the TV set, the rustle of the paper as he turned a page, the clink of her cup as she set it down on the saucer

. . . togetherness sounds, homey sounds.

He had to stop thinking like this.

He glanced at her as he turned yet another page he hadn't read. She was tucked up against one corner of the sofa so that the light was over her shoulder, and she was engrossed in the magazine. Her hair fell forward, obscuring her face, and in one hand she had a highlighter at the ready so that not a fact or an opportunity could escape her.

It was so Francesca. Immediately he had a vision of her in meetings at Shields, armed with heavily yellowed-in pages of data to support her predictions and decisions. She had always been thorough, logical, prepared.

Which had made her decision to quit Shields seem all that much more ill-conceived.

No use going all over that again. The end result was that she had made a success of it, and now, after two years, he was going to eat all his objections for breakfast.

So be it. He was ready.

But he was not prepared for just where the studio was located—in a warehouse north of the Williamsburg Bridge, which she had bought because she could renovate the lower floor into a garage.

She didn't say a word the whole trip, or when they parked inside, or as they entered the cage elevator. Rather, she wanted him to *see*, but she couldn't tell from his impassive expression if any of it was making any impression.

They stepped out into the reception room.

She had furnished it like a living room, with a thickly upholstered sofa and chairs, oriental rugs, low lighting, mahogany side tables, and a matching desk discreetly tucked in the far right corner by the entrance to the studio.

The walls were a soft ivory color and over the sofa there was a three-dimensional representation of the Moonbeam logo: a quarter moon with the studio name angled from it in graduated bold gold letters.

She unlocked the door to the studio and he followed her in.

What he saw was a long corridor off of which there were glassed-in booths with recording and engineering equipment. On the wall, there was a gallery of album covers and publicity photos of Francesca and the artists on the Moonbeam label.

"So this is it," he said, feeling singularly helpless in the face of something he still didn't quite understand.

"This is it."

She entered one of the recording booths, and perched on one of the high stools before an overhead microphone. There was an array of instruments along one wall, and a glass window behind that was the engineering booth.

"This is where we make music," she said, reaching up to the mike and angling it toward her shoulder. "It wasn't easy. It was slow. But inside of a year and half, we had the facility, the tech crew, the first album, publicity, a couple of prestige club dates, a distributor, and a following. Pretty good, huh?"

He didn't want to answer. He didn't want anything to be good for her without him. But he had given up any right to want that.

"That's the glamor part," he said. "What's the bottom line?"

Of course, of course. Always the quantifiable with him. She forcibly pulled in on the jolting anger she felt.

"We rent out the studio to freelancers on the weekend, which helps cut expenses. There's a group coming in this afternoon, as a matter of fact. The per-foot cost here is a great deal less expensive than anywhere else. We put a hundred thousand into it, excluding the equipment. And a lot of sweat, equity, and bartering.

"We produce six artists on Moonbeam, and co-produce a half dozen others. The albums do respectably because the production cost ratio is so good, and the price point is under ten dollars. We have a mail order catalog, and we've gotten a lot of free publicity which has led to a couple of appearances on some local morning shows for me. This market is steady and growing, Nick, but I couldn't plot it out for you on a cost analysis curve."

"And Bobby got the financing."

"That's his business. He understood the niche, the need, and the potential."

"And you gave up Shields for this."

You gave up us . . .

She should have known: It still rankled. He still didn't understand—she hadn't given up anything. She'd walked out and taken control of her life with both hands.

"I didn't give up anything," she said tautly, without thinking how the words sounded.

They hung between them like a puffball, floating there like truth, fragile and destructable. One breath, one more word, and everything would disintegrate.

She eased herself down from the stool. There it was: He still didn't see all she had accomplished and what it meant, and so her silly scheme had come to nothing. He wasn't going to capitulate. It was his way or no way, and he was never going to change.

Fine. As far as she was concerned, everything was self-evident, and if he still thought she had made a mistake, that was his problem.

She didn't need to say another word. She watched as he again took stock of the setup and the surroundings, toting up cost against profit, probably.

She wasn't going to tell him that she lived in an apartment upstairs, a move that had made excellent economic sense to her. He would probably be horrified that she had given up her rent-controlled pre-war apartment on Riverside Drive.

So many things she had done in the past two years that had had nothing to do with him . . .

The engagement scheme had been the only ill-conceived idea, born of emotion and yearning and dreams. Romantic things. Unquantifiable things.

Impossible things.

There was only one thing left to do: She would take him back to Jonathan's so he could have his Manhattan weekend—alone—before he went back to Chicago for good.

And then, within a suitable time, she would end her "engagement" to Bobby, and she would step courageously into her future—alone.

Competent, capable Francesca. Brilliant, beautiful, determined Francesca, who had gone out and gotten just what she wanted.

He was damned impressed.

And damned envious that Bobby had been the one to provide the means for her to accomplish it.

He hated Bobby.

He didn't hate Bobby.

He climbed in the car beside her and watched as she maneuvered into the street and through traffic with the skill of an Indy car driver. The silence was taut and irritating. She kept her eyes straight on the road; her expression was implacable.

He had seen her like that in boardrooms and sometimes the bedroom—oh, damn, the bedroom . . .

"Francesca . . ."

"Fine," she snapped, "why don't you say it?"

There wasn't a thing he could hide from her. "Okay. It's impressive, but I still don't see why it couldn't have been a secondary business."

"Thank you."

At least he was honest. She squeezed the wheel so tightly her hands were shaking.

He still didn't get it.

She felt a crushing disappointment. All for nothing. He was a stranger. She had lost him the moment he walked out the door two years before.

"I'll tell you why," she said, her tone careful and controlled. "Because it's *mine*."

And you were mine, and obviously I couldn't have both.

The sensation of loss was so intense, she could

hardly stand it. She had gambled and lost, something she had done a hundred times as a vice president at Shields.

But the stakes had never been so high, and there was always a way to offset the loss.

She should have just left it alone.

They hit some traffic as they came over the bridge, and by the time she pulled up in front of Jonathan's house, it was almost noon.

"Well." She didn't know quite what to say and neither did he. He had hardly any time left: the afternoon, the evening and the following morning, and then the next time he would see her she would be walking down the aisle with Bobby.

He didn't want to let her go.

"We'll see you this evening," she said finally. "I'll let you know where."

That was final. He opened the car door and got out. One more minute and she would be gone.

As she started the ignition, he leaned into the window. "Come with me."

"What?!" This was definitely out of a romantic dream. Nick was not spontaneous.

"You don't have anything else to do, do you?"

"You might not think so," she muttered. "No, Nick, this is a bad idea."

"It's a great idea. We'll go for a walk. Dad still keeps spaces in that garage down on First Avenue. We'll leave the car there and just . . . walk."

She slanted a look at him. He meant it. She wanted him to mean it. She wanted somehow to erase their disastrous visit to the studio. Just that. Just a memory to carry forward into her new life.

"All right."

An easy decision, really. After she'd parked the car, she grabbed her jacket from the rear seat and dug out a pair of sneakers from the trunk.

"Prepared for every contingency," she murmured as she locked the trunk.

It was one of the things he had always liked about

139

her: the way she meticulously thought everything out and never missed a detail.

"Let's walk."

They walked, up First Avenue to 30th Street and then west to Madison Avenue, into the Saturday crowds and the motion of the city; there was no other place like it, not even Chicago.

They didn't even need to talk, not yet. It was enough to browse in shop windows and watch the passing parade, to walk by the shell that had been Altman's, where he reminisced how his mother had always loved to shop there.

This was neutral territory; nothing personal needed to be said.

They veered over to Fifth Avenue after that, and north in the same companionable silence they had shared that morning.

It was a perfect day with a deep blue sky overhead, and the bright hot sun intersecting the crisp air like a laser.

He liked walking next to her, he always had. She carried herself with a self-confident elegance that made passersby turn to look at her. It was her posture, her coloring, her assurance, her style.

She was made for him, and when he looked at her animated profile, he saw a lifetime of love, laughter, and family. He saw her dressed in white, walking down a church aisle.

But not with him . . .

They sat on the library steps and ate hot dogs. They talked about the weather, the crowds, the exhibits at the library and the Met, sports, his father, her parents, where they should walk next . . . and he wondered what she would say if he told her that he wanted her, that he had never stopped wanting her.

They went on up to Sixth Avenue and north toward the park. They talked about Broadway, the Christmas show at Radio City, the stores.

"It's time to call Bobby," she murmured as they passed a bank of phones.

"So call Bobby."

"You never got to the Met." She punched in the number.

"I guess I didn't really want to go there."

She held up her hand as the phone was answered. "Hey, Bobby. Hi. Yep. We've been walking. Almost to Fifty-ninth Street. Yeah. Up here or downtown? No? Are you serious? All right—I'll do that. I'll see you tonight, then."

She hung up. "No dinner. He's buried in work."

"So we'll have dinner."

"You don't have to—"

"Nonsense. Bobby probably told you we should just go on without him."

"Yeah . . . he did."

"So we'll go up to Lincoln Center and see what we can find."

They found a small, lively restaurant a block from the complex, and a small table in a rear room. They found steak and seafood and burgers and microbrewery beer.

They talked about restaurants, books, music, and they compared the cost of apartments, cabs, the theater, New York versus Chicago.

They sat until the theater goes left for the opera, and remained until they returned.

And finally, at midnight, they cabbed back down to Gramercy Park.

"I'll walk you down to the garage."

She was rummaging in her bag for the key. "But I'm staying over again tonight."

For some reason, that threw him. He hadn't expected it. It was disturbing to think of her being in the house tonight. And it felt too familiar, walking up the front steps with her. Almost as if they had done it together forever.

She looked up at him as she handed him the key, and it was that look, that shimmering, Francesca-in-love look that did it.

He bent down and slanted his mouth over hers, waiting for one heart-stopping second to see what she would do.

141

And then he claimed her. He sank into the sweet heat of her mouth, and he came home.

Oh, no—oh, yes . . . she could not have resisted if her life depended on it; she melted into the kiss, opening herself to his hot, familiar tongue. She had missed this, lord, how she had missed this, wanted this, yearned for this.

He enveloped her as he always had; she loved his bigness, his strength, and the austerity of his daytime persona that translated into this ferocious, passionate demand.

She wanted to drown in it, and, conversely, she wanted to pull him deep inside her and keep him safe.

She felt him shift away from her, fumble with the key, felt him swing her in the door and shut it behind them.

Inside. Privacy. Alone in the semidark hallway that was lit with a cranberry glass bannister lamp.

She groaned as he caught her swollen mouth again in a swamping kiss. She felt her legs give, and then the door behind her, supporting her boneless body as he crowded her against him, closer, tighter, tighter still.

She wound herself around him, seeking connection with every part of his body. This was all she needed, all . . .

They didn't need to talk, they hadn't talked, they didn't need anything else except this . . . this driving, overpowering desire to climb inside each other.

It was enough, it was . . .

"Well, well, well . . ." Bobby's voice, above them. "Dessert?"

Nick broke away from her abruptly, sharply; she felt it like a knife severing a cord.

She couldn't focus as Bobby came slowly down the steps. She sensed Nick moving away from her and she wanted to reach out and pull him back.

"I trust you had a nice evening." Bobby at his sanctimonious worst. The fog was clearing. She blinked and he was there, and Nick was behind him, on the first step, bathed in the roseate light of the lamp.

"Lovely evening," she said tightly. "And you?"

"I can't wait to catch up."

"Let's do that *now*, darling."

"Let's do. Excuse us, Nick."

Nick was so silent. So grim. Bobby's elbow grazed his gut as they mounted the stairs. She saw it, saw his gaze darken, could feel his eyes following them all the way up. All the way. She couldn't say a word to Bobby until they were behind closed doors.

And then: "What the hell did you think you were doing?"

He grinned at her impudently. "I could ask you the same question. Are you nuts?"

She sank into the slipper chair by the fireplace. "I'm beginning to think so."

"I decided to raise his temperature a little, darlin'. How'd it go?"

"Oh." What an actor; she had believed him. "Well, after we left the studio, fine. As long as we didn't talk about *that*."

"As long as you didn't talk, you mean."

She made a face. "So he'll leave tomorrow and that will be that."

"So, we'll just let him stew in his hormones tonight." Bobby grinned at her like an overgrown elf. "Personally, I think he's gotten a pretty good taste of what he's missing."

Chapter Four

He had lost her three times over, and he wondered when a man began to get wise.

Maybe when his life began to fall apart.

Technically speaking, he had no life. He had work, a place to live, events to attend. But a life? He had had that with Francesca, and he had thrown it away.

He sat in the dark in the parlor, where the night before, he had danced, Francesca had played, and a glittering array of guests had celebrated her engagement to Bobby.

She hadn't kissed him like she was engaged to Bobby.

She was upstairs now explaining it all to him. Explaining what? The connection was still there? They still wanted each other? He was still in love with her?

He felt like smashing something.

And tomorrow he would be out of there, a complication that should not have happened.

Or had Missy been right?

. . . don't let her marry Bobby. . . .

If he even thought about that—

But he hadn't kissed her, then.

If he hadn't kissed her . . .

If he stopped breathing . . .

If he just went home . . .

What if he didn't?

No, he couldn't do that to Bobby, or to her.

He couldn't leave, either.

He couldn't . . .

He wouldn't . . .

Sunday mornings at his father's house meant the early service at church, a sideboard breakfast, music, and half a dozen papers spread all over the dining room table.

That hadn't changed since he was a child. There was such a sense of home in this house. Why had he never before appreciated that?

Or what a social person his father was; he loved company, his door was always open, and it seemed to have become a Sunday ritual that a partcular set of friends dropped by to read the papers and to argue the current state of political affairs.

He sat contentedly at one end of the table leafing through the book review and listening to the conversation.

He'd missed this, too; he'd missed so much—too much . . .

And he'd missed Francesca's kisses—

"Good morning, everyone." Bobby. God, when Bobby entered a room, everyone knew it.

And Francesca.

Francesca in jeans and an oversized sweatshirt, her thick hair tied up in a careless ponytail, looking slender, fragile, utterly irresistible.

She sat down across from him and Bobby got her coffee and a croissant, seated himself beside her, and handed her the entertainment section of the paper.

An odd silence ensued as they politely avoided conversation, ate breakfast, and read the paper with the hum of animated conversation in the background.

Fifteen minutes later, Missy arrived. "Hey, everybody." She got coffee and pastry and took a seat next to Nick. "Gee, everyone's so bright and sassy this morning. What'd I miss?" She bit into the pastry and looked around at them. "Oh, my. It must have been good."

Francesca kicked her.

"Umph." She swallowed a quick burning sip of coffee. "Oof." That was way too hot Missy decided, and the atmosphere was way too cool. What the hell was going on here, and what was the right question to dig it out?

She slanted a look at Nick. Too wrapped up in the editorials. Francesca—studiously trying not to look at him. And not succeeding.

Bobby winked at her.

Something *was* up.

She took another bite of her pastry, chewed thoughtfully as she tried to read Bobby's expression, and then she said, "So, Nick, what time are you leaving?"

Nick looked up at her. "I'm not."

Missy shot a look at Francesca, who looked panicky. "You're *not*?"

He followed Missy's gaze. "I thought I'd stay on a couple more days."

"Hey, that's terrific, isn't it, Bobby?"

"Absolutely. We haven't seen nearly enough of my big brother. When did you decide?"

He couldn't tell if the question was malicious, and he didn't care. "Funny you should ask, baby brother. I decided last night."

"Must have been something cataclysmic," Bobby murmured.

"Earth-shattering."

"Sounds critical."

"Bobby!" Francesca pleaded, her voice strangled.

"Well, Dad'll be pleased."

"Could I talk to you, Bobby?" she asked carefully. "In the library?"

"Oh, sure."

There was a fire going in the library, as if company were expected at any moment; the room was warm, cozy, with the morning sun streaming in and spotlighting the pile of magazines and books on the coffee table.

Francesca yanked him inside and slammed the door.

"*What* are we going to do?"

"Hey, that's your problem, darlin'. This is what you wanted."

"I know—but not *yet*."

"Don't lose it, Francesca. It wasn't *that* volcanic a kiss."

She stamped her foot. "It was too. And now what am I going to do? He still doesn't have a clue, and on top of that, I've betrayed you. I can't begin to guess what he thinks you're thinking. Maybe you've been too casual about this."

"Or maybe he's plotting to take you away from me. Francesca—wake up. That's what you wanted."

"I know." But she didn't look happy about it.

"He *did* something."

"I know."

"But . . . ?"

"He *still* doesn't think Moonbeam is viable."

Bobby gave her an exasperated look. "So what do you want?"

"I don't know."

"Sure you do."

"Okay, I do. But what if he finds out this whole engagement was a setup?"

"Darlin', I think you've got to tell him."

She groaned. "Bobby . . ."

"Hey—I believe the end justifies the means."

"You *have* to."

"Francesca—I do love you. But not enough to marry you. So would you please finally get this thing off the ground and take him off our hands?"

But she didn't know quite how she was going to do that. That kiss had absolutely thrown everything out of kilter. It was too revealing. It gave her no room to be elusive or mysterious.

It had told him everything.

She was as naked as if she had gone to bed with him.

And he knew it. It was in his eyes as he watched her pause on the dining room threshold. The hunger, the need, the knowledge. And something else, something indefinable and slightly dangerous.

How was she going to tell him about Bobby?

It was Bobby who followed her into the room and announced, "Hey, Dad—Nick's going to stay on a few days."

Jonathan's head snapped up. "No kidding. Nick, that's great. Come to the office, see what's what. We'll all go out to lunch."

Nick smiled tightly. "I can't wait."

"Nice surprise, Son."

"Surprised me, too," he murmured, his gaze slanting toward Francesca. "But I'm beginning to think maybe I did stay away too long."

He was declaring war.

Damn him. It served him right that someone else had moved in on his turf. Surely he hadn't thought she would pine away for him?

He was like a stallion, pawing the ground. And there was Bobby, having the greatest fun pretending to butt heads with him.

He came right over to her, put his arm around her, and pushed her toward the dining room window.

"Remember, darlin', soft. And retro. With me."

She was feeling anything but soft. But she knew exactly the picture they presented: lovers in intimate conversation. Bobby was going to put on a show, just to raise Nick's temperature.

"I can do that," she said airily.

"He's watching. He's going crazy, count on it."

"Bobby, this is really getting out of control."

"Well, fine—but don't take off that ring yet. All you did was kiss him."

"No, that isn't *all* I did. I also cheated on you."

"If it makes you feel any better, I have lust in my heart for other women—like Missy here, for instance."

"What's going on?" Missy demanded.

"We're in a strategy session. Francesca's having an attack of conscience. He kissed her. I think she kissed back."

Francesca smacked him lightly on his chest.

"I have to say, he looks a lot more decisive today," Missy said thoughtfully. "What happened yesterday?"

"He hated the studio. We walked around midtown. We ate dinner. We didn't talk about music. He kissed me."

"Simplifying to the extreme," Bobby said. "It took master planning to throw them together to the point where they could have conversation."

"As long as it wasn't about Moonbeam," Francesca put in.

Bobby shrugged. "It's a start."

"I thought I was finished."

"Guess not. That must have been some kiss."

"Guess it was," Francesca murmured.

"It'll be okay, darlin'. And you've got Missy to run interference."

"And I have you to *interfere*," she added tartly.

"Speak softly when you say that," Bobby warned.

"So what are you going to do?" Missy asked.

She looked helplessly at her sister. "The only thing I *can* do: I'm getting out of here."

One kiss. One long, delicious kiss and everything had gone to hell. And it changed nothing.

The only refuge was home and work.

She pressed the garage door opener and maneuvered her car inside.

You gave up Shields for this?

149

She felt curiously alone as she rode up the elevator. The studio was eerily empty; nothing was scheduled until early evening.

I don't understand why . . .

She shook off the memory.

Oh, by the way, I never was engaged to Bobby. It was just a ruse. . . .

Worse and worse.

She went into her office at the far end of the long corridor of recording booths, and slipped behind her desk.

One press of a keypad, and she had music. Mozart. Light and airy. At total variance with her mood. Another press and a video popped onto the TV screen across from her desk.

It was their newest quartet, Granny's Attick, a female alternative rap group. Looking good. Booked as the opening act at Asbury Park this coming weekend.

She ejected the tape. There were bills to pay, contracts to send to her lawyer, someone to audition later on that evening, and rehearsal for her own appearance at the Cookery on Friday night.

What did she need Nick Shields for? Criticism? Lack of faith? Little to no support?

Sex . . .

She leaned back in her ergonomically designed desk chair and considered the circumstances. She had planned the whole thing badly, with her heart instead of her head. It was quite obvious that with Nick old hurts died hard, that he didn't easily forgive a betrayal, and that he was as single-minded as an elephant.

Three strikes and you're out.

Well, she was down for the count, and there was no resurrecting the past now.

Her phone rang, and she jumped.

"This is Francesca."

"Franny—it's Missy. I'm right downstairs. I just dropped Nick off in front of the studio."

She went cold. "Why the hell did you do that?"

" 'Cause he's irresistible—and bored—and he wants to play."

"Missy . . ." she said warningly as she heard the visitor bell ring impatiently.

"Duke it out, babe. He would have walked if he'd had to. At least you got a couple minutes' warning." She broke the connection and Francesca slammed down the phone.

She didn't have to press the door release. She could just leave him down there stewing.

He'd probably break down the door.

He'd probably climb walls.

And didn't that thrill her—just a little?

She let him in, and then she slowly walked down the corridor toward the elevator as it creaked up to the second floor.

She was halfway there when it stopped and he emerged. She stopped dead and they just stared at each other. And then he started walking toward her and she started backing away.

"I didn't come here to talk."

"You're right. There's nothing more to say."

"We communicate much better when we don't talk."

That damned kiss . . . "That doesn't solve problems, Nick."

"It solves one problem."

He was too close now. His legs were longer, his determination rock hard. How could she escape him?

"Nick . . ."

Futile protest; and how much did she really want to resist when he had her corralled against the door to her office, imprisoned between his arms.

"Kiss me, Francesca." His voice was so soft and seductive, and his mouth was so close to hers, waiting to swallow her protest.

She couldn't have said a word if her life depended on it. She was shocked by his need, his heat, his urgency.

He kissed her then, pressing her lips softly, gently,

tugging at them, touching them, licking them.

She felt the sensations down to her toes. Her body moved bonelessly toward his, like a flower to the sun. She had no choice. He drew her like a magnet. She wanted to lean into him and absorb his light, his strength, his essence.

He seduced her with his lips: She felt each light, crushing pressure against her mouth, her neck, her ear; each flicking stroke of his tongue scorched her skin.

Slowly he moved his arms around her so that his hands framed her face, and ever so deliberately, he settled his mouth on hers.

Everything inside her melted as his tongue sought hers, hot, forceful, demanding, as she remembered, and as it always had been.

She had always loved his kisses; she lost herself in his kisses. The moment dissolved into swamping sensations of heat and pleasure. There was nothing else so vital, so necessary to her existence.

This was where she belonged, in his arms and at his mercy. She could not get close enough. She pulled at his shirt and slipped her hands against his chest. His skin. The feel of him, so tight and taut, his hair so rough against her palms, his nipples erect as she stroked them.

She knew this body better than her own. She wanted all of him, all his power and his strength. *Now*.

She yanked at his jeans, at the impossible button and impediment of the zipper.

He felt the sinuous movement of her hands seeking him. Francesca, of the molten mouth and silky, milky skin. He had held himself in check, waiting for her, contenting himself with sliding his hands over her clothed body, and feeding off of her lush kisses.

In an instant, he pushed down his jeans and his underwear and gave himself joyously into her hands where he belonged.

And she took him, and she held him tightly as he crushed himself against her. She played with him, with the rock-hard length of him, with the giving, ridged tip of him. She knew him, and she couldn't get enough of him, and she could have held him and explored him endlessly.

He didn't know if he could hold out. He needed to feel her nakedness in his hands.

It took not a moment to slide down her skintight jeans; and another to lift her sweatshirt to get at her heated breasts.

Her body was a dream, unfurling like a flower, every secret place open to his questing hands. Her skin was like cream, opulent and caressable. Her nipples were hot, tight pleasure points.

He was at the mercy of memory and desire. His body hadn't forgotten, not for one moment, the feel of her against his hands and his volcanic need to possess her. Their time apart hadn't diminished his need for her. He was shocked by the depth of it, and by his driving hunger to couple with her.

He wanted to mount her right there, right then, on the prickly tweed carpet, just bury himself in her, as deep, hard, and hot as a man could go, and then ride her relentlessly to bone-melting oblivion.

She was his soul, his life.

And about to become his brother's wife . . .

Dear God . . .

He stiffened. He eased himself away from her and framed her face in his hands again.

And all he could feel were her hands grasping his hardness as if she would never let go.

This was not the time, not for anything. He was breathless and on the brink and the last thing he wanted to do was think of anything else or anyone else.

"Tell him . . ." His voice was a whisper. "You . . . have . . . to . . . tell him."

"Nick . . ." A protest from her soul.

"We can't . . . we can't . . ." He felt his need diminish by the second, his conscience at war with his driving desire. "You know we can't . . . you have to . . . tell him."

153

She was mute. Shocked that all this heat and passion had led to this climax. They couldn't . . .

He couldn't do that to Bobby for anything. And he had taken enough from him as it was.

"You'll tell him." His voice was coming back to normal.

"Okay." She wasn't exactly sure what she had agreed to; her body was flushed and she felt as if someone had turned on the air conditioning, and she wasn't connecting what he was saying.

Even he could see that. "Francesca—you can't marry Bobby."

"No," she murmured, but of course she already knew that. He didn't, and that was what he meant. She got it now.

"You sure?"

"Yes."

"It's okay?"

"Yes," she whispered. But she knew that better than he.

"Okay." He released her and moved aside and began putting himself to rights, while she just stared at him.

The beauty of him. The power of him. It took her breath away.

One more moment, and she would have possessed it.

And now, she could only dream.

She sent him a shimmering look, and then she bent down and picked up her jeans and sweatshirt, and she went into her office and closed the door.

"What am I going to tell him?"

"The truth, of course," Bobby said lightly. "No problem. It'll be okay."

"Okay. We're disengaged. I mean, can't I just tell him that, and not the rest?"

"The problem is too many people were in on this, and someone, sometime, is going to let something slip."

"Well, that will be sometime, Just not now."

"Look, Francesca—everything is working out just the way you wanted it to. A sham engagement is a minor detail."

"Minor? *Minor?* Men have committed mayhem for less."

"You exaggerate. I certainly wouldn't. And if you want, I'll take a vow of silence. Hell, I'll take a vow of celibacy. Anyway, he ought to be flattered we all went to such lengths."

"He'll be furious."

"Probably," Bobby agreed after a moment's consideration. "But he'll get over it."

"Or he won't," Francesca said. "And then, of course, there's the question of when to tell him, and how you should act until then. Morose and depressed sounds good to me."

"So we'll just pile one lie on top of the other. How about I dance for joy because I really didn't want to marry you in the first place, and just took up the slack to please dear old dad."

"Bobby . . ." she said warningly. "This is going to get very sticky. And we don't know how long he's staying, either."

"I've heard you can hold a man with sex."

"*Bobby*—be serious."

"Darlin', I don't know what to tell you. You can't predict the human equation. Of course, I've always said that Nick is less than human . . ."

She threw up her hands. "I can't talk to you."

"Exactly," Bobby said gleefully. "Which is why we never should have gotten engaged in the first place."

"Bobbbbyyyy . . ."

He was no help at all, and it was her duty, her decision, and then it turned out there was no time at all for true confessions because Nick was at the brokerage all day in management meetings, and she was busy at the studio, recording and in rehearsals.

The first night after the "breakup," they had dinner with Jonathan, who handled the whole thing with royal cunning.

The first thing he did was send Bobby back to Chicago since Nick's plans were so indefinite.

"Don't tell Nick," Jonathan counseled.

"Too many people know," she said fretfully.

"Then do it on a need to know basis. What can he do, after he commits himself again?"

"Walk away again."

"Nonsense."

"Don't tell him," Missy said, when Francesca laid the dilemma out once more.

"And what happens if you let slip something about it in the course of sisterly conversation?"

"So you'll explain it then."

"I'm thinking maybe you shouldn't tell him," Bobby said when he called her.

"Damn you, don't do a three-sixty on me. I'm going crazy enough between this and all the hours he's been in conferences and my Friday night gig and—"

"Francesca . . . calm down. Let me put it this way: When the moment is right, you'll know what to do."

"Easy for you to say. You're a thousand miles away. What can he do to you?"

"I rather like it out here, too. And there's lots of opportunities for the company. Nick's done a great job. Maybe we should trade places. I'll become Nick, and he'll become me, and that way you won't have to explain anything."

She hung up on him.

There was no time. That was the whole problem. There was no time, and no privacy, and Nick was leaving her too much alone and giving her too much space, as if she needed to get over Bobby.

God, if he even thought about it, he would know—

But he wasn't. He wasn't looking deeper than sex, and maybe, she thought, that was for the best.

He hadn't felt so energized in years. It was the pulse of the city, the insane speed at which life was lived in the streets, in the boardroom, in the night.

It was all about the night, the forbidden, pounding, pulsating rhythms of the night. Francesca was the night: mysterious, shrouded, his.

Admit Desire

With a minimum of outrage, fuss, and tears, she had ended her engagement to Bobby, and not even his father protested.

. . . don't let her marry Bobby . . .

Nobody had wanted to let her. And no one had said a word.

He kept himself so busy because he wanted her so drastically, and even he couldn't see her hopping from Bobby's bed to his in the space of two days.

There was time, there was so much time. Nothing had doused the flame. And now that Bobby had gone to Chicago, they had all the time in the world for long walks, and dinners, and evenings alone.

Except it hadn't quite worked that way. Yet.

Their lives were very divergent. Jonathan had thrown him into the thick of things at the company and Francesca was working morning till night at the studio and in rehearsal with her accompanists.

There was no time. There was just no time and sometimes he felt as if he were racing just to keep up.

Things would slow down after Friday, he thought. They needed to get to Friday and her performance, and then they could take a deep breath and find their footing.

What he couldn't find was some way to slake his obsession to possess her. He didn't know how he had lived without her for two years. He didn't know how he made himself stay away from her now.

But she needed the space. He had to give her time. She needed to get over Bobby. She needed to sort things out. She was as overwhelmed by and as unprepared for their explosive need for each other as he was.

The scent of her permeated his pores; he couldn't stop thinking about her. His body was tight as drum.

When he closed his eyes, he saw Francesca, naked and melting in his arms.

He wasn't getting much sleep.

Friday couldn't come soon enough.

And then it was Friday night and he was cabbing

to midtown with Jonathan, who kept the conversation on business, politics, and anecdotes about mutual friends, a dozen of whom they found waiting for them when they arrived.

They sat at a table just to the right of the stage and watched the arriving crowd: friends, fans, music lovers, an occasional famous face. There was an underlying excitement in the room that seemed to expand with each passing moment.

They were waiting for Francesca.

At nine precisely, after dinner had been served and they were into the coffee and dessert service, a thin muted light played across the glittery curtains, and a voice boomed, "Ladies and gentlemen . . . the Cookery is proud to present—" the curtains parted —"the innovative music of . . . Francesca!"

She stepped onto the stage, gowned in copper-colored jersey crepe that hugged her body and swirled at the hem with her every movement. She wore a gold bow-shaped clip in her hair, matching earrings, and a gold bracelet.

And she was so stunning, she took his breath away.

The room was as silent as a tomb. The expectation was almost unbearable.

Francesca stood with her head bowed, listening, listening for that one sweet moment when she would begin.

And then her accompanist struck a note, she lifted the violin, and she launched into the music.

Fire and fusion. She was extraordinary, at one with the violin and the music, moving around the stage in rhythm and in love, with the ease of an athlete and the elegance of light.

This was a Francesca he had never seen, never known. This was the Francesca who could not be stifled by the closed-in world of office politics and trendy power suits.

She had enough power to drive the universe in her flexing wrists and pliant body. Her music was supple, her touch was sure; this was her world and as long as she held the bow, she owned it.

And this was what he hadn't understood.

This was her world, and she was brilliant in it, and she needed it as much as she needed to take her next breath.

He saw it now: She had taken that talent and expanded it into something real and possible on every level. She had a plan, she had said, and he hadn't believed that it could encompass both her amorphous dream of stardom and financial success.

She hadn't given up a thing.

Not even him.

He had been the one who had given up . . . what did he know about dreams, or angels like Francesca?

But he had learned enough now to know that he wasn't going to give up again, and he was going to let Francesca teach him.

Chapter Five

She played ten pieces and three encores, and still they wouldn't let her off the stage.

She finally pleaded fatigue and the curtains closed behind her to the sound of tumultuous applause. A moment later, she ducked out from the wings and joined them at the table.

The lights came up and immediately a crowd surrounded her.

Francesca's world . . .

She was as regal as a queen accepting good wishes and enthusiastic reviews of the concert. She told them the CD was on sale at the reservations desk, along with a complimentary copy of the Moonbeam catalog of artists, which they would continue to receive if they left her a card. And yes, they would receive advance notice of concert dates. And she hoped she would see them again soon.

Admit Desire

A different world. He had never been a part of such a world. Music was such a fleeting thing; styles came and went in the blink of an eye. He didn't know how one could build a business on quicksand, but Francesca was doing it.

It just knocked him out.

She introduced him to those of the crowd she knew, and then about twenty intimate friends gathered around the table to dissect her performance.

He was shocked that there was anything to discuss.

Somebody thought the critic from the *Times* had been in the audience.

That precipitated a round of technical talk only an alien could understand.

He walked Jonathan out into the barroom.

"You've seen all this before."

"Oh sure," his father said. "When we got the financing for the studio, the first thing we had to do was get her some visibility. So she played grungy downtown clubs and free concerts at the Y and in the Park, and appearances on local access cable. Well, you get the picture. It didn't take long, as you can imagine. She just went after the audience she knew was there. And now they come after her."

He hated it that his father saw it all so clearly and he hadn't.

"My dear boy, she is the best of everything," his father said, almost as if he had read his mind. "Don't blow it this time."

Now he was just a little scared. The Francesca he didn't know was the one who was coming home with him tonight, the one with the talent and accolades and the burgeoning music career.

It was impossible to keep that out of the equation.

She still had another set to do, scheduled for eleven, which meant they were not going to get back home until two at the earliest.

He'd be drained and dead by then.

And what he wanted and needed didn't matter

161

worth a damn. Maybe it didn't matter to her. There were too many men around her as it was.

. And he had better stop thinking like this or he would destroy the thing before it even got a chance to root.

No, he wanted to root—right between Francesca's long sleek legs—right . . . *now* . . .

He was so immersed in his fantasy, he didn't even hear her say it was time to go.

There was silence in the cab. He wondered why he couldn't tell her how wonderful her music was.

But she didn't particularly want to talk. Not when she was just coming down from the rush of performance. The silence was as comforting as a pillow, and she felt as if she could just lie back against it, against him, and wrap herself in contentment.

And she was going home with him, to Jonathan's house, and this time they walked up the steps together to his bedroom, to his bed.

Oh, yes, now was the time for this, when her body was humming like tuning fork, and every emotion was converging in her soul. She had never wanted to join with him more.

And he had never before taken so much time.

But perhaps it was only right; they had waited so long, and now there was no limit on time and not a single obstacle, nothing to stop them . . . stop him, stop his mouth, his hands, his body.

He stripped off her dress, a matter of a zipper, a hook, a strap, and then the soft slide of material to the floor to confirm that she wore nothing underneath.

And now she was his, naked, in strappy sandals and gold, and he knelt before her as if she were a goddess, and he ruthlessly took what he wanted.

Oh lord oh lord oh lord—he tormented her with his hands and his tongue and words, words like music, words; his hands were everywhere, and there was nowhere that her body was not open to him, inviting him, enclosing him.

She sank into the gyrating pleasure of his carnal

Admit Desire

kiss; he held her so tightly, his fingers digging into her buttocks and pulling her closer and closer to his questing tongue.

She could hardly stand it; she was so wet with it, so wild with the feeling of his tongue, so strong, pointed, poised, delving with expert precision at the very pleasure point she needed, she wanted, she—toppled . . .

Over the edge, over the top, riding him, riding the tip, the very point of her being until she shattered into a thousand pieces. But he caught her, he caught her before she fell, pulling her into his arms, and they tumbled to the floor, and he held her and he protected her from the pain of such soul-wrenching pleasure.

They hadn't moved for a very long time. He had made no effort to get undressed, and she could feel his hardness nudging her thigh.

Definitely a sensation to be explored, she thought, digging her fingers into his waistband and grasping hold of him with one hand and unhooking and unzipping him with the other.

"If you keep doing that, I'm going to come."

"Do it."

He thrust against her hands and crushed himself tightly against her naked body.

She didn't have to do anything; he was primed as a pistol. All she had to do was slip her one hand between his legs, and hold him tightly with the other, and maintain the movement, the movement, the movement . . . just—like—that . . .

And he was gone. He felt himself going, grinding, arching, spilling himself onto her breasts, her belly, her hands; and loving it, loving it, loving it . . . until she had pumped every drop he had to give, just loving it.

"No. No. No." Yes, that was he, feeling raw, relieved, and ready all at the same time, and lounging like a pasha while she carefully and tenderly undressed him.

Thea Devine

The residue of his seed glistened on her body and she shifted onto her knees so he could watch her rub it into her skin and on her taut-tipped breasts.

He got hard just watching her. He marveled at it: He was rock hard and ready just three minutes after spurting all of himself into her hands.

The hands that were already reaching for him to caress him. He loved those hands.

She knew just how to touch him, and just where.

They lay together face-to-face on the thick expensive comforter that he had pulled onto the floor from the bed. His hand was between her legs, his fingers probing deep into her fold; she cradled his sex in her one hand, while she cupped him between his legs with the other.

And they didn't move. She loved the sensation of him just penetrating her with his fingers. He loved the feel of her hands on the most potent part of his body. He would feel those hands there forever. Holding him. Squeezing him. And her shuddering response to just having him in her hands.

He could lie like this forever.

He felt the power gathering within him, the driving force to possess her. Ancient. Elemental. Controlled solely by his will and his desire.

And the heat of her body and the wetness on his hand. Every sensation comingling into a primitive, urgent need to take her.

"Francesca . . ." His voice was ragged. There was no need to stop this time.

"Yes." Barely a breath.

Yes . . . yes . . . He spread her legs, and eased away his hand. She gasped as he left her, moaned as he immediately embedded himself in her, and wound herself around him as if she would never let go.

He felt the weight of her sandaled feet on his buttocks. He felt the heat of her enfold him. He heard the erotic sounds she made as he rocked against her, pushing himself as deep into her as he could go.

He swallowed her voluptuous moans; he covered

164

her mouth and demanded her kisses, her soul, her tongue.

He took her, it was the only word. He took her in lust and hunger and violence and greed to make up for all the time he had lost.

And she responded with the same savage need, her body wild and writhing and reaching for him. As if she couldn't get enough, as she would never get enough of him and only him.

She was all over him. Wherever she could reach, wherever she could touch; she branded him in a hundred places with her greedy fingers. He would never be the same, never. Everywhere she touched, he belonged to her.

Their coupling was tumultuous and explosive. He wanted to pound himself into her and live inside her forever. He wanted her never to know another man, another lover, another life. He wanted to obliterate everything except her awareness of him.

Into the conflagration of his desire, he took her, pushing, demanding, driving her closer and closer to the edge of oblivion.

She surged against him, seeking that pummeling strength to bind with her fragility and her heat. She was on the brink now; she simmered with it—he stoked it, she felt it coiling deep inside her, waiting, waiting, waiting—and then it exploded like thunder, crackling through her body like lightning, gushing like rain.

He couldn't hold her; he didn't want to save her. So he followed her, pitching his frenzied climax into the consuming storm of hers, and riding her all the way down to satiety and to sleep.

One night. They had had one blessed calm-before-the-storm night. One never-to-be-forgotten night, no matter what happened.

Some people didn't even have that much.

She lay still as a mannequin next to him, not daring to move, hardly daring to breathe. Her whole body ached, but she didn't care. She could live on the memory of this night forever.

But for that kind of pleasure, you had to pay the piper. And she knew exactly what the ledger would read: *Betrayal*, it would say, and there was not enough money in the world to wipe that debt away.

It was still deep in the night, the witching hour where doubts and fears lingered, tormenting guilty souls.

And she was more culpable than any. She had loved him beyond all reason, and still she had gone behind his back, made the decision, and done what she wanted. And when she wanted him back, she had concocted a scheme worthy of a sitcom that was going to backfire in her face.

But for one incandescent night of pleasure, it had been worth it.

It *had*. Even if there was only pain and misery to come.

One night. One glorious back-busting, died-and-gone-to-heaven night. With her. The way it used to be. Francesca, naked and lolling beside him, covered with his essence, his scent, his soul.

Francesca . . .

He didn't know how he had ever left her. Francesca was magic; he had always known it, and he had seen it last night. Francesca had translated their love into music and light.

He got it. In the breaking hours of dawn, finally he got it.

It hadn't been a decision against them. It had been a decision to enrich their lives. And he never could have understood it then.

He rolled over on his side and reached for her. "I understand now," he murmured sleepily.

"Do you?" she whispered, fear jolting her to her very core.

"I do."

Less was more. "I'm glad."

In the netherworld between wakefulness and

sleep, it was so mind-bendingly simple: Whatever brought each of them joy enhanced them both.

And if he had realized that two years ago, Bobby never would have had the chance to make her dream come true.

Bobby . . .

Out of nowhere came Bobby, waving his wand, giving her gifts, enchanting her soul . . .

Engaged for a moment and then gone, hardly protesting, allowing his father to ship him off to Siberia . . .

What the hell was going on?

How had she done it? And why hadn't Bobby fought it?

Hell, it didn't matter; she was in his dream, and that was all that counted.

He rolled over, wrapped her in his arms, and fell back to sleep.

Saturday breakfast. A week ago, they had all been cozily ensconced in the library, taking a casual breakfast, reading the papers and watching the weekend news shows.

It felt like a lifetime ago.

Not even a week, and Francesca had broken the engagement and Bobby had gone into exile.

It was early, so very early. Francesca still slept.

He knelt by the hearth in the library and built a fire, and then he took a cup of coffee from the insulated jug that was set up on a tray on the desk. In his father's home he enjoyed every amenity every comfort. He had always loved that.

But he couldn't get the thing about Bobby out of his mind.

He sat cradling the coffee cup and watching the fire build.

She had told Bobby Monday. Monday night, she was without his ring and Bobby was gone.

And the rest of the week, he had been embroiled in the turmoil of the brokerage, with hardly any time to think things over.

Now Francesca was his, and things were just as they should have been if he hadn't gone away.

Why hadn't Bobby fought for her? At all?

And how long had they been engaged, anyway?

He rubbed his hand over his face. He really was making mountains out of molehills. All of that was none of his business. And the only thing that mattered was that he wanted her. Forever.

And as if he had conjured her, she appeared suddenly on the threshold, wrapped in a silk robe, looking sleepy, touseled, and impossibly sexy.

"You're up early." She squinted at the mantel clock. Six o'clock. Horribly early. Ruminate-because-you-can't-sleep early.

She knew it. The thing was over. The minute she turned over and found him gone, she felt that stultifying fear. He couldn't sleep, he was thinking things over, and he had a hundred questions she didn't want to answer.

She poured herself a cup of coffee, to distance herself and to give herself some time, and she took it over to the leather chair by the fireplace.

She would be in shadow there, her back to the window, no lamplight shining on her face. She tucked her legs under her and wrapped her hands around the cup to warm them.

"I was thinking about Bobby."

She felt a flash of terror. "What about Bobby?"

"Just that it's odd that he's in Chicago and I'm here. That it happened awfully fast."

Now what? Now what? "It needed to happen fast," she said finally.

"I guess it did. I just wondered why he didn't fight harder for you."

Oh, dear lord—of course it wasn't going to be that easy. She needed a diversionary tactic, instantly.

"Why didn't *you* fight harder?"

She said it without thinking, the first thing that came into her head, and it just sat out there between them like a rich dessert that was bad for the heart.

She didn't even know it still hurt. She didn't know

she was still bleeding. But she heard the tone of her voice. She saw his face.

"That was different."

"What was so different?"

"You made a unilateral decision that affected us both."

"I made a decision about my career, nothing more, nothing less, the same as you would have. A lateral move that involved some risks, with the possibility of great reward. I had a plan, I thought it out, I projected my income and expenses, and whether I could afford to do it, and how long I could afford it and under what circumstances, and based on those projections, I went ahead. Just like any other start-up business. And though you may finally understand why, I still don't understand what your problem was in the first place."

"My problem was, we didn't talk about it. You made the decision for both of us."

"No, Nick. We couldn't talk about it. You *wouldn't* talk about it." She felt the well of all the pain; she thought she was over the pain, and finished with the analysis. This was the man she loved; not five hours ago, she had been moaning in his arms. And now she felt as if she were racing toward a cliff.

"But you know what—I don't think that was it. I think you just didn't want me involved in something that took attention away from you."

"You went behind my back."

"You didn't allow me to be up front with you." Which wasn't strictly the truth; she could have bulldozed it through. She couldn't get around the fact that she had quit without telling him, and she knew he hated that more than anything else.

"So Bobby did it for you instead," he said bitterly.

"Bobby did it," she agreed, wanting to torture him because he could have done it, too.

"And he just went off and abandoned you."

"A family trait. Maybe it's genetic."

"Just how long were you engaged?"

Another moment of truth. She could have said a

169

week, a month, a year. There was no one to refute it. Jonathan would support her, and Bobby too, but she couldn't count on Missy—or even herself.

She let another long silent moment pass. Who would she hurt by suppressing the truth?

You couldn't rebuild a relationship on a foundation of lies.

"We weren't," she whispered.

He shook his head as if he thought he hadn't heard right. "What?"

She said it slowly. "We . . . weren't . . . engaged."

It took five minutes for it to sink in. Five long tension-fraught moments as she tried to gauge how he was reacting to the implications of her statement.

And she knew he was thinking that first and foremost, she had played him for a fool. And she could almost see him sorting everything out to try to make some kind of sense of it.

"You weren't engaged," he said finally, his voice flat and expressionless.

"No."

"Dad threw you an engagement party for a non-engagement."

"Yes."

"Did he know?"

Here was the kicker.

She sacrificed Jonathan without a qualm. "Yes."

He levered himself off the sofa. "I don't understand what you're telling me."

Time for the bottom line. She took a deep breath and plunged in.

"It was a screwball scheme to get you to come back to New York."

He let that sink in. "What the hell?"

"Well—you did."

He couldn't deny it. He had. It had been like being shot out of a cannon: stuffed in, primed, and exploded across the country, and the detonator was Bobby.

He couldn't get past it. The engagement had been a ruse. "Why . . . tell me why?"

"You wouldn't come back."

"Yeah? And who wanted me back so badly?"

"Me."

She watched his face. The trader's face. No emotion. Just the eyes. And the thinning of his lips. *Those lips . . . hours ago, those expert, knowing lips . . .*

"You should have called."

"So should you have," she retorted acidly. "But you know what you did? You picked up your toys and went away. You as good as said you didn't care, that the relationship was so damaged by what I did that nothing could resurrect it. You didn't consult me. We didn't discuss it. You just did it. You made a unilateral decision, Nick."

He didn't like that. A man just didn't like being cornered like that.

"What's your point?"

"And you didn't call. And you wouldn't come home. Poor Jonathan. He was frantic about you the first six months."

"Fine. He was. Other people weren't."

"Other people got on with their lives," she said pointedly.

"That's quite obvious." God, he was furious with her.

"But other people didn't fall out of love quite as fast."

"So—what? You concocted this desperate scheme?"

"Was it? Desperate, I mean. We all wanted you back. And we found a way to get you back."

Another long silence. He was beyond furious. He didn't even know if there was a word for it. Especially after last night.

"Did you sleep with him?"

"Oh, for God's sake, Nick . . ."

"No wonder he just folded his tent and flew away. I've been acting like a teenager in hormone hysteria, and he's been laughing at me all the time. God—I can't . . . I can't make sense of this. You pretended to be engaged so I would come back home. What if I'd come just for the wedding?"

"Bobby was sure he could press enough buttons to get you home last weekend."

He flashed back to the conversation. "I guess he did."

"I guess I won't say you should be flattered I went to all that trouble."

"My own family," he muttered. "God. Dad too. He sure loves you."

"He loves you more." ·

"You know what . . . I think this was a lousy trick."

She lost her patience then. "Well, you know what—you made a decision behind my back, too, and you went and put something artificial between us to destroy our relationship. I just manufactured something artificial to try to save it. And if you can't deal with it, especially after this last week, then go back to Chicago and send Bobby to me. He's a lot more fun, even without sex."

"I'll tell you what—why don't you get engaged to him for real?"

She bolted off the chair. "Maybe I will. And I hope you regret it for the rest of your life. *I* won't."

She stormed out of library and up the stairs, calming down only after she washed her face and retrieved a pair of jeans and a shirt from a store of clothing she kept at the house.

Well, that was mature and reasoned. They had sounded like two five-year-olds. But she was sane and sensible. She had wasted enough time on this futile love affair. She had things to do, places to go, and a life to live.

He'd probably pick up and run away again. And this time, she wasn't going to try to find him.

His room was redolent of sex and Francesca's scent. Not a place to think clearly or sort out his scrambled emotions.

He wanted to kill Bobby. No, he didn't. He didn't know what he wanted to do.

He didn't want to lose Francesca.

Well, that came through loud and clear.

He picked up the phone.

"Bobby, you shit."

"She told you, huh?"

He envisioned Bobby lolling comfortably in his favorite chair. He pictured his apartment an unholy mess, because Bobby never cleaned up after himself. And he wondered what had possessed him to offer the use of his place to his Judas of a brother.

"You bastard."

"Had you going."

"Yeah."

"All for a good cause, big brother. Don't trash it. It took four good men and women to implement the scheme. If I were you, I'd grab hold of anyone who would go to such lengths, in spite of the way you treated her, and keep her for life."

"Nobody's on my side," he grumbled.

"We're all on your side, idiot. Get over it and go after her."

Get over . . . easy for Bobby to say.

He put the phone down slowly.

"Dad."

"Where's Francesca? Uh-oh, she told you."

"It's that obvious? How could you?"

"I thought it was a dandy scheme."

"Dad—"

"You'll laugh about it in twenty years. Where is she, anyway?"

"Gone."

"Son . . ." Jonathan shook his head. "You're blowing it."

"I'm not going to get over it. I feel like a fool."

"You were a fool for going to Chicago. Get over it and go after her."

Lord, Bobby and his father had the same scriptwriter.

"Thanks, Dad."

No help there. Everyone was on Francesca's side. God, what was it about her?

He knew. He knew. He had fantasized about it for two years. He had dreamed about it, and he had never been able to find a way to return and claim what he wanted that didn't make him look like a fool.

So she had done it for him.

Another unilateral decision.

And what man wanted to have his prerogatives usurped over and over again? And to be tricked into doing what he had wanted to do in the first place?

Damn her.

He didn't want to move from his bed. In his bed, he could inhale the scent of their loving. He could have her over and over again his fantasies as tumultuously as he had had her in his bed.

And after that, what?

He would be alone.

He had never felt more alone. Not even in Chicago.

Check that. He had been successful and miserable in Chicago.

She could have called. He would have come.

Would he?

Poor Jonathan . . . he was frantic about you in the first six months—He should have called. He hadn't been thinking one jot about his father. He had been nursing the wounds of betrayal.

Who wanted me back bad enough?

Me . . .

To go to such lengths, even knowing how he would react when he found out the truth . . . And she didn't have to tell him the truth.

You made a decision behind my back, too, and you went and put something artificial between us to destroy our relationship. I just manufactured something artificial to save it. . . .

He didn't like these home truths.

Get over it . . .

Go after her . . .

Don't blow it.

He finally got it. He got it all. The music. Their

love. Even the screwball reasoning that had precip-itated the ruse to get him back.

It finally made sense. And for one simple reason: He was in love with Francesca and he couldn't live without her.

And she couldn't live without him, and she had moved a mountain to make it happen.

He wished it had been him. He could have been a hero. And his dad was right: He would laugh about it in twenty years.

Once he had made the decision to step into his new life, it took less than a week to arrange everything. His father had waved his presidential prerogative and like magic, Nick had his old job back and a hand-some corner office at Shields and Company, New York. Bobby was going to stay in Chicago, live in Nick's apartment, and run things there.

Nick wasn't going to blow it.

He was going to go after Francesca.

He stood in the back of the cavernous Village club, which was packed with an enthusiastic audience.

This was Francesca's usual Saturday night gig. *Appearing weekly*, the sign had said.

Appearing in the story of her life—without him.

But no longer.

This was the kind of place they used come when they were in their twenties and young and carefree.

The kind of place where everything was possible and everything thrived. It nourished her soul.

He got it now. He did.

The crowd was noisy. And for the first time, he was enjoying the chaos.

And then the disembodied voice boomed: "Ladies and gentlemen, the Cavern is pleased to present— Francesca . . ."

And there she was, stepping into the spotlight, dressed in ivory and lace with sparkly straps on her shoulders.

She stood still for that one harkening moment, lis-tening for something only she could hear. And then she raised the fiddle, the keyboardist struck the note, and she plunged into the music.

Ah—the music . . . rich, soaring, joyous music . . . and her slender body bending, shimmying, stamping, to the music.

There was thunderous applause after.

And under the cover of that, he moved forward toward the stage. He hadn't planned to do it, he hadn't planned anything, but the music had caught him, the music had lifted him.

He wanted the music and he wanted her.

And just as she lifted the instrument to begin the next piece, he stepped onto the stage, startling her, and he took her in his arms and kissed her.

In front of one hundred strangers, he kissed her.

In the spotlight, in public, to the cheers and applause of a crowd of strangers, he kissed her, deeply, wildly, sexily, until she was breathless.

"I want you. I don't care how. I love you."

She had tears in her eyes. "I love you, too."

The keyboardist struck up a romantic waltz as he stood there, holding her as if he would never let her go.

He wasn't going to. She would have to finish the set with his arms around her. She would have to finish her life with him forever beside her.

He bent his head and kissed her again, slowly, deeply, owning her mouth, her body, her soul.

And he began to move in rhythm to the music, a tentative swaying back and forth at first, because he *hated* to dance, and then small confident steps, as he broke the kiss, swung her into the dance, and waltzed her around the stage, down into the wildly cheering audience, and into their future.

The Gold Digger

Evelyn Rogers

*To two friends who are better than fantasy because they
are for real:
Bobbi Smith and Constance O'Banyon*

Chapter One

Susan Ballinger took the Comfort exit off I-10, easing to a halt at the frontage road stop. Her fingers drummed against the steering wheel, and her heart skipped a beat as she considered the possibilities of what lay ahead. Comfort was her destination, all right, and she didn't mean the Texas town on the sign.

Five miles and a couple of turns later, her '86 Chevy, short on springs, bounced along the private road leading to the famous Kitchener estate, whipping past rolling hills, grazing horses and cattle toward a rambling hilltop house visible for miles around.

Bucolic comfort, that's what all this was, fifty miles from San Antonio, fifty miles from San Antonio men.

Ready or not, Bradford Horatio Kitchener, here I come.

Evelyn Rogers

She steered the Chevy through the open gate and wondered why it was unlocked. She had been told to use the car phone and someone would come down to let her inside. Criminal negligence on someone's part, that's what it was, with all the riches that lay at the end of the estate road.

She thought about securing the gate after her. No, she decided. She'd packaged herself just the way she wanted. With the way her luck had been running, any grease within three feet of the lock would find its way onto her clothes.

The drive to the summit was another quarter mile. The house was a simple place, really, two stories with white columns and open porches and at each end an added-on one-story wing. Inside were a reported eight bedrooms and a dozen baths and an art collection she figured to find more satisfying than sex.

It was her kind of simple. Even the three-car garage close to the back entrance bore a red-tile roof to match the house.

She parked in the drive beside a Porsche convertible, bright red and shiny in the April morning sun. Her Chevy, a faded avocado, coughed to a halt. Hopping out, she smoothed the thigh-high skirt of her pink silk suit, straightened the matching jacket, unbuttoned the top of her ivory blouse, fingered strands of ebony hair away from her neck, gave her teeth a quick tongue swipe, and sucked in her stomach.

She was ready for battle. Bring him on.

Something stirred in the shadows on the back of the veranda, where she had been told to report. Kitchener himself should be here, or so her boss had said. She took a deep breath, but instead of the reclusive billionaire, a bear-sized dog bounded down the stairs. Racing past her, the shaggy beast stopped at the edge of the garage and barked for her to follow.

She hesitated. This was crazy. Her future awaited her inside the house, not out on the grounds somewhere. But she was a believer in signs and a sucker for dogs, especially big brown ones with friendly

182

The Gold Digger

eyes. A brisk tail wag and another bark, and she was hooked like one of the Gulf trout her father loved to catch.

Her unexpected tempter led her along a winding trail at the edge of a green pasture, toward a long, single-story building that was clearly a stable. No problem. She liked horses, too. Did Brad Kitchener? One of her many problems was that she knew far too little about the man she was planning to wed.

Her spike heels wobbled on the path's rough surface and her sneaker-spoiled feet cried out in protest, but the uncaring dog bounded on.

A shadowy figure appeared at one of the stable doors, and the dog began to run in circles, shaking all over. Susan did the same, at least the shaking. Whoever the man was, he would prove important to her. She felt it in her bones.

Instead of going for the man, the dog came at her, rising on powerful back legs and planting two big paws on her shoulders. Taken by surprise, she stumbled backwards off the path and sat in what was unmistakably a pile of almost-fresh horse droppings.

Like a fool, she just sat there, too stunned to move. "Naughty girl," the man yelled. She squeezed her eyes closed, hoping he meant the dog.

She sensed more than heard him hurry toward her, and she dared to peek out as he approached.

The first thing she saw was a pair of scuffed brown boots, and faded jeans hugging long, lean legs before stretching across a flat belly. Swallowing, she continued upward to a denim work shirt half buttoned over a sweaty chest with golden chest hair curling damply across some very interesting contours.

She shouldn't have noticed the details, not with a substance warm and soft and smelly clinging to her hips. So maybe her heart should keep its steady beat, too, instead of pounding in rhythm to the dog's wagging tail.

A gloved hand reached down for her. The man's shirt sleeves were folded halfway up his powerful forearms. She forced herself to gaze up the arm, past the corded neck, the square jaw, the smiling lips to a pair of eyes the color of topaz.

With his golden hair and golden skin, the eyes made him look gold all over. It was her favorite color, though she'd never seen it molded so well.

Shaking off his effect, she grabbed for the glove. He pulled her to her feet with such ease that she might have felt graceful if not for the horsehockey coating a major portion of her backside.

"Are you all right?" Mr. Wonderful asked in a rich baritone.

She nodded, eyes closed. Here was perfect humiliation. No, not perfect. Mr. Wonderful could have been Bradford Horatio Kitchener himself, as she had at first suspected, instead of a worker on his estate.

A terrible thought struck.

"You're not Bradford Kitchener, are you?"

His lips curved into a full-scale grin, and she gave up breathing. It was best anyway, considering the smell.

"Do you want me to be?"

She had to think that one over. Here was the guy right out of her midnight fantasies, but their meeting left something to be desired.

And he definitely did not look rich.

"No," she said.

"Then I'm not."

"Not even a relative? a distant cousin?"

"Definitely not."

"Good."

"Why good?"

Before she could answer, his hands spanned her waist and he lifted her back onto the graveled path, turned her back to him, and began to wipe off her rear.

He took the task seriously. So did she, especially since he was finding some very personal nerve endings she didn't know she had. Why was she glad he wasn't Kitchener? As he worked, she tried to frame her answer, but it was close to impossible with her thoughts on the feel of his leather glove as it moved

184

The Gold Digger

down to her legs. His touch was steady, practiced, as if he did things like this every day.

And she was reacting as if no man had touched her quite so intimately before. Which was almost the truth, though she didn't want to think about it now.

"Because I planned to make a good impression," she managed at last.

"You are."

His voice was rich with innuendo. He must be teasing her. What she had really done was make a complete fool of herself. She wanted to die. Either that, or drag Mr. Wonderful through the nearest stable door, stripping them both while she picked out an empty stall, and then ravish him until the cows came home.

Amazing. She didn't even care much for sex, at least not when it was the real flesh-to-flesh coupling instead of an ethereal mating in her dreams.

She should have known those midnight fantasies would get her in trouble one day.

"You need to get out of these clothes."

She started at his words, then got hold of herself. He wasn't suggesting a quickie in the stable; he was stating a simple truth.

She stepped away and turned to face him. "The suit's ruined," she said.

"Kitchener can replace it. His dog knocked you down."

She tried shooting the dog a murderous look, but the happy brown eyes staring back held not a hint of guilt. With a smile and a shrug, she looked back at Mr. Wonderful. She was after more than just the cost of the suit, anyway, though she'd gone without lunch the past month to pay for it.

"Where is he?" she asked.

"Who knows? You've heard what a recluse he is."

That she had. Thirty-two, a loner, the only heir to the investment-rich Kitchener estate, he lived most of the year in Europe and slipped back to his native state only rarely. Or that was how the story went. As far as she knew, he'd never been photographed, ex-

Evelyn Rogers

cept when he was a towheaded boy, and the only gossip she knew about him was that he'd recently been jilted by his longtime fiancée, a Dallas socialite named Bitsy Cochran.

A society column in the *San Antonio Express-News* had quoted the woman as calling him boring. "Time after time I've tried to start a real dialogue between us, but he has no personality to cultivate," she'd said.

After some consideration Susan had decided to give the cultivation a try, especially since a little bird told her he was ripe for a new woman who could be his wife.

In the meantime, here was a far different challenge. Mr. Wonderful pulled off his soiled gloves and held out his hand. "They call me Sonny, by the way."

He had a perfect grip, his skin warm and callused. Of course. "Susan Ballinger," she said, keeping her voice cool, wishing her skirt was longer to cover her shaking knees. "From Martinez-Coleman Associates."

He kept her hand. "Sounds like serious business brought you here."

Very.

Self-consciously, she broke his hold.

"If you think insurance is serious. I have an appointment to appraise the Kitchener art collection for an updated policy. It's been a long time since the last appraisal and Mr. Kitchener's business manager recommended—"

He was watching her in great solemnity, but there was a definite grin in his eyes that unnerved her. *Stop it, Susan, you're talking too much*.

She glanced over her shoulder at her brown-stained rear. "I had an appointment, that is. The fastidious Mr. Kitchener wouldn't care for me traipsing through his galleries smelling up the place."

"Tough."

He moved in fast and scooped her up in his arms.

Despite her surprise, her arm dropped naturally onto his shoulders. His rock-hard, broad shoulders. He was strong and masterful, and while she was after

186

The Gold Digger

a more malleable man, she didn't put up much of a fight.

But that didn't mean she was rolling over and playing dead. She eyed him suspiciously, trying to ignore his outdoorsy charm and the feel of his body every place it rubbed against hers.

"What are you doing?" she asked, while the dog danced circles around them.

"It's time we got you out of those clothes."

"We?"

"A figure of speech. You can undress yourself if that's what you prefer."

Oh sure, she could just imagine doing a solo strip with Sonny standing close by and waiting to help.

The glint in his eyes said he could read her thoughts. She glanced down and found herself staring at the opening in his shirt. Her insides shifted. Steadying her breath, she looked beyond him to the stables.

"The front gate was left unlocked," she said, doing her duty like the good girl she was. "I guess someone ought to take care of it."

"That would be me. I'll get to it later." He didn't sound overly concerned, giving strength to her suspicion that he could be a very bad boy.

"Who are you?" she asked. "You said around here they call you Sonny. Who are they?"

"You're big on pronouns, Miss Susan Ballinger from Martinez-Coleman Associates. I take care of odd jobs, especially the horses, when Kitchener's in town. Don't know where he got off to, but since it was Petunia that did the damage—"

"Petunia?"

He looked down at the dog. Petunia sat on her haunches, tongue lolling, tail slapping against the grass.

"Aunt Bernie's dog. The name came from when the dog was a pup. Petunias are the only flowers Aunt Bernie can grow, and she saw right away the dog would grow as well."

Despite her resolve, she found herself studying

187

him once again. As much as she wanted to hear everything Mr. Sonny Wonderful had to say, she found herself distracted by the tiny lines that fanned alongside his thick-lashed eyes and the way his mouth moved when he spoke. And between the eyes and mouth rested a humped nose that had obviously been broken at least once. Instead of taking away from his charms, it added to his rugged looks.

Suddenly she realized he had stopped talking. She wondered how long ago.

She cleared her throat. "Your aunt owned Petunia?"

He headed for the house, his long stride covering the distance fast as he held her close. "She's actually Kitchener's father's sister, but everyone calls her Aunt."

"The same ones who call you Sonny."

He grinned. Goodness, he had a nice smile.

"The same."

They passed the Porsche and the Chevy. He carried her onto the veranda, and without knocking, through the back door, down a long hallway, and up a winding staircase. All the while she was craning to get a better look at the carved bannister, the crystal chandelier in the front entryway, the paintings on the walls, the oriental rugs on the floors.

The chandelier was a Baccarat, the paintings fine examples of American impressionism, the rugs Kerman, the balusters hand tooled. Nothing but the best for Bradford Kitchener. She'd bet her next paycheck the fixtures in the bathrooms were plated with gold.

As expensive as everything was, it was also light and airy and simple in its elegance. With the scent of the barnyard wafting from her, she felt like an intruder, a soiled Cinderella who would never capture the prince.

Where Sonny fit into the fairy tale, she couldn't imagine. If her plans had any chance of success, she needed to get him out of the story as soon as possible, but first she needed to get out of his arms.

As if he owned the place, he carried her down the

second-floor hall and into what had to be the master bedroom, its four-poster king-size bed, paneled walls, yet another valuable Persian rug, more paintings, brass-and-crystal lamps, antique dresser and wardrobe clearly fit for a billionaire.

She half expected alarm bells to sound at their intrusion, but all was quiet except for their breathing and for the pounding of her heart, which surely he could hear.

He strode through a door at the side of the room, past a clothes-lined dressing room, and into a bathroom the size of her apartment. Here he set her down. She glanced at the marble counter with its double sinks. Gold-plated fixtures, just as she'd expected. Her impulse was to run—right after she inspected the insides of the hundred cabinets and the clothes on the racks.

"What do you think?" he asked with a wave of his hand.

She looked from the marble counter to the skylight to the oversized Jacuzzi to the glass-fronted shower, then back to him. With his denims and boots and his sand-colored hair that brushed against his shoulders, and his width and his height and his open grin, he was as out of place as if he'd ridden one of the horses inside.

"I like," she said, not sure whether she meant him or the room.

Her eye caught her own reflection in the mirror over the sinks. Unable to resist twisting to see her backside, she let out a shriek.

"I said you'd have to take it off."

She wrinkled her nose. "I'll have to burn it."

"Too bad. It fits you just right."

Everything he said sounded like a seduction. The worst part about it was she didn't mind. He was just an employee, for goodness' sake, and she was after richer game. Provided her farfetched plan worked out. Some mistress of the house she would make if she continued ogling the help.

If there was one thing she knew in her heart, it was

that once she uttered the marriage vows, no matter
who the groom might be or the appeal of the men he
employed, she would be faithful to her husband and
forever true.

She sighed. "You must think me a fool to come
here hoping to impress the elusive Bradford Kitchener."

"You're not a fool at all. He's just a man."

She rolled her eyes. "And Everest is just a mountain."

"You plan to climb him?"

She giggled. She, who hadn't giggled in a long,
long while.

"I don't imagine he'd let me."

"Then he's a bigger loser than I thought he was."

"You shouldn't talk about him that way. He pays
your salary, doesn't he?"

"He and I have no secrets from one another. I'd
say the same to his face."

"No secrets?" Her mind started humming. "Is he
interested in someone right now? Of the opposite
sex, I mean."

Arms at her back, she crossed her fingers and
prayed that her little matchmaking bird had told her
right.

His eyes burned their way from her pageboy hair
down to her toes and back to her eyes, lingering at a
few places on the way. She leaned against the
counter for support. The effect he had on her made
her almost forget her smell.

"Opposite sex. I like the sound of that," he said.
"There's one woman who's recently come into his
life. Being the cautious sort, he's not certain where
it might lead."

Her heart fell. So much for little birds.

"Don't look so discouraged. He's keeping his options open. You wanted to impress him, didn't you
say? With a view toward what?"

"Not playing around, if that's what you're thinking."

"He'll be sorry to hear it."

The Gold Digger

"Unless the playing led to something."

"Marriage?"

His blunt rejoinder embarrassed her, but then why should it? He saw the truth, that was all. And she could be just as blunt as he.

"He's recently been jilted. That makes him vulnerable. I want a home. Why not here?"

"So you're a gold digger."

She refused to flinch. "That's an old-fashioned term. I'm a woman with a plan, which happens to include a life without financial hardship. There's nothing wrong with that. Besides, I have things to offer in return."

"Such as?"

She ignored the glint in his eyes. "I'm loyal and trustworthy, a good manager, frugal, although not to the point of being miserly. I love animals and children. My health is good. I love travel, meeting new people, seeing new places, but I can also be contented staying at home. I also know my faults. I'm too impetuous by far, a terrible judge of character, I drive too fast, and I have the worst luck of anyone I know."

"Nothing terrible, it sounds like."

She thought a moment. "And one thing more. Apparently I talk too much to strangers. I never realized it until right now."

"Another minor problem, if it's a problem at all. Miss Ballinger, you are a prize indeed. Brad's a lucky man."

He didn't sound sarcastic in the least. He sounded . . . admiring. She warmed to the *pièce de rèsistence*. "I hope he feels that way. We also share a common bond." *We've both been dumped.* No need for total honesty. "We share an interest in art. At least I've heard he's interested."

"Oh, he is."

Another glint. He ought to have the look patented. "Unless he's looking to marry for money, which is something I definitely lack, he could do worse."

"He certainly could."

"And he's what? Thirty-two? He ought to settle down."

"He tried."

"Ah, yes, Bitsy Cochran. Why did she break off the engagement? Was it really because he's boring?"

"Is that what she said?"

"She was quoted in the paper."

"That sounds like her."

"You don't care for Miss Cochran?"

"She's boring."

"I'll bet she smells good."

"And I'll bet you started out that way."

He turned to study a bank of cabinets along one wall while she, shamelessly, studied his behind. Not bad. Not bad at all.

"Hmmm," he said.

"Hmmm," she said.

He opened several doors before finding what he wanted, a stark white towel the size of a blanket. "Get in the shower. I'll be right back."

He left before she had a chance to protest. Closing the bathroom door, she stripped, stepped into the shower, fondled the gold fixtures, turned on the water, and scrubbed herself down with a newly opened bar of soap. French-milled from the scent of it. Did he ever use a bar of soap twice? She could imagine a charity basket kept in the kitchen just for once-used toiletries and once-worn clothes.

She, on the other hand, used her soap down to a sliver, and she wore her at-home clothes until even Goodwill turned up its nose when she tried to pass them on.

She sniffed the soap, lightly scented with lavender. A thought occurred. Perhaps Brad Kitchener was gay. Could she live with that?

She thought it over. Hormones didn't function forever, and hers had never been all that active anyway. If he was a good man and they were compatible, yes, she could.

A small voice reminded her of her reaction to the stablehand, to the heat and commotion he stirred inside her with little more than a smile. And, of course, there was that stroking hand on her rear. He was an exception, a test thrown in her path to see if she was still alive.

She was. But he wouldn't be around forever. And he was not what she was after. Still, thoughts of him helped steam up the shower. She stepped out to find a neatly folded stack of clothes on the counter. Wrapping herself in the towel, she wondered just when he'd brought them. And how steamy had the glass shower walls been?

She dressed quickly in the bikini panties, spandex biking shorts, and designer tee. Everything fit her like a second skin. The sandals he'd brought were a bit loose—definitely not Cinderella slippers—but they would do.

She found him sitting on the master bed.

"Nice." The look he gave made the *nice* inadequate.

"Whose are they? Bitsy's?" she asked, suddenly jealous that the woman had left clothing in her wake.

"Roberta's."

"Kitchener's sister."

"Right. Since she married her Italian count, she has no use for such ordinary wear. Nor anything beyond the Riviera, for that matter, unless it's Paris in the spring or New York in the fall."

"You disapprove?"

He shrugged. Nice move. "Not up to me. Right now I'm glad she left it all behind. Those shorts never looked so good on her."

He stood and walked slowly toward her. She backed away until she came up against the paneled wall. He moved close, so close her breasts touched his chest, his hands resting on either side of her head.

"I could tell you a lot about what Brad likes, if you're interested. Black hair, straight and sleek to the shoulders, black eyes, a pert nose, full lips." He brushed a strand of damp hair away from her cheek. "He could go for those."

She could barely breathe, and her heart pounded

beneath the Polo insignia on her shirt. "My mouth's too big," she managed.

"Is it?" He studied her from several angles. "Let's try it out."

He brushed his lips across hers. "Doesn't feel too big to me. As a matter of fact—"

He kissed her again, this time with more energy. She pressed her hands against his chest, planning to push him away. Instead, she gripped his shirt and held him close.

This was crazy, and sweetly illicit, so much so her body started pulsing to a dangerous, impulsive beat.

His tongue touched her teeth ever so gently. The pulsing settled low in her stomach, and lower. The tongue passed her teeth, aiming deeper. Sweet. Very sweet. She just about lost control . . . until a woman's voice pierced her fog.

"Sonny, I didn't know we had guests."

With a sigh and a grimace of exasperation, he broke the kiss, no easy feat considering his involvement, and he eased away. She, on the other hand, pressed herself harder against the wall, wishing she could melt into one of the panels.

"Aunt Bernie," he said, turning toward the door. She could swear he adjusted the fit of his jeans. "Let me present Miss Susan Ballinger of Martinez-Coleman. Susan, this is Bernadette Kitchener, Bradford's aunt."

"Hello, my dear," the woman said. "How nice to meet you."

A man stood behind her in the shadowy hallway. Neither made an attempt to enter the room.

"She had an appointment with your nephew," Sonny said, "but he doesn't seem to be around."

The woman blinked. "I see," she said, somewhat vaguely, then smiled at Susan. "Were you looking for something to insure?"

Susan stared at the woman, as dumbfounded as she was embarrassed. With her short, buxom figure, her soft gray hair, and her long print dress, and especially with the kindly warmth in her eye, Bernie

194

The Gold Digger

looked like Everyman's aunt. But she wasn't. She was Kitchener's aunt, for heaven's sake, and she'd caught her nephew's wannabe bride diddling with the help.

Behind her, the silent man in his cutaway coat and striped morning trousers looked like a British butler right out of central casting.

Neither appeared the least bit surprised to find the stablehand embracing a shorts-clad woman beside the master bed. She opened her mouth to speak, but not a sound emerged. She didn't have a clue how to respond.

Chapter Two

"Sonny, you're a naughty boy."

Brad Kitchener grinned at his aunt across the breakfast table. "Yep."

"Lying to that girl was wrong."

"I told her what she wanted to hear."

"Still—" Bernie's expression turned sly. "She's very pretty."

Images of Susan sprang to his mind. She'd been gone almost an hour, but the details were as clear as if she were sitting in Bernie's place. Great hair, great eyes, great figure. And the mouth she thought too big was great, too. Couldn't he think of a better description? He'd never been at such a loss for words. Why should he worry? *Great* covered everything about her from her smile to the good-natured way she'd taken her fall into the horse dung.

Everything except maybe her ambition. But then

again, maybe it wasn't so bad. True, he was tired of avaricious women, most of whom lied about what they really wanted from him. Bitsy Cochran headed the list. He'd dodged that marital bullet just in time. At least Susan was up front about her purpose.

And as to her front—

"Sonny, I was thinking."

Uh oh. Brad loved his aunt as much as he did anyone in the world, including his flighty mother and social-minded sister, but he also knew to beware when Bernie adopted a cause.

The two of them were having a cup of tea in the breakfast room. Douglas, the British butler Aunt Bernie had hired on her one trip to England five years ago, hovered in the background, studiously trying to look as though he weren't eavesdropping.

"Maybe you ought to tell her who you are," Aunt Bernie said. "That way she could learn what a fine man my nephew really is. You're not in the least boring."

"You must have read the paper."

"I always do."

But she seldom remembered anything, except when the Kitchener name was involved.

"Are you matchmaking?" he asked.

Bernie concentrated on stirring her tea. "Whatever are you talking about?"

He reached across the table to squeeze her hand. "You're a terrible liar."

"I want only what's good for you."

"I know. That's what has me worried. Promise you won't tell Susan the truth when she gets here tomorrow."

"But—"

"I'm not going to hurt her. That's the last thing on my mind."

Making her feel good was more to his purpose, in whatever way he could. Just thinking of her sent desire knifing through him. He couldn't even stand right away or else Aunt Bernie would know. A maiden she might be, but she wasn't stupid.

Reluctantly, she promised what he asked.

Brad looked past her to Douglas. "You, too. Not even a hint of who I am. As far as our visitor is concerned, I'm Sonny the stablehand."

Douglas raised his permanently arched brows a couple of notches. "I am the soul of discretion, Mister Bradford." He said the name as if he were saying *m'lord*. Poor man, living in the past. He ran the Kitchener estate with great efficiency, Aunt Bernie finding the particulars of management beyond her, but Brad knew he dreamed of London's Mayfair district, where he once had served.

Everybody had dreams. His was to find a good-hearted, generous woman, a devoted mother to the children they would have, a helpmeet, a loving, lusty creature who reached in his pocket to fondle more than just cash. Why he thought Susan had potential, he didn't know, given her frank admission about wanting to marry money.

Maybe it was because she didn't blame Petunia for her ruined suit. Maybe it was the can't-fight-the-feeling way she returned his kiss—his poor man's kiss, he amended.

Oh, yes, she had definite potential, as long as she didn't find out who he was. His subterfuge was more than just a lie. He was protecting his other self, the sought-after wealthy Bradford Horatio Kitchener. This time money wouldn't get in the way of pursuing a woman. This time he would find out if she could ever be really interested in him and him alone.

And not just any woman. The predator's blood of his money-making ancestors pulsed in his veins. He was a hunter, and he had Susan Ballinger in his sights. He must be crazy, chasing after an admitted gold digger when he ought to be running the opposite way. But then Susan drove him to craziness. He couldn't remember ever being so intrigued.

He would investigate her more tomorrow, as thoroughly as she would let him. He would let her see his real self, the one that didn't turn from the smell of horse manure, the one who liked to work with his hands. He was a simple man, really, except for the worldwide investments he'd inherited. And the chateau in Lucerne, the villa in Tuscany, the London flat.

Treating a woman right was something he'd taught himself. Lately he'd had far too few chances to enjoy his skills. Bitsy had turned out to be a cold fish. Susan Ballinger was warm-blooded. And he'd seen enough through the shower door to know she had great places to explore.

Aunt Bernie was right. He really was a naughty boy.

With that thought in mind, he excused himself to use the telephone.

Susan stopped by her downtown apartment to change out of the tee and biking shorts, then went to the office to report her day's work. What exactly she should reveal was still not settled in her mind; the entire truth of all that had transpired was far from being one of her options.

Martinez-Coleman Associates was a two-block walk from her apartment-house door, a good thing since the Chevy could scarcely have endured for very long an expressway journey twice a day. Like the apartment, the office was housed in one of the restored nineteenth-century buildings that gave downtown San Antonio its appeal.

Joseph Martinez was the sole owner, Coleman having long gone to his actuarial reward, but he'd kept the original name because of the agency's fine reputation. M-C handled the insurance for some of the wealthiest estates in South Texas, but none wealthier than the Kitchener holdings.

In sending her out to appraise the Kitchener artwork, Martinez had entrusted her with a very important assignment. She couldn't let him know how she'd totally messed up—and been totally messed up—within five minutes of reporting for work.

She wasn't sure herself the seriousness of her situation. She was going back the next day with hopes of meeting Bradford Kitchener himself and with absolute dread and excitement that she might see Mr. Sonny Wonderful again.

Martinez's secretary, Alice Roberts, greeted her from behind her reception room desk.

Though they'd worked together for little more than a year, Alice had become Susan's best friend and closest confidant. She was also a smart-talking, no-nonsense woman whose filing system was so hopelessly complicated Martinez would have to keep her employed forever if he wanted to maintain the high level of his business. She used a computer, but she'd come up with data files so complicated they would defy the understanding of Bill Gates.

In her midfifties, a decade older than her boss, she was tall and formidable of figure, with gray-streaked brown hair, brown eyes, and a wise I-know-your-secret expression that could be unnerving. Like right now.

"You got the wedding announcement ready for the *Express*?"

Susan rolled her eyes. "I'll have to meet my fiancé first. Just so we can get the wording right."

"Kitchener didn't show?"

"Nope. It was quite a disappointment, especially since a little bird told me he would be practically waiting on bended knee for me, a poor stranger come to perform a menial task."

"Hmmm."

"What, my dear canary, no other songs to sing? Let's start with who told you he would be delighted to meet me."

"I've already said. I heard talk. For all his money, he's lonely and he's shy. He wants to get married and settle down."

"Ripe for the plucking, I believe was the way you put it. Was that the exact wording you heard? Well, guess what? He wasn't hanging on any tree I could find."

"So he wasn't there?"

"That's what I'm trying to tell you. If he was anywhere around, he was in hiding. Maybe he got a look at my car. Maybe he got a good look at me from one of the upstairs windows and cowered in one of the closets. Maybe he broke out in acne and didn't want to be seen. Any number of things could have happened. What didn't happen was instant romance."

An image of Sonny suddenly burned into her mind. She dropped her eyes. Too late. She could feel Alice tense.

In the moment of silence she knew Alice was looking her over. "That's an old skirt and blouse. I thought you were going to wear the new suit."

She dared to look up. "I did, but—"

Her hesitation was fatal. Under the secretary's penetrating stare, she went from aggressive to defensive, her usual shift when cornered, and found herself making an almost full confession, playing up Petunia and the fall from grace, scarcely mentioning the person who had helped her up. She deliberately left out the part about the bedroom and the shower and the kiss.

It wasn't that Alice would misunderstand. Quite the contrary.

The two women came from similar middle-class backgrounds: Alice's parents were operators of an icehouse at the edge of town, Susan's father, a Brownsville bus driver until an accident with a watermelon truck left him injured just enough to draw disability. He spent much of his time fishing. He'd even bought a charter boat to take out groups seeking marlin in the Gulf, but it was mostly a labor of love. Susan and her housewife mother called him Skipper, a title he brushed aside but secretly adored.

Her parents had scraped enough money together to send their only child to the University of Texas in Austin. It was there, while working at whatever job she could manage, that she'd decided to marry a rich man. She would take care of her parents in their old age, just as they'd cared for her, and in so doing she would take care of herself.

At twenty-eight she was still searching for riches.

Twice she thought she'd found what she sought, once in college and once in San Antonio. Both men found someone else, someone part of the "in" crowd, someone who could add to their wealth. She would have admired their style if their leaving hadn't hurt so much.

Alice, on the other hand, had been married four times, all for love, she swore. Unfortunately, each husband had been cursed with the bad luck of meeting an early death.

Widowed and childless, Alice had taken Susan under her wing. Right away she'd guessed her ambitions. Joe, as she called Martinez behind his back, hadn't a clue.

Martinez chose that moment to stroll out of his office. He was a distinguished looking man, his dark hair gray at the temples, his stature short but perpetually erect. Proud of his physique, he worked out everyday at noon at a downtown athletic club. A devoted family man, he dabbled in local charities and fancied himself somewhat of an intellectual.

"Ah, Miss Ballinger, done already?"

"Not quite." She avoided looking at Alice. "I'm to return tomorrow. The assessment may take longer than we estimated. His possessions are exquisite and quite unique."

She could have been describing Sonny. She thrust the thought from her mind.

"Just make certain you are thorough. Don't be so swept up by the beauty of the collection that you overassess its value."

"I won't be swept away by anything, I assure you."

"Good. Take as long as you need."

Of course he would say that since the extra time would cost him nothing. Instead of being a full-time employee, she worked as the M-C art consultant whenever she was needed. In order to get the Kitchener account, which Martinez had threatened to assign to one of his regular agents, she'd agreed to a flat fee rather than her usual hourly wage.

Martinez shifted his attention to Alice, and Susan

202

stepped toward the door. She needed to get home and select her next day's armor, the battle dress that would bring Bradford Kitchener to his knees.

"Susan, I almost forgot. You had a phone call earlier."

Something in Alice's tone caused her to turn in dread.

"Someone named Sonny."

"Oh?" Even the mention of his name turned her stomach upside down.

"He said Mr. Kitchener might want to ride tomorrow and you should dress appropriately. Unless you want to borrow some more clothes. He mentioned someone named Roberta, but I didn't get the connection."

Alice was all innocence as she blinked her eyes at Susan. "I assume you know what he was talking about."

Susan nodded curtly, sharply aware of Martinez's stare.

"He had a very nice voice," Alice added.

"I didn't notice." She glanced at Martinez. "You know how eccentric these billionaires can be," she said with a fake little laugh. "I suppose if Mr. Kitchener wants to ride, that's exactly what we'll do. It won't, I promise, interfere with my work."

With a killer glance at Alice, she made a hasty departure. There was no telling where Bradford Kitchener was, but she doubted he was sitting around the house thinking up ways to spend the day with a woman from an insurance agency. No matter how lonely he was. Even in her moments of wildest optimism, she knew she had to actually meet the billionaire before she could interest him in any way.

Sonny was the one who wanted to ride. Remembering the way he'd kissed her, she wondered if he meant her or a horse.

By the time she made the short walk to her apartment, she still hadn't come up with a satisfactory answer. The sight of Ralph Johnson, the building superintendent, standing before her open door, drove the question from her mind.

Ralph was her father's age, a retired policeman who'd taken an avuncular interest in her. His presence usually comforted her. But not today. Not after all she'd been through.

"What's wrong?" she said as she hurried down the third-floor hallway.

Ralph shrugged his broad shoulders and ran a hand across his balding head. "Fellow said he had a delivery to make. He was from one of those fancy boutiques over in Alamo Heights. Since you weren't here, I let him in. No need to worry. I kept my eye on him the whole time he was bringing in the boxes."

"Boxes?"

"They're on your bed. He's gone, left not five minutes ago. I was just about to lock up when I saw you."

She thanked him and secured the three deadbolt locks he'd installed on her door the week she'd moved in. The boxes were piled high on her bed. She opened them and spread their contents on the cover her late grandmother had handquilted when Susan was just an infant. By the time she was done, not much could be seen of dear Granny's quilt.

She pulled up the dresser chair and collapsed, staring in amazement at the sight of silk suits, a mountain of them, an army lined up in formation across the bed. Okay, she exaggerated. Actually there were only five, each a different color, the pink identical to the one she had ruined, and then copies in yellow, blue, red, and black. An invoice from one of the boxes—without any mention of money, of course, just a handwritten "paid in full"—indicated the one in hunter green was out of stock and had been back-ordered.

And then there were a half dozen pairs of bikini panties and a dozen pairs of hose. Not panty hose. Old-fashioned hose packaged with two garter belts, one red mesh, the other black lace. Her mother would have been shocked. Not Granny. Granny would have wondered where she could buy "one of those whatchamacallits" for herself.

Susan's reaction fell somewhere between the two. The note was tucked inside a pair of black lace panties.

"Arf, arf," it read. "I'm sorry."

It was signed with a paw print and a scrawled "Petunia."

It should have read *Sonny*. Brad Kitchener was surely paying for all of this, probably without his knowledge. The idea had come from Mr. Wonderful. It had the Wonderful touch.

She hugged herself to hold in the heat the thought of him aroused. He needed strangling with one of the garter belts. He, of course, would have other uses for it in mind.

Throwing the cursed undergarment across the room, she went to take another shower. This time she would keep the water cold.

Chapter Three

The wind whipped through Susan's hair as she galloped down the incline of a shallow ravine, across a dry creek bed, and up the far side, the hooves of her black gelding kicking up dust and small clumps of dirt and the dead leaves that had fallen the previous autumn.

She reined the horse to a halt in the shade of a live oak tree, her companion close to her side. Heart pounding, she looked at him and felt a rush of exhilaration that had nothing to do with the ride.

"You've got a good seat," Sonny said. The white gelding he was riding bobbed its head in agreement.

Susan stared at him as long as she could without losing her cool. She lasted ten seconds. Looking away, she couldn't erase the picture of him that burned into her mind. He was dressed pretty much as he had been yesterday, but somehow he looked

The Gold Digger

even better, his shirt sweaty against his chest and back, his jeans tight, his skin as tan as his buff-colored boots. The only difference was the narrow-brimmed Stetson he wore low on his forehead, but the eyes staring out at her from beneath sandy brows were the same penetrating topaz.

She couldn't imagine him in anything but denims and boots, unless it was without any clothes at all. In conjuring up this new image she fell woefully short of details. For all her limited experience where naked males were concerned, she knew he would look like no other man.

She smoothed the gelding's black mane and stroked his neck. "I used to ride along the beach when I was a little girl. It must be one of those things you never forget, like riding a bike."

"What beach is that?"

"South Padre. I grew up in Brownsville, close to the Mexican border, about as far south as you can go and still be in Texas."

"I'll bet you were a tomboy."

"Oh, I was. Long skinny legs, stringy hair, more than my share of bruises from getting into scrapes. Skipper—that's my father—said he didn't need a son as long as he had me. Mother said I'd turn into a girl someday."

"Mother knew best."

The way he was looking at her, she didn't feel like a girl. She felt like a woman. Even with her wind-blown hair and her jeans and her fringed leather vest over a plain blue shirt—the best riding clothes she'd been able to come up with on such short notice—she'd never felt so feminine in her life.

So much so, she felt her nipples pucker. This was ridiculous. She was twenty-eight years old, light years past adolescence. Her hormones should have been behaving themselves. They weren't. With Mr. Wonderful's golden gaze settled on her, she could barely sit still in the saddle.

What would she do if he touched her? If he kissed her again? Best that she never find out.

She glanced toward the sun, which was heading fast for a spot directly overhead. She'd arrived at the estate at midmorning. Douglas the butler had directed her to the stable, where Sonny had been waiting with the saddled geldings.

"Brad's been called away," he'd said. "He had to make a quick flight to Dallas. He could be back later in the day."

She knew there was a landing strip on the western edge of the estate, and a hangar to house Kitchener's private Cessna.

Her first reaction had been pure pleasure. Then she jolted herself back to reality. This was not good news.

"Will he be seeing Bitsy?"

"If I've read him right, he plans never to have anything to do with her again."

"Never?"

"Never. Believe me, I'm right on this one. And don't worry. I'll take you on that ride he promised."

"If you insist," she'd said, trying to tamp down her eagerness, trying even harder not to look like a panting Petunia ready for a romp.

"Unless you'd rather stay here and work."

He'd looked so innocent, waiting for her answer. But she'd fast learned he was seldom innocent.

"Let's ride," she said.

He'd gone from innocent to smug. Okay, he had a right. One more day with Sonny, she'd told herself, with a few hours stolen away from him for her work, and she would be ready to concentrate on her real undertaking: the conquest of Bradford Horatio Kitchener.

It would be like going on a diet. She'd have one last satisfying meal. Looking, of course, not tasting, not devouring, not licking, not . . .

She had stopped herself. How, she'd asked herself, was she coming up with these ideas?

They had been touring the estate for more than an hour, her companion pointing out details of the land and its stock, always staying close by her side, always unsettling her with a grin and a watchful gaze.

When she wasn't looking at his face, she was stealing peeks at his thighs, noticing especially the way they gripped the horse. Images kept rising in her mind. Unladylike images, un-Susanlike pictures of her on her hands and knees while Sonny—

"Hungry?" he asked, stirring her from her reverie.

"Oh, yes," she said with more enthusiasm than was appropriate. At least she had the decency to blush. She'd once thought her dreams erotic; they were nothing next to what her mind conjured up with Mr. Wonderful at her side.

"I like a woman with a good appetite," he said. "I'm pretty hungry myself."

Why did everything he say sound like a come-on? Perhaps, she decided, because it was.

"I'm not on the menu, you understand."

It was a little late to sound huffy, but maybe he didn't know that.

"Would I take advantage of you just because you're sexy as the devil in those jeans and I've been staring at your luscious backside for the past hour?"

Having studied his luscious thighs, she gave up fast on trying to look shocked. "You might."

He made a Scout's sign. "I won't do anything you don't want me to."

Which was exactly what she was afraid of.

"Aunt Bernie packed us a lunch," he said, nodding toward the bundle tied behind his saddle. "I have no idea what we've got."

He clucked at his mount and headed down a path that led from the trees. She followed across an open pasture covered with bluebonnets to a pair of tall cottonwoods surrounded by shrubs, and down another incline, this time to a shallow creek that ran through the secluded shade. Reining in her horse beside the water, she breathed in the cool, green-smelling air.

"Beautiful," she said.

He threw a long leg across the saddle and slid to

the ground. "Yep," he said in a fine Gary Cooper imitation.

She dismounted quickly, before he could offer to help, and handed him the reins. He staked the horses downstream where they could crop the thick grass, then returned with the food bundle in his hand.

The first thing out was a blanket. She helped him clear rocks from a patch of ground and spread the blanket. He tossed his hat and gloves on one corner, and the bundle on another, then dropped to his knees. Everything he did, he did with grace. He even looked wonderful with hat hair. She wanted to ruffle the crease left by the Stetson. Just a little, just a touch . . .

"If you want to wash up or whatever, there's the creek and lots of bushes for privacy."

She took advantage of the offer, reminding herself all the time she was gone that she was going to be a very good girl today. When she returned, he was staring down at a half-dozen foil-wrapped packages.

"Aunt Bernie has outdone herself," he said.

Throwing her gloves beside his, she ventured to unwrap one of the packages and stared at the small tin can resting on the foil. According to the label, it contained pheasant pâté with pistachio nuts. Along with it Aunt Bernie had enclosed a plastic bag of crackers and a small silver knife.

"I don't think I've ever eaten pheasant pâté before," she said. "Mother used to fix gooseliver sandwiches, but that was as exotic as it got down on the border."

"It's not bad."

"You've had it before?"

"Sometimes I eat in the big house."

"You make it sound like a prison."

"It can be."

He sounded serious, totally unlike the Sonny he normally presented to her. He even had an uncharacteristic frown on his face, but only for an instant.

"How? You're free to come and go. You can quit your job any time you like, can't you? Unless you've signed a contract, which seems unlikely. I don't think stablehands normally have work contracts, do they?"

"No, but—"

He seemed to want to go on, but whatever he planned to say was lost in a shrug and his killer grin. Something inside her stirred, and it wasn't because of the smile. She wanted to know more about the frown, more about the dark thoughts that lurked beneath his golden glow.

But they didn't have that kind of relationship. Goodness, they shouldn't be having any kind of relationship. She must not allow herself to care.

"Enough talk," he said. "Let's eat."

She concurred.

He went on to unwrap another package, this one with small slices of a dark dried meat which he identified as *canard*. Duck, he translated, then went on to the remaining two packages: herbed goat cheese and two small loaves of crusty bread in one and a bag of carrot sticks in the other.

"Kitchener got a care package from France this week. All except the carrots. They're pure Bernie."

"Roberta sent him food?"

He shook his head. "His mother lives outside of Paris. She thinks he's terribly deprived."

"Do you think so?"

"Nope. This kind of food is all right at a sidewalk cafe on the Left Bank, but out here a man likes his barbecue."

Last from the bundle was an insulated wine holder and a pair of plastic wineglasses.

"Chateau Chandon Cabernet Sauvignon," he said, reading the label.

"Sounds expensive."

"Don't ask how much. Just enjoy."

Which she did. Everything. Barbecue was fine, but she wouldn't mind an occasional meal of herbed goat cheese and pheasant pate, washed down by a wine that probably cost more than her silk suit.

Which reminded her . . .

"The clothes were delivered yesterday."

"Clothes?"

Evelyn Rogers

"The suits and the . . . other things."

Panties and hose and garter belts, things like that, things she couldn't bring herself to mention because he'd probably ask her to model them and then where would she be? He didn't look like a man to take *no* for an answer, especially from a woman who really wanted to say *yes*.

In truth, she had the black lace panties on under her jeans. Not, of course, for modeling purposes, but just because . . . well, just because.

"I really ought to send everything back," she said.

"Why? You want to marry the man but you won't accept a few clothes from him as an apology? He really was sorry about the dog. Petunia's never done anything like that before."

"Don't try logic on me. Mr. Kitchener can shower me with whatever he wishes after we're married." She sighed. "That sounded terrible. Change that to after I've introduced myself to him and we've gotten to know each other and he has subsequently decided to make me his wife. If, of course, he does so."

"Oh, yeah, that's a lot better."

"You're laughing at me."

"I just can't get a picture of Brad Kitchener turning you down."

"He wouldn't be the first."

The words popped out. She couldn't believe she'd said them. It must have been the wine.

"Want to tell me about it?" He sounded very serious.

"Nothing to tell."

"Liar."

She sighed. "I got engaged in college, okay? And again after I moved to San Antonio. Both guys decided to marry money instead. To add to what they already had, you understand. Both were what the Skipper calls sailors in smooth financial seas."

"No rough waters, is that it?"

"You got it. Not that they wanted to say good-bye. I was supposed to be their side sweetie."

"Side sweetie?"

212

The Gold Digger

She cringed at the memory. "My words, but you get the idea. After I told them off, I decided they had the right idea. Not the side sweetie part, but the marrying for money. Once I've gone through the ceremony, I intend to be faithful and true to my husband."

She looked directly at him as she spoke. Just in case he was getting ideas.

"No poor man ever caught your eye?"

She thought about the art students she had known at the university, and the artists she'd met through her membership in the San Antonio Art League. Poor as the proverbial church mice, most of them, and more than one thinking to marry her so that she could support them while they painted or sculpted or whatever.

No one had been interesting or charming enough to tempt her into giving up her ambitions. But why explain all this to a man who probably had an eye for every woman who came along? He wouldn't understand.

Unwisely, she asked for a refill on the wine. He divided what was left between their glasses. They stared at one another as they downed the rich, red liquid. It could have been jug wine for all she tasted it. But she sure felt its effect.

"He's not gay, is he? Kitchener, I mean. Not that I'm judging, you understand, but, well, I just wondered."

"He's no more gay than I am."

Sonny moved close and took the glass from her hand. She rose to her knees; he did the same. Somehow he managed to push all the lunch fixings aside and take her into his arms.

"Allow me to demonstrate."

He kissed her. His lips were moist from the wine, warm, and very, very sweet. His tongue found its unerring way past her teeth. Not that she wasn't cooperating. She grabbed his shirt front. He lowered her to the blanket until they were lying side by side, his

213

arms still around her, her hands still holding on to his shirt.

He shifted until he was half on top of her, and he was kissing her with A-plus thoroughness, and she was rubbing her hands across his chest, wondering how to get inside his shirt and how she could manage to get him inside hers.

His hand slid under her vest and cupped her breast. They were thinking alike. They were both breathing pretty heavy, too. He broke the kiss, sat back, and played a moment with her vest.

"Leather fringe. I like."

At the same time he eased her out of it.

"We shouldn't be doing this," she said. Weakly, but she felt the words ought to be said.

"Why not?"

"For one thing, we don't know each other."

"I'm working to change that."

"For another, I'm betraying Mr. Kitchener."

He grinned, but he didn't stop fiddling with her clothes. This time he went for the buttons on her shirt.

"How can you betray a man you call Mister?"

"All right," she said, with no inclination to stop him, "I'm betraying Brad."

"He should have stayed around. Besides, you said you'd be faithful and true after the ceremony. You didn't say anything about before."

"That's a technicality," she said, with great difficulty on the last word.

He tugged the shirt from her jeans and opened it wide. He stared down in silence, but his eyes said all she could ever want to hear. She, who had undressed in the dark when she'd been with her two ex-fiancés, practically arched her back so he could get a better look.

He kissed the valley between her breasts. Her nipples vibrated like the tines of a tuning fork.

Get a grip on yourself, she screamed inwardly.

What she gripped were his biceps.

Oh, my.

The Gold Digger

He rolled one hard little peak between thumb and forefinger, watching her reaction.

She stared at his parted lips. "Don't," she said.

He shifted to the other breast.

"That's not what I meant."

Each word came out breathy. The wine turned hot in her veins. She squeezed her eyes closed. He kissed the valley and pressed his palm against her abdomen. Her insides did a rumba to a hot, rhythmic beat. She almost came up off the blanket, not—pitiful person that she was—to get away, but to show him just how available she really was.

She whimpered. He hesitated, then pulled away.

"What's wrong?" he asked.

"I don't want to like this."

"Why not?" he asked.

"Because I never have before. Not so . . . passionately." She'd never said *passion* or any of its forms ever before in her life, not boldly, not out loud, where it just hung in the air. Now it was the only word she could think of.

He closed her shirt. Such a gentleman, or maybe he'd gone as far as he wanted to go.

"I'm driving you crazy, am I?"

She ventured a quick peek. He was not grinning. He was looking very serious indeed. And he looked as if he really did want a great deal more.

"Crazy doesn't begin to describe what you do to me."

"What's wrong about that?"

"Bad timing."

"Ah, you mean Brad."

She nodded. She felt his hands working at her buttons. Somehow he kept touching her skin, and even when he didn't, she could feel the heat of him through the cotton fabric. Her body rhythms quickened. Passion—there was no other word for it—pulsed from her toes to her ears.

"What if you meet him and can't stand him?" he said. "Will you be looking for another roll on the blanket?"

He didn't sound angry. He sounded interested.

"No." The word came out too fast for either of them to take as the truth.

She sat up. He did the same. With a trembling hand, she smoothed the hair from her face. He caught a rebellious strand and pushed it back with the rest. Again he touched her skin, and she shivered.

Bending her knees, she cradled her legs against her chest. Defensive maneuver, pure and simple. It kept both of them from unfastening her shirt again.

"I don't know anything about you," she said. "Not even your last name."

"A fair complaint, since you told me about yourself. My last name is Hardcastle. I work hard, I like animals and children, I'm a loving son and brother, I don't do drugs or an excess of alcohol, I'm clean of disease, my teeth are my own, I have no major debts, I believe in a long list of good causes, and I rarely cuss. What else is there to know?"

"No flaws? I told you mine."

"I've got plenty. I'm impatient, I walk out of plays and movies that bore me, I like to get my way, although I'm open to compromise if the other party is reasonable. I tend to take matters far too casually, which drives do-gooders up the wall, and I'm forgetful. Which probably means I've left out a flaw or two."

None, she decided, that showed.

"And one more thing. I'm looking for a good woman to marry, and I find you absolutely, completely, totally captivating."

She swallowed hard. "You don't know me."

"If you recall, I was working on that when you made me stop."

"I don't mean *know* in the biblical sense."

"It's a start."

"But what's the finish?"

"A happy ending, I hope."

"Surely you're not proposing marriage."

"Not yet."

The Gold Digger

Her head reeled, and she knew it wasn't from the wine.

"We just met yesterday."

"Haven't you ever heard of love at first sight?"

"I've had fantasies of the sort."

"The guy is always rich, right?"

"When I'm awake. When I'm asleep, well, money doesn't seem to matter."

She couldn't believe she was telling him so much. But it didn't matter, did it?

Did it?

"That's encouraging," he said.

Uh-oh. She hadn't meant to encourage him in the least.

He stood and helped her to her feet. While she tucked in her shirt, he scooped up her vest and handed it to her. "I'll get the horses," he said, and she watched as he strode toward the creek.

Goodness, he was efficiently put together. Lots of hard, sleek muscles working beneath those jeans.

Two days, and he'd turned her upside down and inside out and almost done a whole lot more. And he'd done it all with respect. Now that was a novel concept. Practically stripping her by a creek the second day they'd known each other, coming at her with soft insinuations and warm hands, and all of it accomplished with respect.

She began to pack everything away, carefully setting aside his hat and gloves lest she crush them to her chest and inhale his scent. He'd surely see her and take it the wrong way, thinking maybe she was smitten with him. She couldn't be, not in a hundred million years.

Love at first sight.

Who was he kidding?

What was it he'd said to her question about a proposal?

Not yet.

What a line. And yet he'd said it with respect.

Respect and passion, she whispered to herself as she stood and girded her loins. For a basically lonely woman who'd never had much of a sex life, the combination was proving deadly.

217

Chapter Four

The next two and a half days were the best and worst of Brad's life. Best because Susan was close by for long hours at a stretch. Worst because he'd vowed to keep his hands to himself.

"Don't even smile at me," she'd ordered when they got back to the stable after that almost incredible ride.

Hard to do, when he wanted to giggle and chortle and chuckle whenever she came into view. Right before he dragged her off to bed.

But a promise was a promise. For a liar and a fake, he was an honorable man.

For two and a half days she'd examined every room, every painting, every vase, every decoration in the twenty-plus rooms, taking photos, writing notes, whispering to herself, seemingly unaware he was lurking and watching.

The Gold Digger

But she knew he was there. He could see the tension in her shoulders and the way small lines formed between her beautiful eyes any time he came into the room.

So he was driving her crazy, was he?

She was doing a number on him, too.

His only moments of peace came when he stole into the small office she hadn't yet discovered and faxed and e-mailed and talked to his various companies around the world, caring for the money his rascally grandfather had accumulated and passed on to him. He usually found this part of his daily routine boring. Not now. In the world of commerce he found order. He was in charge, if only because he was the player with the most money. He'd told her he liked to have his way. He hadn't lied.

More than riches, he wanted his way with her. But he couldn't have it. He was learning patience, not one of his strong suits.

One of his problems—aside from an overactive sex drive—was a conscience that kept lecturing him about telling her the truth. Sometimes it came in the form of a nagging inner voice that wouldn't let him rest.

Hardcastle, it said more than once, *how did you come up with a name like that?* He rather thought one of his London managers was named Hardcastle. Whatever the case, it was the name that had popped into his mind by the creek.

Other times his conscience took a more corporeal form, namely, Aunt Bernie.

"Tell the poor girl the truth," she said the the second day after the ride. It wasn't the first time she'd brought up the subject, but it was the first time she'd put it in the form of an order.

"I will. The time isn't right yet."

They were sitting on the back veranda, Petunia at her mistress's knee.

"What's not right about it?"

"We're getting to know one another without the issue of money getting in the way."

"She's a smart girl. She'll forgive you for being rich." Aunt Bernie scratched the dog's broad head. "She's going to get away."

"Maybe. Maybe not."

"You know I want to see you happily married."

"You've mentioned it a time or two."

"Not married to Bitsy, though. She wasn't right. This one is."

"We barely know her," he said, venturing to test her auntie instincts.

Aunt Bernie's rocking picked up steam. "I've been appraising her the way she does the paintings. She's a classic. Works hard, doesn't ask for anything, stops to talk when I interfere."

"Which you've been doing regularly."

"We've got a great deal in common."

"Such as?"

"You."

"Aunt Bernie, if you've—"

"Don't worry. I know how to lie, too."

Brad shuddered to think what little secrets she might be keeping from him and what she might have revealed to his maybe bride.

"And she talks to Douglas, you know. He never talks to us. He just nods and does that thing with his eyebrows. Around Susan he opens up. Amazing." Aunt Bernie smiled. "We can't let her get away, you know. We'd never forgive ourselves."

A faraway look came to her eyes. Brad went on full system alert. "Don't do a thing. Not a thing. I'll handle the situation to everyone's satisfaction."

Aunt Bernie sniffed. "Do you hear him, Petunia? The man's an out-and-out scalawag."

The back door opened, and Susan walked onto the veranda. The expression on her face said she'd heard little of their conversation, otherwise she'd be bolting toward her Chevy, or else beating him about the head and shoulders with her clipboard.

She was wearing the new pink silk suit. He liked it on her even more than he'd liked the first one, but then he'd liked the blue one she wore yesterday, and he would like the yellow one she had promised to wear tomorrow.

She was wearing them, she'd told him, as a thank you to Brad Kitchener, should he ever choose to make an appearance.

"Not that that seems likely," she'd said. "I'll be in my dotage before he gets back from Dallas."

Brad figured he would soon have to come up with another excuse. Maybe he would break his leg—fictitiously, of course—by slipping on a slick floor in one of his banks.

"Come on out, my dear," Aunt Bernie said. "I was just telling Sonny what a scalawag he is."

"In what way?" Susan asked, avoiding his eye, a habit she had developed to perfection.

A sly look crossed his aunt's face. His alarm grew.

"He hasn't told you the truth about himself."

This time she looked directly at him. "Oh?"

Brad came halfway out of the chair. "Aunt Bernie—"

"He hasn't mentioned a thing about his cooking."

He sat back down and stared at his aunt in amazement. He could muck out the stables with the best worker on the estate, but as far as kitchen chores were concerned, he couldn't boil water. He didn't even know where the water-boiling pans were kept.

"He was supposed to ask you to join us for dinner. I so had my hopes raised that you would agree." Aunt Bernie looked down at Petunia, who dutifully returned a soulful gaze. "It gets so lonely out here."

What a crock. The woman could live anywhere she wanted. She chose rural Texas, but she was connected on the Internet with friends all over the world. When she wasn't on the computer, she was beating Douglas in one of their silent chess games. She'd told Brad the only thing missing to make her life complete would be a dozen grandnieces and grandnephews she could spoil.

"I don't want to impose—" Susan began.

"Please," Aunt Bernie said in a wheedling tone.

"It's no imposition. You've been working far too hard. You need a reward."

Susan's dark eyes darted to Brad. He settled back in the chair and stretched his legs in front of him, offering himself should she choose to take him. Her gaze wandered down the length of his body. Good girl. She was still interested.

She looked back at Aunt Bernie. "If you really want me to stay, I suppose I could."

"Now I don't want to force you into anything. You don't have any other plans, do you? I wouldn't want to interfere. Perhaps you have a young man . . ."

His aunt's voice trailed off.

"No." She sighed. "I can stay. Thank you for asking." She looked at Brad. "Are you fixing barbecue?"

"What else?" he said, rising. "I'd better get started."

He promptly went inside and signaled the ever-hovering Douglas to join him in the kitchen. The mother and daughter who came in from Comfort three days a week to clean and cook had already departed for the day.

"Call the nearest smokehouse and get the works sent out right away. Chicken, beef, sausage, potato salad, beans, you know."

"Of course, Mister Bradford," Douglas said without raising his brows.

"Have them call from the gate. Someone will go down to get it."

"Of course, Mister Bradford." Douglas turned on his heel and departed. Brad could have sworn the butler was muttering under his breath, but then, so was he.

He returned to the porch to ask that everyone stay out of the kitchen while he worked. The truth was, he needed to scout out the place. It was large, with enough cabinets and equipment and stoves and ovens to service Maxim's in Paris. He clattered and banged for a while, opening and shutting doors, shaking pots, rattling pans, then settled back on a barstool next to a center island and sipped at a beer.

Douglas returned to announce his mission accom-

The Gold Digger

plished. Nothing to this cooking, Brad decided. You just had to know who to call. He gave himself fifteen minutes to relax, then went out to the veranda to take the drink orders. He found the two women in a heated game of chess.

Aunt Bernie glanced up at him. "She's winning."

"I see," he said.

"She's letting me," Susan said. "I'm rotten at chess."

"Pooh," said Aunt Bernie. "I'm not nearly clever enough to cheat."

"Hah!" Susan and Brad said at the same time. They looked at one another and smiled. In that instant he knew for sure he was in love. It came at him like a burst of warmth, only it came from inside, burgeoning, billowing, filling his heart and his mind with sunlight, obliterating all the world except for Susan Ballinger, insurance appraiser, admitted gold digger, horsewoman, temptress, the most beautiful, wonderful woman in the world.

He was also in lust. He wanted to play games with her and cheat whenever he could, but he wouldn't use a chess board and they wouldn't be out on the veranda with Aunt Bernie looking on. Strip poker came to mind. Oh yes, he would definitely cheat. He could do it very well. He'd been taught by one of the most notorious gamblers in Las Vegas.

Forget the drink orders. He wanted her in complete control of her faculties so that she would know what was happening between them. No wine for Miss Susan Ballinger. He preferred her full and sober cooperation. He wanted to ravish her until dawn, and then he wanted to propose marriage and ravish her again.

Somewhere in all that ravishing, when the time seemed right, he would tell her who he was.

First the meal. He forced himself to return to the kitchen. "Can you make iced tea?" he asked of Douglas, who was getting plates out of one of the cabinets.

Douglas shuddered. "If I must."

The butler considered the beverage an abomination, but dutiful man that he was, he would serve his master poison if requested.

"Teach me," said Brad, thinking he ought to prepare some part of the meal.

Douglas came as close to smiling as he ever had, but one had to know him well to see it.

"First you boil the water."

"Yeah, well—"

Without so much as a sigh Douglas showed him how. He also taught him the proper way to set the table, although Brad had eaten enough formal meals to know where a butter knife went. Why they were using butter knives in the first place he couldn't imagine, but he was in such a good mood he would humor anyone with any request that didn't separate him from his intended wife.

He went so far as to don an apron and, when Douglas arrived through the front door with the food, he even smeared a little barbecue sauce on the bib, giving his appearance a downhome touch.

The trouble didn't start until Susan was summoned in for dinner. They were to eat in the breakfast room just off the kitchen. Douglas had declined to join them—actually he'd shuddered in genuine alarm when the invitation was put to him—so there were only three places.

But Aunt Bernie didn't show. Susan didn't know where she was. "After Douglas came out, she just disappeared."

Susan had taken off the jacket to her suit. The pink silk skirt stretched nicely across her thighs, and the ivory silk blouse clung to all the appropriate places across her breasts. Her hands were small, but her fingers were long and tapered, her nails rounded and polished with a pale pink. She wore a narrow gold watch and gold stud earrings, no other jewelry. She was class. Brad forgot the sausage. He wanted to gnaw on her for a while.

Petunia joined them and settled in one of the corners of the room, her wide brown eyes never once leaving the table. An opportunist, that's what she was, but then so was he. They were both presented with a feast.

Brad sat in a chair at Susan's left. She looked over the platters and bowls of food that covered the linen-and-lace tablecloth.

"You really cooked all this?"

He opened his mouth to lie.

Nope slipped out. "Smoky's Barbecue in Comfort delivers. I had a hard enough time making the tea."

"Why would Aunt Bernie brag about how you could cook?" She thought a moment. "Does she want us to be together? Is she matchmaking?"

He couldn't help himself. He took her hand. "Looks like it. Anything wrong with that?"

She stared at their entwined hands. "You promised."

"Yeah, well, I've been good for three days."

"Two and a half."

He grinned. "So you've been counting. So have I. Longest two and a half days of my life."

She pulled free and stood. "For me, too. This is insane. I've got to leave."

Petunia must have thought she was being invited to join them. She moved in fast, resting her big head on the table next to the beef. Her tongue snaked out. Susan jerked up the platter. The meat, covered with warm sauce, slid down her front, down the white silk blouse, down the pink silk skirt, and onto the floor, where Petunia promptly did her duty and started to clean up.

Susan looked at herself in horror. "I've done it again."

"Not quite the same. Last time you sat in it."

The look she gave him was not kind.

"I'll never wear pink again."

"Yeah, well, I guess we'd better get you out of that."

She stepped away from the table, away from Petunia, away from him. "I can take care of myself."

"I'm not so sure. Besides, I've been good as long as I can."

He scooped her up in his arms and headed for the

front of the house, taking her up the winding staircase, down the long hallway on the second floor, and into the master bedroom. She didn't struggle, but then she didn't cuddle, either. If he had to describe her attitude, he would have said she was resigned.

He set her down in the bathroom.

"I know the routine," she said. "I get undressed while you bring me a change of clothes."

"Wrong. This time I stay."

"Sonny—"

He unbuttoned the top of her blouse. She backed against the counter. He came after her.

"It's all right," he said. "I love you."

She didn't look particularly happy. "You can't mean that."

"Oh, yes I do." He moved to the second button. "Let me show you the ways."

"Love is a lie. I thought I was in love twice, and it didn't feel anything like this."

He broke another promise. He grinned. Button number three. He could see something lacy lying against her milky skin.

"How does this feel?" He stroked the fullness rising from the top of her brassiere, just in case she didn't get the point.

She closed her eyes. She bit her lip. She sighed.

Three strikes. She was out, and he was in. Or soon would be. He forgot the grin. He loved her so much he thought he would explode from the pressure. She had to love him, too. He would give her no choice.

"This is wrong," she said, her voice low and husky. "You're not what I want."

"Oh, yeah?"

He kissed her eyes, her cheeks, her chin, her throat, and then he licked his way back to her lips. By the time he got there, she was openmouthed and ready for him. Her hands stole around his neck. He hugged her to him and commenced the kissing, thrusting his tongue deep inside her, and then slipping in and out, letting her know exactly what he had in mind.

The Gold Digger

She eased away long enough to finish working at her blouse. He took it off her. The brassiere came next, fast, with her help. Still holding on to one another, they dropped to the floor and stretched out on the thick bathroom carpet. He kissed her without plan or thought, her shoulder, her ear, her neck, her breasts, wanting to taste everywhere, feeling her heat rise and get inside him, raising his blood to the boiling point.

He had too many clothes on. So did she. And he didn't want their first time together to be on the bathroom floor.

But he couldn't stop kissing her. He tried to take off his shirt and got into a tangled mess. Forcing his lips from hers, he looked down to see she was smiling.

"Are you laughing at me?" he asked.

She grew solemn. "Not really. I'm enjoying you. I'll bet you're usually good at this."

"I'm out of practice, but that's not the problem. I've never wanted anyone or anything more in my life than you, Susan Ballinger. I'm all thumbs."

"Not *all* I hope."

Her eyes smoldered. She helped him with his shirt, and then she started kissing him the way he had been kissing her, without pattern, nibbling and licking, and running her lips over his bare skin, playing around his nipples with her tongue, kissing his neck and throat and then coming back to his lips. This time she was the one who thrust in and out.

He almost lost it. They were both naked to the waist, and she was rubbing her breasts against him, and he knew if he didn't do something within the next five seconds, he would be taking her on the bathroom floor.

The first time ought to be in bed.

The second time they could move back to the floor.

He was a captain of industry, a manipulator of fortunes, a mover and shaker, a world traveler. Surely he could get one slender, willing woman from one room to another. But he couldn't stop touching her,

227

Evelyn Rogers

kissing her, rubbing his palm over her silk skirt, easing it up until he could feel the garter belt and the hose and when he investigated further the cool slipperiness of her panties.

Calling upon the strength of his robber-baron grandfather, he broke away, picked her up and carried her to the bed. Good thing she couldn't see the way his knees were shaking. She'd think he lacked the strength to do what they both wanted.

She would be wrong. He was nervous and eager, that was all. He was Atlas. He was Zeus. He was Superman. He would prove himself if it took all night.

She looked down at the satin coverlet. "The master bed?" she asked. "We can't."

"Better than the master floor."

She looked at him. The heat in her eyes ratcheted up a few degrees. "Right."

She insisted they pull back the covers. She wasn't neat, but who was judging? They both finished undressing—she took a long time with the garter belt and hose, but he didn't complain—and fell onto the satin sheet. The room was in semidarkness, the draperies pulled against the oncoming night, a bedside lamp turned low. Its light was like moonglow against her naked body. She was beautiful with her pale skin and dark nipples and black pubic hair, her body long and sleek and yielding as it curled against him.

Everywhere they touched they sizzled. And they touched everywhere. With hands, and lips, and tongues, skin rubbing against skin, neither showing the least inclination to inhibition.

Once he looked up from her navel, where he was spending some time, to tell her he loved her. She looked pained and maybe glad at the same time. He decided not to tell her again, not until she confessed the same to him.

Back to pleasure. He licked his way down through her thatch of hair, found his destination, and brought her to climax with his tongue, having no fear he could not do the same to her the more ordinary way.

228

The Gold Digger

What was ordinary? What could be wrong between them? Only the denial of pleasure and of their destiny. They were meant for each other. They would have children. They would grow to old age at each other's side. He owed her good times through the years.

Beginning with their first time in bed.

She gave as good as she got, using her hands, showing she understood what he especially liked, the caress of his buttocks, the hard strokes on his sex, the hot breath on his neck that made him shiver.

He paused to get himself ready, using a condom from the bedside drawer, part of the stock he'd purchased when he thought Bitsy was a real live human being. He hadn't been called upon to use a single one.

When Susan lay back and opened herself to him, he entered heaven. They both climaxed within a half dozen thrusts. She held on to him tightly, breathing hard, as if she were afraid he would leave. Silly woman. It would take a crowbar to get them apart.

She pressed her lips against his ear. "I've never done that before. Not—you know. I didn't know it could feel so good."

"With us, my little chickadee, it'll happen every time."

"Little chickadee?"

He forced himself to pull away a few inches and look at her. "You prefer honey or baby or sweetie?"

Her lips curled into a delicious grin. "Chickadee. Definitely chickadee. I guess that makes you my cock."

She looked surprised by her own words.

"You got it," he said. He excused himself for a minute, then hurried back from the bathroom, stretched out beside her and pulled her back against his front. "I promise before dawn your cock will be rising and ready to crow again."

She giggled.

He lifted her hair and kissed the side of her neck. "You don't do that often enough," he said.

She held still for a moment and he gave up on the kissing.

"This isn't the real me," she said. She sounded far too serious, as if she were ready to analyze what had happened between them. Like his telling the truth, the analysis was coming too soon. He wasn't through showing her a good time.

He cupped a breast. "Feels real to me."

She caught her breath, then let out a long sigh.

"Rest," he said. "I need you at full strength."

She giggled again. "You're the one who needs to rest. I'm ready right now for whatever you have in mind."

"Insatiable wench."

"I prefer chickadee."

"Okay. Insatiable chickadee."

He started to add something about insatiable cock when he heard a rustling outside the bedroom door. She drew in a sharp breath. "Maybe it's the master of the house returning to claim his bed."

Nothing in her voice indicated she was glad.

"I'll check." He padded naked to the door, opened it a crack, looking up and down the empty hallway, then down to the silver tray piled high with food and a pitcher of fresh iced tea. This had to be Aunt Bernie's idea, she was keeping up his strength, caring for Susan, making her feel at home.

Silently he thanked her and carried the tray to the bed. Susan sat up, the top sheet tucked modestly over her breasts. Her hair was tangled and her lips were swollen and her cheeks were reddened by his late-day bristle, and she was lovelier than ever.

He settled under the sheet beside her, both of them cross-legged. He eased the tray close and picked up a long, thick link of sausage. "What do you suppose we should do with this?"

She took the sausage from him and licked the end. "Ummm, good."

He felt the impact in his zero zone.

She held it out to him, but he shook his head. "No, it's all for you."

230

She licked it again, then thrust a good portion of it in her mouth, pulling it in and out, finally biting off a chunk.

"Ouch," he said, but he didn't feel like *ouch*. He felt like *wow*.

Her tongue swiped the barbecue sauce from her lips and she chewed. She swallowed, and he watched the play in her throat. When she started to take another bite, he moved in and took the bite for himself, finishing off the sausage in two gulps.

He started to lick the sauce from his mouth. "Let me," she said. She did a thorough job, and he returned the favor by licking her hands clean.

He got the tray off the bed fast.

"Is it dawn already?" she asked.

He eased the sheet down from her body and lowered himself to her side. "Fair warning, my little chickadee, your cock is again ready to crow."

Chapter Five

Susan overslept the next morning. Sonny had already showered and gone downstairs. Through a fog of complete satisfaction she'd heard his movements maybe an hour ago but had found stirring too difficult a maneuver to undertake.

She had every right to oversleep, after the night she'd been through. The best night ever. The best a night could be. She couldn't believe she'd done some of the things she'd done. Her task now was not only to handle a certain soreness she'd never experienced but also to convince herself she'd done nothing wrong.

Sonny had called whatever it was between them destiny. She wanted to believe him, but she'd been burned before. It could be just a line.

She nestled down in the covers. She had to quit being so cynical. He wasn't like other men. He wasn't

232

trying to get her in bed. At least not just that. He loved her. He had declared that love several times.

Her heart told her he wouldn't lie, not to her, not about something so serious.

Would he love her this morning with the same almost scary intensity as he had loved her last night? She meant the emotion, not the activity. She had no doubt he was physically capable of anything he chose.

Did she love him? Fool that she was, she did. She couldn't. He hadn't any money, and money had been her longtime goal. He went light years beyond the lover of her midnight fantasies, but he fell far short of her fantasy husband. She had her standards, no matter how low they might seem to some people. She had wanted to sell out.

And she'd fallen head-over-heels in love with a poor man. A poor man she'd known less than a week. She had no sense.

Finding the biking shorts and tee shirt in the bathroom in place of her ruined clothes, she showered, dressed, and was about to go downstairs when she heard someone walking in the hall outside the bedroom door.

"Bradford," a woman called out.

Susan stopped in her tracks, her hand gripping the doorknob. Here was a voice she didn't know.

"Bradford, come on out. I know you're in there. We need to talk."

Susan stiffened her spine and opened the door. She faced a petite blonde, maybe twenty-five, pert nose, pursed lips, narrow, suspicious blue eyes. Cute, she would have called her in high school. Cute and critical. The woman was dressed in a beige linen pants suit that made her look squat instead of tiny. Her red nails, the brightest thing about her, were almost an inch long.

"You must be Bitsy," Susan said, taking a chance. "Mr. Kitchener's not here."

The two women stared at each other. Bitsy broke the stare to look Susan over.

"You can't be Roberta," the woman said. "I've seen her picture."

"You're right. I'm not."

Don't give the enemy too much tactical information. Not that Bitsy Cochran was her enemy. Over the past two days Susan had gradually given up on Bradford Horatio Kitchener as a possible pursuit. But she'd once considered the former fiancée her opposition, beginning the moment she'd read about her in the paper and continuing to this week, and old habits were hard to break.

Bitsy attempted to look past her into the bedroom.

"I told you," Susan said, "he's not here and he hasn't been. Not for days. He flew to Dallas. Didn't you see him there? Oh, sorry, I forgot. Your engagement is off, isn't it?"

Bitsy sniffed. "It's a negotiable point, though I can't see how it's any of your business. Who are you? What are you doing in his bedroom?"

"I'm working here."

Bitsy smirked. "I'll just bet you are. Bradford does have animal tastes."

Susan felt a rush of sympathy for the missing billionaire and a rise in her own usually dormant temper. All right, so matters could never have worked out between them, despite the urging of her little bird Alice, but that didn't mean he deserved a wife like Bitsy. Not a man with an aunt like Bernie, a dog like Petunia, and a hired hand like Sonny Hardcastle.

Hardcastle. He certainly was well named.

She looked past Bitsy to see Sonny coming down the hall. She started to wave. He came to a sudden halt, turned on his heel, and disappeared. Strange. Apparently he didn't care to talk to Bitsy. She couldn't blame him, but she couldn't help thinking it was cowardly of him to leave his little chickadee in the company of a coyote like this.

In truth, she was a little disappointed. She hadn't wanted to be greeted with flowers and breakfast in bed, but a good morning kiss and a little reassurance that he really meant what he'd said would have been nice.

The more she thought of it, the more she decided *nice* wasn't the right word. *Essential* came to mind.

Suddenly in the bright light of day everything looked different to her. She was seeing herself through Bitsy's eyes. Well, sort of.

What had she done in the shadows of the night? Had she made a fool of herself?

All the warmth and beauty of the morning fled. She felt foolish. Sonny had abandoned her twice this morning—their first morning after their first night. If she were going to give up all her plans for a life of leisure, she at least wanted to be pursued.

A woman in love, she realized, was a fragile being indeed.

"Excuse me." She stepped around Bitsy, gesturing toward the bedroom. "Go on in. Look under the bed if you want. He's not there."

She went downstairs to gather her purse and her briefcase. Douglas informed her Aunt Bernie was plugged in to the Internet and had left orders not to be disturbed.

"She wanted to make some sort of announcement, I believe she said. She seemed quite determined."

"And Sonny?"

"He left rather hurriedly a moment ago. He left word for you to meet him in the stable."

"Oh, he did, did he?" What did he want, a little roll in the hay? They'd discussed the possibility sometime in the wee hours of the morning, but she'd thought it had been some more sex talk.

"He expressed regret that Miss Cochran had appeared," Douglas said. "I owe you an apology, Miss Susan. She darted past me at the door. I really couldn't stop her short of, well, a physical assault."

"Not your style, I know," Susan said with a reassuring pat on his hand.

She went out on the veranda, down the steps, and over to the Chevy. Except for a hawk circling overhead, no other living creature was in sight. Even Petunia had disappeared. Probably suffering stomach problems from all that rich barbecued beef.

At least the dog hadn't gotten to the sausage.

Susan blushed when she remembered the sausage particulars from last night. She had lost her mind. She'd become a sex fiend. If Sonny didn't show up and soothe her fears, she'd have to go into therapy. Not that she would get over him, not ever.

She spied Douglas still standing on the veranda. "Tell Sonny I had to go home."

Where was home? Her small downtown apartment? Her parents' place in Brownsville? Suddenly she felt very much alone.

She got in the car, gunned the motor as best she could considering its age, and careened down the winding private road, through the gate, and over to the expressway, getting the most out of the Chevy as she zipped the fifty miles to downtown San Antonio. She thought she made good time. But a bright red Porsche pulled up beside her just as she drove into the small strip parking lot beside her building.

The Porsche must have been behind her on the expressway. She hadn't seen it. Not that she had been crying, but her eyes had been blurry and her vision impaired.

She was dry-eyed now. Roberta's sandals flapped on her heels as she got out of the car. Hands on hips, she stared at Sonny as he emerged from the Porsche.

"You stole Kitchener's car," she said.

"He wasn't using it," Sonny said.

He was dressed in a black tee shirt and cutoffs and sandals, and his legs were long and strong and fuzzy with short golden hairs, and his chest was broad, his neck strong, his skin golden, his eyes darker than she had ever seen them.

She swallowed and fought for resolve. "How did you know where I lived?"

"I've followed you home the last few nights. To make sure you got here safely. Can't be too careful, you know, a woman alone."

The Gold Digger

"I can take care of myself. I've been doing so for the past ten years."

"Are you mad at me?" he asked.

"I don't want to talk about it." With her briefcase and purse clutched to her bosom, she walked around him, in the front door, and onto the stairs.

"You have to talk about it," Sonny said as he bounded after her. "Tell me what's wrong."

They'd almost reached the second floor when a downstairs door opened and Ralph Johnson, the friendly superintendent, stuck out his head.

"Is this man bothering you, Susan?"

Oh, yes.

"No," she said. "I can handle him."

"Ha!" Sonny barked.

She rolled her eyes and continued her journey to her front door. When she fumbled with the locks, he took the key from her hand and turned it easily. The door still refused to open.

"There are still two more," she said with childish satisfaction. He found them in short order and gestured for her to enter as if he owned the place.

She threw her belongings on the sofa and went into the narrow kitchen. There was barely enough room for one person to move around between the sink, the refrigerator, and the table. Sonny made himself fit beside her.

She stared out the kitchen window, which opened onto a brick wall. She turned on the cold water, then turned it off.

"What are you doing?" he asked.

"I'm getting something to drink."

"Don't you need a glass?"

"I can't get to it. You're in the way."

"I'm sorry I left you with Bitsy. I was a coward. I don't get along with her."

"And you thought I could?"

"I had faith in you." He stroked her arm. "Have a little faith in me."

Tiny little bumps jumped out along her flesh. She took a deep breath and closed her eyes. "I'm scared."

"Of what?"

"Of you. Of me. I'm not used to all this. It's not what I wanted. It's not what I expected. It's too much."

"My little chickadee—"

"Don't call me that. That's bed talk. We're in the kitchen."

"You don't think we could make love in here?"

The suggestion in his voice turned up her body heat.

"Of course not," she said.

"Are you challenging me?"

Her heart stopped, but all her other parts seemed to be working, including a few that ought to be too sore to react.

"No," she said fast. "No challenge. Definitely not a challenge."

"Too late. The gauntlet has been thrown."

He backed her up against the refrigerator and ran his hands down her spandex-covered thighs.

"You'll never get these shorts off my body. I could barely get them on."

"Motivation, that's the key. You didn't want them on. You wanted to lie naked in the bed and wait for me. I was on my way when Bitsy showed up."

"You didn't have to leave."

"I went down to order breakfast. We missed supper last night, remember? Douglas was going to bring it up, along with a big pot of coffee. In an hour or so. I figured you would be starving by then."

"We had the sausage."

"How could I forget?"

By now his hands had worked their way around her thighs and locked onto her behind. He held her against him. Boy, did he know how to fit their bodies together, even when they were dressed.

She was already ready for him, and he was ready for her. She'd learned all the signs.

He shifted his hips, rubbing himself against her to wondrous effect. "Marry me," he said.

"I don't know you."

238

The Gold Digger

He chuckled and rubbed some more. Then he stopped and put some space between them.

She panicked. "No."

"No what? You won't marry me?"

"No, don't stop."

"Have I got a bargaining point here?"

As hot as she was, she had to smile. "You're a very bad boy."

He kissed her and rubbed just a little bit more.

"Do you love me?" he asked.

"Love is more than just sex," she said just before she nibbled at the side of his neck.

"I know," he said, his voice getting thick. "I'd love you without it, but why should I when we're so good together?"

For emphasis, he grabbed hold of the waistband of her shorts and tugged. Before she could say *stop* both shorts and panties were down around her ankles. What was a girl to do? She stepped out of them and even managed to slip out of her shoes.

He shifted her to the table and dropped his cutoffs. She lay back and he did to her what he had done countless times during the night. Actually, not countless. Six was the number that burned into her mind.

He did it just as well as he had in bed. The legs of the table bounced against the floor. She cried out from the sheer, explosive pleasure he brought her. She was especially glad that he did the same. He held her while she trembled against him, loving him with all her heart and filled with joy that he had pursued her as she had wanted.

But finally she had to speak.

"I don't mean to sound ungrateful, but the edge of this table is putting a new crease in my behind."

"Can't have that," he said as he pulled her to her feet and cradled her against him. "I like your creases just the way they are."

They were both a little messy. Lovemaking like this wasn't neat, but that didn't detract from it. She hugged him and rested her cheek against his chest, listening to the very satisfying pounding of his heart.

"You've got to marry me now," he said. "I didn't bring any protection."

"Unfair."

"Yeah."

She sighed. "I was going to marry you anyway. Otherwise you would never leave me alone."

"Even if I'm broke?"

She thought that one over. "Even if you're broke. We'll get by somehow."

He kept silent for a moment. "I'm not without a few resources. Don't worry. You're right. We'll get by."

A fist pounded at her door. The sound traveled through the small apartment. "You sure everything's all right in there?" Ralph yelled.

"Yes," she called back. "I'm fine."

She looked up at Sonny, who was staring down at her with a smile of triumph on his face.

I'm fine, she repeated to herself. She'd known him less than a week. He was poor and she was greedy and they shouldn't be together, but she knew she would never find happiness without him.

Soon, very soon, she had to become his wife.

Chapter Six

Two days later, on a brilliant April Sunday afternoon, she found herself walking with Alice Roberts along the narrow street that led to the downtown chapel known as the Little Church of La Villita. Nestled among the quaint old homes that had been converted into artists' shops along the River Walk, the chapel was a popular place for weddings.

"This is too soon," she said. "I've known him for seven days and I haven't seen him for two of those."

Alice rolled her eyes. "You love him, don't you?"

"I think so. All right, don't look at me that way. I do."

"And he loves you. What's to worry about?"

"My sanity. And his."

Alice looked her over. "There's nothing wrong with his. You look great."

She was wearing the white silk suit and pink silk

blouse he'd had delivered to her apartment yesterday.

"I've reversed the order of the colors, my little chickadee," he'd written in the accompanying note. "Your luck is about to change."

The truth was she was scared. She loved him so much he was all she could think of. She couldn't eat, couldn't sleep, couldn't draw a breath that didn't bring thoughts of him.

After the table episode, which she was still trying to put a name to, she'd fixed them both breakfast, and he'd told her to come to the chapel two days hence. He had assured her all would be well.

"I know there aren't any blood tests in Texas, but we still need to get a marriage license. Doesn't that take three days?"

"I'll take care of it."

"The chapel is very popular. It's probably already reserved."

"I'll take care of it."

"My parents can't get up here in time, and neither can your mother and sister. Didn't you say they live out of state?"

He'd hesitated over that one. "We'll visit them as soon as you like. I promise. I can take some time off. I've got a surprise honeymoon in mind that I think you'll like. Pack light. You won't need much."

She'd seen he would come up with an answer for every question she raised. But that wasn't why she had given in. She'd done so because she loved him so much she couldn't stand to be away from him. He was an illness, an obsession, a life force that kept her systems working. She must have been storing up her love for the past years because it was overflowing them both, like a tidal wave sweeping them to the altar.

But that didn't mean she wasn't scared. She was too hot. She had to cool down.

Alice squeezed her hand. "Quit worrying. You're doing the right thing."

"You've certainly changed your mind. A week ago

The Gold Digger

you were telling me Brad Kitchener was mine for the asking."

Alice's eyes shifted away to the horde of tourists walking past them and on to a shop offering hand-crafted jewelry for sale. "I changed my mind. Sonny's the right one."

"You haven't even met him."

"I've got instincts about these things. I married four good men, remember?"

The particulars of Alice's marriages, particularly her four-time widowhoods, cast another shadow over the imminent proceedings.

"I couldn't even tell Mother and the Skipper what was going on. They didn't answer the phone."

"Call 'em after the ceremony."

"It's not the same thing. Do you know who's going to give me away? Ralph, my apartment super."

"I'm sure he'll do a fine job."

They came to the steps leading into the old stone chapel. Organ music drifted through the closed doors. Alice went ahead of her and opened the doors, then stepped aside and gestured for her to enter. She walked into what was supposed to be a practically empty chapel. Instead the back pews were filled with flowers of all colors and kinds, mountains of flowers, a rain forest of greenery and blooms, and beyond them a crowd of people stood and turned to face her as the organ music soared into the familiar strains of "Here Comes the Bride."

Alice appeared beside her, brushing a tear from her eye as she placed a bouquet of white and pink roses in her hand.

Wide-eyed, Susan took one step and then another, staring first at all the flowers and then at the people, some she didn't know, some she did. She saw her boss, Joseph Martinez and his wife and their two children, the elderly couple that lived in the apartment down the hall, a few friends from the Art League, and off to one side one of the sculptors she'd befriended along with his significant other.

Beyond them she saw Aunt Bernie standing beside

Evelyn Rogers

Douglas on the right, and on the left Ralph the super and—

She blinked. It couldn't be. There were her parents, her mother in a blue dress, a lace handkerchief clutched in her hand, and her father in a tuxedo, looking like the proudest man in the world.

Her mother was wearing an orchid the size of a small shrub, but it was the tuxedo that got her. The Skipper had never worn one in his life.

She stifled a cry. The whole chapel seemed to be whirling around her. She grabbed the back of a pew. She must not faint. She had to think.

And then she saw her bridegroom striding down the aisle toward her. He, too, was dressed in a tuxedo. She'd thought he looked great in jeans. She'd thought he could never look better. She'd been wrong.

Her heart twisted in a knot. He came right up to her and took her hand.

"I don't understand," she said.

"I love you. That's all you need to know. Except, maybe, for my real name."

He pulled a piece of paper and a pen from an inside pocket. "You'll have to sign this. The county clerk himself waived the usual wait and brought it here."

She looked down at the marriage license. She zeroed in on the signature of the bridegroom: BRADFORD HORATIO KITCHENER.

She looked around the chapel, and then she looked at him. The truth hit her. "You?"

"Afraid so. Brad Kitchener, bridegroom, man in love."

"But you didn't . . . you told me . . . I thought . . ."

He frowned. "Maybe I shouldn't have surprised you like this."

"Maybe you shouldn't . . . oh!"

She dropped the license and pen, threw the roses at him, and turned on her heel, dashing for the doors and down the front steps. He caught up with her in one of the lanes that trailed off between the shops.

The Gold Digger

Tourists were here, too, but they scattered fast as he took her by the arm and turned her to face him.

"You're crying."

"I'm furious."

"You're sorry I'm rich?"

She brushed the tears from her cheeks and fought for control. "I'm sorry you lied. How could you? How could you?"

"I told you what you wanted to hear."

"You didn't have to keep telling me."

"I thought that I did."

"Why?" She started to cry again and stopped herself. "Why? Why?" She was practically shouting, but she didn't know how to stop.

He dropped her arm and stepped away. "Because I wanted you to love me. I knew it the moment I saw you sitting in the horse manure." He attempted a smile, but this time he failed. "Call me a romantic, but that's the way it was."

His smile, even forced, did what it always did to her. The tightness in her, the confusion, began to let go. She fought to get them back.

"I could have loved you knowing the truth."

"I wasn't sure. I'd had a few bad experiences with women—"

"With gold diggers, you mean. I admitted that I was. That didn't bother you?"

"You were honest about it. The others weren't."

He turned solemn and she saw that even billionaires could have trouble finding true love.

"You should have been honest, too. Now look what you've done."

"What? Turned out rich instead of poor? I thought that's what you wanted. When I decided to make it a surprise, I hoped you'd be pleased."

"Surprise? The flowers were a surprise. My parents were a surprise. You're a shock."

She tried to run a hand through her hair, remembering too late the small white hat perched on the top of her head. She knocked it askew.

"You look adorable," he said.

"I feel like a fool."

"Aunt Bernie told me you'd feel this way."

More humiliation. She closed her eyes. Her cheeks burned.

"She must think I'm an idiot."

"She thinks you're the girl for me. She and Alice have been conspirators even before we met. They somehow hooked up on the Internet, bemoaning the fate of their two unmarried loved ones."

"That's why Alice told me to get out to Kitchener's—to your place." A new thought occurred. "Oh, she knows, too. And Douglas. How about Ralph?"

"Ralph didn't know until I called him yesterday. I told your parents, of course. I had them flown to San Antonio. You wanted them here, didn't you?"

She groaned. "And I ran from them. What must they be thinking?"

"We ought to go ask."

"I can't go back in there. I can't face all those people. I don't know what to do."

"It's simple. Marry me. Unless you don't think you can love a rich man. I'll give it all away, if you ask. Well, most of it. We have to live."

She looked away from him, staring at the stucco and stone walls that lined the lane. She found herself smiling. Suddenly she saw matters from his point of view; at the same time she saw them from hers. Not love a rich man? She'd told herself for years she could do just that, and she couldn't admit she'd been wrong.

They stared at one another. His eyes grew warm. They melted her heart.

"I love you, Sonny—" She stopped herself. "I ought to start calling you Brad."

"If you like. It seems to me a couple of nights ago you came up with another name, my little chickadee. Best not use it around your parents. They might be shocked."

"Oh, they definitely would. My late Granny would have been. I'll bet she's looking down from Heaven right now and grinning."

The Gold Digger

She couldn't contain herself any longer. She threw herself in his arms and kissed him.

"I love you, and I don't care who you are. If it's my fate to marry a billionaire, then so be it. You told me more than once we can't fight our destiny."

"Glad you were listening."

He straightened her hat and, arm in arm, they went back to the chapel.

The newly married Brad and Susan Kitchener, the subject of gossip columns from San Antonio to Paris, honeymooned in Brad's Swiss chateau, went on to his villa in Tuscany, and after a visit with his mother and sister in Paris, settled for the summer in his London flat. They saw plays and they did the tourist bit, but mostly they stayed to themselves, learning to know one another, deciding with each passing day and night that they were the luckiest two people in the world.

In the autumn they returned to Texas to await the birth of their first child, conceived, Brad was sure, on a table in a kitchen so small they had to mate to stay in the same room.

Every time Brad grinned at her or kissed her or simply walked into the room, Susan became more certain that all her fantasies had indeed come true.

A Quiver of Sighs

Olivia Rupprecht

For Nora and Stephanie and Laura and Molly

Teh Path unfolds a ribbony maze of roads
revealing poems without rhyme,
passion plays of life
to impulsively relish or wisely decline

Daughters of my heart
sisters of the pen,
let truth be your compass
it lies within

P.S. Five rules for the road, girls:

1. *Believe in yourselves*
2. *Reach for your dreams*
3. *Hold fast to each other*
4. *Honor the gift*
5. *Because I'm the Mama and I said so!*

Chapter One

Valerie Smith was getting desperate. She had to be to stoop this low. Sitting at the linoleum and chrome kitchen table, she chewed another antacid tablet and told herself she had nothing to lose but her self respect. With a potential check to gain, she began to type:

Last Tuesday began as any other day. Little did I realize a secret fantasy was about to become a reality.

I was on my way to work and running late when a taxi stopped at the corner. Briefcase flying behind me, I reached the handle at the same time a large, masculine hand gripped the metal. What happened next was destined to change my safe world forever and thrust me into a wild, sexual adventure!

Valerie dropped her head in her hands. She peeked through her fingers to scan the words. And shuddered.

"It sucks," she muttered. "I can't do this." She jerked the page out, wadded it into a ball of disgust, and took aim at the overflowing trash can.

"Hey sis, are you trying to deplete the national paper supply? It's starting to look closer to a Chicago snowstorm in here than summer in L.A."

"Hi, Sarah," Valerie dully replied, and drummed a thick stack of pages, seeking what comfort she could. Second novel, half done, while the first was pleading for attention in New York. Ten rejections and counting. If she was lucky maybe an editor was using her labor of love for a scratch pad or a place to rest a coffee cup. "Any luck with the audition?"

"Same old, same old. 'Don't call us, we'll call you.' I keep telling myself even Marilyn Monroe was a starving actress once and maybe she was worried the director couldn't hear her over the growl of her stomach, too."

"Tell me about it. The muse decided to take the day off and I'm beating my brains to pabulum so I can come up with next month's rent. If I don't make a sale soon it's back to punching a clock."

Visions of returning to Iowa were ample incentive to roll in another blank page. She'd done all the right things, gone to college, worked her tail off for five years, and even dated a doctor. Only the doctor had been a dud, her degree in English lit was fairly useless, and her job was going nowhere. Had it been only a year since she'd ditched it all to move in with Sarah and chase after her dream? A dream so elusive, it was like searching for the end of a rainbow. Like believing Mr. Right was out there somewhere. Yeah, right. Not a single date in the year she'd lived here. Even Dr. Dud was starting to look good.

"Whatcha working on, Val?"

Sarah looked over her shoulder. Valerie scowled. She hated for anyone to watch her work. It was like performing a self-labotomy while the observer gawked at her naked brain.

"Not much. There's supposed to be a big market for sexual experience stories."

"You? Writing about your sexual experiences?" A snicker was followed by an affectionate tug of Valerie's long strawberry-red braid. "Hey, that oughta fill up half a page."

"I have a very vivid imagination." Val indignantly sniffed. "And besides, at seventy-five cents a word my half page could put a dent in the rent."

"Know what I think?"

"Yes and don't say it!"

"Val, you really need to get out more," she said anyway. "I mean, how can you write about emotions and things like sex when you stay holed up with a bunch of imaginary characters instead of living in the real world with real people? It only makes sense that personal experience would bring a lot more to your writing than all that research you do at the library."

Valerie glowered at her sister, who had a way of picking at those fears and insecurities she secretly harbored. But what was she supposed to do? Throw herself in front of a car to experience terror? Go to bed with a man she wasn't in love with for a taste of passion? Hope someone she cared for died so she could fully grasp the meaning of grief and sorrow? Or maybe she'd really luck out and fall in love only to be betrayed so she could write with authority about rage and heartbreak.

"Excuse me, Sarah, but I have work to do."

"Just let me read it when you're finished. I sure wouldn't want to miss the next Anais Nin's epic work of sleeze." Sarah took off and giggled as several well-aimed wads hit her retreating behind.

Valerie watched her go, all tanned legs and spritzed blond hair. Looking down at her own long muslin skirt and embroidered peasant blouse, she wondered how in the world two women could be so different and still thrive on sisterly love. Lord knew

Olivia Rupprecht

they had to thrive on something. Especially when she didn't have a carnal seventy-five-cent word in her head.

A wisp of warm California breeze flirted with the curtains in their tiny kitchen. Shoving away from the table, Val latched onto a floppy straw hat. Maybe a long walk would get the creative juices flowing. Couldn't hurt.

Half an hour later, it hadn't helped, either. A string of quaint shops beckoned and she told herself perhaps some spark of inspiration would find her as she browsed.

Then again, talk about inspiration! And *envy*. Her gaze riveted to a couple kissing outside an elaborately carved wood door. In the middle was an oval stained-glass window with the word KISMET beveled around the arch.

Moving past the lovers, Val wished desperately that she was in an amorous clench. If she'd had more of those maybe she'd be pounding out a lusty story instead of looking for treasures she didn't have the money to buy.

A wind chime tinkled overhead, announcing her arrival. There were no other customers. No clerk in sight, either. She glanced around the unfamiliar surroundings. Strange. She thought she'd scoured all the second-hand stores in this area. Kismet was apparently a new one since she definitely would have remembered it.

Dust motes filtered the air around a menagerie of antique books, vintage clothes, and an assortment of paintings and knick-knacks. It had a warm, weathered texture about it that breathed a gentle welcome. The musty scent of age mingled with cloves and lavender and old lace.

"Hello," Val called, gliding her fingertip down the edge of an aged mahogany table. No one answered and she was struck by a displaced feeling, a sense of having stepped into a wrinkle in time.

A brass candelabra caught her eye, and she tapped a crystal prism hanging beneath a white taper. The crystal hummed as though she'd flicked the rim of a Baccarat flute.

"Not cheap," she muttered. Just out of curiosity she looked for a price and found none. She did notice the heavy layer of dust outlining the vacant space. And next to that was—

"A cupid!" Carefully replacing the candelabra, she lifted the tiny statuette. The delicate porcelain, painted in soothing pastels, had a special feel to it that seduced her imagination. Was it the way Cupid seemed to smile at her with a mischievous wink? Or perhaps it was the carved wood bow holding the tiny arrow he pointed straight at her heart. She responded with a twinge of sadness. One of Cupid's wings had been broken. It seemed a travesty to mar such an exquisite work of art.

Even the quiver on his back was painstakingly detailed, right down to the arrow nestled into the filigreed sack.

"Must not have heard the bell. Got to get this hearing aid checked out."

Cupid in hand, Val swung around at the grainy sound of the old man's voice. He was a curious looking fellow, bald pate, long white beard, and a tropical shirt over a pair of bermuda shorts. Santa Claus laid back and doing L.A.

"I love your store," she said with a rush of passion that surprised her. "I don't know how I missed it before, but I'm glad it found me."

"Kismet has a way of finding those who need to be found."

His cryptic remark seemed to coincide with the general strangeness of the store itself. Fodder for the writer's imagination, Val decided. Why else would she feel a surge of energy spark off the cupid and ignite the muse?

"How much for Cupid?" Breath held, she possessively fingered her priceless find.

The old man studied her until Val had the queerest sensation, one that caused her toes to curl into her sandles. He was sizing her up.

"Hard to put a price on that one, missy. The cupid's special."

"Yes. Yes, I know."

He pulled at his beard and asked, "How?"

Stroking the chipped wing, wishing she could mend it, Val impulsively kissed the miniature head. The cool porcelain felt warm to her lips. They . . . throbbed. As if she'd been thoroughly, wantonly kissed. Which made no more sense than feeling as if Cupid was pulsing to life in her hands.

She *had* to have it. She was stone broke, but taking Cupid home was suddenly more imperative than having groceries for the week.

"I can't explain why," she honestly admitted. "I just have a feeling he belongs to me."

A pleased, satisfied smile broadened the grooves in the proprietor's lined face. "In that case, he's yours."

"How much?"

"No charge." He raised a hand to quell her objection, then shuffled to the door and held it open. "Time to call it a day."

Too elated to wonder why he was closing shop in midafternoon, she quickly went for the exit.

"Thank you." Though she was tempted to throw her arms around his neck in gratitude, she poured her heartfelt thanks into another *"Thank you."*

"Just remember one thing, missy. Cupid's had a lot of practice and rarely misses his mark." He reached out a gnarled hand and patted her cheek. "Listen to your heart, but be prepared to pay the price. Dreams are never free."

Chapter Two

Val shot up in bed. She was shivering, burning up. Her nightgown clung to wet skin, twisted around thighs still parted. She didn't need to touch herself to know she was wet there, too.

Her heart pounded so hard it felt like an urgent rap against her chest. Panting, she reached blindly for the lamp switch.

A dull glow spread over the cupid. His cherubic face smiled up at her, his arrow pointed her way.

Her unblinking gaze fixed on the tiny statue as jumbled visions of torrid lovemaking with a man she'd never met meshed with words and more words tumbling through her brain.

Throwing back the covers, she got up on shaking legs. Taking Cupid with her, she hurried to the kitchen, sank into her chair, and put fingers to typewriter keys. *Dreams*, she typed. Paused. Listened.

Olivia Rupprecht

Then felt a white-hot rush as her hands raced to lay down the words she heard:

Dreams are never free. They take flight, and me along with them. Enfolded in their silken razor wings, I feel my body dip and soar until I am embraced by the untender fury of my lover.

He comes to me now, gliding on a whisper of lust, the promise of pleasure's unwavering devotion. We are enslaved, held prisoner by emotions and tactile exploration that is at once frenzied and curious and painfully slow.

The jolt of his mad thrust matches the rapacious greed of our mouths. The heady succor of tongue against tongue, the flowing moisture of sweat and passion's juices seal our undulating hips and chests into a bond beyond the physical. It is too beautiful, too poignant, and too base to describe.

But it is our destiny, riding to the climactic confrontation of tortured groans of ecstasy, binding us as one only to tear us apart.

The raven enfolds me into his keep and spirits me away as I cry for the lover left behind. He is my own, pulled from my embrace while I plummet back to reality from sleep.

Shakespeare once said it is better to have loved and lost than never to have loved at all. As I lay here, too empty and alone, I weigh his words against the ache in my breast.

"Dreams," I whisper, "dreams are for the lonely." We wake up, we pay the price. We relinquish them only to wish them back. The morning cash register rings up. It spits out the grand total. The receipt glares its hazy bottom line like a cool whiff of blue mimeograph ink from a grade-school exam. I lick the tip of lead with my tongue, then poise the pencil, ready to pit my loss against the test:

The tally is my return to reality.

The score is always the same. The zero sucks

*me into its black, seamless O, leaving me blind
but for the glimmer of sleep's borrowed light.*

*Night falls once more, promising escape into its
sweet carnal prison. Yet again I am shackled to
ecstasy's nocturnal warden, laid bare and plundered by his shadowed caress until we writhe
upon waves of rippling splendor.*

*Now I lay me down to sleep, I pray the Lord my
soul to keep. I die a little each time I wake, upon
a pillow of dreams that my wide-open eyes may
never partake.*

Valerie slumped over the typewriter, tears flowing
down her cheeks. Crazy as it was, she felt as if she
were mourning the loss of a lover she'd never met.
Even after committing him to ink, he was no more
tangible than a wisp of her receding dream.

"It was just a dream," she told Cupid. Swiping
away the tears, she couldn't help but laugh at herself
for talking to a figurine. But she supposed it wasn't
much different than speaking aloud to her characters, which she did a lot.

Hesitantly, she rolled out the paper and prayed the
results would be as good as she thought. Struggling
to remain objective, she read the marching lines.
With a sigh of relief she decided it was either wonderful or she was delusional. Unfortunately, the lat-
ter was always a possibility.

With practiced efficiency, she inserted another
sheet and pounded out a cover letter, addressing it
to The Editor, *Fantasies* Magazine. They were close
to, but not quite as raunchy as, *Penthouse Forum*, so
she deemed her chances of acceptance better there.
And at seventy-five cents a word she could make a
cool 300 dollars in exchange for ten minutes' time
and a piece of her soul.

She felt a little like a prostitute asking *Fantasies* to
pimp her work to their Johns who liked it down and
dirty. And hopefully tastefully erotic since *"Dreams,"*
as she'd entitled it, didn't meet the typical standards
of smut.

Olivia Rupprecht

An innate respect for her true literary calling gave her pause as she began to sign off with her name. Deciding a magazine that catered to men would react more positively to a male writer, she went with V. A. Smith. Sounded male enough.

She kissed the envelope for good luck. Then kissed Cupid for whatever luck in love he might bring her way.

"Hey, Jake, get a load of this."

Jacob Larson looked up from the pile of riffraff cluttering his desk. With a bored yawn and a grimace, he accepted the submission his best editor was waving.

"Don't tell me, let me guess." After two years in this editorial hell, Jake figured it was an easy gimme to surmise, "It's another 'I Never Believed the Stories You Printed Until It Happened to Me' confession and he had sex while flying a Cessna."

"Nothing that predictable. Either this writer doesn't read our stuff or she's decided we need a new format."

A woman? That much was promising since they tended to focus more on emotions and sensations than graphic descriptions, which was what always gave them away even when they got creative with their names.

"You mean it's actually good?"

"Depends on what you call good." Charles pumped the air with a loose fist, and shook his head. "Not good for our average reader. But for someone like yourself, it's damn good. We couldn't print anything like this but I thought you'd enjoy reading something closer to home."

Though he appreciated the thought, Jake didn't need any reminders of his prestigious career biting the dust. Booted out of Publisher's Row, he'd ended up serving time in California, consigned to the literary prison of porn. Like the tabloids, prestige was zilch and fiscal return highly lucrative. Which was why he made good money for wading through trash day after day, but it was like a steady diet of the humble pie he'd refused to swallow in New York.

Taking a swig of his coffee to wash down the bad taste he got everytime he thought about the injustice of it all, Jake scanned the two pages, neatly typed. The coffee lodged in his throat.

He laid the pages on his desk, and tapped his pen against them while he let the effect sink in. Then he studied the words again. Savoring the refreshing flow, a slow, appreciative smile nudged out the grim set of his lips.

"Buy it. Cut the last paragraph and keep the rest as is," he instructed. "When you send her the check be sure to add a request for more of the same. Oh, and kick in an extra hundred for some incentive."

"*What?* Jake, our readers won't go for anything like this."

"Give 'em a taste of caviar and they just might realize sardines are as cheap as they smell. No way to tell unless we take the risk." He reluctantly pushed the pages away. "Let me know when Ms. V. A. Smith makes another submission. I hope she's got a drawerful of this stuff we can get our hands on."

Charles stared at him as if he'd lost his mind. And maybe he was a just little crazy making a decision on the basis of editorial integrity. It had cost him a job before and he could be out on his duff again. Integrity didn't rank too high with the *Fantasies* publisher; profits did.

"Maybe you should think about this, Jake. Something tells me Gino might have a problem with it."

"I'm sure he will. Which is why I want to slip this in without running it past him. Hell, he probably won't even notice. Gino's too busy schmoozing to read his own magazine. That's why he hired me—who hired you, remember?" He wasn't adverse to pulling rank when necessary. Jake deemed it necessary now. "As Executive Editor, I give the marching orders around here. Hup! Two, three, four. Get your ass out that door. Cut the check, send the letter, and don't sweat it. I'll assume full responsibility for any repercussions."

Charles swiped up the pages and shook his head. "Have it your way, boss. All I can say is you must like living on the edge."

Jake watched the door shut and indulged in a grin. Charles was right. He *would* have it his way, and that's how he liked it. Almost as much as he preferred living on the edge to putting out the same old crap. He did love the rush he got from taking a risk.

Of course, those qualities had landed him in this cracked leather seat. It was a dubious throne financial survival had dictated he mount. Just as the pen he currently wielded was a damn poor substitute for the scepter of power he'd been stripped of in New York.

The Wishy Washy Laundromat was busy for a Friday at six P.M., and Valerie resented the crowd. Not only had she waited for a dryer, the noise made it impossible to concentrate on the erotic short story she was struggling with.

The money she'd received two weeks ago had gone the way of rent. She had to come up with another submission before the landlord came knocking again. There were no guarantees *Fantasies* would buy it as quickly as the first, or buy it period, despite the request to send more. So far all she'd been able to come up with was an idea about a vampire. Named Victor. Victor the vampire. At first she'd thought it a clever bit of alliteration but it had begun to sound more and more stupid. Same for the story that in her head had seemed like a sexy fantasy until she'd tried to tell it.

The words were stumbling all over the page and she was tempted to ditch the whole mess, start from scratch on something else—only who knew what because she sure didn't—and give Victor another chance later. Maybe when she felt as inspired as the night she'd penned "Dreams." Had it not been for the

A Quiver of Sighs

copy she kept and the check from *Fantasies*, she'd lay odds that writing it had been only a dream. Whatever magic was at work that night had yet to make an encore. Unless she counted her . . . dreams.

Her dream lover, that was. Only it seemed he was a flirt who liked to tease her with the briefest of appearances just before she woke up. None of that mind-bending, soul burning, passionate ravishment stuff. Nope. Once was apparently enough for him. Not for her. If he didn't do more than whisper her name, steal her breath with a sexy smile, kiss her cheek and leave with the promise he'd see her soon, well, if he didn't make good on that promise and quick she would . . .

What? Proposition Cupid? Now there was an idea. If only he was better endowed and talked back—though there was something to be said for a man who could listen to a woman as well as her sweet little Cupid did.

She smiled at the thought of him and the dream lover—who'd better show up soon or she would throw herself at the feet of the first hunk she passed on the street. With a sigh, Valerie folded the last of her lingerie and heaped it on the laundry pile.

Jostling the wicker basket along with her purse and notebook, she headed home. On foot. As much time as she sat on her butt, walking was her preferred mode of transportation. But ten blocks with a laundry basket was really too much, and within five minutes Val could only wonder what she had been thinking? She should have driven. Then she wouldn't be peeking over the top of her underwear and hoping it didn't blow into the intersection.

Unable to see the curb, she stubbed her toe on the hump of concrete and down went the basket as well as her balance.

Hurtling to the sidewalk, her vision was a flurry of spilling laundry, a stop sign, and cars whizzing past. She was a second away from kissing the pavement when firm hands locked under her arms and swiftly lifted.

Olivia Rupprecht

"Caught ya."

"Thanks, I—" Had she hit the concrete after all, passed out, and was about to wake up since . . . that's when he always came to her? She must be dreaming. But what a wonderful dream it was, so real she could swear his hands had really moved to her waist and held her steady as her knees gave way.

His warm but incisive blue eyes, his sharp, angular features, so familiar, were better defined in the light of day, making her realize the soft focus of sleep hadn't done him justice. His complexion was darker than she'd realized, the color of amber, contrasting sharply with her own fair skin, lightly dusted with pale freckles. He was also a little older than she'd thought him to be.

It wasn't so much the actual age—he still struck her as in his mid-to late thirties—it was the maturity marking a face that suggested an excess of life. Too much packed into too little time.

A wisp of dark hair, a medley of deep brown and black with a sprinkling of silver threads, fell over his brow. It furrowed as he peered down at her, clearly concerned.

"Are you all right?" His voice was the same, only slightly deeper and with more of a clip to his words.

Val managed a faint, "I think so. I'm just . . . stunned." Her focus settled on the lips she knew as well as her own. They pulled into something close to a smile and she forced her attention to his gaze. It rocked her like a velvet blow.

"I'm sorry," she heard herself say, and could only hope more words would spring from wherever those had come from. "I don't mean to stare, but I've seen you somewhere before."

His scrutiny was intense, as was the persona he projected. He made his decision quickly with a shake of his head. "No. I would have remembered you. And I'm sure I won't be forgetting you any time soon."

His smile was as sexy as ever, but spiced with a

A Quiver of Sighs

sageness that might have passed for wickedness in more innocent days. He let go of her waist and bent to retrieve his briefcase. The outside pocket was stuffed with papers. Several white pages were scattered on the ground.

When she bent to pick them up, he caught her wrist. His touch set off a jolt too vivid to pass for a dream.

"I'll get it." He let go and glanced at his fingertips. "Just some work I'm taking home for the weekend." He stuffed the papers back without regard to their condition. His movements were brusque, agitated, and she scrambled for a ploy to extend their meeting.

"You must be from the East," she said, hoping against hope her observation would get him talking.

"Either you're psychic or the accent gave me away."

"The accent's faint. It's more the way you handled your briefcase. No nonsense and in a hurry to get it done." Those were the things she noticed most about people. Their movements, inconsistencies, or in this instance, the way he kept a brief silence before a decisive extension of his hand.

"I never could resist a woman who threw herself at my feet to meet me. Jake Larson. And you would be—"

Did he feel it too? A kinetic fusion at the instant of contact that raised the fine hair on her nape.

"Valerie Smith. My friends call me Val." Did she sound too eager, too quick-let's-be-friends? "In time," she added.

"Val, in time." He chuckled. "It's not every day I meet a Valintime." *Or feel like I just got zapped by one mother of an arrow*, Jake thought. Bull's-eye! Straight through the chest, past the drop of his stomach, and lodged in his groin. If there was such a thing as Cupid, the little bugger was a mean shot. Turned on by a handshake. He'd begun to wonder if a glut of smut could adversely af-

267

fect testosterone levels. It had been a long time since he'd felt a twinge and suddenly he had an aerobics meet going on in his pants.

Reluctantly letting go of the hand he had to thank for assuring him he was still very much a man, Jake insisted, "Let me help get your laundry picked up. No nonsense, just with my usual efficiency."

He got to it before she could argue. Not that Valerie was so inclined, since she was still reeling from the slide of his finger down the middle of her palm before he'd released her hand. The subtle gesture had been acutely sensual and far more provocative than any overt pass.

As Jake scooped up a runaway blouse, she threw in jeans on top of T-shirts and mismatched socks, hardly cognizant of what she was putting where. The laundry was heaped to overflowing when she spied a bit of lace Jake was picking up.

She lurched and grabbed her panties just as he snared the crotch. Nevermind that he'd had his face buried between her thighs in the dream, she could feel her cheeks go as crimson as the panties flapped between them on a breeze.

Claiming them with a tug, she pushed the most risque underwear she owned under a towel and confessed with a groan, "I have never been so embarrassed."

"Why? You've got good taste in lingerie and I should certainly know about—" He broke off and his lips thinned as he settled his briefcase on top of the basket. Lifting it, he asked, "Which way?"

"To the right." Even with his unweildy load, she had to quicken her steps to keep up with his long, brisk stride. The trek home she'd dreaded earlier was now much too short. Desperate to know more about him, actually everything, right down to his own brand of underwear, Valerie tried hard to keep her voice conversational.

"What kind of business are you in, Jake?" Given his suit, a smart, double-breasted pinstripe, she was

A Quiver of Sighs

certain he was a businessman of some sort.

"Let's just say I'm something of a broker who deals with public commodities and shuffles a lot of paper."

"An executive, then."

"Executive? Well . . . yes, executive goes with the position." Without offering more, he turned it back to her. "And just what do you do, Val? I know it's creative, something to do with the arts."

"What makes you think that?"

"I used to deal with a lot of creative people. They usually have this vague kind of quality about them, like they're there, and then their eyes get a little unfocused and you know they're suddenly somewhere else. That was the first look I saw on your face. So, are you an actress? L.A. has a few of those."

"I'll say. My sister's part of the drove. She's been here for five years and hasn't landed more than bit parts. But she keeps at it, and don't ask me why because I have no idea why I keep plugging for pennies either."

"Maybe because you believe in something that means more to you than money," he suggested.

"Obviously." Val stopped in front of their L.A. flat that would qualify for a step above ghetto status in Iowa. "We're here."

"No," he disagreed. "I'm here, you aren't. You're doing that vanishing act again. Thinking about a painting or a potter's wheel that's waiting for you to get rid of me?"

"Hardly." Laughing at that, she confessed, "I was plotting, asking myself, 'What if I told this man I so appreciated his help that I'd like to invite him in? Will he accept? Or will he politely decline and I'll pretend not to care while I watch him go and wonder if I'll ever see him again.' I usually ask myself what if this or that happens, but now I'm thinking what if it doesn't? Happen, that is."

Jake simply stared. Certain she'd lost him on the convoluted path of her thoughts and afraid he was considering whether she was some kind of flake, Val

269

took a deep breath and put it to him as straight as she could.

"I guess what I'm trying to say is I'd like to see you again and I hope you feel the same way."

He made a sound between a chuckle and a groan, and wrapped it around a long-suffering smile. "You're a writer."

Val nodded. Somehow she couldn't bring herself to say she was a writer. It's what she did ten hours a day and had put in enough man-hours on the page in her starry-eyed lifetime to earn a doctorate. But her meager sales didn't give the title much credibility, especially considering the latest source. If only she had a byline in *Omni* or *National Geographic*, just something she could be proud of, but she'd rather die than admit to being a *Fantasies* rag contributor.

"Had anything published yet?" he asked.

Val inwardly cringed. She detested that question. It was usually the first question asked when she admitted to her true calling, which was why she rarely admitted to it. There was nothing worse than feeling like an imposter and that's how she felt when the typical response was a dismissive "Oh" to the reply of, "Nothing worth mentioning."

"Anything's worth mentioning," Jake surprised her by saying. Equally surprising was the authority with which he asserted, "Even getting a poem published is an accomplishment. I don't care how obscure the journal. Competition is so fierce, even Grisham had a tough time breaking in. Did you know *A Time to Kill* was turned down by sixteen agents and a dozen publishers? Good thing John hung in there." Jake gave her a wink. "Good luck hanging in there, too."

"John," she repeated. "Don't tell me you actually know him."

"We met a while ago." Leaving it at that, Jake nodded at the door. "Now if you'll let me in, I'll not only park your basket inside, I'll park my buns long enough to find out what you've got perking on your desk. Then you can watch me go and wonder what to wear the next time you see me again."

His voice dropped to a murmur, and her dream lover revealed himself as a very earthy man, sure of his sensual finesse. "And in the meantime I'll be wondering whether or not you're wearing some of the prettiest red panties I've ever seen. Almost as pretty as your hair."

Val's throat went dry even as she felt a moistness gathering between her thighs. The whisper of fate tickled her ear with a single word: *Kismet*.

Chapter Three

They were still locked in a battle of wills when he pulled up to the curb facing Val's apartment the next night.

Jake cut the engine and leaned closer to the other side of the already close quarters of his Porsche convertible. Deciding his dogged insistence that he read her writing was sounding closer to a we're-on-a-deadline-cough-it-up dictate, he tried a more logical approach to get the goods he was after.

"C'mon, Val, be reasonable about this. You're too close to the story to be objective. There could be holes in the plot, lack of motivation, or the characters might need fleshing out. Any or all of those things could be right there and you wouldn't see it. That's why a fresh eye can be invaluable. Just let me have the manuscript for a few days and I'll give you my take on what you've got."

A Quiver of Sighs

"No." The shake of her head was even firmer than the one before. "Absolutely not, Jake. I'm too attached to the book, and for you to read it would make me feel more exposed than parading down Main Street naked. It's discouraging to have enough rejection slips to paper a wall, but at least I don't have to see an editor cringe, or even worse, laugh at my work. They're faceless strangers, you're not. I might feel less intimidated if you hadn't been an editor yourself at one time, but you were and that means you'll see all the flaws."

"It also means I'll be able to see the strengths you have to build on," he pointed out. When she didn't budge, he compromised the truth about his credentials a little more, hoping it would get him what he wanted: *His hands on an honest-to-God manuscript again.* "And you're making too big a deal out of my little stint in New York. Sure I've got some background in the business, enough to be helpful, but I haven't worked there in years."

Two years, five months, and four days to be exact, but he wasn't about to tell her that any sooner than discredit his actual abilities by owning up to being an executive—Executive Editor of a major player in the porn industry, pandering graphic sex for fiscal gain. He got a sweet salary but the price had been his pride.

The morning cash register rings up. It spits out the grand total. The price is always the same, sucking me into its black seamless O . . .

The words continued to haunt him, an echo of emptiness he couldn't get out of his head. They grew louder sitting here, filling himself with Val's face, so fresh and naive she still believed in her dreams. Had he ever been that young?

Little did she realize how much richer she was than he, living in this hole-in-the-wall on next to nothing with a pure passion for something she believed in. He lived in an upscale condo but it was devoid of passion, his ability to believe in something sullied.

The brutality of reality had taken its toll: He suffered from a bankruptcy of the soul.

He wanted, *needed* some of what Val had. She could give him at least a small portion. A book that came from the heart. He didn't give a damn if it was fatally flawed.

"I miss my old job sometimes, Val." Sometimes? *Constantly.* "I'd really enjoy the chance to see if I still remember how to work with a book. And a writer."

"Well . . ."

Was she weakening? Had his honest appeal hit a soft spot that logic and aggression had missed? Of course it had. She was a writer for Pete's sake! Man, he *had* been away too long. He'd forgotten how to work them.

"Did I mention I think the concept's intriguing? And the title's great!" Praise, they ate it up. Thrived on it like kids scarfing down candy. *"The Secrets That Bind Us.* Love it. It's dramatic but not over-the-top. Sounds commercial, too. Very important."

Even in the shadowed interior of the car he could see her eyes light up. Definitely on the right track. Good thing, since he wasn't leaving without those three hundred pages that could possibly use a new title. And the best way to seal the deal?

With the kiss he'd been aching for all night—and judging from Val's longing glances at his mouth and the coral-slicked lips she kept wetting, she was past ready for one, too.

"You can think about it while I walk you to the door," he said in a low, husky murmur that was intended to seduce her agreement to more than a kiss. A prelude, actually. By the time he got through with those delectable lips of hers she'd be amply senseless to agree to anything.

She reached for the handle and he caught her wrist. Stroking a thumb over the delicate underside, he could feel her slight tremble. Innocence. Such a heady aphrodisiac to jaded sensibilities, and few were more jaded than his.

"I'd rather you let me get the door. It's been one of

the more refreshing aspects of the night, being with a woman who's comfortable with her femininity and doesn't feel threatened by a simple courtesy from a man."

He brought her hand to his mouth. Flicked his tongue into the center of her palm. He could hear the catch of her breath as he teethed the fleshy mound, giving as a woman's breast. His gaze fixed on the quick rise and fall of the bosom he wanted to press his head against.

In a city filled with starlet hopefuls, Val truly stood apart. There was a lot more to her than Barbie doll proportions and he liked what he saw. Inside and out. She was *real*. As real as the ivory skin that hadn't seen a sunbed and the light-gold freckles she didn't try to hide.

Jake felt himself fully distend as he imagined his teeth gently clamping her nipple and tugging it a fraction beyond comfortable before releasing it with the same tiny bite he applied to her palm.

The bodice of her little black dress revealed two beading juts. Were they the same bright ruby shade of the panties he'd wondered all night if she was wearing? And were her aerolas the color of strawberries needing another week to ripen, just like her hair?

"I love your hair." He wanted to get his hands in it, bury his face, bind her wrists, wrap it around his neck, his waist, his shaft, just lose himself in the long, lustrous hair that was as unpretentious as Val.

"It's a mess." She combed a hand through the tangles. The car's top had been up when he arrived but Val preferred the rush of the wind over coiffed perfection. So different from the women of his past— no wonder she fascinated him.

"It's a gorgeous mess. When did you last cut it?"

"My freshman year at Iowa State. In other words, longer than I care to remember." She laughed self-consciously and twirled an end that fell just below a breast.

Jake wasn't sure what was the greater urge. To fill

his hand with that breast or tickle her nose with the end she was twirling. He really liked her nose. A little upturned, it suggested an impish nature. Once she let her hair down, that was. She was a little nervous. And very vulnerable.

Oh yes, Val was just what he needed to get some sense of his own humanity back.

"Stay put," he told his Valintime. Jake wasted no time in getting to the car's other side, even less in promptly pulling her to him.

He crooked a finger under her chin and lifted it in tandem with his own descent. But he didn't kiss her, not yet. The anticipation was too sweet, as was the quiver of her sigh.

"I thought you were going to walk me to the door."

"I'm in no hurry. Especially when there's too much light and I prefer my kisses in private. What about you?"

She nodded, but he wasn't satisfied. He wanted more. Something deeper, which got at the heart of what this impending kiss was really all about.

"Tell me, Val, what does kissing mean to you? Beyond the ritual thing everyone seems to do after a date."

"I never really thought about it before, but now that you ask . . ." Her gaze softened and she stared at him, yet into some distant realm he couldn't see. Again he wondered just where it was people like Val went to gather their thoughts and weave their creations. When they emerged, as she did now, he was always curious as to what they'd found.

"I think kisses are only as meaningful as the people involved," she decided. "Because when you get right down to it, kisses are about feelings. All kinds of feelings, good, bad, or indifferent. I mean, even if it's an unpleasant kiss, that says something about your feelings for the other person."

"And if it's exciting?" *This* was exciting, this peek into her head more arousing than the slip of a tongue.

"Then there's more going on than simply swapping

276

some spit. I don't particularly like that phrase, it's a little crude, but kisses that lack affection, respect, some honest emotion *are* crude. At least I think so. But I'm a woman—"

"So I noticed," he whispered en route to her neck. With the instincts of a homing pigeon, he found the soft nook where she'd dabbed a fragrance that suited her. Not too sweet, not too heavy. Fresh and subtle and sensual as the shiver that went through her and rippled hotly through him.

"And—and you're a man—"

"Oh yeah, you better believe it." *Feel it*, he silently bade her, fanning a palm at the small of her back and locking her against the evidence that he was not only a man, but a man she stirred in no small way.

"And men, well, they're different, and I'm not sure if they need all those things to make a kiss . . . good," she finished faintly as he brushed his lips once to hers.

"Hush," he told her, and went in search of more than swapped spit. He wanted a kiss and not just any kiss. He wanted *her*. Every emotion she possessed, every sexual impulse between her thighs, every libidinous thought in her head. Indeed, he was a man and the differences between them certainly weren't lost on him.

The hesitant glide of her fingers through his hair, his hungry fondle of hers. The little whimpers she made, rousing a deep groan, a primal need to take himself out, put himself in and . . . stay.

What was this? Jake vaguely wondered as she tilted her pelvis closer and delicately rubbed. Like a kitten softly sashaying around an ankle, seeking a scratch of its head, a stroke of its back, some sign of affection. And amazingly, that's what he felt. Affection. And more. More than the need to rut, to hump, to tear up the sheets until they were drenched with a mindless release.

Not that he didn't feel such an urge. He did. And gave silent thanks to Val for reviving those urges. She'd also given life to something he struggled to name. Alien as this radiant feeling in his chest; warm as the breath he sucked from her lips. Refreshing and tingly as the peppermint he culled from her mouth and then passed back.

Back and forth went the mint, guided by their tongues. In and out, a playful, intimate game. Play had become as foreign to him as intimacy. Perhaps that's why he was sorry when the mint had dissolved and by some silent, mutual agreement they ended their kiss.

The game was over. Jake couldn't say who had won. In truth, he couldn't say anything when she gave him a shy, kittenish grin, licked her lips as if the moisture he'd left was finer than cream, then straightened his tie.

So much for rendering her senseless to get his way. *He* was senseless, unable to do more than thrill to the sensation of her arm around his waist, his around her shoulder, and wonder if that mint had been laced with crystalized youth. He was thirteen again and just got kissed. First time, heart going like a tommy gun, whooping at the moon he could surely reach with the head-over-heels thrust of a cartwheel.

Wait. Head over heels? No. Not possible. He was too wise to the ways of the world, the wiles of women, to buy into a hearts-and-flowers dream. It was unrealistic, juvenile, a hopeless romantic notion he was too savvy to entertain.

So why did he feel as if the controls were being jerked from his grip, as if he were free-falling into a vast unknown?

"Now who's the creative type?" Valerie lightly teased. She snapped her fingers, a hypnotist bringing him out of a trance. "It's fun in there, isn't it?"

No, he thought, no it was not fun realizing that one kiss had sucked him in and down, and another kiss would surely render him over his head.

"I'll call," he said, more curtly than he intended, in an effort to regain some control over the situation.

Her look of surprise gave way to obvious dismay

at his cowardly male evasion. She'd expected better of him.

He expected better of himself. Yet that kiss had shaken him. Apparently far more than Val. She wasn't letting him off the hook that easily and she dangled the bait he couldn't resist.

"Is your offer still open to look over my book?" Her tone was brisk, leaving him to wonder about her decision. Was it a ploy to see him again despite his trite good-bye that had ruined an otherwise wondrous evening? Or was it because the kiss had been good-but-not-that-great for her and his opinion no longer had the capacity to hurt?

"It is," he assured her, while suddenly wishing for some assurances himself.

"Just a minute, then." She was gone and almost immediately back, hugging the thick stack of pages to her.

"Here. Take it. Quick, before I change my mind."

His eager grip rivaled her reluctance to let go.

"That's my dream you're holding, Jake. Please be gentle with it." There was such aching in her voice that he wanted to hold her, reassure her that he wouldn't spit on her dream.

She turned as he reached out a hand. Before he could say good-bye with another kiss to make up for the one he'd tarnished with two words, the door closed . . .

Leaving him with a load of regret, the disturbing magic of a kiss, and the knowledge that dreams were never free.

Chapter Four

"Bastard," Val muttered with another pound of her pillow. *How could he?* How could Jake kiss her like that then say "I'll call?" Male lingo for "Don't hold your breath, babe, 'cause I'm outta here."

If they hadn't had such a wonderful time . . . If the conversation had run dry instead of running nonstop . . . If the chemistry weren't there . . .

If, if, if. She'd been tossing and turning on a dozen ifs or more since throwing herself on the bed and wanting to weep for what felt like a betrayal. And it wasn't just Jake. She had betrayed her beloved book by using it to lure a man who could desecrate her dream.

He was capable of it, of that she was sure. There was a cutting edge in him that could draw blood. It was one of her curses wrapped in a blessing, her ability to sense people out, and in Jake she sensed a hardness of heart. And had he not proved an ability to turn cold? *I'll call.*

She flinched at the memory of his curt dismissal. She wanted her book back and her dream lover, too. He couldn't hurt her, reject her, or trash her work.

Neither could he leave her lips so tender she couldn't doubt the reality of a bone-melting kiss or a blatant erection lightly pressing between her thighs. And she'd wanted Jake there, damn him, wanted *him* so much that she'd met his subtle thrusts with an inviting rub. That wasn't like her, not like her at all. She'd never behaved so shamelessly on a first date, or even a third—but it hadn't felt like a first date.

"What does kissing mean to you? Beyond the ritual after a date?" It wasn't something she'd given conscious thought to until Jake wanted to know. And if he didn't care what her feelings were about kissing, then why would he ask? Besides which, kissing worked both ways and no way had she been the only one moved by that heart-pounding, earth-shaking kiss.

Val considered the kiss. Words could lie, kisses couldn't. She lay there until her thoughts about kisses and Jake's mixed messages propelled her out of bed.

Damn, she was confused. Writing always helped. No need for a shrink when she could psychoanalyze herself on a page. Grabbing up Cupid, she shot him a scathing glance.

"We're going to work," she informed him as she plunked him beside the typewriter. "If Jake Larson is your idea of some kind of dreamboat, think again. Thanks to him, I can't sleep. Therefore, neither will you. Now, let's hope you're better at inspiring the muse to strike than you are in picking out a man. I'm very disappointed with you at the moment so feel free to suck up with something I can sell."

Val rolled in a piece of paper and her eyes drifted past Cupid, looked within that place Jake had led her to. Where kisses were more than just that and their meanings worthy of consideration. . . .

The Kiss

Consider the kiss. What an odd, intriguing, and absurd concept, this pressing of lobes, this mating of faces.

Who decided it was to be the mouth, rather than the eyes or the ears or even fingertips for that matter? And who extended the landscape to include teeth and tongues, limited only by what the imagination can conceive?

Ah, the kiss. Obscene and brutal? Or magnificent, erotic? A tribute? An insult? Whatever the form, it does span mouths and hearts and time.

There are too many kinds to count, this mirror of emotion, purveyor of desire:

The Judas kiss, low as a snake and deadly as sin. The obligatory kiss to Aunt Mabel, whose breath is stale with age and cigarettes smoked to the butt. The perfunctory peck upon the cheek, a greeting here, perhaps sincere but perhaps not. A parent's worried lips to the child's fevered brow. And what of the kiss of comfort, the one that absorbs even a little grief while a loved one sleeps in a silk-lined box? Kisses sweet, brief, given without thought or considered at length. An apology even, when the words are too hard to say.

The lover's kiss: prelude to passion each mortal strives to perfect with varying degress of success. Mustn't be too sloppy or too dry; the timing is crucial, too; when to begin as important as knowing the moment it is meant to be over.

Is it tentative or hungry? Is it reciprocated, or rejected with the turn of a cheek, mauling the ego more deftly than any two-fisted blow? The cheek will not do, not when lips are destined to meet and seek a fit as intimate as hip to hip.

He traces her lips with the tip of his tongue, fitting it neatly at the top should she possess a small, sexy groove. Dip. Taste of the tender, fleshy lobes, around, under, and finally between. She takes his tongue into the dark, moist chamber of her mouth. Textures there, be it raw silk or rough as a kitten's tiny bumps coated with cream.

Does he hear her accelerated breathing; is his ragged, harsh, a little raw? Their breaths mingle, exchanging flavors of mint, longing, the boozy whisper of whiskey and wine.

Her teeth close, claiming his tongue. She bites, just a tiny pressure, letting him know she finds this part of his mouth much to her liking. A groan. A sigh.

They reverse their exploration.

And then their eyes peek open, affirming this curious rapture is mutual and unfeigned.

Now the deepening of it, the slanting of lips, the tongue thrusts, the increasing wetness and carnivorous nibbles as they devour each other . . .

It is delicious. Absolutely divine.

Skimming down to her chin, he sips at the delicate jut. Unwilling to relinquish and yet feeling the natural course playing to the end, he sucks her smooth flesh in the final moments.

Their eyes open and meet and no words are needed. If it is good, it is the best part of heaven; if not, they part knowing the kiss was fatal and this is good-bye.

Consider the kiss. A concept worthy of thought, though one better pondered with nimble lips rather than words.

Jake put aside the pages and barked an order at Charles.

"Get me Ms. Smith's return address. Take your time, say, fifteen minutes. I need to think."

"That's good news. I've kept my mouth shut, just like you 'asked' but production's talking. Do us both a favor? Decide a rejection letter's in order. Her writing's good, better than buh-tah. But we know which side our bread's buttered on and eating words doesn't buy dinner or cut the check to pay the tab. Hope you'll think about that, too."

Olivia Rupprecht

Charles left, and Jake returned his attention to the pages he didn't have to think twice about accepting or rejecting. The only thing he wasn't completely sure of was the author's true identity, though that had nothing to do with the decision he'd already made. "The Kiss" did not belong in *Fantasies*.

Which was precisely why he was putting it in. He'd compromised his ethics until he could hardly look at himself in the mirror. Printing an erotic essay was a small redemption and one he needed as surely as he needed Val.

And while she might be better off without him, her book was in dire need of his direction. It wasn't the writing itself—her talent was obvious from page one. He'd known that, of course, before offering his services, since he would never put himself in the position of telling a woman he had a thing for to get a real job and bury the dog. Only a fool would do such a thing and he was no fool.

He had, in fact, been rather sly. Val wouldn't let him touch her precious stack of pages, even after he'd carried her laundry. Therefore, he simply arrived early Saturday night—had it only been five days ago? Forever seemed closer to the count—and while Val had finished getting ready, he'd taken the liberty of scanning the first chapter.

He'd seen enough to know she had potential. And now that he'd read the entirety of what she had, he had a revision letter in the works. Three single spaced pages so far, another two and she'd have the tools to turn that puppy around. Man, was he having fun! He was also more homesick than ever for where he really belonged. In New York. Buying books like . . . Val's could be. After some work. A lot of work.

In its present state she would have no takers. Editors were spread too thin to skim something like this off the slush pile and funnel their too-limited time into such an amorphous piece of . . . a dream.

The book lacked focus and had holes in the plot big enough to put his fist through. But Val had that special something that couldn't be bought, couldn't be taught: magic. The storyteller's gift.

A Quiver of Sighs

She could reach out of a page and grab the reader. Unfortunately, she kept losing her grip with a lack of dialogue and a propensity for prose.

Prose that sounded suspiciously familiar to the voice in "Dreams," and now, "The Kiss." And the familiarity extended beyond the narrative tone.

Jake drew a finger under the lines that jumped out at him. Yes, he did remember tracing her lips with the tip of his tongue then fitting it into her neat little groove, sexy and how.

As for exchanging flavors from their mouths, it just so happened that he'd had Jack Daniels, she'd had white zin, otherwise known as whiskey and wine. And let him not forget the mint! *As if he could possibly forget it.*

He skipped over the groans and sighs, too generic to qualify for evidence. But the chin sucking, *umm-umm*, the chin sucking, now there was a clue—especially since "in the final moments" coincided with his own timing.

No words had been needed. It had been the best part of heaven—until he'd screwed up with such a fatal sounding good-bye. Jake scowled and returned to his favorite part.

A fit as intimates as hip to hip.

Was that how Val thought of their tongue play, imagining him inside her? Women's libidos. Fascinating. And frustrating because they made it damn near impossible to get inside their heads, where a man could stroke more than their soft thighs.

He was hard. He felt like a voyeur looking in on the bedroom of Valerie's mind. Would she admit to such thoughts? He deemed it about as likely as her proudly telling him about her second sale to *Fantasies*, given that the first was considered "nothing worth mentioning."

Jake buzzed his secretary. "Tell Charles to forget the address. And please see that I'm not interrupted for the next hour."

No, he didn't need Ms. V. A. Smith's address to bet his retirement fund on the odds that Val had a chain

285

smoking, old Aunt Mabel with bad breath and to
whom only duty could force a kiss.

Disdaining the work he'd come to well and truly
despise, Jake finished what remained of the revision
letter, smiling all the while. Then it was over too
soon, and with a heavy sigh he started to print out
the work he coveted. A spark of mischief gave him
pause. Long time since he'd felt mischief at play.

It felt almost as good as the title he'd reclaimed of
Deputy Publisher. Then just to make sure she
thought it a joke, he substituted the name of his ex-
employer with:

Valintime Publishing.

Chapter Five

"I'll call," Val sullenly mimicked. Here it was Thursday, and she was still listening to the phone not ringing.

With a vicious rip of yet another lousy page, she decided Victor the Vampire had nothing on Jake the Jerk. And that said plenty considering she was fed up with Victor. Despite her pleas and cajoling, he didn't care she desperately needed more than a campy Dracula knock-off to make a sell, especially if "The Kiss" cashed out with a rejection from *Fantasies*.

Too soon to tell but she didn't have the luxury of waiting for a response and *damn* why didn't the phone ring?

It was all Jake's fault she couldn't work. His fault she could hardly sleep for thinking about him, replaying their date over and over in her head. Everything had been great and then *boom*, something went wrong. After he'd kissed her. But *what* could she have said or done to give him cold feet?

"The horse is dead, Val," she told herself for the umpteenth time, "So quit beating it and get to work."

Giving up on Victor, she tried to concentrate on the book she never should have let Jake have. It was agony, pure agony, wondering if he'd read it yet, if he hadn't called because he hated it or—

No. She was *not* going to torture herself like this. Five straight days on the rack was enough, and if Jake was into mind games then he could find someone else to play with. She was getting her manuscript back. Not that she needed the extra copy, but the principle of it demanded she do so.

Besides, she'd have an excuse to call him. That's right, he'd find out she wasn't one of those mousy little wimpettes who'd let a man kiss her, dump her for no reason—*no reason at all!*—and act as if her work was of such little worth he could keep it for all she cared.

Well, by golly, she did care and her characters were a lot more dependable than Jake the Snake had proved to be. No wonder she'd rather spend time with her invisible friends than "real" people who turned out to be phonies.

The phone beckoned. She was madder than hell and glad of it since anger fueled her nerve to dial—

Rats! His home number. He'd told her where he lived and the phone book had confirmed that his honesty extended to a non-bogus address and an active listing. Just to make sure, she'd called yesterday when he was bound to be at work.

Which was probably where he was now, doing whatever executives did at 3:30 in the afternoon on a Thursday. Five days, five *lousy* days since the little weasel said he'd call! Oh yes, outrage felt much better than the hurt and self-pity she'd been wallowing in for the *five horrible days* he deserved to get shot for. Now she just had to hold on to that thought for another three hours instead of making stupid female excuses for him and chickening out before he got home.

In the meantime, she wasn't getting a thing done and her thighs could use some exercise. Destination? A strange little shop named Kismet might add some intrigue to a totally wasted day and, who knew, maybe that strange old man would have some weird cosmic message about the cost of dreams.

"They sure ain't free, Cupid." With a weary sigh she picked up the figurine. "And this pay-as-you-go plan is turning out to be a real bitch. Why *can't* dreams be free, huh? It's not so much to ask, is it, just to have one teensy-weensy dream be a freebie? You know, like getting a simple little phone call from Jake where he ends up apologizing and wants to see me again and by the way, he's read my stuff and thinks it's great."

Dream on, she thought. At the shrill ring of the phone, she jumped.

Cupid still in hand, Val raced across the floor, telling herself all the while *it's probably a soliciter or Sarah or her latest boyfriend or Mother, so why are you running? It's not Jake and if it is, then you shouldn't even bother picking it up, much less try to catch your breath so you can say—*

"Hello?" *Oh puh-leese, did you have to blow out the word like you're in the phone sex biz and answer with a kiss?*

"Val, is that you?"

Though her head was suddenly so light she didn't feel like herself at all, she said, "Yes." Then added, "Who's calling, please?" as if she didn't know.

"It's me, Jake. Look, I'm really sorry about taking so long to get in touch. I would have called sooner but didn't want to take the chance you'd say 'Gimme that back' before I was through reading. Finished it up last night, late, so anyway that's why I waited till today. I, um . . . well, I hope you didn't get the idea I was avoiding you."

"Of course not," she lied, before lying some more. "I didn't think anything of it."

"Good." He sounded relieved. "But I do hope you thought about me, at least a little. Did you?"

Bruised pride demanded and justified the biggest whopper she'd ever told. "A little."

"Makes two of us, then. Only you've been on my mind a lot. I had a wonderful time Saturday night, Val. And as for that kiss . . ."

He paused and she could hear the ruffle of pages. *Her manuscript?* He'd read her manuscript, all of it, without getting so bored he put it down! Only he hadn't said anything about it yet and she was dying by inches to know what he thought of her cherished characters, the plot she'd worked and reworked for months, all the words she'd sweated bullets over trying to get just right.

She gripped the phone tighter so it wouldn't slip from her grip. The suspense was torture and Jake's voice, lowering like the dip of a woman to the floor, murder on the cool she struggled to keep.

"Remember me asking what kisses meant to you? I wish I'd asked again, after the fact. It's something I keep wondering about, how you felt about our kiss. Were you disappointed, was it just okay? Or was it good for you, so good you want more? Tell me."

"It was . . ." The moisture in her mouth, her throat, suddenly migrated to her palms, the liquid pulse between her legs. Two words, surely she could manage two words. "Good." Followed by, "You?"

"It was . . ." Jake's pause was different from her own. While she battled a case of hormonal apoplexy, he seemed perfectly calm. Maybe it was his seductive chuckle or the faint sifting of pages, coinciding with an easy, "What the hell, I'll tell ya the truth. Val, it was . . . *heaven.*"

Heaven, ohmygod, he thought their kiss was heaven! For a moment she was too stunned to do more than stare dumbly at Cupid. Had he cast some kind of spell?

If so, the spell wasn't holding. It wavered on the cusp of a dream.

Her dream. The book Jake hadn't said squat about.

A Quiver of Sighs

Their kiss was obviously of more interest to him, which raised the suspicion he was killing time *before* he dissed her book.

Because if he dissed her book first the only kiss she'd want to give him was a smack in the choppers.

Dreading to ask, hating how bare she laid herself, Val forced the question. "What did you think of the book?"

In the pause it took him to weigh his words, she blurted, "You hated it, didn't you?" She was humiliating herself, she knew it, but the words kept rushing out. "I knew I shouldn't have let you have it. Look, just send it back through the mail and I'll get over it eventually and after I do then maybe we can go out again—"

"Tonight."

The single word cut through her rambling, and Val wondered if her distress was to blame for what sounded like a command appearance, not a date.

"Look, Val, if you have other plans, we can reschedule, but I'm free tonight if you are. I've made a few notes I'd like you to look over before we discuss this."

"You made notes?" He was actually taking an interest. Which had to mean he didn't hate it. "That was very thoughtful of you, Jake."

"Just doing my job." Another chuckle, though it wasn't exactly seductive. More like he'd made a joke and she hadn't gotten the punch line. A noise in the background brought a quick end to his humor and he said brusquely, "When do you want to meet?" I'll come by.

"Tonight's fine. Say, around seven?"

"I'll be working late, so let's make it eight."

"Eight o'clock. It's a date."

Jake's low, confidential pitch let her know someone was in his office and he wasn't comfortable being overheard.

"I'd like to make one for this weekend, but not tonight. This isn't a date. That's something we'll need

Olivia Rupprecht

to talk about, how to separate business from pleasure."

"Business?" she repeated. Jake made this sound serious. And thrilling as it was for someone to take her work seriously, she wasn't so sure about putting business before pleasure with Jake.

Especially if he was as bossy as he came across with a decisive, "We'll talk later."

And then he proceeded to eradicate every uncertainty she had about Jake Larson with an equally decisive, "By the way, the book's good. But you can make it even better. Val, you have a great gift."

Chapter Six

Maybe it wasn't a date but that didn't keep Jake from nearly getting into an accident so he could get home in time to shower, shave, throw on his best California casual attire, and slap some cologne on the neck Val would surely want to hug.

Actually, he deserved a lot more than a hug for all the hours he'd spent reading, editing, and putting together one hell of a revision letter. But he wouldn't push for more than the hug—and however many kisses she'd want to cover his face with—since this was, after all, a business meeting. Personal feelings had to be put aside. Affections and egos couldn't get in the way of turning out the best book possible.

Lucky for Val, he hadn't been able to put all his affections aside. He could have torn her work to shreds. His letter, however, was tactful and encouraging, yet honest.

Jake was honest with himself as he knocked on her door, briefcase in hand. Applying his skills to a manuscript he wouldn't have spent five minutes on a few years ago had given his ego a much needed boost. He still had the touch. And the best revision letter he'd ever written to prove it.

The door swung open. Just as quickly, work, his letter, the rules they needed to set no longer existed. There was only an urgency, strong and primal, to fill his hands with her hair and ravish her mouth to his content.

"Jake, come in!" Her gaze went to his briefcase while his attention remained on her lips. They were moving again, saying, "Please excuse the mess. After you called I was so jazzed I got back to work and whipped out more pages than I've done all week. When I looked up, I realized you were due in half an hour and it was either make the place look decent or do an overhaul on myself. Wash my hair, put on some makeup and—and . . ."

Her tongue flicked over lips already slicked a moist peach, begging him to sink his teeth into the fleshy bottom lobe, swirl his tongue inside and sample the finest nectar any connoisseur ever tasted.

"Why are you looking at me that way, Jake?"

"What way?" He booted the door shut, dropped his briefcase, and stroked the arms she chafed. "Like you're the best thing I've seen in five days and you're even more delicious than I remember? Like the first order of business is kissing you until that lipstick's so smeared you look as indecent as you make me feel?"

Her eyes were saucer wide. Jake shook his head, hardly believing what he'd said. What had come over him? So much for the calculated tactics of a man who knew the art of seduction to be a game of innuendo, suspense, and the patience to wait a woman out until she played into his hands. Those hands had always kept a firm hold on the reins, inevitably tossed aside once he tired of the game.

With no more than a vivid blush, Val had yanked

the reins from his grip. She was out of her element and suddenly so was he. Jake had no idea where they were but it had to be the big leagues. Emotional terra incognita. Scary. Especially when she pressed a kiss to his cheek and it felt like the lash of a velvet whip bringing him to his knees in supplication for a dozen lashes more.

"My lipstick's smeared," she whispered. A lightly teasing whisper, like that of a new playmate suggesting a game they might both enjoy. "At least it's smeared on you. Right . . . here." Her thumb stroked the remains she'd left and Jake endured the burning intensity of a branding iron leaving an indelible mark on his skin.

He turned his lips into her palm and watched her eyes narrow to dreamy slits, watched her head fall back in provocative invitation. "Do I look indecent yet?"

"Inviting? Yes. Indecent?" He framed her jaw with the span of one hand while the other hovered over her breast. Not touching, and there was the beauty of it, to feel the leap of her heart, the warmth of her skin, even the thrum of her blood suffuse the air between them. "No. You're pure."

"Then why don't you do something about it? Make me feel indecent, Jake."

Make me feel pure, he silently entreated with an openmouthed kiss. No flirting, no preliminaries, this kiss was about hunger, need, and . . . anger, that she could do this to him.

Demanding penance, he took her mouth with the aplomb of a thief ransacking a church, unlocked, bidding all who entered to find some comfort within its hallowed walls. He pillaged at will. But then came a knock at the chamber door.

That knock was his heart. To linger would be to risk discovery. The time to escape was now.

He told himself to stop this kiss and take the spoils with him. He told himself not to be greedy, but her little moans were like silent pleas to be fondled and so he cupped her breast, gently squeezed.

She pressed deeper into his hand. He departed with a slow draw, a tiny pinch of a distended nipple.

"Jake . . . *Jake*."

"I love the way you say my name." Even more, he loved the way she clasped his hand, kissed it. Head bowed, her hair fell like a bright cooper cape he could get lost in. Hell, he must be lost already. Why else would he hear himself confess, "I feel too comfortable with you and that's something I'm not too comfortable with."

"Why not?" She nuzzled against his chest and imparted even more of the connection he craved.

"It's unfamiliar. I find it easier to keep a distance than to get too close. As for why, who knows? My family wasn't ever what you'd call demonstrative but so what? Sure I got my heart broken a couple of times but nothing too traumatic. I like my autonomy, Val. Guess it's just the way I'm wired. So you can imagine I'm having trouble coming to terms with meeting a special someone who's easy to be close to, talk to, and I find myself wanting things I never really wanted much before. Like a hug, holding hands."

She touched his lips; her own curved into a smile so sublime it dazzled his eyes and did very strange things to his insides as it cut a path straight to his toes. Tingling toes—whoa, boy—trouble with a capital T. He wasn't ready for this.

"So you're a tough guy, huh?" She knuckled his jaw, causing it to clench. "So tough you don't need hugs or your hand held like the rest of us do. That's baloney, Jake. We're all wired a little differently but you're a human, not a machine. You need your space? Well, guess what, I covet my solitude. Though lately I'd rather be with you so it's a real relief to know you feel the same way. Anyway, what I'm trying to say is . . ."

Her voice trailed off and Val could only wonder what she'd said or done now to provoke such a look. Amazement. Dismay. A scrutiny so intense it gave her the urge to squirm.

"Well, you get the idea." Val could only hope so

since she had no idea what she'd intended to say. "You know, writers write because they can't talk half as well, at least that's the case with me. Actually, I don't have this much trouble usually but you seem to do something to my wiring. It's like my mental circuits get scrambled when I look at you and all it takes is a touch and *zzzzt* I'm blowing a fuse."

She laughed nervously but Jake didn't join her.

He said nothing beyond a prolonged gaze, perplexing in its wariness and yearning. He appeared torn between eating her alive and racing for the door.

Jake abruptly reached for his briefcase. "We'd better get to work."

She grabbed his arm. "Why? Is it because you're more comfortable working than getting personal with me?"

He stared at the fingers biting into his biceps. Slowly his gaze lifted. What she saw was so starkly sexual and emotionally incisive it hit her like a slap.

Val jerked back her hand.

"You want to get personal with me?" Jake's low chuckle mocked her swift retreat. "Then you've got more courage than good sense. I understand lust, Val, and I'm relieved to understand that much about what's happening here. I feel like I'm twisting in some very strange winds, so the familiar looks really safe at the moment, never more enticing."

Jake glanced down and she followed the path of his attention. Her throat went dry. A sharp pang of answering arousal felt like a finger put to her cleft, slid inside her, then reaching up until she jerked from the clutch, the shiver of her womb.

Realizing her glance had lengthened to an out-and-out ogle, Val could only hope Jake hadn't noticed.

The lift of a dark brow, accompanied by a knowing half-smile, assured her otherwise. Half-smile turning to a fully wicked grin, he reached into his pocket and withdrew a coin.

"Heads, we get to work. Tails, we get personal." He flipped it into the air and the silver turned end-over-end in tandem with her stomach. Jake slapped the coin onto his wrist. He kept it covered and her anxiety mounted.

Heads, she silently pleaded, *please let it be heads because Jake's turning out to be a lot more than I bargained for and if it's more than kisses he's got in mind, I'm not ready for this!*

He lifted his fingers ever so slightly, just so he could see. A darkly sensual twist of his lips made him seem even more imposing, more worldly and out of her league. He was James Dean on a tear and she was Peggy Sue primping for a prom. He knew his way around the bedroom; she'd gotten around, too—if fumbles and gropes and some heavy petting in the backseat of a car counted.

As the seconds ticked past, Val wondered whatever had possessed her to open this Pandora's box. Jake Larson wasn't a man to toy with and she silently willed him to say—

"Get to work."

Chapter Seven

He exposed the coin and heads it was.

Instead of relief, Val felt a surprising surge of disappointment. Not only in the outcome but in herself. She'd wanted to crawl into her cocoon of safety rather than risk a taste of unbridled passion.

Sarah was right. Pretend heroes were a poor substitute for the real thing. Only Jake was a far cry from a fairy-tale hero, a self-admitted sexual creature who didn't know much about love. But he did have feelings for her. And she did long to find her guts and do more than lust in her heart for him. The problem was, she wanted to have it all but that didn't mean Jake had it to give.

"Catch!"

Val caught the coin. She turned the silver from side to side and her heart gave a little leap of hope. He didn't love her and maybe he never would, but

Jake Larson had just assured her that his feelings definitely went beyond lust.

"What's this? Your lucky quarter?"

"Can't lose when it's heads both sides." His voice dropped as if he were sharing a secret. "I won it in seventh grade for a consolation prize at a talent show."

"What was your talent?"

"Piano. Chopin. The teachers loved it, but the students? Suffice it to say I couldn't keep pace with a bad rendition of 'Stairway to Heaven' by a wannabe Zeppelin band."

"You should have won."

Jake shrugged. "That's life." He curled her fingers over his prize and she felt a tingling thrill.

Her own seventh-grade year had been spent hiding behind a book, ugly glasses and baby fat placing her in the ranks of social misfits; high school hadn't been much better. Jake's gift bore the significance of the class ring she'd never received with a tenderly spoken, "It's special to me and so are you. I want you to have it."

"Are you sure? You might miss it."

"I don't think so." He brushed a kiss to her knuckles, then patted his briefcase. "Something tells me you're a good-luck charm that'll put that one to shame."

Val stared after him, too amazed to move. Until Jake snapped his fingers at the kitchen doorway.

"Hop to, sunshine! You might have time to spare but I'm not getting any younger."

Val wasn't sure how she got there since her feet still hadn't hit ground when she plopped into the kitchen chair Jake held out—like a date displaying his best manners to impress the girl of his dreams.

Yes, it must be a dream she was truly living at last. The kitchen table was a pumpkin transformed into a coach. And the piles of paper seemed like so many snowflakes beneath the bridge of meeting hands.

Fingertips grazing fingertips, then lingering on a thin vista of white, Jake murmured, "I'd like to say this is entirely business but it's not. From me to you, a letter from the heart."

Her own heart turned over. A love letter? She'd never gotten a love letter before, much less from a seductively dark prince like Jake. Was she falling in love? Impossible. Their relationship was too new. But if love took a heavier toll on her senses than this, she'd surely be courting a coma.

"Go on. Read it."

The first paragraph revealed a love letter beyond her wildest dreams. Praise for her book, her talent and skills, the belief she was destined for a stunning career.

In that moment she felt rapture. Jake was saying everything she'd ever dreamed of hearing. Eager for more, she raced onto the next paragraph.

And stopped at the first word: But.

One shoe dropped, and she braced herself for the next to fall. Val skimmed the first page. She shut her eyes and prayed the remaining pages wouldn't empty out the equivalent of Imelda Marcos's closet.

By the end of the second page her heart had bottomed out. Her palms were slick with sweat. Her hands trembled so hard she could hardly turn the paper.

She got through the third page and wondered if she could endure any more of these horrible, horrible words leaping out at her:

Slow pacing, rev it up . . . plot, too contrived, try this twist . . . nice characters, too nice, give them some flaws, bad judgement, more dimension, get the reader into their skin . . . lack of conflict and dialogue, see notes on manuscript . . .

And on and on and on. *Slap. Slap. Slap.*

Eyes smarting, stomach queasy, Val could hardly make out the last paragraph. The gist of it seemed to be some kind of pep talk about revision being an art in itself and she had the stuff to pull it off with professional aplomb.

Her head felt attached to rusted hinges on her neck, rebelling against the jerky little movements required to face Jake. He was smiling benevolently. It was too absurd. How could he smile like that after mutilating her work?

She wanted to lunge at him, scratch his eyes out, scream "GET OUT" at the top of her lungs.

Val rose and whispered, "I think you should go."

"Go?" he repeated. "We just got started."

"We just finished." Unable to bear the sight of him or his traitorous letter, she marched into the living room and opened the door.

"Okay," he said uncertainly. "If you need some time to think all this through, we can pick it up later. Maybe over dinner Saturday night?"

Though "fat chance" seemed the politest reply she was capable of, a part of her realized she might regret such rashness. Better to take what mean pleasure she could by curtly informing him, "I'll call."

The door shut in his face. Not exactly a slam but loud enough for Jake to know he'd somehow pissed Valerie off.

Just in case she had a change of heart, he waited beneath a tree on the small plot of grass fronting her apartment. Twirling an errant dandelion, Jake blew it like so many dreams in the wind while struggling to figure it all out.

What a night. Nothing had gone as he'd planned and Val's reaction to his letter wasn't even half of it. Never in his New York minute life had he expected to kiss a woman, look into her eyes and suddenly *know*.

It had hit him out of left field and maybe if he'd gotten such a slug before he would have been prepared.

Jake rubbed his temples, trying to relieve the pressure. It didn't help. The tree looked awfully tempting. Maybe if he banged his head against it until he passed out, he'd wake up sane again.

He had to be losing his mind. Actually sitting here, crushed because Val didn't appear and belatedly thank him for the letter he'd labored over. Not so much as a glimmer of appreciation. Instead, she'd

A Quiver of Sighs

seemed so upset he almost apologized, which was crazy because if anyone deserved an apology it was him!

That's right, he had feelings, too. He just couldn't afford to get temperamental the way some writers did. Val didn't know how lucky she was to get his input but he'd sure like to tell her just who she was dealing with.

Deciding to go lick his wounds elsewhere, Jake got to his feet. Took a step and stopped cold.

A primal scream from Val's apartment raised the hair on his nape. Cringing, he looked this way then that.

There was no intruder, of course. Only himself.

He was the intruder, confronting her with the often brutal realities of publishing. Despite his best efforts to be kind, she was shaken.

But surely no more shaken than he.

Jake Larson was in love for the first time in his life. And he didn't need to pick any flower petals to know whether "she loves me, loves me not" when he heard Val yell at the wall between them, "Damn you, you bastard!"

Chapter Eight

Val stared morosely at the phone. What a crummy way to spend a Saturday, cleaning the toilet and baking cookies she had no appetite for, just to put off the inevitable.

She had to call him. Swallow her pride and apologize. If Jake didn't want to see her again, she had no one but herself to blame. The terrible truth was, Jake hadn't been cruel. He'd been honest. And how did she repay the time he'd spent, hours and hours surely, the unerring advice he'd offered?

A door in his face.

Steeling herself for the worst—that Jake would cut her off and disappear from her life, taking the heart he'd stolen along with him—she pressed Cupid to the dull thump of dread in her chest. And called.

He picked up on the first ring.

Without so much as a return greeting, she rushed

out, "I'm sorry, Jake, really sorry about the other night. I was rude and immature and the only excuse I have is that I was upset by all the things you were saying in your letter and I just didn't want to believe it was true, so I showed it to my sister so she'd be mad at you too, but she agreed with you instead. So then I was mad at both of you and I really wanted to stay that way but I ended up being mad at myself for being such a twit, such an awful writer, for—"

"Val, enough. You're a very good writer and I got a little carried away playing editor, so put the whole thing out of your mind and think about a kiss to make up, instead."

Almost giddy with relief, she asked in amazement, "You mean you're not mad at me, that you want to see me again?"

"Are you kidding? I've babysat this phone all day, hoping my Valintime would call. I've missed the hell out of you. And I've been kicking myself for letting this come between us. Much as I'd enjoy the chance to work together, it's not worth messing things up with you."

"But they won't get messed up again," she promised. "I really need your help, Jake."

A pause pulsed between them before he filled it with a quiet passion, a frank demand. "Need me for more than my help. Need my company. My kisses. Need *me*."

Val squeezed Cupid in gratitude for whatever role he'd played in bringing this marvelous man her way. An intensely arousing man who groaned softly when she confessed, "I do."

"How soon can you be ready?"

She looked like hell. Her eyes were puffy from crying and her hair could have been a mop it was so ratty and stiff from a runny nose and salty tears.

"I need a few hours to get myself together, Jake."

"Make it two. Which is two hours too many for me."

My, but he was impatient! Val liked that, she liked it a lot. He was aggressive, decisive, and *he wanted her.* It was incredibly heady, being wanted by such a worldly man, and the temptress in her—there was actually a temptress in her!—couldn't resist making him wait.

"Two and a half, and not a minute sooner, Jake."

"That sounds like a challenge." He laughed quietly, seductively, and with a hint of amusement. The sound was a challenge in itself to go ahead, take him on, make his day. "So tell me, what's going to happen if I don't obey?"

"Then I won't wear my red panties tonight."

"In that case, I'm already gone."

Realizing her blunder, she gasped, "No, Jake! That's not what I meant! I meant I'd wear something *besides* my red panties. Like white briefs or, or—"

Jake burst out laughing. "Okay, you win. I wouldn't dream of showing up early and have to spend my time with a woman who's got on ugly underwear."

"You think I'm naive, don't you?" She made it sound like a flaw, a personal embarrassment.

"I think you're priceless." Gone was his mirth, he'd never been more serious in his life. "You're like a buttercup springing up from a wasteland of weeds." It had to be the sappiest thing he'd ever said. Nonetheless, it was true.

"Oh, Jake," Val sighed. "That's the most romantic thing anyone's ever said to me."

Buttercups. He had to find some before their date to prove just how romantic he could get. Showing up in a limo wasn't a bad idea, either; they could get cozy in the backseat. From there he'd sweep her off her feet with candles and champagne and playing footsie under a table draped in white linen. Winding up the night would be a grand finale beyond her wildest dreams: strolling violinists serenading them to her door. They'd dance and kiss and then he'd spring the biggest surprise of all. Rather than try to get her into bed, he'd do the tango for Val. With a rose between his teeth.

Mr. Romance, move over!

A Quiver of Sighs

He had to hustle. "See you soon, sunshine. Wear your best dress and get ready to do the town in style. Bye."

"Jake, wait!"

"Yes?" He tapped his foot, ready to go.

"I hope you don't mind but if it's all the same to you I'd rather have some time alone instead of pretending we're alone in a crowd. I'm not a super great cook or anything but I'd really like to cook you dinner."

"You would?" There went his grand plan. But he could put it on hold, especially when he liked Val's idea even better. The image of Val cooking him dinner and then the two of them doing dishes together further softened the once hard knot in his chest that hadn't quit pounding since the day they'd met.

"You've carried my laundry, Jake, taken me out for a night on the town already, and slaved over my manuscript without a single word of thanks for it. I want to show my appreciation by doing something for you this time."

"What are you cooking?"

"What do you want?"

He bit his tongue to keep from saying "You. On a table, on the floor, on the couch—even better, in bed. Bring out the whipped cream and we'll lick each other off for dessert. Then let's do something really novel. Forget sex and make love."

Jake licked his lips. He could taste her already. "Do you cook Chinese?"

"Only if it's chop suey."

"Never sounded better. I'll bring the plum wine."

"Great! Could you bring a video, too?"

She wanted a video on the VCR, not a Broadway play. Wow oh wow oh wow. Maybe he'd bring an engagement ring along with the video. Better X that out. He might be in a hurry to cut to the chase but scaring Val off was no way to get there.

A little fright could work to his advantage, though. Forget a predictably romantic video—he'd have Val crawling all over him before the final credits rolled.

"Video, no problem. Want me to bring the pop-corn, too?"

"Got some already," she chirped. A morning gale's song, music to his ears.

He was still hearing it when he knocked on her door.

Jake shuffled his feet like some kid with a crush, waiting for the girl of his dreams to let him in . . .

With buttercups, plum wine, and a Bela Lugosi video in his hungry hands.

Chapter Nine

The Dracula flick gave Val the chills but even more frightening was sharing the couch with a man who made her feel too much. Too needy and vulnerable. Too elated and fearful of the spiraling intensity between them.

A look and she melted. A touch and she burned.

He touched her with a look, a light caress now. A hot chill slinked down her spine. She wanted to turn to him, confront this thing of alarming proportions leaping between them from the briefest of contact. His arm settled around her shoulder, and her hand gripped his knee as if the sight of fangs descending onto a neck provoked her need for his protection.

In truth, she'd never felt so unprotected in her life. Defenseless, that's how she felt. Defenseless against the strange and wondrous emotions unfurling within her, this wild streak of desire so fierce it was wonton.

A kiss and she'd willingly fall into bed with him. Lay herself open to a man who could tear her heart out, such was his hold on her.

The thought wasn't comforting. Neither was Jake's full attention on her profile. Did he think she was actually watching Bela seduce a victim with a mesmerizing stealth and grace that had nothing on Jake?

Unable to bear the tension a moment longer, Val muttered, "You're staring at me."

"Uh-huh."

"Why?"

"I like what I see." He stroked the pulse point of her jugular and she knew a sudden kinship with the actress being drawn into a dark embrace, then succumbing to a force greater than she. Would this thing suck the very life out of her? Or would it give her life as never before?

Jake's teeth lightly scraped the side of her neck. A sybaritic sigh escaped her lips and she wondered at the sound he so easily called from her, the intoxicating rush of sensation coinciding with an almost painful squeeze of her heart.

She was terribly afraid she might be in love with Jake Larson. And just as her dream lover wasn't at all what she had expected, neither was love.

Love took courage. It was exhilarating, an ecstasy high. It was intimidating, unruly, and potentially dangerous. Love was a very powerful thing, capable of taking a person over.

No one in love was beyond bartering. Sex for affection. Sex for a proclamation of love. Even sex for the sake of sex. It was a bad bartering system. And she wasn't immune.

"I know you're afraid of something," he said against her neck. "I can hear it in your silence, the shake of your breathing, even taste it on your skin." He took another lick. "Tell me what you're afraid of."

"You," she confessed. "Me. Of what you make me feel, of feeling more than you do."

A Quiver of Sighs

"That's a relief."

"It is?" Val looked straight at him for the first time since they'd finished the dishes and he'd untied her apron with the proprietary touch of a lover. His pat to her behind had been tender, familiar, and left her yearning for an eternity of such domestic bliss.

"Believe it. Because Val . . ." He searched her eyes and in his she saw truth. "I feel the same way you do."

Her audible *whew* drew a chuckle from Jake. A very short chuckle that gave way to a groan when she inched her hand higher on his leg.

"I want you, Jake. I've never come out and said that to a man before, but then again, I've never wanted a man the way I want you. Beyond reason and with every reason there is."

Jake bowed his head and tried to decide which body part to listen to. His erection surged and demanded immediate action. His brain bounced from "Take her, she wants you, c'mon go for it!" to "She could regret it tomorrow and then you'll both be sorry!" Loudest of all, however, was the voice within, insisting he'd gone to bed with women he cared little for and his values of intimacy had been cheapened over the years of one-night stands and passing flings. Val was not one of those women. He cared for her deeply and for once there was something more important at stake than getting sex.

His gaze lingered on the skirt he swore he wouldn't take off. It was simple, white, long. A wedding dress for a child of the Earth with her head in the clouds. All Val needed for a bouquet were the buttercups she'd gathered to her earlier, proclaiming them more gorgeous than a roomful of roses. As for a sanctuary he saw not a church but a glade, her bare feet gliding over soft grass, a vivid green to match her eyes.

The movie played on. Jake muted the sound just as Dracula spread his cape with a flourish and proceeded to suck.

"You want me?" he asked, just to be sure Val hadn't changed her mind while he made up his.

Olivia Rupprecht

A nod. Too stilted to be convincing. Was she sorry already for an impetuous admission? If so, he'd change that.

"You don't want me enough. Want me more." Determined to give and only give, he ran a finger up her skirt. Her thighs locked and he soothed, "Easy. That's how we're taking this, slow and easy. Now relax and let me touch you."

Val tried, tried really hard to do what he said, but *how was she supposed to relax?* The only prelude to passion had been an endless silence from Jake before he put his hand up her dress! That's not how it was supposed to happen. He was supposed to kiss her and murmur sweet nothings then carry her into the bedroom. This wasn't at all what she had envisioned.

"Second thoughts?" he surmised.

"Yes."

He didn't move his hand from between her thighs. Then again, he could hardly do that with her legs clamped tight as a vise. The problem was, if she opened them Jake would have access to what she'd offered before wanting to take it back.

"Jake, I . . . I know what I said, but suddenly I'm not very comfortable with this and I hope you don't think I'm a tease because I'm not."

"I know. And neither am I, not with you. Which is why you can take my word that we won't be getting naked tonight. Maybe not for a while. So . . . relax. And open your legs."

Val wondered at the ebb and flow of her desires. They were returning, making her want him even more now that he was apparently in no hurry to do more than touch her.

As her legs parted, she admitted, "If that's one of your seduction techniques, it's definitely working." When he stroked, simply stroked the tender interior of a thigh, she softly moaned. "That's working, too."

"Works even better when you watch. Here, I'll show you."

It wasn't a suggestion, rather an enticing insistence from a dark prince of sensual pleasures. Yes,

A Quiver of Sighs

Jake was the darkness, and the path he was leading her upon, enlightening.

Slowly he lifted her skirt, higher, higher, and she felt her excitement rise inch by decadent inch. By the time he arranged the bunched gathering of material into a provocative white pool over her scarlet panties, Val was gripped by a fever and that fever was lust.

So powerful, so blinding, she couldn't think past the certainty that she'd go mad if Jake didn't lay his hands on her.

And then he did.

"Look." His gently spoken command feathered her neck yet seemed to come from a great distance. Even the riveting sight of dark amber fingers playing against the ivory of her skin appeared strangely detached.

She felt as if she were watching a movie, soft focus. Watching the sweep and sway of his hands move like phantom shadows over the body she had no control over.

It was his to command, to possess and how assured was his command, how compelling his possession. If he'd asked for her very soul in that moment, it would have been his.

Yet all he asked for was a kiss. A most intimate kiss . . .

"Of your panties," he coaxed with a light flick of the crotch. Val nearly came off the couch. Her hips arched up and in one smooth move Jake was on the floor, his thumbs hooked into the thin band of silk as he slid the panties to her knees. She couldn't tear her gaze from him.

He let go a long *ahhh* and who was she to deny him when he asked with a groan, "May I have these?"

"Take them." *Please take them!* Impatient with his agonizingly slow removal, she gripped his wrists and shoved down, nearly ripping the panties in half to get them off.

Was this really her? she wildly wondered. Had she actually become this carnal creature who stripped

313

off naughty underthings and brazenly pleaded, "Kiss me there, too" when adroit masculine fingers sifted through tight, red curls?

Those fingers, oh my, *those fingers* what they did to her. Fanning open the lips which sheltered the pinnacle of flesh he exposed to them both.

"You're beautiful." He blew the words into the moist hollow of her thighs and she could only marvel at the exquisite sensation, the reverence of his whisper.

His cheek rested on her thigh, allowing her to behold the stunning vision of his tongue tracing her. She saw herself watching a man make love to her with his mouth, saw a stranger emerge. That stranger was her. She was sensual, sexual, and bold in her demands.

She led his hand to where she most ached. Inside. So empty, so desperate for some fullness to grasp. "Please," she moaned. "*Please.*"

He lifted his head. His eyes glittered with pure prowess. His lips, wet with the juices he'd stirred and culled, parted slightly. He led her hand to his mouth, suckled a finger.

"Please yourself," he whispered as he led her further down the path, his path, and invited her to share the dark pleasures. She hesitated, uncertain if she could go through with this.

"I . . . it's . . ."

"Forbidden?"

"Yes."

"All the more reason to bite the apple, Eve." He nipped her neck. "Do it," he coaxed. "For me."

How could she be doing this? Actually touching herself while he slipped a single digit, then two, into her and gently pressed . . .

As they watched, touched, pleasured her together.

Then she wasn't watching any more, she couldn't with her head thrown back, mouth open and eyes closed in ecstasy. She wasn't a civilized being with conscious thought of her actions, her words. Her body was seized by an overwhelming rush of exquisite sensations, leaving her feeling completely undone. She was at the mercy of the arms lifting her up, holding her close.

"Where's your bedroom?"

"It's . . ." she didn't want to tell him, wasn't ready to venture there with him. He was a dark stranger; she was a stranger to herself. *Who was she?* Jake had turned her into a wild woman, devoid of reason.

"I can't . . . what happened . . . what did you do to me?"

"Not half of what I'm aching to do now." He found her room and navigated his way to the bed. No light, only night shadows illuminated his path.

He spilled her onto the bed, touched her cheek. Then moved away until the shadows swallowed him up. He was the darkness, no more than a voice, sad and haunting, drifting like tendrils of fog from her door.

"What have *you* done to *me*? I don't want to leave you, don't want to go home. It never seemed that empty before but lately, and tonight I know . . . so damn lonely."

Chapter Ten

A Drop of Ecstasy

He was the darkness.

So damn lonely in the darkness that he was. There was no crypt-mate to share the daylight slumber, no female creature to exchange love bites, to trade sips of wine-dark blood.

Victor Jakes studied his image in the mirror as he shaved. He didn't look so different from anyone else . . . unless he smiled too broadly. It amused him that people believed his sort had no reflection—not that mortals, in their ignorance, believed such things as himself existed at all.

The straight razor nicked Victor's eternally bronzed skin, which looked a bit peaked since he had yet to dine.

"What a waste." He sighed, wishing for the lap

A Quiver of Sighs

of a woman creature's tongue to suck the crimson drops. Ecstasy, that's how it tasted. And felt. If humans only knew how scintillating the experience was they'd line up to offer their necks.

He wiped the trickle of blood off the skin that had already mended. Drawing his lips into a full smile—as he was careful not to do until he was alone with a dinner companion—Victor brushed his teeth, giving special attention to his two sharp incisors. Even after more than a century they fascinated him, the way they extended just far enough to pierce a vein, the tiny holes that allowed him to drink.

They responded to his attention, lengthening a fraction and glistening diamond-bright in the fluorescent lighting.

"Yes, yes," he said, acknowledging the burning thirst.

Knowing he had to grab a bite before keeping his evening date, he drew on his powers of speed: In seconds his thick dusky hair was brushed, his designer jeans and loafers were on, starched white shirt and silk tie exact.

Just as quickly, he left the house and leaped twenty feet, making a perfect landing in the driver's seat of his sleek, silver Porsche.

Victor gunned the engine and peeled out of his circular driveway. He glanced at the gate and it obeyed, silently clicking shut behind him.

He had to hunt quickly. A mortal friend he hadn't seen in twenty years was expecting him at eight. Even if he himself had all the time in the world, he thought it rude to be late when his friend's time clock was ticking fast.

Once a safe distance from his lair, he scanned several miles' radius with his senses. His internal radar locked in on a lone figure leaving a deserted business. His nostrils quivered. L'air du Temps cologne. The lingering hint of hair spray. And, of course, the heady scent of healthy blood.

A woman. Good. Food was food but given his

sexual preferences, he gravitated to the opposite gender.

Unfortunately his car couldn't fly as fast as he and discretion was always wise. And so he pulled to the curb, scoured the immediate area with a laser's accuracy, and took to the air undetected.

Had anyone been watching they wouldn't have believed their eyes anyway. He was no more than a streak whistling a missle path through the cloak of night.

She was opening her car door when he dropped soundlessly behind her. It was cruel to frighten a victim and he didn't care for an extra shot of adrenaline to season the taste of her sustenance, so he infiltrated her mind with a black curtain command.

The woman slumped against her sedan and he pulled her against him. Pliable. Limp.

Ah, delicious. Vulnerable. Succulent.

"So glad you could join me," he whispered into her ear. Victor brushed aside her long hair, red as the nectar he could hear humming a siren song, and efficiently exposed the tender length of neck.

His kiss was soft but the breasts in his hands were even softer. He caressed them gently while his teeth pierced the slow throb of a vein.

Her blood flowed into him in the sweetest undulation. He could feel the pulse of her organs contracting with the pull of each gulp. She was nearing thirty, a single secretary with dreams of love and a family. She adored poetry and plum wine.

As he absorbed the knowledge of who she was and how she'd gotten that way, he was glad to feel the threat of bloodlust subsiding . . . for he did find her a pleasant feast. She tasted of heart and life and loneliness. She longed for a lover but had none.

As much as he craved to devour each precious red drop, Victor slowed his sucking and denied himself the ultimate ecstasy while he gave it to her.

She came to a shuddering release.

A Quiver of Sighs

He took delight in the tremors racking her unconscious body and allowed that much of the experience to slip between the ribbons of her brain.

He was done. With only a little more than a pint taken, he knew he'd have to feed again before calling it a night.

Victor stroked her breasts one last time, concealed the tiny neck pricks with a wisp of his fingers and released her mind to consciousness at the instant he streaked to the sky.

As he dropped easily into his still-running Porsche, his vision cut through trees and houses and highways and he smiled, watching her get into her car with a confused shake of the head.

She was feeling a little woozy, but most definitely erotic and good. He noticed she touched her breasts and shifted in her seat, aware of the liquid pulse between her thighs.

"Till we meet again," Victor said into the darkness, chuckling as he sent his farewell in a flash through her stunned psyche.

He sped off to his destination, still whistling when he rang the doorbell. He could kill, and he had, and doubtless would again. But he didn't like waste and greed had always seemed an insufferably bad quality. Blood did replenish itself, and he liked to think his sense of ethics compensated for some of his ill-mannered colleagues who depleted the food supply.

As the door swung open, Victor thought most humans deserved to live. Even if it was just a wrinkle in the fabric of time that mortal hearts sustained their fragile, finite beat.

Thanks to Val, his heart had never been more fragile. Nor his job more finite, Jake thought, as the latest issue of *Fantasies* hit his desk.

"And just what is *this*?"

Jake shrugged. "Looks like your magazine, Gino."

"That's right, *my* magazine!" Gino's fist came down on the expanse of wood, and given his glower, Jake wondered if his jaw might be the next target of Gino's wrath. "What the hell is going on here? I go to Europe for a month and this is what I come back to! Jesus, Jake, I count on you to run this place and pay you damn well to do it, so what do you do? You try to ruin me, that's what!"

"Far from it, Gino. I want you to succeed. Which is why I upscaled some of the material so we could try pulling in new readers who—"

"Screw new readers! Now you listen to me, Larson," he seethed. "There *is* no magazine without subscribers and our subscribers expect us to deliver fantasies about fetishes, not stupid little ditties about vampires and dreams and kisses. Am I making myself clear?"

So, Gino, you not only read the latest issue, you did some belated homework. From procurement to print it took two months and in the two that had passed since he'd bought the "Ecstasy" piece, he'd acquired several more from Val. Did Gino know about those? If so, they'd be yanked out of production and surely one Jake Larson's butt would be out of this chair.

Since Gino hadn't fired him yet, Jake figured his boss was still ignorant of those additional sins he could summon no guilt for.

"I understand, Gino." And indeed he did. Either he pulled Val's stuff himself or come the next issue, he was out of a job.

"You'd better. Otherwise, I'd advise you to get your resume out and don't bother to use me for a reference."

Slam! The room reverberated with the force of Gino's exit. Jake cringed. But not because the big guy was angry and his paycheck was on the line.

It was the snapshot of Val in a gold frame commanding the middle of his desk that had him wincing. He should have stood up for her, the merit of her work, and those editorial ethics he had regained while helping her reach for her dream.

One that was extremely close to becoming a reality.

The revisions were done, then redone and done again until he'd pronounced them perfect. They'd

A Quiver of Sighs

had a few skirmishes and a dandy of a fight along the way but he'd loved every minute of it even if Val had wanted his head.

No doubt she'd be in the market for a guillotine after tonight. The manuscript was nearly finished. She had about fifty pages to go and should be able to wrap it up in a few weeks. But first she needed to fix the latest chapter she'd sworn was the best thing she had ever written.

He could still see her beaming when she'd presented it to him at the table in her kitchen, where that silly little cupid with the broken wing had taken up residence. Hell, you'd think she couldn't write without it, she was so attached to the thing. As for himself, the figurine gave him the creeps. Not exactly the creeps since he didn't believe in curses or spells or any kind of hocus-pocus like that, but the cupid did give him a weird feeling for some reason.

Maybe it was jealousy. She called Cupid her good-luck charm and every time she did, he wanted to demand, "Hey, what about me? I'm the one putting in time and a half to get you on the bestseller list and it's sure not a piece of porcelain buying that other stuff you keep hush-hush about so you can pay your rent!"

But he didn't say it. He didn't dare. Val was insecure about her talents and would think he had bought her work out of favoritism, not because it was good. And just as she was too embarrassed about the source of her income to fess up, so was he. His pride wouldn't let him tell her the truth.

His conscience had been slugging it out with his pride of late. Those pieces he'd bought weren't just bits of imaginative whimsy. They were intensely personal insights into their evolving relationship.

Jake recalled the poem she'd submitted last week. "He Takes Me There." Val was shameless, really, in gutting up her private sentiments about him for public consumption. It rubbed him that she would share with others—in return for money of all things—what she wouldn't confess to him.

Ah, the psyche of the writer. He'd thought he

understood them until Val had proven how grossly
he had underestimated their subterfuge, emotional
honesty, and willingness to prostitute their very
souls for a story to tell. And sell.

Nothing was sacred. Not kisses or orgasms or confessions of loneliness from the darkness that he was.
Or had been before Val turned him to mush and
filled his life with the light of a thousand suns.

Mush, definitely mush. With the exception of one
perpetually stiff organ, the rest of his insides had
about as much substance as the Pillsbury Dough
Boy. Yep, that was him, Dough Boy with a hard-on,
secretly enjoying Val's secret fantasies instead of
confronting her with the evidence and enacting each
and every one.

Actually, Gino would probably like the bondage
fantasy she'd spun. That was a legit sort of thing for
them to publish, even if it did have her trademark
penchant for prose. So pretty the way she painted
the page, Val made bindings and spankings seem far
from perverse. Yet he did find a certain perversity in
her fascination with the forbidden only to shy away
whenever he suggested such intimacies of interest to him. Like a few weeks back when they'd
been talking books and happened to be at his place.

He liked her there because she brightened the
spaces and he could smell her long after she was
gone; he liked seeing her in posh surroundings
rather than in a dump that bothered him more by
the day. He wanted to provide for her, give her the
best, wrap her in the love he still hadn't professed.

He'd tried. Many times. But those three words refused to emerge. Maybe if his parents had said them
more, maybe if he'd said them more himself, it
wouldn't be so hard. Then again, if Val said them first
he'd surely be able to cough up something better
than "ditto."

How to lead up to such a revelation? Their mutual
passion for books and each other had seemed a good
place to start. So he'd reached for a book—not Val.
To reach for her was to invite yet another "Jake,

A Quiver of Sighs

please!" and a struggle to remember his chastity was a self-imposed purification process. Restoring one's sexual integrity didn't happen overnight for a one-time bed hopper who longed to turn back the hands of time and be as innocent as the love of his life.

While his intentions were pure, all that self-denial had created a never-ending want for what he wouldn't let himself have. Perhaps that's why Madonna's *Sex* had seemed an excellent choice at the time. Raunchy yet thought-provoking, it also represented the sort of professional liaison he and Val had forged, albeit unbeknownst to her.

Hey, just the book to pave the way for all sorts of confessions, right?

Wrong.

His great idea had bitten the dust with the turn of a page. A bondage pictorial. "Hmmm . . . interesting," was all he'd said.

Val had made no comment beyond an eye-popping stare, several agitated breaths, and a quick exit to the balcony to make sure the red peppers and shrimp on the grill weren't burning.

Go figure. Val had gone to check the grill and he'd held himself in check only for her to pen a steamy bondage fantasy, giving herself away as the reluctant yet all-too-eager virgin with no choice but to be gently savaged and ecstatically devirginized by his saber.

He could always see himself in her work. As for his Peeping-Tom view of her delightfully libidinous brain, he was hooked. Kinky, even for him. Let Val in on that and she just might decide he was a little twisted. That could give her pause once he got on bended knee.

Mrs. Jake Larson . . . Valerie Larson . . . V. A. Smith-Larson . . . Valerie Smith-Larson. Yeah, that fit. Jake considered the dips and sways of ink, the riot of hearts around the title looking like so many puckered kisses and mutated buttercups.

With a sigh he tossed his doodling into the trash. It hit the heap and bounced onto the floor. Trash and more trash, he couldn't stomach putting such sala-

Olivia Rupprecht

cious dreck to print much longer. The only way he could hang on was to go for his own dream while helping Val reach hers.

One in the same, really. When it came to love, dreams were meant to be shared.

And nightmares, too, he supposed. But while he wanted to be there for Val when she most needed him, he didn't want her to know his job was in jeopardy or how deeply that disturbed him. Unemployment had been a humiliating experience and he couldn't bear the thought of going through that again, even with plenty socked away for a rainy day.

He'd learned something about himself the last and only time he'd been out of work.

Jake Larson without a job was not a nice person. He was moody, angry, and had a mean streak. A real jerk.

The darkness that he was could come back with a vengeance. Give him a few months of scouring the want ads and he'd be capable of lashing out, admitting to Val that she was the primary cause for his dismissal.

That was something she must never know. And knowing what he did about himself, no way would he be popping the question without gainful employment elsewhere.

"They're *not* stupid little ditties, Gino," he snarled. "They're pearls thrown before swine and you're the biggest porker of all. Yeah, bastard, I've got a dream. To be a major player on Publisher's Row again and take Val with me before you drop the ax I can already hear coming."

Chapter Eleven

"What do you mean it *has* to go?" *Don't cry*, she silently ordered herself, *don't you dare fall apart.*

"I mean it's got to go," Jake bullishly insisted, punctuating his point with a tap to her finest chapter.

"But it's the best thing I've ever written," she weakly protested, hating the way he so easily undermined her confidence. What was left of it anyway. She'd gotten her first rejection from *Fantasies* today.

She shouldn't be surprised that "He Takes Me There" didn't make the cut but with each sale she'd grown more courageous, taken greater liberties with the erotic envelope she pushed. Erotica, not smut. One was subtle, a suggestive whisper wooing the libido; the other crass, explicit, raw. Porn lacked heart and without heart there was no heat.

No wonder few women read such magazines. Including her. Then again, maybe their sales had gone

325

Olivia Rupprecht

up since she'd given voice to those females who liked it hot but not trashy.

Well, by golly, she was a damn hot writer and the four grand she'd earned in the last several months proved it. Still, she had to admit the poem Jake had inspired probably wouldn't sizzle any senses besides her own. So she shouldn't be upset by the rejection. But she was. And the blow to her writer's ego sure didn't need another smack from Jake.

"You have to put your ego aside, Val." He said it like a loving parent to a simpleton child who was starting to tax his patience. "The writing itself is beautiful but all that beauty's hiding the guts you need to expose. Step away and think about it. Then give me some guts. You can do it."

He was patronizing her. She hated to be patronized.

Throwing something would feel good. Throwing something at Jake would feel really, really good. Her new word processor? Too heavy. Her best chapter she was *not* changing? Too light.

Val's gaze settled on Cupid. She always looked to Cupid when inspiration failed. Tempted as she was to fling it at Jake—who had certainly inspired her to do so—she feared the other wing might be knocked off or the arrow broken.

Besides, throwing Cupid or anything else would be an act of violence. She abhorred violence.

". . . and it's really a simple fix. All you have to do is ditch the pretty prose and get down and dirty here. That's honest, the other's a cheat."

"No it's not!"

"Oh, yes it is. When people feel they've been betrayed, they don't have a civil conversation about it and then kiss and make up. Maybe in the best of real life they do, but not usually, and never in compelling fiction."

"And just what are you suggesting?" Her hands balled into two fists beneath the table. Beating him to a pulp, how sweet the fantasy. He actually expected her to toss twenty of her best pages. No doubt

326

he'd say the same about the ten she'd written today.

"A knock-down, drag-out. Accusations flying like shrapnel, they're cutting each other to pieces. She walks out, he goes after her and *cut*. Next chapter, she's slapping him, he gets a little rough. Make it nasty. Remember, he just found out she's been sleeping with his brother."

"But she *hasn't* been sleeping with his brother!"

"True. But Marcus doesn't know that and Leigh's so offended by his accusations she won't deny them. Now's the time to hash it out."

"They do," she haughtily reminded him. "He confronts her with the evidence and she explains it's all a blackmail scheme to tear the family apart. Marcus believes her instead of his brother because he knows she would never lie to him and Drake could lie for a living. He's sneaky and manipulative and deceptive. A total jerk."

As she ticked off Drake's flaws, Val noticed Jake's jaw clench. She couldn't imagine what she'd said to set him off, but he suddenly slapped her beloved pages.

"Get rid of it," he snapped. Not a suggestion, a dictate. "This is crap, absolute crap. You make the human condition out to be sweet and nice and tidy. It's not. People are people and great fiction lets them be just that. These aren't people! They're cutie-pie cardboard characters who don't know the meaning of passion. Of emotion or hurt or doubt in each other, not to mention themselves. You've got a plot, another five subplots, and this is the best you can do for the black moment denouement?"

She couldn't speak. If she did she'd surely spew enough hateful words to pass for Regan in *The Exorcist*. So she let her eyes say how much she loathed Jake Larson in that moment; willed him to see the daggers shoot from her pupils and crucify him as surely as he'd crucified her characters.

He didn't seem to feel so much as a nick to the leather jacket he flung over his shoulders.

"A last suggestion, sweet Val. The nastier the bet-

Olivia Rupprecht

ter. I know it's a real stretch of the imagination for you, but most of humanity can relate to a good wallow in the muck. True, it lacks the sacchrine ambiance you apparently prefer yourself, but a fight to the finish in the sack can make for a really great scene."

"You don't actually expect me to—"

"Nix the kissy-kissy yuck stuff and get creative with some raw sex and anger? That's exactly what I expect you to do. It's honest."

"It's *pornographic*."

"Not if it's appropriate and in this case, it is." His smile made her cringe; talk about sacchrine. "Do what I said and you've got a riveting climax that'll turn those last fifty pages faster than the flip of a silver Ben Franklin. Let the characters be as real as they were before this cop-out and nobody will put down the book. Not an agent, not an editor, not a reader, not nobody. On that note, I'll leave. And you can get to work."

Get to work? After this she was supposed to *get to work*? Cut out the heart of her book—hearts were loving, forgiving, they heard what ears did not, right?—and go play in the gutter to keep the pages turning since Jake had proclaimed himself God of All Editors and believed humans related to characters who stooped to the lowest of lows.

He strode out of the kitchen.

Val went after him. "Jake!"

He kept going. By the time he reached the door, she knew he was really leaving, acting as if she didn't exist.

Incensed, she whipped him around with the force of her rage. "Talk about crap," she heatedly whispered. "I refuse to trash the meaning of what love is and for you to suggest such a thing is *wrong*. I care for you, Jake, but don't ask me why when you have such a capacity to disgust me."

"Get real," he clipped out. And then he laughed at her. Actually laughed at her! "For an empath of humanity, you sure don't seem to know much. Emotions are messy and I can tell you right now if I

328

thought you were sleeping with my brother you'd be amazed at my capacity to get ugly. Anyone pushed past their limit can become monsters they don't even recognize themselves, that much I know about life. As for love—"

"You don't know much," she flung back. How could she love this man? He was cold and calculating and twisting everything around to get his way.

"Maybe not," he said with an unnerving stillness that only seemed to verify that he didn't love her, at least not the way she loved him, so fiercely and deeply it hurt. "But I do know what makes for a damn good read. Now you can either respect my expertise or find someone else to edit your work. If that's your choice, better latch on to your cupid because you'll need all the luck you can get."

Had he slapped her? She could hear the crack of a palm to a cheek splinter the air. But her head didn't move, it couldn't move with so much fury filling it.

Jake's face rocked sideways. Then slowly returned, pinning her in place with an expression so smugly satisfied and livid, she was mute with horror.

"You want a fight?" he asked in a lethal whisper. "You've got it. Just remember you're a writer and take notes."

Before she could beg his forgiveness for what she couldn't believe she'd done, his mouth came down on hers, hard. His lips punished her own until they throbbed.

A shudder went through her. Heat mingled with the chill. It was a strange, disturbing alchemy of adrenaline and the rush of hormones creating a primal, sexual impulse.

This couldn't be her, she couldn't want Jake this way. He was the dark stranger she occasionally glimpsed and retreated from, even as she shunned the decadent darkness within herself. He called to that part of her now, and she answered, returning the kiss as fiercely as it was given. He groaned and she realized he liked the taste of savagery, the way she struck back.

She liked it, too. Her excitement rose and so did her confusion. How could she enjoy this? How could he? What was wrong with them? *This wasn't right.* This wasn't a kiss, nothing like kisses were meant to be.

As disgusted with herself as she was with him, Val struggled against him. His assault intensified and she pulled at his hair, pounded his back, but on he went as if to encourage her to fight harder, dirtier. *Nastier.*

She jerked her knee between his legs.

Jake caught it, held it still against the groin she could feel tense in self-protection.

He freed her mouth. His eyes glittered with an almost feral hunger. He smiled. A taunting, licentious smile that seemed to say he'd fallen from grace, see how low he could get, and how lovely for her to join him.

"You like it this way. So do I. It's honest, artless. Reminds me a bit of that night on your couch. You know, the night we don't talk about because you'd rather pretend you've got status-quo tastes in bed instead of a taste for the forbidden. You hide from yourself, Val, the same way you hide behind pretty words. That's the unvarnished truth. So is the fact that you enjoyed having your mouth at the mercy of mine. Deny it and you're a liar."

Though she longed to slap him again and ravage his mouth this time around, she swiped the back of her hand over her lips. They felt swollen, tender, consumed.

"Get out, Jake."

"Sure, I'll get out." He let her go. Only to lock the door and lean casually against it. "After we finish hashing this out. Civil conversation, anyone?" When she gaped at him in disbelief of such audacity, he chuckled. "Didn't think so. How about cutting to the chase, then? Forget talking and get right to the good stuff. You know, kiss and make up."

"How *dare* you," she seethed.

A Quiver of Sighs

"Oh, I dare plenty. Lots more than you ever *dreamed*, buttercup."

"Don't call me that, you—you—"

"Bastard?"

"Yes! Not only that, you're a—"

"Son of a bitch?"

Damn him! He wouldn't even give her the satisfaction of calling him names herself. She wanted to scream them at him, do justice to the epithets he stated with the enthusiasm of a yawn. Just as nonchalantly, he pushed away from the door.

A step toward her and she took two back.

"Come, come, Val, such unimaginative slurs. You're the wordsmith, surely you can do better than that."

"Guttersnipe." she gladly obliged. And retreated as he advanced. "You're a pig, worse than despicable."

"Why sufferin' suckatash, move over Sylvester. Ouch, you really hit me below the belt." Jake unlatched his buckle and her heart doubled its beat, then raced even faster as he whipped off the leather. His belt went to the floor and he went for his zipper.

She turned from him then, blindly, thinking no further than escaping to her bedroom, with its beckoning light, lock, and soft bed. She'd go there, curl up under the covers, forget about this ugliness—

The grip on her hair, starting as a single yank and then becoming a slow pull, stopped her short. He reeled her in, then held her prisoner by her hair.

Her back flush against him, she could feel him thick and bulging from the open wedge of jeans.

"Going somewhere?" he murmured.

"I . . . I—I'll scream." Could she? Her vocal cords were so tight she could barely whisper.

"I'm sure you will," he assured her. "Because I'm not leaving until you do."

Chapter Twelve

Giving his promise substance, Jake rubbed intimately against her, whispering, "You'll scream with pleasure. And what pleasure for me to hear you say 'Jake, *please*' like never before after all those nasty things you said about me."

"I take them back, Jake. Now let me go."

Despite her demand, she didn't try to break free. Too bad. He really had enjoyed their little chase and wouldn't mind another. His blood still pumped through muscle and vein that fed the rush to his groin. Was she just as hot? Given her moan, the swish of her tush, he believed so.

"No need to take back what's true. I can be all those things. And more." Manipulative, deceptive, a total jerk. With the exception of possessing a conscience, he could be Drake. But maybe even a weasel like that could fall in love.

A Quiver of Sighs

After all, if it could happen to Jake Larson, it could happen to anyone.

The bed was close. The floor even closer. Even the wall looked tempting. He wanted her back to it, her legs wrapped around his waist and the feel of her gripping, convulsing around the bulk of his thrust.

That's what he wanted now, right now. But what about tomorrow? What about those months of self-denial that were culminating in a rapacious greed for a fast-and-furious consummation? It wouldn't be fair to Val or to him, throwing it all away on an impetuous whim. Gone would be his fantasy of carrying her over a honeymoon threshold and plying her with the skill of a seasoned lover who had won his virginity back.

"Jake?"

Her tremulous whisper nearly made him come undone. He had to back off. Fast. Or kiss his most cherished fantasy good-bye.

Jake stroked her hair, pressed a kiss to her nape, and forced himself to let go.

"I'm sorry, Val." Saying he was sorry had never come easy. How amazing that it was so much easier to say than a heartfelt profession of love. Then again, maybe not. His heart had been hardened for a very long time and after years of a flat-line reading, he was so alive, so vulnerable, that he still shook from the jolt of an arrow hitting its mark.

"Where are you going?"

Her voice was at his back ; he knew better than to turn, to gaze at the mouth he had rejoiced in devouring, without the veneer he presented to the world, to Val, to himself.

It had begun as a lesson, an attempt to make her understand that she had to bleed from her fingertips, put her guts on a page. In the end, he'd exposed his.

"I'm not sure where I'm going." To find his belt, good place to start.

"I want you to stay. I want to talk about this."

"Later. When I'm not nursing a problem in my

pants and we can have a civil conversation about what happened to put it there."

"Damn you!"

Suddenly, he hit the floor. *How did she do that?* Jake vaguely wondered. How did she manage to push him down while he reached for his belt, roll him over and straddle his hips?

Stunned, he stared up at a vision. An angel. And some halo she had, her hair so wild and disheveled the ends stuck out like lit sparklers bristling on end.

"Damn you, Jake Larson. You have no right, no right whatsoever to do this to me."

"Do . . . what?" He had no idea what she was talking about, couldn't think past the realization that she'd yanked the belt from his grip and was efficiently cinching his wrists to the leg of the coffee table.

It was wobbly. He could pull free. But what man in his right mind would make more than a token resistance when his sweet, virgin angel had turned into a sultry siren consigning him to hell?

"You can drop the innocent act, Jake, just drop it and join me for the hell you put me through every time you touch me, then leave. You've done it for nearly four months and I've had enough. You want me to admit I have a wild streak that makes me squirm, naughty ideas that make me blush even when I'm alone? Okay, I admit it. Now say good-bye to Little Miss Sunshine because I'm ready to take a stroll on the dark side and you're coming with me. Understand?"

"Uh . . . okay."

She stood over him, legs braced on either side of his hips. And proceeded to strip. Holy . . . ! Had she taken lessons from Gypsy Rose Lee?

One-by-one, she dangled blouse, bra, skirt, and panties over his head, tickling his nose, then flirting with his lips until he claimed the bait with his teeth.

And then her little game was done and she gave new meaning to sensual torture with the drape of her hair over his chest, the back-and-forth swish of her silky red whip lightly chastising him as she stroked his length.

"You're so beautiful. Why do you keep this from me?" Ruby lips took him inside and he almost lost control.

"No," he gritted out. His fantasy, the fantasy of all fantasies, was at stake. A new job, a proposal, a wedding, meeting her parents, all those things had to come first. He couldn't let her do this, couldn't let her rob him of his secret dream. "Please, no. This isn't the way I want it to be, not how I've imagined it to be."

"Then imagine this." She rose up, put his tip to her entry. Then her head, hips, fell forward as one and he was inside her. Less than halfway, yet she winced.

"Stop," he groaned. "Stop before it's too late. I don't want to hurt you—"

"But you do hurt me." She opened her eyes, opened them to him, let him see all the way to her soul, the womb he could feel crying for him to reach. "You hurt me every time you take me there with your hands, your mouth, and refuse what I want more than anything I've ever wanted before. You, Jake. All of you. Now I'm taking you there, where you're as much mine as I am yours."

Head thrown back, crescent arcs of ecstasy, she plunged down. Jake commanded himself to be still, to let her body adjust and take what was hers already, what would always be hers and hers alone. Him. All of him. The good, the imperfect, and oh, how imperfect he was.

His body, out of control, was heedless of his need to touch and kiss and soothe the tender flesh he must be ripping with the jerk of his hips.

"No, no . . . no . . . ." His protest against the force of nature, the force of Val's breasts slapping against his chest as she sobbed his name, made him know too well the true meaning of impotency. He was impotent against the love he felt for her, the lust she summoned, the fate that had brought them together and whatever fate awaited. He ached to hold her but even his arms had no say in the matter.

Val had gotten the final say.

"Untie me . . . sunshine." The face she lifted to him did shine, with tears and joy. How could she beam like that when he wanted to cry?

"Only if you say 'Please.' " She sniffled.

"Please, Val."

"With sugar on it?"

If only she knew he'd give her every sugar plantation on Earth if he had it to give. Hell, he'd give her the world if he could. But he couldn't do that any more than undo what she'd done and have his fantasy back.

Dreams were never free. Val didn't know what it was costing him to give this one up. Even strolling violinists, a rose between his teeth as he did the tango solo and made a fool of himself was an easier dream to put aside for another tomorrow than the dream she'd taken, never to be recaptured.

"With sugar on it," he said dully.

"You're not happy."

"No."

"Why not? I am."

Jake considered that. Even if he wasn't happy—make that totally depressed—Val was elated. Love. He considered that, too. He loved her so much, couldn't he find some happiness in hers? And being the source, shouldn't that make him feel good?

"Now you're happy." She kissed him soundly and undid the belt. Holding her now, sifting his fingers through her hair, feeling her heart beat so close to his . . . yes, he was happy.

So happy that he laughed, freely, without so much as the first coat of a shellacked veneer.

Val joined him. But once they sobered, she asked, "By the way, what was so funny?"

"Let's just say, if you were taking notes O. Henry should have nothing on what you've got to put in your book."

"Hmmm . . ." Val pursed her lips, twitched them

from side to side. So cute. He loved to watch her brain work. "You know, Mr. Editor, maybe that last chapter could use an overhaul. Something along the lines of Rhett having his way with Scarlett—but with a gender-bender twist."

"I like that idea even better than mine. And, I'm sure, so will the audience. Even from the men—especially the men—I don't think you'll get any hate mail." Mail. She'd probably gotten the rejection letter today. Damn, if he hadn't been so preoccupied with his own work situation, he would have remembered that and been less of a bully.

More than anything he wanted to tell her everything, including the fact that he personally adored her poem and had kept a copy, but he just couldn't stretch the content of *Fantasies* that far. But now was not the time for such confessions. Not when she felt so soft, so right, in his arms.

And not when her leg was wedged between his and she could have a knee-jerk reaction to the extent of his hidden agendas.

"Um . . . Jake. Is this a civil conversation?"

"So far. But I'm definitely up for a repeat of some very uncivil behavior."

"I'm on the pill." She bit her bottom lip as if exposing a deep, dark secret. Secretly, he was disappointed. "I thought this would happen sooner than it did, so I went to the doctor and got a prescription. The pills make me moody."

And to think he'd chalked it up to artistic temperament. Jake knew he should appreciate her taking the responsibility, so why did he feel so temperamental himself at the moment?

"Then quit taking them. I don't mind rubbers much if they're of the lambskin variety and I don't mind any variety at all if you're the one putting them on me."

Val got that distant look in her eyes. "Good line. Maybe I'll use it sometime." He popped her behind and she jumped. "Hey! What was that for?"

Olivia Rupprecht

"For all the lines you've probably already taken the liberty of using."

"What makes you think that?" she asked innocently.

"I know how you writers work," he hedged.

"Then you must also know that it's wise to stay on our good side. A word of warning, Jake?" She wagged a finger at him. "I don't get even, I write you in."

"Yes, my dear . . ." He gave a sharp nip to her finger and met her startled gasp with a knowing smile. "I'm sure you do."

Chapter Thirteen

He had the ring. He'd bought it in New York two weeks ago when his prospects looked good and Cartier had never looked better. Things didn't look nearly so great now that Tavern on the Green was a memory and so was his job.

As for those prospects, they proved to be as empty as the desk he was cleaning out. The calls had come shortly after his return, all of them sounding pretty much the same:

"Jake, you're great and I did what I could, but the market's so tight and positions for someone like yourself even tighter . . ."

Of that he was sure. A golden boy turned pariah didn't merit special treatment—especially with his latest credential. His old colleagues had been tactful enough not to point out the obvious. Maybe because they knew that with a twist of fate it could be them.

Olivia Rupprecht

But it wasn't. It was him. With a ring in his pocket, no job, an empty desk, and Val's latest submission in his briefcase. As Editor-in-Chief his last decision had been to reject "The Picnic." It was too personal to put to print. Val didn't need the sale anyway.

Her manuscript, also in his briefcase, was finished. It was to die for; he'd seen to that. After he made sure she had the best agent in the Big Apple, she wouldn't need him anymore. Not professionally anyway. She'd still have need of him otherwise, but that was borrowed comfort when she had bright tomorrows ahead and his own future was bleak.

Jake left his office without a backward glance. Eager as he was to put this chapter of his life behind him, he stopped at Charles's smaller office.

Charles met his grip over the desk. "You're leaving. Does Gino know?"

"He does if he bothered to read my letter of resignation. But my guess is he's too busy checking what just came off the presses to notice."

"He will soon enough. The rag needs you, Jake. Gino's sure to realize he can't replace you in a year, much less in a day."

Jake summoned an appreciative smile. Yet it was weary. Even if by some miracle Gino didn't fire him, he simply couldn't continue here. "Maybe you should start cleaning out your desk too, pal."

"Probably. Accessories to the crime don't warrant much slack but maybe Gino'll hire me back once he realizes—"

"That you're the heir apparent for my job? He'll realize it once he reads my letter. I let him know you stood up for the magazine as it was before I started putting my own spin on it and suggested he let you fill my shoes for a few issues. Without anyone else to do it, you betcha he will."

Charles had the same look of gratitude and determination he'd worn himself when the Big Break came years ago. So many years ago, it seemed a past lifetime away.

Those years stretched into a distance so vast he

A Quiver of Sighs

could only wonder at the fate that had brought him full circle to the place Val had returned him to. Back to the pure joy of a job well done on a story without the need to dismiss those with promise because they weren't the shortest way to the top.

Several hours later his second glass of scotch was hitting empty. Val would arrive soon, here in his upscale condo, which wouldn't be his much longer. Several half-packed boxes were in the foyer, ready to move. Where to, he didn't know, but he sure couldn't afford this kind of rent.

Val's place was much too close to the digs he could be in if he couldn't land more than freelance work in a couple of years. It could happen.

His skills were highly specialized and the positions he qualified for were, for now, nonexistent. He wished he could have faith in the celestial as Val did. She even believed her cupid had brought them together. He highly doubted that, but who knew? Loving Val had taught him there did exist higher powers unseen.

In retrospect, he saw too well. He should have come forward with the whole truth and nothing but months ago, should have acted on his tango fantasy and all the other wildly romantic notions he'd dreamed up.

At least their picnic had been a fantasy realized. How he wished they were still there. Then he wouldn't be sitting here, drinking, dreading what he had to do. No rejection letter with Charles as the front man; he would personally return Val's latest—and last—submission to *Fantasies*.

He tapped the pages to his chin. "The Picnic." A slice of their intimate life that would never see print, yet it was indelibly etched in his mind. How well she had captured their outdoor tryst—except for the ending. His favorite part. Pure fiction but such a dream. His dream. And apparently Val's, though she'd stayed true to form and hadn't made him privy to certain secret desires he found out about anyway.

And when Val found him out? He shuddered to

341

think. And so he wouldn't. He'd pour himself another drink and escape to where they'd been, where he dreamed to go . . .

The Picnic

It is a perfect day for a kidnapping. I shiver as a man binds my hands, his capable fingers wrapping a swash of raw silk around my wrists and securing a loose knot in the region of my lap. Deft and agile are his movements; fleet and sure is his thumbing of my cleft beneath a white muslin peasant skirt.

I make a whimpering sound. He smiles, wickedly, and withdraws the teasing friction.

"Where are you taking me?" I ask as he insistently leads me out the door and to a low-slung convertable.

No answer.

My gaze gravitates to a suspicious-looking object, covered with a blanket in the minuscule back seat.

"What are you hiding in there?"

"Dark strangers don't give away their secrets." He presses me into the leather seat. Smooth as a glove and warm as a hot toddy after absorbing the rays of the midmorning sun. The seat imparts a stimulating message to the backs of my thighs, the cheeks of my buttocks.

The engine roars to life and leaps forward to the tune of Percy Sledge crooning about a man loving a woman. The dark stranger's hand works the stick shift with the same ease he recently worked me.

City traffic sounds give way to rolling green countryside and I raise my face to the sun to welcome the whipping wind, kissing me senseless.

In the middle of nowhere, he stops the car.

Not a word is spoken between captor and captive as he gathers the blanket and hoists a basket onto his shoulder, then leads me to a deserted glade. Long, soft grass, a willow weeping, picture-postcard perfect.

Beneath the gnarled branches of an old oak

dripping moss, he lays out a satin coverlet. And then he slips the knot, unwinds the raw silk that caressed rather than chaffed my wrists.

Thrusting the bindings aside, he whispers, "We're all alone and I'm feeling dangerous." His mouth finds my neck and he tongues the runaway pulse in its hollow. "I'm also very hungry. Time to get rid of these clothes and enjoy the feast."

I can't outrun him. I can't hide. Both are moot points since I have no inclination to do either.

His fingers, electric against my skin, brush over my breasts to part the thin cotton of my blouse. Then he removes the even thinner shield of my panties.

The frustrations of the workaday world drop from me, leaving me gloriously naked and open to discovery with a man who gently commands, "Lie down."

This captive obliges. Anticipation runs high.

"Are you hot?" he asks.

"The temperature has seemed to zoom in the last few minutes."

"Then shut your eyes and pretend we're on a sandy beach. Can you smell the coconut oil?" He squeezes some into his open palm and massages the scent of summer into my skin. My breasts slide and part beneath his touch; he cups and molds pliable woman flesh with a sculptor's sensitivity.

"I feel like clay." Yes, that's how I feel. "Clay that's been thrust into a kiln. God, I'm on fire."

"The last thing I want to do is dry you out." Digging into an ice bucket, he swirls the cubes around, rubbing them like dice between his palms. "Cold. Wet." He holds a chip over a nipple, watches the transparent drip . . . drip . . . drip onto a puckering peak. "Stimulating."

"Warm me." I am shaking, so cold, so hot, as his tongue teases me to mindless sensation, the need for more.

"More?" he asks, his smile a taunt. "But my dear, appetizers come before the entrée. Look in the basket and see what you'd like to eat."

I probe and plunder. Then decide, "I'd love a banana. Feed it to me?"

My lips part to take the fruit while I lift a cherry tomato to his mouth and feed him in turn.

His teeth bite into the smooth red skin. Juicy, the tart sweet pulp sliding over his tongue and dribbling down his chin. The tiny seeds, slick between his teeth, apparently put him in a mind for . . .

"Caviar?" he suggests, leaning me back. "I left the plates at home. You won't mind lending me a serving dish, will you?"

"Not as long as you're the rest of the spread."

The cool jellied lumps fill my navel and he dishes it up with a silver spoon.

"Good and salty," I pronounce with approval. "It tastes a lot like you."

"Then taste me."

He substitutes the spoon for his finger and I suck at it with a hungry tug.

I reach up to steal a kiss, but he gently pushes me back down.

"Not yet. The picnic's just getting started."

I watch as he makes two matching sundaes, swirling whipped cream round and round each heavy breast. Plop. Plop. The tempting garnish of plump maraschino cherries, their stems long and curved and so agreeable to plucking, trail a white-streaked path up my throat, around my chin, between my lips. He tidies up, alternately licking and rubbing the whipped cream's journey into my skin.

I hear my sighs of wet arousal, his catching groans of labored breath. They echo the sounds of our starvation. So hungry, the grip of teeth squeezing the fruit. We savor the trickle of sweetness that is nectar, the cherry's texture of giving flesh teethed and shared and swallowed down the throat.

His tongue laves the rich cream filled with fluffed air. He is merciless in his tiny tortures. I stroke the hardness between a dark stranger's legs; my thighs open wide.

"The main course," I demand.

A Quiver of Sighs

In one hand he dangles a raw oyster. In the other, he holds the complement of cocktail sauce.

"A perfect match in your current position. This could have been molded from you."

Laying the oyster over my feminine nook, he matches the pearl-like nub within the oyster's body to mine.

He says my scent is that of the ocean, briny and clean. He spreads the red sauce on my inner thighs. He's licking the sauce. Tasting the oyster with a vibration that leaves me shrieking.

He balances the shellfish on his tongue; it slides down his throat. Then he kisses me and he tastes of woman. He lays himself on me.

Our coupling is too frantic to be making love. It is too poignant and caring to be considered mindless sex.

Body textures, lust words, and lingering erotic tastes blend in tandem until we call each other by name and embrace the sweetest death.

My hand glides languorously over his sweat-slicked chest. I sigh in contentment. "That was some dessert."

"I hope you saved room for more." He feeds me a bite of wedding cake. Giggling, I paint his lips with frosting.

He looks silly and achingly handsome. He moves me with a warm gaze, a whisper. "Happy anniversary, sunshine."

"Happy anniversary, darling."

"Tell me what you feel," he softly commands.

"Lust. And Love. So much love."

"The two best ingredients," he assures me with a wink.

"Even when life's no picnic."

Val's knees were literally knocking. It was more than she could say for the knuckles hovering over Jake's door.

He'd read the final copy but didn't want to discuss it when he'd called that afternoon. His voice had sounded strained, distant, and she'd asked, "What's wrong?"

Olivia Rupprecht

A long pause, then, "We have to talk but not on the phone." Jake was no alarmist. He had bad news.

And she had a very queasy stomach after four hours of imagining what could be so wrong that Jake had spoken with the gravity of a funeral director. It wasn't about her manuscript. As many times as he'd played drill sargeant to whip her book into shape, he would have said something on the phone.

For once she wished the problem was with her book. As much as she loved it, she could never love anything or anyone so much as she loved Jake. That's what this visit was about—she knew it. He had bad news of a personal nature.

Had he gone to a doctor for a checkup only to find out he had a fatal disease? She couldn't bear the thought because life without Jake would be no life at all. She needed him the way she needed to breathe.

She was having trouble breathing. Had he met another woman during those few days he'd been in New York? Seeing to business, he'd said, but what if that business included an old flame? Or a new one? When he returned he'd been excited but evasive, and preoccupied ever since. Even when they made love lately, he wasn't all there. *Was there another woman*?

The idea hadn't occurred to her until Jake called today. And until today she'd never thought herself capable of murder. Jake was right about the human condition. If there was another woman, she'd kill her. Then she'd kill Jake.

As she'd nearly gone mad imagining Jake dying by disease or at the hand of a jealous lover, a last possibility had emerged. It seemed the most logical, but no less distressing.

A new job. A move. Back to New York. Without her. He hadn't said he loved her and from the tone of his voice she knew he didn't want to see her for the purpose of proposing.

"Cupid, please help me. I'm scared." So scared she'd brought him along in her purse, knowing she'd never needed the kind of luck she needed now.

Bracing herself for the worst, Val knocked.

Chapter Fourteen

She waited for an eternity of seconds, then knocked again. The door opened. Val stepped back, stunned.

She hardly recognized him. Jake looked haggard. Even his smile seemed to belong to a scarecrow, with stitches of thread animating a too-still face. His eyes were bleary.

"And heeere she is," he slurred. "My Valintime. Who is, according to my watch . . ." He squinted down at it. "Late."

Jake liked his drink but he never got anywhere close to sloshed. *What was going on?*

"I stopped to pick up some plum wine." Memories, she'd scrambled for every one she could get her hands on before coming over. Even a duplicate pair of red panties. Memories bound people and she'd been desperate to seal their bond by any means she could. "From the looks of you, I should have picked up some espresso instead. You're drunk."

"Gettin' there." He gave her a wet, sloppy kiss and scooped her into his arms.

"Put me down, Jake! You'll break our necks!"

"Only if you keep squirming, so in the interest of our mutual safety, be still!"

A kick to the door and he wove into the living room, only to knock his shin on the marble coffee table. A curse and a stumble later, she landed on the couch with an *ooomph*. Val struggled to sit up and get her eyes refocused.

The sight of several half-packed boxes filled her vision. *He's moving. That's why he's drunk—he's moving without me and this is good-bye.*

With surprisingly steady hands, much steadier than her own, Jake reached for his briefcase.

"First, the good news." Her manuscript, its weighty pulp held intact with big rubber bands, landed on the sofa. "You'll have the toughest shark in business agenting you within a week. A couple more to put it into the right hands, a week for Publisher's Row to go into a feeding frenzy, and voilà. In a month, you're writing your own ticket. This baby's gold, sunshine. You're gonna be rich. Count on it."

Count? On what? If she couldn't count on Jake to be in her life what did anything matter? She could only look from the boxes to him and dash tears from her eyes.

"Hey, what's this? You're supposed to be thrilled, jumping up and down and—"

"What?" she demanded. "Just what am I supposed to be thrilled about?" Pointing a trembling finger at the boxes, she accused, "You're packing." He confirmed the worst with a short nod. "You went to New York to get your old job back, didn't you? You love to edit, I know you do, so you went there to get your old job back, right?" Another nod. "So, while you were there, did you look up an old lover, did the two of you—"

"What?" His bellow coincided with the smack of his fist to his palm. "Where the hell do you get off even suggesting such a thing? Answer me, dammit!"

"I—I don't know, but you went there and you came back and you haven't been yourself and now you're leaving and going back to your old job and—"

"I am *not* going back to my old job." He picked up a half-empty bottle from the floor, took a swig, then held it out to her. "Forget the plum wine. A special occasion such as this merits something a lot stronger. So take a drink. Take several. Hell, have the whole bottle. As you can see, I've had enough. Enough booze, enough secrets and half-truths. Time for an outing, way past time actually, and believe me it's not gonna be a picnic. Now you drink. I'll talk."

As she took the bottle, his fingers grazed hers. Even in this terrible, terrible moment, his touch was a singe. She'd never had scotch and in a single sip, knew she didn't like the taste. But she welcomed the burn to her throat. It was real and she needed something real when everything around her seemed so surreal. Jake, the boxes, what he'd said about her book that might or might not be true and how could he know such things anyway? Nothing made sense, and what a strange time to remember Jake saying the difference between fiction and real life was that fiction had to make sense.

"I misled you, Val." This did not make sense. Did that make this real life, was she really hearing Jake? "I told you I used to be an editor. True enough, but I wasn't just any editor. Three years ago I was Deputy Publisher of one of the most prestigious houses on the Row. I was up for another promotion when I pissed off one of the biggest bestselling authors out there and he threatened to leave if I didn't. What immaculate timing. I'd pushed for an enormous advance on what I thought was a sure thing and the sure thing fizzled on the racks. Thanks to me, we took a very expensive bath."

This was the half-truth, the big secret? Flush with relief, she held out her hand. "I'm sorry about what happened, Jake, it must have been a nightmare. But I'd be lying if I said I wasn't glad it brought you here."

He didn't take her hand. Instead, he reached inside his briefcase and withdrew some pages. "You might change your mind about how glad you are once you see this."

He tossed it to the table and the pages splayed before her disbelieving eyes.

"And what have we here, my dear? Looks like our own black moment denouement to me. Agreed?"

Speechless, she couldn't even form a coherent word much less a sentence to describe the utter horror of seeing her most private thoughts exposed so nakedly on Jake's table. It didn't matter that he was the man on the picnic, in truth and in her written expression of it, this was her work, her latest submission to *Fantasies*, meant for readers who had no idea who she was, how she really felt, who would assume she was a faceless writer simply spinning a tale.

"When you topple from the top and land on ground zero, where does one go? L.A. looks pretty good when the snow starts to fly and the salt under your feet seems warm compared to cold shoulders and a knife in your back."

Had Jake just plunged one into hers? Or maybe it was her heart taking the blow as he bowed and said with a preposterous formality, "Allow me to introduce myself. Jake Larson, Editor-in-chief of *Fantasies* magazine. Sorry, kiddo, much as I enjoyed your latest submission, I just couldn't buy it."

Put together every rejection she'd ever received, enough to paper a room with, and they didn't amount to anything compared to this. Not only had Jake deceived her, accessed the most hidden chambers of her mind and her heart, he had rejected more than her work. Only two pieces had he—*he*, not some editor named Charles—rejected. One, a love sonnet. And this, "The Picnic." Pretty hot stuff and since he'd bought her other hot stuff, it must be the ending he couldn't buy into.

"I think I get the picture." She laughed to keep from crying. A hollow, brittle laugh. Val picked up

A Quiver of Sighs

her manuscript, picked herself up from the couch and prayed she wouldn't collapse on the floor. No, she couldn't do that here. She had to get home, then she could fall apart.

Two steps and her legs buckled. Jake moved with an amazing speed and seemed more coherent than this madwoman screaming at him, "Get your hands off me!" and pounding his chest with her beloved pages. That's all she had now, a story demanding to be told, only now that it was told she didn't even have her book, just her racking sobs. "I hate you for this. Do you hear me? I hate you, *hate you—*"

"No you don't." He shook her and then his face was in hers and he was forcing her to look at him. "You love me, Val. You know and I know it. You do."

"But I don't want to." Never were truer words spoken. And never would she forgive herself if she didn't lay down the rest. "You used me, Jake. You got your editorial fix and now that it's over you're ready for another literary virgin to play Svengali with. You really get off on that, don't you? You like the mind games, the power plays, and what an extra treat it must have been to get some sex on the side, not only on the floor but between the pages."

She took a steadying breath but it was more a dry heave. "You never said you loved me. Now I know why. You don't."

Jake stared at her, unblinking. The blur of his eyes cleared. No man had ever looked more sober.

"Not love you?" he repeated. Again he shook her, only this time there was anger, passion, hurt in his grip. "What are you, crazy? How can you sleep with me, work with me, play with me, talk to me, look in my eyes, and not know? I do love you, Val. Love you so much that you're the best part of my days, my nights. Even my dreams are spent wondering how I ever lived my life without you, wondering why it's so damn hard to say three simple words to describe the most complex emotion I've ever encountered. With you, only with you."

He choked up and suddenly Jake seemed close to

351

joining her while she cried. With joy. "And—and now that you're on your way, how will I live without you while I go mine . . . sunshine?"

"You love me," she whispered, then shouted, "You love me!" Throwing her arms around him, *The Secrets That Bind Us* pressed between their chests, she kissed him, kissed him. And when she was done, she held his face in her hands and fully claimed the daring woman within. "Marry me, Jake."

"I'd give anything to, but . . . I can't." He nodded toward the boxes. "I gave my notice yesterday. It seems I'm out of a job again and as much as I like to think of myself as a progressive, modern man, I can't marry you until I get another job. It could take a while and meanwhile your career's going to soar. All I can do is dream that you'll still have me by the time I—"

"But I don't want to wait. I want you now. Maybe you're wrong about the book, maybe it won't sell and I don't even care." Her dream. At one time it had been everything, but without Jake in her life, it meant nothing. She had to make him see. "I don't care if you're pounding the pavement and coming home with no more than a buttercup you picked out of someone else's garden, it's enough for me. As long as we're together, it's enough."

He shook his head sadly. "Maybe for you, but not for me. I know myself and that self isn't nice when he's out of work. I wouldn't wish me on anyone, much less you."

Damn, he was stubborn. And smart and ambitious and the best editor ever. She didn't want another editor and she didn't want him to hand her work over to some agent she didn't even know, maybe even one of the dozens who had rejected her before but might take her on now that Jake had . . .

Wait a minute. The light went on the way the best ideas came, out of nowhere but surely heaven-sent.

"So, you *will* marry me once you have a new job, right?"

"So fast it'll make your head spin."

A Quiver of Sighs

"I think it's spinning now."

"Uh-oh, I know that look. You always get that look when you're plotting."

"The plot's already hatched and all you have to do is agree with me for once instead of arguing." She cut to the chase. "You said I need an agent. You said you need a job. You'd make a great agent, Jake. Please don't step back and think about it. Just say you'll be my agent and then, according to what *you* said, we can say 'I do.'"

Jake thought about it. An agent. He'd never really thought about being an agent before, but . . . nobody knew the business better than he and the best agents around had been editors at one time and . . . Val was right. He would make a good agent. A damn good agent. As for clients, he'd have plenty after landing on the map with a bidding-war auction. Nobody would ever fight for Val the way he would, and after he proved he could swim with the sharks, his reputation would be better than restored. No need for his old job when his new one made him a power broker who could forget a grudge.

For a king's ransom, that was.

"Before I go along with this plot of yours—a very fine plot, I might add—I think we need to discuss how to separate business from pleasure. We never did get around to that but marrying my client might present some unique conflicts with the characters involved. Especially if you get irked and decide you want to fire me—or vice-versa. Not an option, Val. Neither is divorce. Till death do us part, understood?"

"Now who's the boss?" she teased.

"Got a two-headed quarter, by chance? Heads, we split the difference and seal this deal in bed."

It was to bed he carried her and in that bed new fantasies were shared. But none so richly realized as the ring he placed on her finger in the wee hours, the joy of her assent to be his wife, his lover, his most cherished friend.

Val gazed at the ring and wondered at the mystery

that was love. Even if Jake didn't believe in cupids and such, she did. Her heart hadn't quit singing since he'd aimed his arrow and made her pay through the nose for the dream she claimed now. Nose-to-nose, an Eskimo kiss, her little Cupid should be with them to celebrate their victory.

"Where are you going?" Jake demanded as she slipped from his hold and, decadent temptress she was, pranced stark naked into the living room. Jake was on her heels and sounding much too like his bossy self, ordering her to get back in bed.

"Impatient as you are, always no-nonsense and in a hurry to get things done, I'll make this quick." Reaching into her purse for the luck she no longer needed, Val presented Cupid to Jake. "From me, to you. An engage—"

A hum like the *ping* of Baccarat crystal filled the air.

She gasped; he gaped. "I see it, but I don't believe it."

Val could only nod. She didn't believe it either but there it was, the broken wing, no longer broken. The arrow aimed from Cupid's bow? Gone. As for the arrow in his quiver, it had company. Now there were two.

"This is too weird," Jake muttered.

"Definitely weird," she agreed.

"Uh, Val, much as I appreciate this particular engagement gift, and though I don't buy into superstition or anything like that, if it's all the same to you, think we could get rid of this thing?"

As much as she adored her Cupid, Val wanted to get rid of it, too. But not because Jake had goose bumps prickling his skin. It was just a feeling, an absolute certainty—like the one she'd had when she first touched Cupid and knew he belonged to her—that he no longer belonged to her.

Jake belonged to her. But not Cupid.

Epilogue

A wind chime tinkled overhead, announcing their arrival. There were no other customers in the strange little shop.

"You're back," a familiar, elderly voice said in greeting. "A day late, but not to worry. Cupid can move quickly when he has to. Another mission complete, it's time for him to fly."

"I know." Val pressed her lips to the porcelain head and regretfully handed Cupid over. Gnarled hands replaced the figurine in the spot where she'd found him.

"I don't know who you are, but thank you." She gave the cryptic old man a hug.

Jake shook his hand and solemnly echoed, "Thank you."

As they stood outside, embracing, a man stopped and gazed wistfully at the lovers.

A wind chime tinkled overhead, announcing his arrival to the realm of Kismet . . .

Where Cupid awaits with a broken wing and a potent arrow drawn from his quiver of sighs.

A Quiver of Sighs

He Takes Me There

He takes me there
with his light and his
magic
Hands sweeping over me
in a moving caress
A gently whispered
Come
come to me
in the night
Stay till morning shines bright
as buttercups
falling on the moonbeams
I hold to my breast
Beguiled by the magic
that is this man
taking me there yet again
to that place which is
Love
borne on a shadowed caress
revealing my heart
undressed
As his love lies watching
my own unfold
then reaching to embrace
that place where quivering
sighs of his name
trespass my lips
like savored sips
of celestial champagne

Anne Avery, Phoebe Conn, Sandra Hill, & Dara Joy

WHERE DREAMS COME TRUE...

Do you ever awaken from a dream so delicious you can't bear for it to end? Do you ever gaze into the eyes of a lover and wish he could see your secret desires? Do you ever read the words of a stranger and feel your heart and soul respond? Then come to a place created especially for you by four of the most sensuous romance authors writing today—a place where you can explore your wildest fantasies and fulfill your deepest longings....

_4052-2 $5.99 US/$6.99 CAN

THEIR FIRST NOEL

DON'T MISS THESE FOUR HISTORICAL ROMANCE STORIES THAT CELEBRATE THE JOY OF CHRISTMAS AND THE MIRACLE OF BIRTH.

LEIGH GREENWOOD
"Father Christmas"

Arizona Territory, 1880. Delivering a young widow's baby during the holiday season transforms the heart of a lonely drifter.

BOBBY HUTCHINSON
"Lantern In The Window"

Alberta, 1886. After losing his wife and infant son, a bereaved farmer vows not to love again—until a fiery beauty helps him bury the ghosts of Christmases past.

CONNIE MASON
"A Christmas Miracle"

New York, 1867. A Yuletide birth brings a wealthy businessman and a penniless immigrant the happiness they have always desired.

THERESA SCOTT
"The Treasure"

Washington Territory, 1825. A childless Indian couple receives the greatest gift of all: the son they never thought they'd have.

__3865-X(Four Christmas stories in one volume)$5.99 US/$7.99 CAN

Dorchester Publishing Co., Inc.
65 Commerce Road
Stamford, CT 06902

Please add $1.75 for shipping and handling for the first book and $.50 for each book thereafter. NY, NYC, PA and CT residents, please add appropriate sales tax. No cash, stamps, or C.O.D.s. All orders shipped within 6 weeks via postal service book rate. Canadian orders require $2.00 extra postage and must be paid in U.S. dollars through a U.S. banking facility.

Name_____
Address_____
City _____ State _____ Zip _____
I have enclosed $_____in payment for the checked book(s).
Payment <u>must</u> accompany all orders.☐ Please send a free catalog.

A VALENTINE FOR YOU—
TWO HEARTWARMING ROMANCES
FOR ONE LOW PRICE!
A $7.98 Value For Only $4.99!

Only The Present by Noelle Berry McCue. Maureen Connolly was sheltered and innocent until the night steel-eyed Daniel Lord took her in a night of passion and then coldheartedly left her. But now, years later, Daniel is suddenly back in her life, determined to make her his wife, and Maureen wonders if his sudden reappearance is the beginning of a new love song, or just an old—and treacherously seductive—refrain.

The Face Of Love by Anne N. Reisser. Breck Carson is a commanding businessman who always gets what he wants—and he wants Andrea Thomas. Andy swears she will never surrender to his heated advances, but one look in his piercing blue eyes makes her doubt her resolve. She longs to lose herself to his masterful touch, but will she be just another victim of his devastating charm?

__3571-7   **(two unforgettable romances in one volume)** Only $4.99

Dorchester Publishing Co., Inc.
65 Commerce Road
Stamford, CT 06902

Please add $1.75 for shipping and handling for the first book and $.50 for each book thereafter. NY, NYC, PA and CT residents, please add appropriate sales tax. No cash, stamps, or C.O.D.s. All orders shipped within 6 weeks via postal service book rate. Canadian orders require $2.00 extra postage and must be paid in U.S. dollars through a U.S. banking facility.

Name _____

Address _____

City _____ State _____ Zip _____

I have enclosed $_____in payment for the checked book(s).

Payment <u>must</u> accompany all orders. ☐ Please send a free catalog.

Enchanted Crossings

Three captivating stories of love in another time, another place.

MADELINE BAKER
"Heart of the Hunter"

A Lakota warrior must defy the boundaries of life itself to claim the spirited beauty he has sought through time.

ANNE AVERY
"Dream Seeker"

On faraway planets, a pilot and a dreamer learn that passion can bridge the heavens, no matter how vast the distance from one heart to another.

KATHLEEN MORGAN
"The Last Gatekeeper"

To save her world, a dazzling temptress must use her powers of enchantment to open a stellar portal—and the heart of a virile but reluctant warrior.

___51974-7 *Enchanted Crossings* (three unforgettable love stories in one volume) $4.99 US/
$5.99 CAN

BETRAYAL Evelyn Rogers

By the Bestselling Author of
The Forever Bride

If there is anything that gets Conn O'Brien's Irish up, it is a lady in trouble–especially one he has fallen in love with at first sight. So after the Texas horseman saves Crystal Braden from an overly amorous lout, he doesn't waste a second declaring his intentions to make an honest woman of her. But they have barely been declared man and wife before Conn learns that his new bride is hiding a devastating secret that can destroy him.

The plan is simple: To ensure the safety of her mother and young brother, Crystal agrees to play the damsel in distress. The innocent beauty has no idea how dangerously charming the virile stranger can be–nor how much she longs to surrender to the tender passion in his kiss. And when Conn discovers her ruse, she vows to blaze a trail of desire that will convince him that her deception has been an error of the heart and not a ruthless betrayal.

___4262-2 $5.99 US/$6.99 CAN

"Evelyn Rogers delivers great entertainment!"
—Romantic Times

It is only a fairy tale, but to Megan Butler *The Forever Bride* is the most beautiful story she's ever read. That is why she insists on going to Scotland to get married in the very church where the heroine of the legend was wed to her true love. The violet-eyed advertising executive never expects the words of the story to transport her over two hundred years into the past, exchanging vows not with her fiancé, but with strapping Robert Cameron, laird of Thistledown Castle. After convincing Robert that she is not the unknown woman he's been contracted to marry, Meagan sets off with the charming brute in search of the real bride and her dowry. But the longer they pursue the elusive girl, the less Meagan wants to find her. For with the slightest touch Robert awakens her deepest desires, and she discovers the true meaning of passion. But is it all a passing fancy—or has she truly become the forever bride?

_4177-4 $5.50 US/$6.50 CAN

WICKED
Evelyn Rogers
An Angel's Touch

"Evelyn Rogers delivers great entertainment!"
—*Romantic Times*

Gunned down after a bank robbery, Cad Rankin meets a heavenly being who makes him an offer he can't refuse. To save his soul, he has to bring peace to the most lawless town in the West. With a mission like that, the outlaw almost resigns himself to spending eternity in a place much hotter than Texas—until he comes across Amy Lattimer, a feisty beauty who rouses his goodness and a whole lot more.

Although she's been educated in a convent school, Amy Lattimer is determined to do anything to locate her missing father, including posing as a fancy lady. Then she finds an ally in virile Cad Rankin, who isn't about to let her become a fallen angel. But even as Amy longs to surrender to paradise in Cad's arms, she begins to suspect that he has a secret that stands between them and unending bliss....

___52082-6 $5.99 US/$7.99 CAN